None Shall Sleep

T.D. ARKENBERG

outskirtspress
DENVER, COLORADO

Outskirts Press, Inc.
http://www.outskirtspress.com

Paperback ISBN: 978-1-4787-6231-7
Hardback ISBN: 978-1-4787-6688-9

Outskirts Press and the "OP" logo are trademarks belonging to Outskirts Press, Inc.

PRINTED IN THE UNITED STATES OF AMERICA

To Louise,
Happy Birthday.
In memory of a wonderful adventure in
Fidenza.
And of more to come love from Eleanor.
Percy x

For dreamers everywhere—

For Jim, the best fan I could ever want—

For my parents who believed anything was possible—

And for Gia, whose bold quest inspired this story

Also by T.D. Arkenberg

Final Descent
Jell-O and Jackie O

None Shall Sleep

No-one shall sleep!
No-one shall sleep!
You too, oh Princess,
In your cold room, watch the stars
Trembling with love and hope!

—*Turandot* (Giacomo Puccini)

Part I

Isa's Adventure

Chapter 1

San Benedetto, Italy

Their voices tormented Isabella Fabrini. Didn't they understand that she pressed her eyes shut for a reason—to lock them out? Yet, the four prattled on without mercy. Her dressing room, Isabella thought as she reclined on the sofa, was supposed to be a refuge.

The licorice-laced breath of her voice teacher puffed in her face. "Pre-concert jitters are bourgeois, my pet."

"Maybe so, Leech," her sister Gina said, "but bullying won't push Isabella onto that stage. She's stubborn. Always has been." The irony and menacing tone of her older sister tested Isabella's patience.

"Oh my, my. There's the audience to think of. Flown in from the four corners of the world, they have." Kate Mahoney's brogue raced with the Irish penchant for hyperbole. "Poor, poor darlin's."

Ana caressed Isabella's shoulder. "Hush! If Isa doesn't want to perform, she doesn't have to." Ana's gentle tone sent Isabella over the edge. She expected, perhaps even wanted, her younger sister to push her onto the stage instead of greasing an escape from her debut.

Bloody hell, Isa thought, glaring up at the fretting quartet. They meant well, but she needed time to think, space to figure things out. Withdrawal had always been her tactic in times of crisis. "Out, out, out!" The crackle in her voice surprised her.

Richard Leech went white; he began to shake. "Isa, my pet. Your voice! You must take care of the voice."

"Here, darling," Ana said, pulling what looked like a prescription bottle from her jeans pocket. "Miracle workers for my creative juices."

Before Isa could decline, her younger sister thrust the bottle into her hand. At Gina's loud gasp, Isa dropped the tube between the cushions.

"Artists!" Gina growled, foot tapping, arms crisscrossing her chest. "Drugs, always drugs."

"*Get out!*" Isa bellowed, hating herself at once for the wounded looks that flashed on every face including Gina's.

But really, who do they think they are? This wasn't their concert, their life. Their necks weren't on the block. Fighting an urge to surrender, to apologize, Isa glared at the lot of them, willing them out the door with a sneer. With theatrical flair, she moved a quaking hand toward a vase of freesias. She wanted them to believe she'd throw it. Maybe she would have. Smashing those damn flowers would provide a secondary benefit—venting anger at the one person she wanted at the concert…but wasn't.

Hell, if fear, embarrassment, and a swirling cocktail of emotions keep me off the stage, at least I can play the prima donna in my own dressing room.

The threat worked. They fled. Maybe she had the makings of an actress, after all. But no sooner had she kicked the door shut than her relief withered away at the sound of Leech's sobs from the hall. Her heart sank, picturing him quivering, lifting a lavender-scented handkerchief to his ruddy, bulbous nose. She hoped he wouldn't faint. As her teacher, wasn't he heavily invested in the concert…invested in her? He'd traveled all the way from London.

And what about her sisters? Nothing could keep precious Ana, the free spirit, away from the concert. Of all people, Ana so much like their father, understood an artist's sensitivities. Or did she? Ana's financial blunders were vexing, but Isa gloried in her younger sister's embrace of life—freefalling into things like a skydiver. Isn't that why Isa bailed her out so often? She told herself that she looked after Ana for their papa, but perhaps she had another motive. Maybe she secretly wanted to be Ana.

Ana always scolded her for thinking too much. Did Ana think less of her for failing to jump onto that stage, view her as an artistic lightweight—all talk, no guts?

And she had Gina to consider. Surely, Ana tried to render their older, cynical sister guilty enough to leave her family in Buenos Aires. But was a concert the *quid pro quo* for the trip to Italy? Isa was, after all, godmother to Gina's eldest, sending money, even during hard times, to give her niece music lessons that Gina deemed fluff. Choosing a path to please Gina was pointless. Her older sister never needed an excuse to ascend her self-righteous pedestal. She was the image of their mother as she scurried from the room, the words *I told you so* formed on her thin, pursed lips. No, Isa thought, better to cancel the concert before she embarrassed herself and suffered Gina's endless ridicule.

As for Kate, certainly the Irishwoman would view her friend's implosion in the context of their journey of self-awareness. Not as a shortcoming of Lighthouse to prepare Isa, and certainly not her personal failure. No, as an ardent Lighthouse disciple steeped in the self-help program's intoxicating elixir, Kate would rationalize Isa's fear as a short circuit in her hard-wiring—something in her history that paralyzed the subconscious. Kate wouldn't prescribe less Lighthouse *but more*. More courses, more group hugs, more barefoot walks on hot coals to shake off the fetters chaining Isa to the past. Besides, concert or no concert, the merry Dubliner would make the most of her Italian weekend.

What shall I do? Isa buried her face in her hands. Her mind wandered to the friends and family descending upon San Benedetto. She'd already seen the throngs sipping cappuccinos and eating gelati in the main square, strolling the high street, and dashing to the Terme for spa treatments. *She* brought them there. They came to hear *her* sing, to witness a mid-life conquest, her transformation from drone to...*diva*. Oh, how she hated that word—pretentious, egotistical, *undeserved*. What a fool she was to believe she could change careers at forty, especially for a role as demanding as that of opera singer.

And for all those who traveled so far in support, her heart ached for the one person who wasn't there. Isa wanted him to hear her sing, to witness her hard-fought triumph, to share her joy. She thought he wanted the same things. *Why did Luca abandon me when I need him most?* One hand soothed a souring stomach while the other brushed her forehead, cold and damp to the touch.

Isa tried to shake the faces and hurt from her mind, tilting her head back until it came to rest on smooth satin, gloves for one of the evening's gowns. On the wall, a clock, cruel in its unrelenting march forward, glared at her from its post between prints of Maria Callas as Norma the Druid priestess, and Renata Scotto as Lucia descending into madness. Five hours till curtain time. Her groans rose toward the ceiling. "I can't do this, I can't."

Leech, Kate, and her sisters, she knew, hovered out of concern. Despite her theatrics that suggested otherwise, she found comfort in their support. They believed mere stage fright afflicted her—easier to let them think so. Perhaps a debut in front of friends, family, and a hometown audience did rattle her nerves. But she'd fallen on her arse plenty of times before…and would do so again. No, her reluctance to go on stage had deeper roots that confounded her.

How had she allowed her emotions to spiral out of control? Had she bungled her entire life? Was the desire to become an opera singer at her age merely another in a long line of quixotic quests? Surely her poor judgment in men subjected her to ridicule. Laughter at her performance was only a minor worry. No, the prospect of an audience mocking Isa's entire life terrified her.

With eyes closed, she was overpowered by the scent of freesias. The delicate white blooms were her favorite, but now, now she hated the sight and smell of Luca's offering. Their pungent sweetness nauseated her. Instead, she craved for the earthy bouquet of something more practical… more intoxicating.

After several minutes, the pounding in her head subsided. The sobbing noises from the hall gave way to hushed whispers. Her voices of conscience, she assumed, plotted their next volley. She lifted her head, her gaze wandering to the dressing table.

Isa grinned from ear to ear. "Katie Maureen Mahoney! God bless the Irish and your marvelous dose of Dutch courage."

As she reached forward to grab the bottle of Jameson and a glass from the table, she gasped. Her reflection jolted her. Untamed raven strands, dark desperate eyes, and a round face, pale as the Snow Moon, made her appear more like Verdi's Lady Macbeth than his Violetta.

Inching from the horrid mirror, she wiggled backward onto the sofa, pushing aside her red gown. With glass in hand, her legs cradled the whiskey bottle as she twisted the top. After setting down the cap, she watched it vanish between red velvet cushions.

"Damn!"

But the odor of vanilla, honey, and caramel ascending from the amber well revitalized her.

"Brilliant," she cooed.

After filling the glass and placing the bottle on the floor, she raised the whiskey to her nose. She savored the scents that freed her from the traitorous and sobering freesias.

"Damn Luca and his bloody flowers," she grumbled. "He can take his silly card and… How could he not show up?" As tears welled, she pushed the slight from her mind. The potion beckoned.

She waded into her indulgence slowly, first wetting her lips with a gentle splash and letting the liquid dribble onto her tongue. She sighed. "Just what the doctor ordered." She took another sip, and another—*heaven*. Kicking off her slippers, she almost toppled the open bottle.

She thrust her hand down between the cushions. "Where's that damn cap?" Probing fingers failed. Capping her savior could wait. Instead, Isa refilled the glass.

Uncooperative feet foiled her attempts to return the bottle to the dressing table. But she didn't want to spill whiskey onto the rug or, God forbid, her gowns, the value of a month's mortgage. "Theater management will think I'm a 1-lush," she muttered with a snicker, before collapsing backward into the cushions.

Plunging her hand again into the void, Isa redoubled her efforts to find the cap. *God only knows what lurks in the underbelly of an opera house sofa.* Her fingers gripped something, a cylinder of sorts. "Of course," she mumbled. "Ana's magic pills." She studied the salvaged treasure. *Look, then decide.* The top popped off and shot across the room, sending her into a fit of giggles. She gazed down. Adorable, satin-coated pink pills mingled at the bottom of the bottle.

Had they been larger, coarser, or clinical white, she'd have distrusted them at once. Her interest in the whiskey cap faded. She took a few more sips of the liquor as she contemplated a relationship with her new, tiny, pink acquaintances. *Friend…or foe?*

A knock drew her focus to the door.

"Isa, you okay?" She recognized the velvety voice with the Argentine accent. "It's me, Christina. Let me in."

So the little angels had raided their arsenal. And a powerful weapon indeed—Isa's oldest friend in the world, Dr. Christina Negroni. *What to do?*

"This isn't a good time." Isa projected her voice toward the door—less anger, more control. She didn't want to give the good doctor cause to barge in.

"Let me in, Isa," Christina said as the doorknob rattled. "I've come so far."

"No!" Isa shouted, surprised by her intensity. "Sorry, dear," she said, softening her tone. "Come back later, *please*. I need time alone…time to think."

Isa looked down at her hands, clutching the whiskey and pills as if they were lifelines. She didn't want her old friend to see her like that, or worse, pluck her from the turgid water of despair…just yet.

"Tell me you're okay." Concern laced Christina's voice.

"Yes, yes dear. I'm fine, fine, really I am. Come back in a bit."

"Only if you promise you're okay."

"I'm okay, Christina."

"All right then, I'll give you fifteen minutes."

"Thirty," Isa answered. "And so very sorry to cause such a fuss."

"You wouldn't be Isabella Fabrini if you didn't stir the pot. Brava!" Christina said with a lilt in her voice and a clap of her hands. "You're acting like the consummate diva."

Isa winced. *That damn word again.* If not talent, then maybe tantrums had earned her the title.

"Thirty minutes," Christina added, her tone more relaxed.

"Deal!"

Isabella Fabrini believed in the power of the universe. When it spoke, she listened. Why else had the caps for the whiskey and magic pills vanished? This wasn't self-medication. A greater force doctored her. She plucked one, two, then a third innocent pastel pill from the bottle and poured two fingers of Jameson into the glass.

Isa stared at the pink trio in her palm. "How did I get into this mess?"

Chapter 2

London—Three Years Earlier

"We agreed to six months," Isabella Fabrini said into the phone. She was working inside her flat when the call came in. "I turned down other jobs. Yes, I understand receivership, but apologies don't pay bills."

The Warsaw job was her first big break, a chance to lead a major consulting engagement. The prospect of turning around a slumping manufacturer and saving thousands of jobs energized her. She'd already spent weeks designing a leadership program for the firm's management team. Besides the potential boost to her résumé, she needed the money.

Isa slammed the phone onto the desk. Failing to conjure up a Polish curse, she settled instead for a "Bloody hell!" delivered to an empty flat—small by most standards but large for London. Concerns over her mortgage—small by London standards but large for the world—frazzled her. The loft represented her dream, or rather, her compromised ideal. She stretched her budget for the *pied à terre*. When her sister Gina called it *a quaint little cell*, Isa grumbled, "Christ! She and Mama make it sound like a working-class bedsit complete with metered heat and communal toilet."

Floor-to-ceiling windows, a fireplace surrounded by bookshelves, a demi-loft above the entryway, *and* a private bath endowed her treasured space with airiness and grandeur. She imagined the flat as the townhouse study of a rich merchant or the library of a solicitor's country estate. The single room represented all that she acquired in a long career, like a curio cabinet brimming with her modest mementos.

Unlike some silly women she knew, Isa didn't have the temperament to sit on the sofa with starry eyes over a cup of tea, conjuring up a dream home beyond those four walls. Imagining the musings of such dreamers, Isa affected an upper-class accent. "Through there stands the grand staircase," she said, gesturing toward a closet. "Mustn't miss the library or third-floor playroom." She shook her head and laughed. *Fantasies are for fools.*

The dashed promise of a paycheck slashed from six months to two stirred Isa's late lunch of Marks & Spencer shepherd's pie. She shuffled to the kitchen, grabbed a glass from the cupboard, and poured the Cabernet, pairing the wine with milk-chocolate digestives snatched from the counter. She set down her comfort companions on a table beside the window before walking to the stereo and flicking through a pile of CDs, stopping at Solti's recording of *La Bohème*.

"Perfect." She hit the play button, picturing herself as a destitute Bohemian.

She dropped into a chair, took a gulp of wine, and listened to Act One. Opera relaxed her. Music flowed through her veins or maybe she simply recalled her papa's exuberance for all things Italian. From self-imposed exile in the New World, Papa Fabrini clung to his native culture as if it were a shipwrecked wayfarer's rock. Argentina may have provided financial opportunity as it had for many other Italians after the Second World War, but Isa's father never abandoned his love for Italy. Isa closed her eyes, listening to Placido Domingo. In her mind, she saw her papa caressing the cheeks of his three little principessas before twirling each of them in the air and belting out his favorite arias with comic vibrato— *Figaro qua, Figaro la, Figaro qua, Figaro la...*

As the act closed with Mimi and Rodolfo's duet, Isa brushed a tear from her eye. She looked through the rain-spattered windows toward Kensington High Street. Pedestrians bustled about in their own worlds with no regard for anyone whose path crossed their orbits. The anonymity of London suited her—most of the time. But she found the weather ghastly—that afternoon, merely another in a string of gloom that entwined the summer. While ceaseless mist nurtured her complexion, humidity curled her hair and psyche. Biting into a biscuit, she recalled the path that brought her there.

Three decades earlier when Isabella was a child of eight, her papa seeded her roving ways when he packed up the family and moved them to Argentina. "Italy may be fantastic for making music and love," he said, garnering his wife's scowl, "but it's no good for making money. We must eat!"

Tears gushed when the family boarded the freighter in Genoa—family and friends left behind. But after one day at sea, Papa Fabrini had Gina, Ana, and Isa singing Spanish ditties in a make-believe world of handsome gauchos, brave señoritas, and magic horses. "*Prisa, prisa caballo!*" he taught his little girls to shout as he hoisted them onto his back and galloped around the ship's deck. Only once did Isa's mother, Angelina, who spent the crossing fretting with a rosary in their cabin, surrender to Papa Fabrini's exuberance.

"*Diavolo!*" Isa's mother shrieked with a giggle when her husband spun her into a dip on a makeshift dance floor in the freighter's canteen.

"*Diablo, mi vida, diablo,*" he said with mischievous grin, translating *devil* from Italian into Spanish. Isa and her sisters giggled throughout the tango, imitating their parents' steps in a corner of the room.

On their last morning onboard, the family gathered at the ship's railing and gazed across the Rio de la Plata. As the family's adopted country grew on the horizon, Isa's mother wore a mask of misgiving. Her dark moods and quick temper intensified as they sailed farther from San Benedetto, the only home she'd ever known.

As soon as the ship docked, Ana dashed down the gangplank. Papa Fabrini followed in mad pursuit. Isa hesitated. Glancing behind her, she saw her mother with Gina clutched in her arms. Doubt had given way to fear. "It'll be okay, Mama," Isa said, squeezing her mother's hand. A child's squeal drew Isa's focus back to the pier. Papa Fabrini had corralled Ana. Waving wildly, the pair beckoned the rest of the family ashore. Taking a deep breath, Isa picked up her suitcase, squared her shoulders and descended to the pier.

Two decades later, and spurning her mother's advice to find a man and marry as Gina had done, Isa returned to Europe. She did so on her terms—to attend business school. Despite the pull of her heart to the sun, warmth, and passion of Italy, she heeded her father's fiscal warning and listened to her head. She chose Europe's financial capital. She quickly learned, however, that London's weather and its men were cold and inclement.

After completing her degree and careening through a series of multinational companies, Isa considered herself a Londoner. "Not English, mind you. Heavens! Never English," she would say—simply a prudent inhabitant of the world's most cosmopolitan city. She even learned to endure the rain with the stoicism of a native.

Her decade-long run in the employment of others, first in marketing then later in leadership development, ended nine months earlier along with the promise of a paycheck. "Next year's budget will be tight," her impeccably tailored boss said in his Swedish accent. "Revenues aren't supporting our overhead." That was his roundabout way of announcing her redundancy without invoking his wife's jealous accusations.

Isa recalled his surprise—raised eyebrows, creased forehead, and flushed cheeks—when she barged into his office days later. "I quit!" she shouted. "I've given you three years of my life. The job's a bore and the sex is shit." The fact that she didn't hold out for a generous severance package to soften her landing in the unemployment line shocked him. In retrospect, perhaps the show of bravura was self-indulgent.

But she'd planned her exit for some time. She wanted to branch out on her own, no longer bound by corporate constraints or patronized by chauvinistic supervisors. As much as Isa loved her father, she sympathized with her mother's plight, pulled from home and family. Isa would take the reins of her own future. Many of her business school chums had started consultancies when they hit forty. Some found success. So, she hung up her shingle and waited for clients.

Schoolmate Jamie Stuart, a Glaswegian living in London, counseled her. "It'll be a slow go establishin' yourself, love. But once ya build a base, momentum will carry you." All that carried her in the first six months were odds and ends, and sloppy seconds from sympathetic friends. Then came the big break—a job for the Polish manufacturer. But six months had been slashed to two. Isa groaned, her mind returning to her Kensington flat.

Mimi's plaintive lament refocused Isa's ears on the stereo music. *Are they gone?* Mimi sings. The dying heroine desires privacy before confessing her eternal love for Rodolfo. Isa listened as the lovers recounted happier times amid the pain of lost opportunity—then Rodolfo's raw grief. Isa couldn't help but cry.

As she dipped the milk-chocolate digestive into the Cabernet, Isa wondered whether she was destined to drift through middle age, a failure in business and in love.

Nothing was more pathetic, she believed, than finding herself old, destitute, and alone. *Poor Mimi had the good sense to die young.*

Isa considered the insipid prefix, *poor*, grafted forever to her name. "Poor Isa this, or poor Isa that." She seethed. "Bloody hell!" she cried toward the rain-speckled windows, "I don't even like cats."

Chapter 3

Milan—A Few Months Later

That Christmas, Isa flew to Italy, unemployed, rudderless. She welcomed the escape from London. After the Warsaw assignment collapsed, she scraped through the fall working odd jobs begged from other consultants. She hated losing control. Although viewing such a move as surrender, she began to consider a return to the corporate world. A starving master was as unappealing a fate as that of a well-fed slave.

Isa hadn't visited San Benedetto since her parents, homesick in retirement, had returned from Argentina. After landing in Milan, she caught a bus to the city center. She arranged to meet her younger sister, Ana, near the station. The sisters could catch up and fortify each other before they faced their mother's inquisition. Ana had been abroad for two years, involved in some project that took her across the globe, bringing art to refugees. Germany was simply her latest stop.

From prior business trips, Isa knew of a spot opposite the central station run by a kind-faced Milanese and his Russian wife for whom she assumed the café, La Russa, was named. The arrival times of Ana's train from Berlin and her flight from London gave the sisters three hours to enjoy a casual lunch before their onward train to Bologna and the connection to San Benedetto.

Isa arrived at the café first. Savory smells of cabbage, borscht, and blintzes mingled with onions, garlic, and sauce Bolognese. The décor, in shades of red, harmonized the native cultures of the restaurant's husband and wife. A silver samovar gleaming on an antique chest at the entrance, however, was unmistakably Eastern.

Isa asked for a table with a street view to watch for her younger sister.

"Nice to see you again, Signora Fabrini," the owner, Matia, said with a smile and nod. "Permit me."

"*Sì, grazie.*"

Matia pulled the coat from her shoulders and folded the fluffy red wrap over his arm. He began to drape the fur over the back of the other, vacant chair.

"Oh, no," Isa said holding up a palm. "I'm expecting someone."

Matia's eyebrows arched. "*Mi scusi, Signora Fabrini. Certo*, of course."

Isa remembered the frequent scoldings from Matia and his wife, Olga. "Lovely lady like you," they said, "should never dine alone. This is Italy!" Invariably, one or the other walked away, head shaking before returning with a glass of wine. "On the house," they would say with a sympathetic squeeze to her shoulder.

"A very lucky man, indeed," Matia added, recalling Isa to the present.

Isa chuckled. "You're hopeless. I'm waiting for my sister."

"*Bene, bene,*" a blushing Matia replied, holding Isa's chair as she sat. "I keep my eyes open for another lovely lady. She looks like you, *sì?*"

"Heavens, no! My sister's a classic beauty. When you gasp and your eyes nearly pop out of your head, you'll know Ana's arrived." Isa laughed as anticipation mounted on Matia's face before he retreated with her coat, his heels clicking on the black and white tiled floor.

Isa didn't understate Ana's beauty. Big brown eyes, a perfect complexion, full lips, and a shapely figure brought her younger sister plenty of attention. Men doted over her. But Isa didn't harbor any jealousy. She left that to their older sister. In addition to her name, Gina inherited their mother's genes. She was short and stocky with a low center of gravity. Her round face held coal-black eyes surrounded by dark circles. Thin lips set below a flat nose gave a permanent sneer. As the middle child, Isa bridged the genealogical gap with features balanced between her sisters' extremes. Perhaps Ana's good looks would have threatened her if she used them to hurt others. But Ana was like a sprite who fell into her beauty unaware of its potency.

Olga appeared. The sturdy Russian, a head taller than her husband, extended her customary greeting—two kisses on the cheek and a hardy Russian bear hug delivered as Isa remained seated. "From the way Matia goes on," Olga said with a nod toward the curtained entrance, "I expect a goddess to walk through our door."

"My sister's quite a looker. You'll see."

With arms folded across a generous bosom, Olga looked down. "Don't undersell yourself. You just gotta…meet the man halfway." With her foot, the husky, graying blonde poked Isa's black leather boots. Round blue eyes scanned the red knit suit. "You got the goods, signora."

Feeling her cheeks warm, Isa avoided Olga's stare. She didn't want to admit that the outfit was new, bought especially to impress Ana—a small dose of sisterly rivalry.

"Believe in yourself, then you find your man…or better yet, he find you." Olga tapped the tabletop. "How you think I get skinny Italian man to import big Russian wife, her mama, *and* two sisters from Moscow?" Her laugh was as big and as warm as her personality. "Now, what I get you while you wait?"

Isa craved *vino bianco* but didn't want her sister to find her drinking alone. Besides, she still felt a little tipsy from the airplane wine. "Cappuccino."

Ana's train must be late, Isa thought as she stared out the window. She didn't mind. Train stations and airports fascinated her, wanderlust no doubt inherited from her papa. She could sit for hours watching flurries of people come and go from the station. For many, she assumed, this was their first glimpse of Italy. The excitement in their faces gave them away.

A movie from her youth popped into her head. Barely a teenager, Isa sat through three showings in a smoky Buenos Aires cinema. The vintage film, shot in Venice, made her homesick. In the story, a middle-aged secretary suppresses her Midwestern morality to taste romance with a sexy Italian. As her train departs, the deflowered spinster stands at an open window, glancing back to the station. As hope of seeing her lover one last time fades, he appears. Their eyes meet. He darts down the platform, racing the accelerating train. Will they have one last kiss?

The first time through the film, Isa cried, drawing taunts from Gina. Isa thought for sure the lovers would get their kiss if not reunite in happily-ever-after bliss. American movies always had happy endings. But instead, the man reaches the platform's end without catching the train. Wistful resignation spreads across the woman's face: this was merely a summer fling. As the gap between the lovers widens, the man's face lights up. He pulls something from his jacket and waves it in the air. Squinting, the woman recognizes the object—a gardenia, *their* flower. She smiles, content. A passionate memory is hers forever…if not the lover.

"Christ!" Isa muttered into her cappuccino cup, drawing a leer from a café patron. *How pathetically maudlin.* She was no spinster. She had plenty of flings. *But none lasted*—the words echoed in her head along with an image of the fluttering gardenia.

Seeing Ana stroll toward the café, Isa mumbled, "Thank heavens." She'd finished her coffee and didn't have the stomach for another. She needed something stronger.

No sooner had Isa's sister stepped into the café than Matia pounced. Ana wore a beige wool coat with fur collar trim, matching hat, and large round sunglasses. She looked like a movie star. The sisters locked glances, exchanged waves. In Matia's excitement to usher Ana to the table, he left her trailing several paces behind.

"Sorry to be late, darling. Rescued another helpless soul frantically searching for his train. Didn't speak a lick of Italian."

Isa should have known that a man was behind her sister's delay. He probably spoke perfect Italian too. The sisters embraced while Matia hovered to the side. Isa figured he wanted an introduction, eager to unwrap her sister to see the hidden treasure beneath the cloak.

Ana pressed Matia's arm. "I'd kill for a martini, but I'll settle for white wine."

"Me too!" Isa said. "Bring a bottle."

As Matia hurried away, they both giggled. "Probably trip over his scampering feet," Isa said. Reaching for Ana's hands, she stared at her sister. "Still the face to launch a thousand ships."

"Me? You're the one who looks marvelous—stunning. Love the new style." Removing her sunglasses, Ana brushed auburn tresses from Isa's eye. "Adore the color. You're gorgeous."

Ana didn't disappoint. Isa could count on her sister to notice any little improvement to her appearance. Still, she blushed. "Thanks, Gattina," Isa said, using her pet name. As children, Ana's playfulness, big eyes, and delicate features reminded Isa of an adorable kitten. "But your hair's still the loveliest of all."

Ana's shriek of laughter startled Isa and Matia who had returned to the table with the wine. Isa looked around the café before staring at Ana whose brilliant eyes danced. But what else did she see?

Isa waited for Matia to leave before leaning in and whispering, "What's gotten into you?"

Ana's face took on the same impish expression their father adopted as a prelude to mischief. With a flourish of her hand, Ana pulled the fur hat from her head. Isa's hand flew to her open mouth. Ana's silky, blonde hair was gone, replaced by fine, purple stubble.

"Go ahead, touch it," Ana said, grabbing Isa's hand. "Don't be scared," she added, navigating her sister's fingers to her scalp.

Was this one of Ana's whimsical pursuits? Simply another exhibit, her body transformed into a living canvas? Isa wanted to believe that, but something told her this was no simple art project. She didn't have to wait long for Ana to confirm her suspicion.

"It's cancer, darling. Let's get that right out into the open."

Isa felt as if she'd been punched in the stomach. Her eyes welled with tears. "My precious Gattina. Why didn't you tell me?"

Ana pulled a tissue from her purse and dabbed Isa's eyes. "Hush now. I won't allow cancer to define me. And I surely won't let it come between us."

Isa grabbed Ana's hand, squeezing tight. Had she been too absorbed in her own problems to take notice of her sister's plight? Pangs of guilt washed over her. "You should have told me."

"Darling, not much more to tell. German doctors are the best. Chemo and radiation seem to have beaten back the cancer as well as my hair." She pointed to her scalp. "Dye job was my idea, and quite frankly, against their orders. Tattoos too," she added, pushing up the sleeve of her sweater to reveal a pastel stamp. "Dragonfly."

"Looks more like a butterfly."

Ana shrugged. "Tattooer was high, but then again so was I. Show you the others, later." Mischievous laughter intimated the additional tattoos' immodest placements.

Ana spent the next thirty minutes recounting her ordeal. "Scared as hell," she said, "but who has time for death?" Ana made her illness sound like an adventure. Her strong will to live comforted Isa who couldn't imagine life without her beacon of light. The sisters cried, giggled, cried some more…and finished the Pinot Grigio. Isa extracted Ana's promise never to keep such secrets from her again.

"So you see, darling, there's really nothing more to say. Nothing more to worry about either." Ana held her finger to her lips, flashing a stern expression followed by a wink. She was the image of their father who used the same tactic to end debate. "Enough about me. Spill your exciting news."

Ana assumed everyone lived A-list lives. She spent one summer sheathing the Eiffel Tower in fabric. Another time, she assisted a photographer who snapped herds of naked people in public places across the globe—an art project and lover du jour.

Isa studied her sister's face. Cancer was cruel. Why did it choose her little kitten? She sighed. "My problems are nothing after what you've been through."

"Nonsense. Won't budge till you reveal every juicy morsel." With her elbow on the table, Ana rested her beautiful face in the palm of her hand.

Isa hadn't planned to bare her soul to her kid sister or anyone else for that matter. Her dark moods, bouts of sadness, and anxiety were her business. She felt helpless, even ashamed, clueless as to cause or cure. Sometimes, she even blamed herself for the gray, paralyzing spells that rolled into her head like a fog, lingering for hours or sometimes days. Surely they'd run their course. She didn't want to spoil the Christmas holiday. But she couldn't lie. Not now, not after Ana had been so candid. But how could she describe something that she herself couldn't explain?

"I'm lost," Isa said looking into her sister's kind eyes for reaction. Grasping Isa's hands, Ana nodded for her to go on. "For the first time in my life, I'm scared to death." As she shared her festering burden, Isa felt liberated. But she couldn't believe she was confessing silly insecurities to a woman who embodied courage.

But Ana didn't judge. She offered validation and empathy. "Not silly, and certainly nothing to be ashamed of," Ana said. "Everyone goes through patches of doubt and despair. Sure we fear death, but most are terrified of life."

"I've made a mess of things, Gattina. No husband, no children, and now not even a steady job." Those words had echoed in Isa's head for weeks in anticipation of the grilling from her mother.

Ana laughed. "Darling, I don't have any of those things either."

"But you live, Ana. You live life to the fullest, just like Papa." Isa sighed. "No, afraid I'm like Mama and Gina."

The irony was clear. Facing death, her sister embraced life more fully than Isa ever could. Ana didn't fear the future like she did—maybe that was her secret.

Ana squeezed Isa's hand. "Darling, you're no more like Mama and Gina than champagne is to grape juice. You've got Papa in you."

"Nonsense! You embrace life. Take it on your terms. No regrets."

Ana shook her head, her sparkling eyes fastened on Isa. "No regrets? Wherever did you get that idea?"

"What could you possibly regret?"

"That I'm not more like Isa, my big sister."

"That's absurd."

"You got the best of both. I'm all Papa. You're grounded like Mama. Educated, a career, independent. Take your London flat."

"Neither my flat nor my career is on solid ground at the moment."

"Temporary setbacks," Ana said, squaring her shoulders. "I've every confidence your consultancy will soar. Patience."

Isa studied Ana's face. "You said, 'best of both'?"

"You carry Papa's spark. Funny, you don't see it. Perhaps, you simply lack the confidence to let yourself go, to embrace your passion."

"As much as I love Papa, I could never be like him, or you for that matter."

Ana's eyebrows arched. "Have you tried?"

Isa closed her eyes, trying to pull something from her past to prove her point. "Yes!" she said, after several seconds. "Remember how Papa played piano? Sang his favorite arias?"

Ana nodded; her cheeks dimpled. "Fondly. You and I on the piano bench with Papa between us. We raced each other to turn the music. Our squeals drove Mama and Gina crazy."

"Called us wild cats."

Ana cleared her throat. "Still waiting."

"Huh?"

"Your artistic flop?"

Isa tapped the table, nodding smugly. "Piano lessons."

"And?"

"Utter failure. Couldn't even master *Chopsticks*."

"Pshaw," Ana said, swooshing the air with her hand. "Anyone can fail at piano. But not everyone can fail at opera. Sing, my dear Isa, sing."

Chapter 4

London—One Month Later

"Christ!" Isa muttered just outside the door of her flat. *Am I losing my mind?*

She was winded from climbing the stairs for the second time in as many minutes. First she'd forgotten her mobile, then the directions. She pushed the key into the lock, opened the door, and marched across the room. Snatching a note off the desk, she read aloud, "Amore, 10 Tavistock," before thrusting the paper into her pocket.

"As if," she grumbled, pulling the door shut—repeating the restaurant's name and address was pointless.

Had this bout of absentmindedness sprung from a fortnight spent with family in San Benedetto? Perhaps shaky finances jumbled her mind. Or just maybe, mental barriers sabotaged her.

As she descended the staircase, Isa tripped over dog leads held by a neighbor, a retired professor pulling two white dogs. Isa avoided a fall by sitting abruptly on the hall bench. Squatting beside the Westies, who looked none the worse for the tussle, the professor wailed, "Darcy, Lizzy, my poor, poor babies." Isa cleared her throat, twice. "Oh! Oh, oh, my apologies, Miss Fabrini."

Rubbing her backside, Isa continued down to the next landing where she came upon Mrs. Grimm watering potted plants. *Just a matter of time,* Isa thought, staring at the drooping ferns. She responded with a polite nod to her neighbor's complaint about the nasty cold spell, resisting an urge to snipe, "It's bloody January." Relations between the women soured when Mrs. Grimm and her cats, named after *EastEnders* television characters, suffered through Isa's failed attempt to master piano. Only twelve feet and a thin layer of plaster separated the neighbors. Buying and repotting several sets of drowned ferns was Isa's self-imposed penance for the angst she caused her neighbor. But her anonymous gesture had unfortunate consequences. Believing she had a green thumb, Mrs. Grimm watered away.

"You can do this." Isa's voice and clicking heels echoed through the empty foyer.

The short stroll to the Kensington High Street Underground was cold, but not unbearable. The chill didn't annoy her as much as the perpetual gloom of a London winter—eight short hours sandwiched between dawn and dusk. *A person tired of London isn't so much tired of life; just bloody fed up with gray*, she thought, waiting with a handful of others on the platform.

At Gloucester Road, Isa changed trains to the Piccadilly line for the short ride to Covent Garden. As the train rumbled under central London, she questioned the wisdom of following Ana's prescription for mental well-being. Was she about to make the biggest blunder of her life?

Thus far, her younger sister's persistence had beaten back second thoughts. At Christmas on the train to San Benedetto, Ana had repeated her suggestion that Isa take up opera. Their papa, whom Ana enlisted in her crusade, nudged Isa throughout the holiday. "Follow your passion, *principessa*," Papa Fabrini said. Perhaps Ana used the operatic quest to divert conversation away from her illness, mention of which sent their mother into sobbing fits and their papa into uncharacteristic sullenness.

Although Ana and her father wore down her resistance, Isa made up her mind only after Gina and her mother gave their opinions. "You're forty," Gina said. "Your voice is untrainable. And you!" she added, turning toward Ana with fire in her eyes. "Might have guessed you put the silly idea into her head. Isabella's consultancy, foolish as that may be, is her life now."

Papa Fabrini frowned. "Opera is life."

Their mother glared at him. "Life? A husband and children are life. But that's never gonna happen." With sniffles and a finger wagging in Isa's face, her mother added, "Don't waste your time in a make-believe world."

By the time Isa left San Benedetto the week after New Year's, she and Ana had found a London-based chorus of opera enthusiasts and the name of a respected voice teacher. Papa Fabrini slipped Isa several LPs from his opera collection when her mother wasn't looking. "Inspiration," he whispered with a peck to her cheek. She didn't have the heart to tell him that she didn't own a turntable.

"Richard Leech." Isa repeated the name as the train pulled away from the Green Park platform.

She didn't care that her voice drew a glance from the smart couple with shopping bags seated across the aisle. *Richard Leech*—the name sounded operatic. Certainly, this Richard Leech wasn't the American tenor. Couldn't be, at least she didn't think so. *Her* Richard Leech— *Heavens! Had she already laid claim to the man*—spoke with occasional bursts of a Liverpudlian accent and blamed a chronic cough on a lifetime attraction to tobacco. Yet, his credentials were stellar. Not only had he sung professionally in his youth with the Royal Opera, but he also taught voice for many years at the University of London. Former students included members of European opera companies. Covent Garden, the organization that sponsored the amateur chorus, listed him among their preferred instructors. Her stomach soured. *Richard Leech will take one look, turn away, and trot off without so much as a scoff or nod.*

As the train sped forward, Isa recalled the last day of her Italian holiday. She and Ana spent the afternoon scouring Milan's trendiest boutiques for a wardrobe worthy of what Ana called, Isa's *stage persona*. "You're as good as anyone," Ana chided after Isa threatened to back out. "You face that Richard Leech as if you're auditioning *him*." Ana made anything seem possible.

Isa smiled, recalling how Ana dragged her to the piazza in front of La Scala. Spinning her reluctant sister to face the opera house, Ana formed Isa's hand into a fist and lifted her arm. "Repeat after me," Ana said. "I shall not rest until my heart sings." Isa, feeling somewhat sheepish, repeated the vow only after her sister threatened to disrobe on the spot.

Unsatisfied with Isa's whisper, Ana added, "Scream as if your life depends upon it."

The plea reminded Isa of Ana's own courageous battle. She kissed her sister's soft cheek. Then with arm raised and fist formed, Isa bellowed at the top of her lungs.

Closest I'll ever come to an opera house, Isa thought as the train screeched into Covent Garden. With a deep breath, she lifted herself from the seat, minded the gap, and headed toward a new adventure. Exiting onto James Street, a whoosh of cold air revitalized her. She turned, navigating toward the market's familiar colonnade.

In any other month, a crush of tourists darting into shops and circling the colorful bands of street performers would have slowed her progress. But in the bone-chilling dampness of January, a gold-sprayed Mad Hatter wore a frozen frown without an audience to bait him out of character. Ten paces down the cobblestones, the head of a floppy-eared man-dog, whose human torso lay hidden under a prop table, stirred and snorted as Isa walked by.

"Throw me a bone, lady," the street performer growled in a voice more Rottweiler than retriever.

Had Fido once aspired to artistic grandeur? Isa shuddered. She pictured herself sheathed head-to-toe in silver lamé, pimping for tourists as Venus or Salome. Reaching into her pocket, she pulled out two coins, eliciting a whimper as they clanked into the street performer's bowl. She winked at the mutt, hoping her tribute would bring good karma to her own pursuit.

With her hands buried deep in her coat pockets, Isa continued toward the market, scanning in the direction of Bow Street. Although she'd attended many performances in the nineteenth-century auditorium, the sight of the Royal Opera House sent her stomach somersaulting. Eliza Doolittle first met her Professor Higgins in this very spot.

Would Richard Leech take her on as a student and would the opera house accept her into its choral program? She remembered Ana's pledge—*No rest until my heart sings.* Would she ever enjoy a full night's sleep again?

With a shake of her head, Isa turned from the building, squared her shoulders and marched toward the Amore restaurant.

She'd passed through Covent Garden often, but never heard of Amore before Richard Leech suggested the restaurant as a meeting place. "Like to meet prospective students on neutral ground," he said between coughing fits in their initial phone call. "Don't want a Steinway to come between us. Or worse, let a ghost-filled hall stifle our chat." His informal manner soothed Isa's nerves.

Turning into Tavistock Street, she passed Mozart's Wine Bar and the Oscar Wilde Pub before finding her rendezvous point. From the outside,

Amore looked like every other schmaltzy Italian restaurant that catered to tourists. Its uninspired name oozed sentimentality. *Owned, no doubt, by a couple from Belfast or Birmingham offering mediocre food and clichéd décor.* She opened the door expecting checkered tablecloths, Chianti bottles dripping with wax, and the sounds of Sinatra.

"Buona sera, bella signora," said the man behind a podium.

"Good evening," Isa replied in her most proper English. While the man's Italian sounded authentic, she wasn't about to be drawn into false familiarity.

"Is madam dining alone?" he asked. Although he spoke in near perfect English, a pleasant voice between tenor and baritone betrayed a genuine Roman accent.

"No." Isa scanned the restaurant although she had no idea what her dinner companion looked like. Linen tablecloths, Murano candlesticks, an upmarket clientele, and Vivaldi gave the room sophistication. "I'm meeting Mr. Leech. Assume he's made a reservation."

"Sì. Signor Leech, one of our regulars. But I have bad news for the lady."

Isa's heart sank. Had her Henry Higgins gotten cold feet? Did he realize the futility in transforming a forty-year-old consultant into an opera singer? She tried to find a clue in the man's heart-shaped face but his big, brown eyes only crinkled with kindness.

"Signor Leech phoned. Sends his apologies. He's running a little late—a fiasco at the opera house." The host replaced a sympathetic pout with a reassuring smile as he offered to take Isa's coat.

Isa exhaled. *Leech hasn't abandoned me just yet.* "But a fiasco? That could take hours."

"You don't know Signor Leech?" he responded with a congenial laugh as he grabbed two menus. "With him, *everything's* a fiasco. No worries, signora, he'll come."

"To meet his next fiasco."

The host cocked his head. *"Scusi?"*

"Nothing, nothing." Isa covered her mouth. She hadn't intended to speak aloud the doubts and insecurities that swirled through her head. Competing for clients convinced her that fear and vulnerability were liabilities. Rich veins of chauvinism still seeped through most layers of business. Like a tortoise, survival required a hard, impenetrable shell.

At the table, the host held Isa's chair and placed a napkin on her lap. The draft from a passing waiter blew out the candle. *Was that a bad omen?* "Please relight that," Isa said, nodding toward the center of the table, a hint of panic in her voice.

"Signora is, perhaps, superstitious?"

"Certainly not!"

After fulfilling her request with a lighter pulled from a pocket, he paused. Isa felt the intensity of his stare. "May I get the signora a glass of wine? Courtesy of the owner."

What compels everyone to offer me free alcohol? "Never met the owner."

"Permit me to change that at once." With a slight bow, he added, "Luca Caruso at your service, lovely signora."

"Isabella Fabrini," she replied, extending her hand. "Very well then, I'll take that glass of wine, thank you."

Caruso, she thought as he walked away, *trumped up alias if ever I heard one*. But whatever his name, she admitted to herself that the distinguished man with wavy salt-and-pepper hair looked splendid.

Isa pulled a makeup kit from her purse. Holding the mirror to her eyes, her gaze drifted to a man seated at another table. While the face had aged and the hairline receded, the curls were the same, only silvered—and of course, the scar under the eye. Given his scrawny frame, she'd doubted his claim of earning the jagged mark in a spirited rugby match.

Isa hadn't seen Willy Epson in years. They last ran into each other two years out of business school at a fundraiser in the City, a pet charity for one of the lesser royals. Willy made a splash during the auction, the high bidder for a gaudy piece of jewelry, a crucifix studded with semiprecious stones. He drew a mild rebuke from the podium when he upped his own high bid. After doubling over in laughter, Willy waved a hand at the auctioneer. "The bid stands," he shouted, basking in the ensuing applause. "It's only money." Obviously, Willy's job as an investment banker paid well.

Further studying the reflection, Isa didn't recognize the young blonde seated with him. She wasn't the same woman presented as Willy's wife at business school. *Hell, nine years ago, that woman was barely out of diapers.*

With Isa's consulting business floundering, networking wouldn't hurt. Her savings were hemorrhaging, and that was before voice lessons. Intent on reintroducing herself, she turned in her chair. Willy must have seen her first. He sprang to his feet and walked over to her table.

"Isabella Fabrini," he said with a wide smile. "It's been years."

"Yes, can't remember when we last saw each other." Isa fibbed as Willy bent down to kiss her cheek. "I don't often hobnob with the City's power brokers."

His lips turned up slightly, not one of those shy, half-embarrassed smiles but rather a flash of pride at the label. "I'm waiting for someone," Isa said. "Can you sit for a moment?" She nodded toward his companion. "And your…"

With a bit of nervous laughter, Willy flashed his same prideful look. "Fiancée. Eva. Well…er, not quite fiancée, *yet*. Still married to Lenore. You remember Lenore?"

Isa nodded, wondering if Lenore knew that her days as Mrs. Willy Epson were numbered. Was she supposed to congratulate him? "Oh, terribly sorry."

"I'm not. Best for both of us…long time coming."

Luca Caruso, delivering Isa's wine, interrupted the conversation. Without looking up, Willy barked an order. "Bourbon and soda."

Isa offered the restaurant owner a sympathetic smile before responding to her old school chum. "A healthy perspective, perhaps, but a loss nonetheless."

"Gotta recognize a loser, lost cause. Too many people hang on long after they've mined the value."

"Are you speaking personally or professionally?" His comment sounded to her like an investment strategy.

Willy's gray eyes narrowed. After a few seconds, he laughed, dusting the table with his hand. "I know it must sound cold, but business and marriage are just two sides of the same coin."

Isa guessed Lenore had learned that lesson, but wondered what Eva might say about her presumptive fiancé's philosophy. "Don't need to ask about you," Isa said. "Your name's always popping up in the newspapers." In fact, she'd recently heard his firm linked to a shady investment scheme but chose discretion. She wanted his help, not his wrath.

"Things couldn't be better. Embarrassingly high returns. Customers banging down the door."

Isa would have killed for one client scratching at hers. Many in the City were swimming in cash. Willy graduated at the top of their class. She assumed he rode the crest of the wave of new millionaires with nary an atom of embarrassment.

As Willy spoke, Luca deposited the bourbon on the table with a silverware-rattling thud. With a glance at the simmering host, Isa forced herself not to smile.

After downing half of his drink, Willy extended his jaw, a gesture that exaggerated his pointed chin. "What about you? Still the good corporate soldier? Assuming you never married."

Aware of Willy's curious gaze, Isa covered her ring finger. With the conversation's tilt toward her, she guessed that Willy had exhausted his litany of accolades. Isa didn't bore him with a career history, and she certainly didn't respond to his rude comment about her marital state. Instead, she fast-forwarded to the present and described her consultancy. "I'm doing okay." She lied, before digging in her purse for a business card. "But always eager to take on new clients. Management triage and leadership development are my specialties."

Willy stared at the card. "Not easy to reinvent yourself. Takes guts. Constant target for enemies eager to see you to fail." Tilting back his head, he finished off the bourbon.

Isa felt his sincerity for the first time since he sat down. She detected sadness in his voice, but didn't press. They never had that kind of a relationship. Besides, Willy was terribly British—stiff upper lip and all. But he had opened the door.

"My consulting business is nothing compared to my new venture… actually more *ad*-venture," she said, before taking a sip of wine. "Reason I'm here." She enjoyed watching the expression that met her announcement— cocked head, furrowed brow.

He rested an elbow on the table and leaned forward. "Do share."

She described her plan. "Not an international star, mind you. I'd be happy for a shot in the chorus."

Willy winked. "At school, Isa Fabrini pushed the professors, countless what-ifs, fantastic scenarios—project-of-the-year. You'll make the chorus. Might even aim higher."

Isa wished she shared his confidence. "First things first. Need an invite into the chorus and a voice teacher. Feel a bit at the moment like a draggle-tailed guttersnipe."

A blank expression told her that the reference to *Pygmalion* flew over his head. "Stick with your dreams," he said. "Bet you'd never guess I wanted to be a painter. But dear old father…" With fingers tracing his facial scar, Willy's expression careened between rage and sadness. "Ah, that's all ancient history. If all else fails," he added, transforming back into an investment banker, "and you fancy *easy money*, invest with me." With a nod toward Eva whose thumping fingers and tapping foot drew both their attention, Willy rose from the table. "Honestly—*big* returns. Some of our old school chums are clients—Jamie Stuart, Walter Benchley."

Isa's stomach sank. She had taken years to push Walter's name from her mind...and heart. She cleared her throat, pretending she hadn't heard. "Feel free to throw me clients," she said, cringing at the echo of the street performer's words, *throw me a frigging bone.*

No sooner had Willy left than Luca approached her table. His broad shoulders practically eclipsed the figure Isa detected trailing behind him. From their phone conversation, she recognized the cough of the voice teacher, still invisible except for his protruding belly handles. She gulped the rest of her wine.

"Signora Fabrini, your Mr. Leech." As Luca stepped aside, wafts of bergamot and lilac touched Isa's nose.

Most artists she knew were a bit crazy—eccentric, especially the good ones. Richard Leech expressed his idiosyncrasies with color. Orange eyeglasses, yellow pants, and a violet scarf snaking down to his calves comprised his personal rainbow. A moon of a head topped with a thinning mop of lavender-rinsed hair connected, without visible evidence of a neck, to a pudgy torso. Short legs reminded her of a stick-figure drawing while turquoise shoes that curled at the toes covered his feet.

He extended his hand, palm down. "Call me Leech." But before Isa could respond, he turned away. *"Caro mio, grazie."* He rose on tiptoes and kissed Luca's cheek. "Extra for good measure." He planted a third kiss and swatted the seat of Luca's trousers before the blushing restaurant owner retreated.

"Love that man," Leech trilled as he turned back to Isa. "So, you want to be an opera star?" As he sat, he squeezed Isa's hand and didn't let go. "Tell me about yourself."

The very opener she'd rehearsed for days. "First off, call me Isa. Everyone does." She began her history: birth in Italy, childhood in Argentina. She plodded on, undeterred by Leech's coughing fits.

When she got to business school, Leech raised both hands. "Stop, stop! *Enough.* Backstories bore me. Tell me where you're going."

"Excuse me?"

"Dear Isabella, you've got a lyrical name, beautiful face, sensuous speaking voice, and excellent diction. Above all, you're Italian. You are Opera!"

Isa felt herself blush. Surely the interview couldn't be that simple?

"But to guide you," Leech added, "I must know where you wish to go."

How to answer? A feeble response would gut her chances.

Luca's return gave her time to think. The handsome host set down a tray containing a second glass of wine for Isa and what looked like a lab experiment for Leech: a glass, two bottles—one green, one clear—a silver spoon and a bowl of sugar cubes. "Absinthe," Luca said, no doubt seeing her bewilderment.

Isa watched Leech prepare his concoction. He placed a sugar cube on the spoon and rested it over the liquor-filled glass. Next and with eyes focused, he poured the water over the sugar. Both watched in silence as the cube dissolved. "Calms my cough." Leech sipped his drink, closed his eyes, and tipped his head backward. He sighed before breaking the silence. "I'm waiting, Miss Fabrini. Where is it you wish to go?"

She writhed in her chair, willing herself not to hyperventilate. A vision of Ana in front of La Scala inspired her with courage. Her voice rose just above a whisper. "I want to sing opera."

Leech sat up. His little blue eyes peered at her from behind the orange-framed glasses. "*Want* to sing opera? Not good enough. I suggest you figure it out before either one of us wastes our time."

The guttersnipe would never make it to the Embassy Ball. Isa reached for her purse. "I believed discipline and a need to sing would be sufficient. Sorry, Mr. Leech."

The liquor glass paused at his lips; his eyes seemed to spark. "Whatever for, my pet?"

"I've obviously wasted your time. I'm better suited as a flower peddler."

She started to stand but Leech squeezed her arm. "Nonsense!"

"But you said—"

"Said what, my pet? I say a lot of things."

"You said, 'Stop wasting any more of our time'."

His hand flitted over the table. "Merely a figure of speech. I don't mean half of what I say. As for the other half...well...no one listens anyway. Opera's full of drama. Get used to it."

"I don't understand. No, yes, maybe?"

"Your *wants*, my pet, are pretty little ribbons. But your *needs*, ah, your needs are a gift, true north on your personal compass. Should have said you needed to sing opera in the first place. Would have saved ourselves all this senseless banter." He studied her over his eyeglasses. "But in all truth, you're not getting any younger."

Isa gasped. Should she laugh or cry? She felt her biological clock lurch forward—visions of collapsing lungs and snapping vocal cords, not to mention arterial hardening and the onslaught of senility. "Perhaps I should meet with an undertaker?"

Leech patted her hand. "We've no time for jokes or self-pity, we must begin at once."

"I'm in?" she asked, still uncertain.

"Of course you're in…*with me.*"

Reaching over the table, she hugged him. As his perfume enveloped her, she stiffened. "You said, 'With me'?"

He nodded. "A voice teacher's one thing. Our next hurdle…Lady Blatherwicke. We've only a few weeks before your audition."

She sat back, slumping in the chair. She'd forgotten about the chorus. Of course there'd be an audition. But she'd never be ready so soon. "Is this what you'd call a fiasco?"

"Worse!" His lips puckered as he sighed. "Not a pleasant experience, not pleasant at all. The chorus may be amateur, but Lady B guards the gate with the ferocity of Cerberus."

Familiar with mythology, Isa shuddered at the reference. Cerberus, a creature with three heads, a serpent's tail and a mane of snakes guarded the entrance to the underworld.

They finished what remained in their glasses before Leech broke the silence. "Auditions begin in one month and conclude four weeks later. No exceptions! With luck, I can worm you into the very last time slot." Leech thumped his forehead. She sensed his mind turning, devising tactics to make that happen.

The emotional roller coaster exhausted her. However, she had to trust, Leech. She admired brutal honesty—knowing the path, difficult though it may be that lay before her. Too many people stumbled through life happily deluded—that whole ignorance-is-bliss crap. *None of that for me.*

Leech handed Isa a card with his studio address and phone number. "Thursday, six p.m." His licorice-scented breath blew out the table candle.

Chapter 5

After a fitful night's sleep, Isa spent most of Thursday leaping through emotional acrobatics at the prospect of her first voice lesson. As soon as she pumped herself up, convinced she had the mettle to succeed, doubts crept into her mind and thrashed her self-confidence. The distraction almost kept her from meeting a client's deadline for details of a mentoring program they engaged her to design. She kept finding herself glancing to the corner of her desk, and the violet-hued business card. She recognized the address as a street in the West End. *Silly to have imagined Leech's studio inside the opera house. Of course he'd need his own space.*

After climbing the steps from the Underground, Isa gazed across Piccadilly Circus. How many times had she passed Eros, perch for tourists and pigeons alike, without a glance? Yet since meeting Leech, she became reflective—hypersensitive. She scrutinized everything, especially herself, through a fresh lens. The quirky voice teacher had stoked the smoldering embers of self-confidence. A flickering glow illuminated a purposeful future.

Isa waited with a throng of pedestrians at the traffic signal. Lights from giant neon billboards shimmered on the sides of double-decker buses and black cabs that snaked up Regent's Street. Stores brimmed with customers enjoying late-night Thursday. She crossed Sherwood Street and made her way up Shaftesbury Avenue.

A light drizzle began to fall, but didn't stifle the odors wafting from stalls that sold pasties, kebabs, and Chinese takeaway. She quickened her pace, dodging a wall of umbrellas and skipping over puddles leftover from the last downpour. As she gazed up at the street sign, a passing umbrella nearly impaled her rain hat.

Rupert Street was home to a cluster of adult bookstores, sex shops, and stores with blackened storefronts (what the latter housed, God only knew). The seedy area known as Soho was on the edge of the West End, a place where legitimate theater mingled with its bastard cousins—peep shows and strip clubs.

"Brilliant!" Isa said, reaching the address. The building's ground floor housed a clothing shop, Drag Strip. Window mannequins modeled gowns, go-go outfits and vintage cabin attendant uniforms in every color of the rainbow. Isa wondered whether Leech enjoyed a tenant discount.

One floor above the shop, the voice teacher opened the red-lacquered door to his studio. "Isabella, my pet. You're here."

She detected surprise in his tone. Was he impressed with her navigational abilities or stunned that she had the nerve to move forward?

"Call me Isa—" She cut herself off, remembering Leech's shortlist of her artistic assets—a lyrical Italian name…and little more. "Nice location, Mr. Leech," she said instead. Her eyes scanned the room—a motif best described as shabby chic. Plush chairs and a camelback sofa in bright velvets were set on angles facing the fireplace. Original art covered the walls, selected it seemed, more for bold color than for composition. The studio impressed Isa as a place where form and function melded, a room equally suited to students of high opera, Andrew Lloyd Webber, and lap dances.

"It's the shits," the voice teacher replied, "but the rent's cheap and the neighborhood feeds me a steady flow of students." Leech responded to her puzzled expression with an explanation. "Opera may be my fave, pet, but aspiring divas are only dessert. West End choristers and strippers keep the wine flowing and my tummy full." He patted a belly bulge under his purple caftan. "Everyone's got a dream."

Piercing blue eyes stared at her, then darted to the heavily draped window in front of which sat a baby grand piano topped with framed photographs and other treasures. What had he seen in her face? Perhaps her tightened brow and wrinkled nose betrayed her judgment on those 'working girls.' *Absurdly unfair of me, small minded.* Hadn't she after all, rejected Gina's and her mother's head-shaking scowls when she shared her dream? Leech was right. Everyone had a right to seek a better life—a chance to pursue passion.

But what drove the interesting Richard Leech? She'd have to wait for that answer.

Leech took her hat and coat, hanging them beside a green cape. An assortment of head covers mingled on the shelf above the wardrobe hooks—an orange fez, a studded cockney cap, and one with a plume *à la* Robin Hood. Leech motioned her to sit on the cherry-red sofa beside which stood a small table topped by a pitcher of water, a drinking glass, and a vase containing a single rose. The voice teacher sat opposite, studying her.

"Up! Up, up, up!" he shouted, sitting forward. "I must teach you to breathe."

"I know how to breathe. Been doing it all my life." *Oh God, did I just say that?* She often masked unease with sarcasm and humor.

Leech didn't react to her gibe. He rose, extended his arms, and lifted her to her feet. "Breathing is the second most important thing you need to succeed."

"And the first?"

"An outstanding teacher, of course." He laughed, provoking a coughing fit. "A little joke, my pet, a little joke. Good health, that's what's most essential. Sound mind, body, voice, and all that shit."

She controlled an urge to roll her eyes—such a philosophy coming from a chubby chain-smoker.

"Breathe!" He grimaced. "No! Like this." He stood erect, neck straight, back arched. Stomach muscles flexed. "Now you...better, better," he said stepping beside her and applying pressure to her back and abdomen. "Feel that? From the depths of your soul."

Soul! In the name of creativity, she let his reference to religious gibberish slide. Leech after all held her fate and diaphragm in his hands.

"No! No, no, no!" he shouted, pushing down her head. "Vocal cords run front to back, like this." With his hand, he sliced a line on the side of her neck from Adam's apple to nape. "A chin too high or low strains the vocal folds. Think of a string pulling upward from the crown of your head."

She'd become a marionette, Leech's puppet on a string. But the image and lesson stuck.

Despite Leech's admitted addiction, Isa caught only a slight whiff of cigarettes when she brushed passed the opera cape. Her scan of the room didn't turn up any telltale signs—ashtray, match, cigarette box. "Given up smoking?"

Leech's hand fluttered like a butterfly, a gesture Isa first noticed during their initial meeting. "No, my pet. Wouldn't dare bring that filthy habit into my studio." After allowing her a drink of water, he returned to his drill. "Breathe, Isabella, breathe."

Another thirty minutes passed with her doing nothing except inhaling and exhaling. Bending her forward at the waist, he placed his hands on her lower back. "Breathing low is like filling a tire. Feel the air filling all the way around."

Isa stood up, pessimism sweeping over her. "I must say something."

Leech sank down onto a chair and motioned her to sit. "What is it, my pet?"

"At best, we've seven more sessions before I face Lady Blatherwicke, at worst, three."

His tiny eyes enlarged to the size of pound coins. Twitching with delight, he clapped his hands several times. "Seven weeks, Isabella, *seven*. Good fortune is ours. You're set for the last day of auditions. I was saving that little *bon bon*."

Pressure lifted from Isa's sagging shoulders. She applauded. "You did it? You snared the last slot?"

He shrugged; a blush rose in his cheeks. "Well, second to last. Gwilly Bowser snatched the final slot," he said, seething with a frown. "But good enough. Gives us a sporting chance."

"How did you ever manage it?"

He lifted his hand to his mouth. "Not usually one to tell." He leaned forward, eyes twinkling. "Called in a favor from Lady Blatherwicke's assistant." His blush deepened.

Isa's euphoria vanished. With downcast eyes, she picked at invisible lint on her slacks. "Seven weeks may as well be seven years."

"Confidence!" he replied. "You've got Leech."

As Leech reviewed vocal exercises for home, loud knocks at the door ended the session. "Blast! You in there, Leech?" bellowed a voice from the hall. "Friggin' door's bolted."

On his feet, Leech scurried to the door. His billowing caftan knocked the table, the teetering vase steadied by Isa's quick hands. "Coming, Ivy," Leech shouted. He spoke to Isa over his shoulder. "My next student. Works up the street at Ramon's."

Isa retrieved her coat and hat. "Rather impatient, isn't she?"

"Ivy dashes from our lesson to the theater. She's used to an open door. Didn't have anyone in this slot before."

Leech's frenzy and stammering made Isa smile. She found his use of the term *theater* to describe a stripper bar *très charmant*. Expecting a glamorous showgirl, Isa stood with breath held and eyes fixed. But instead of a tall, willowy blonde with fishnet stockings and stilettos, Leech opened the door to a plump woman dressed in grays and blacks, no taller than the voice teacher.

"Apologies, my angel. I've got a new pupil," Leech said, gesturing toward Isa.

"Isa—Isa*bella*," she said, extending her arm.

"That explains the *friggin'* door," the newcomer said, accepting Isa's hand. "Irene." She beamed a smile that dimpled apple-dumpling cheeks. "But call me Ivy. Leech says it's *lyrical*." Isa looked to the teacher whose cheeks crimsoned.

The next seven weeks progressed much the same for Isa. On most days, consultancy work occupied her from morning to midnight with two hours squeezed in for breathing and vocal exercises. One Sundays, in addition to an entire morning dedicated to training her voice, she took long walks through Hyde Park. The fresh air cleared her mind of business clutter in order to concentrate on music.

Though she hadn't thought about it in years, her drills for Leech recalled the many years spent in youth choruses back in Argentina. While her mother pushed her into the church chorus, her papa bartered his tailoring skills to send Isa and her sisters to voice lessons with another Italian immigrant. At their father's direction, the plump woman whose home smelled of anisette cookies exposed the girls to Puccini, Verdi, Rossini, Donizetti and other Italian composers. Isa tapped into that training to prepare for her weekly voice lesson.

Thursday was all Leech—body, mind, and voice. The sixty-minute drill ended with Ivy's grand entrance—a friggin' this or a friggin' that. At the end of Isa's second lesson, Leech assigned more homework—a cool down exercise—Amore restaurant.

"Compulsory," Leech said, guiding her out the door. "One glass of wine, or two, or three, and pasta are your rewards, my pet. Luca offers student discounts."

"More backdoor bartering," Isa said with a smirk.

Saturday was Isa's day—reading, shopping, cinema, theater, opera—wherever the mood carried her. And always a call to Ana once Isa tracked her sister down to Berlin, Venice, Barcelona or…she couldn't keep track.

Ana began every call the same. "Mesmerize me."

"Doing my best," Isa said. She knew better than to admit her insecurities to her younger sister. She didn't want Ana flying to London for some emergency handholding. She had her own life, her own problems.

Ana ended the calls the same way. "Shout it out!"

Isa knew what Ana wanted—better to get it over with. "*No sing, no sleep!*"

After the shout, Isa pressed her ear to the phone. She braced for an argument, a complaint that she shortened the vow to a trite chant. Ana would say that Isa had ripped the heart out of the pledge. *But seriously, "I shall not rest until my heart sings." Who am I supposed to be, the Queen of England?*

Hearing Ana's gasp through the phone, Isa cringed. *Here it comes.*

"Fantastic," Ana said. "Love, love, love."

"You do?"

"It's so you. I picture you beating your chest."

Isa giggled—she couldn't help herself.

"Besides," Ana added, "it's your vow, not mine. I'm so proud of you, darling."

From that moment, Isa owned the vow. She shouted, "No sing, no sleep" in her flat to the chagrin of Mrs. Grimm, the professor, and all her neighbors. The chant became her battle cry.

"My job's done. Tomorrow's up to you," Leech said at their last session before Isa's audition.

Isa stopped sliding sheet music into her portfolio. "Any final words?"

Beneath a red and gold Gandhi cap, Leech beamed from ear to ear. "Don't be frightened."

"I'm nervous as hell."

"Isa," he said using the diminutive for the first time, "you'll be fine. Just remember *everything* I taught you." Isa patted his hand. "But don't be cocky. Lady Blatherwicke relishes her reputation as a ball buster. Remember, balance…balance."

"What about unbridled exuberance?" Leech used that phrase repeatedly during lessons to push her performance.

He rested one hand on his hip while the other wagged in Isa's face. "Exuberance must wait, my pet. It's *balance* until you're accepted."

She kissed his cheek. "A third for good luck. You're a darling little man."

Holding her shoulders, he flashed a coy smile. "Now, off to Luca's with you."

"I couldn't eat a thing. And I wouldn't trust myself near alcohol... not tonight."

His hand fluttered in her face. "Nonsense, my pet. Luca expects you." She felt the pressure of his hand on her back as he guided her toward the door. From the threshold, she glanced back into the studio. What had she forgotten? Leech solved her conundrum.

"Where's Ivy?" he said. "Not like my little angel to be late."

Leech's concern was that of teacher for student. Isa's interest was pure selfishness. Ivy Vine also planned to audition. In fact, in yet another deal with Malcolm, Lady Blatherwicke's assistant, Leech secured a slot for Ivy immediately prior to Isa's audition. *A strategic placement,* Isa thought, grasping for any advantage. She assumed Lady Blatherwicke would welcome Isa's staid repertoire as a salve for the *friggin'* wounds inflicted upon her refined ears by the stripper. Ivy simply had to show. She was the squeak that would grease Isa's slide into the chorus.

Isa spent the morning of her audition popping out for this and that. She picked up her dress from the cleaners, nothing too fancy—tea-length knit in red. Next stop, Sloane Square and a darling boutique for black Italian shoes with a medium heel she'd ordered weeks before. Leech's *balance...balance* rang in her ears. Besides banishing the gray and trading auburn for raven black, Isa instructed the stylist, "Definitely not Margaret Thatcher, not Diana either—glamor." He poofed Isa's hair into a style reminiscent of Joan Collins or Elizabeth Taylor. Skillful applications from the Harrods cosmetologist along with nail polish and lipstick in modest shades of red completed the makeover.

As Isa made her way up the stairs to her flat, Mrs. Grimm opened her front door. "Delivery for you." The older woman produced a vase of roses wrapped in cellophane. "Something to do with your singing." Her nose inched toward a card that resembled a scroll of sheet music.

Offering a thank you, Isa took the flowers. Through the closed door, she heard the older woman grumble, "No sing, no sleep? *Bollocks!*"

Upstairs in her flat, Isa tore open the cellophane. "Ana? Leech?" She hadn't told anyone else about the audition. When she unrolled the scroll, her eyes welled with tears.

Per la mia piccola principessa, Canta con tutto il cuore! Papa

She hadn't mentioned the tryout to her father. Why disappoint him if she failed? Ana must have shared her secret. She felt lighthearted as she inhaled the air sweetened by the scent of her papa's roses. She whirled around on the balls of her feet and grabbed her music—"Musetta's Waltz" from *La Bohème.* Her audition piece had to be Italian. Her papa would demand nothing else from his little princess. "Bollocks, Mrs. Grimm, bollocks!" Isa shouted before singing Puccini with all her heart.

Staring past the driver through the windshield, Isa fretted, worried that the taxi might not get through Friday afternoon traffic in time. "Bloody hell!" She hadn't meant to utter the words. If anything, she was to blame for not leaving earlier. Swearing only made the driver go slower. Her mind was jumbled with fear. Opera began to give her life purpose, an artistic vocation beyond grubbing for clients and a paycheck. Leech and her ripening voice awakened her confidence. The mental fogs that blanketed her spirit hadn't vanished, but they rolled in less often.

The taxi pulled to the curb—ten minutes to spare. Auditions were held in a building next to the Royal Opera. An amateur chorus, Isa assumed, even one under the auspices of Lady Blatherwicke, wasn't compatible with the dignity of the main opera house. Frantic after trying three locked doors, Isa finally remembered Leech's instructions about the side entrance. A comatose elevator forced her to run up four flights of stairs. "Ivy, please be there," Isa mumbled, getting winded by the third landing. She ran down the hall, sliding to a stop in front of the audition room, its door closed. Dropping onto a bench, she held her stomach and grabbed for her purse.

"No, no, no!" A woman's voice boomed from behind the door.

Isa checked her face in the makeup mirror. "Poor Ivy."

Still the rants came from inside the audition room, intermixed with hushed whimpers. "You can't sing. Next year? This is an adjunct chorus of the Royal Opera, not a prison glee club." Even for Ivy, the criticism was harsh. Isa felt surging sympathy for the poor woman. The voice bellowed again. "Goes against my better judgment, but Malcolm says—"

The opening of the door prevented her from hearing the rest. Lavender wisps of hair and a crimson nose preceded the appearance of Leech's round face. He peered down at Isa, cheeks red, sweat dripping from his forehead onto the polished wood floor. "Isabella, thank God you're here. I was worried. Fifteen minutes. We had a…" He paused, looked back over his shoulder into the room, then returned his gaze and whispered, "Fiasco."

Isa began to speak, but Leech shook his head. Sweat beads flicked through the air. The head vanished; the door slammed. Her prior glee faded. Had Ivy poisoned the entire well?

The sound of pounding came from the room—wood against wood. "Begin!"

Isa shrank in her seat. The piano began. She recognized the opening measures of "O Mio Babbino Caro." She smirked. Poor dear chose Puccini. Soho diction was no match for native Italian.

The singing began. Isa held her breath. The first note cracked. Isa smiled. The second and third wavered. She exhaled and looked to the ceiling. But in a matter of seconds, her mouth dropped open.

"*Sì, sì, ci voglio andare!*" Ivy's voice was magical. She hit her stride and Isa's stomach soured.

Several minutes passed before Leech retrieved her. "What's wrong?" he asked, enveloping her in his arms. "You're shaking."

Isa's knees buckled. Thank God, he held her. "If Lady Blatherwicke treats an angel like shit, what hope do I have?"

Mumbling reassurances, Leech pulled her through the doorway. She almost didn't recognize the showgirl. Frump had surrendered to fairy. Radiant in midnight blue, Ivy appeared years younger because of hairstyle and makeup. She chatted with a young man with short, dark hair and intense brown eyes. Isa thought him more beautiful than handsome. He wore fitted jeans, a T-shirt accentuating his chest muscles, and a dinner jacket. She surmised this was Malcolm. Leech had told her that the assistant assumed the accompanist role for auditions.

The only other person in the room had to be Lady Blatherwicke. The chorus mistress stood in a corner holding a walking stick, her back to the door. Her judge was no dowager. A pink Chanel suit hugged a slim and shapely figure. Leaning over a desk, she spoke into a box.

Leech saw Isa staring. "That's her," he said in hushed voice. "Sorry for the delay. Gwilly Bowser rang up in the middle of Ivy's audition."

Of course, a speakerphone. Isa realized her error. Ivy wasn't the target. Lady Blatherwicke had been ranting at Leech's archrival, Gwilly Bowser. The two voice teachers competed for students as well as bragging rights over which had more of their protégées in the amateur chorus.

Leech snatched the sheet music from her hands. "Last time Gwilly gets her private number, I can assure you. Insolent bastard." Leech walked toward the piano and the dashing Malcolm.

Ivy, looking more beautiful up close, came up to her. "Good luck, Isa. You're a stunner." And she was gone, floating out of the room like a ballerina. Isa felt her face warm with the heat of embarrassment.

"I abhor tardiness," Lady Blatherwicke said, turning to face Isa.

The indictment stung although Isa couldn't fathom how the woman could possibly blame her. Leech had coached Isa to maintain eye contact—"Shows your mettle," he said. The imposing figure approached. Long blonde hair framed a creaseless oval face. If Leech hadn't revealed the woman's age, Isa never would have guessed the grande dame standing before her approached eighty.

Stopping five paces short of Isa, Lady B looked her up and down. "Mature."

"But driven, bursting with passion, I assure you," Leech said, head bobbing and hands fluttering.

The chorus mistress turned to him; walking stick pounded floor. "When I want your opinion…"

Leech nodded. He appeared to shrink within his five-foot frame.

Isa reached for the other woman's extended hand. "Isabella Fabrini."

"Real name? Doesn't matter. It's good." She snapped her fingers.

"I'm all set," called the voice from Isa's side. She turned to see Malcolm, dimpled cheeks and cleft chin, seated at the piano. He flashed a brilliant smile.

"Ready, Miss Fabrini?" Lady B's voice recalled Isa to her mission. Reestablishing eye contact, Isa nodded her response. Stick pounded floor. "Begin!"

"Quando me'n vò soletta per la via, La gente sosta e mira…"

Isa didn't know how she managed or from where the inspiration sprang, but she sang with a clear and strong voice. When finished, Isa looked over at Leech. He beamed. Malcolm rewarded her with a wink. But giddiness vanished when she turned to the only person in the room whose opinion mattered.

Lady B lifted her chin and stared at her. Her hands rested on the walking stick, the head of which glistened in the chandelier light like a diamond. "Thank you, Miss Fabrini." She didn't move.

Neither did Isa. Leech mentioned the high probability that Isa would learn her fate immediately. The last slots usually did.

Lady B kept her eyes fixed on her. "Admirable." Isa brightened. Lady B's eyebrows rose as she continued, "Admirable for a woman of your age and experience, but mediocre at best."

Leech gasped. Before his head bowed, Isa saw him mouth, *fiasco*. She squared her shoulders. She'd done her best, that's all that mattered. She overcame insecurities and conquered her fears. *Bloody hell, there are other choruses.* As she turned to go, an exaggerated cough came from the piano.

Lady B's stick rapped the floor. "You're not excused, Miss Fabrini."

Isa flinched. She readied her return volley, but Leech's wide eyes stopped her. Color returned to puffy cheeks.

The chorus mistress scowled. "We'll have to discipline your voice."

Isa's head bobbled between Leech and Lady B. Excitement and fear electrified her entire body. "Are you saying I'm in?"

"Conditionally," Lady B replied. "I owe Leech for sending me the voice of an angel."

"I don't understand."

"You, Miss Fabrini, scooted in on the *brilliant* coattails of Ivy Vine."

Chapter 6

London—One Year Later

*B*rainchild of a sadist. If reunions were truly the jubilant affairs promoted in glossy invitations and alumni newsletters, why hadn't antiquity recorded their genesis? Perhaps archaeologists would someday unearth a stone tablet in an Alpine cave:

> *You're cordially invited to the twentieth anniversary of the sacking of Rome. Mingle with fellow pillagers. Relive those magical years of mayhem. See what became of the Barbarian voted most likely to civilize.*

"Damn! Ten years and nothing to show for it." Isa had sat at her desk staring at the invitation for so long that sunshine faded to shadows inside her flat. Her eyes wandered to a bank statement. She managed cash flows with the nerves of a gymnast teetering across a balance beam—a tilt to the credits, a totter to the debits. Thus far, she managed to keep from tumbling onto her bum—odd jobs, barter and raids on savings. A lengthy illness or drought of clients meant overdrafts, the stigma of failure, and the loss of her flat. The looming threat to her independence terrified her.

A ringtone interrupted the silence. Lifting her head from her hands, Isa answered the telephone.

"Isa? *Amazing* to hear your voice. Guess who."

"Danny Chance." She recognized the rapid-fire delivery and accent of her old school chum. Danny fit the New York stereotype—polished, pressed, driven. He spoke as if he had mere seconds to recite the entire Manhattan phone directory.

Isa liked Danny even though at times he reminded her of a runaway party balloon. He attended only the first half of the two-year program in London, returning home to finish his degree. He didn't want to be an ocean away from landing his dream job on Wall Street. "Right time, right place…then pounce," Danny said when he announced his departure. Isa admired the confidence that attached itself so freely to him and his countrymen.

"Don't have much time to talk," Danny said. "Lunching with a Saudi prince and his London bankers. Looking to repatriate a few greenbacks for a chunk of Midtown."

"Be sure to check the serial numbers under the oil smudges, Danny." Isa snickered, recalling how he bristled at the diminutive.

"Never knew you were such an Arabphobe."

"I'm not. It's English bankers I distrust." She toyed with him, but the image of Walter Benchley in a Savile Row suit erased her smirk. "Mustn't keep you from the prince."

"Yes, yes, to the point. I'm coming to the reunion. Want to make sure you'll be there." His words clicked in staccato.

She glanced at the invitation and cringed. "Er—"

"*No* is not an option. It's all settled then, I'll send you my itinerary." His tempo slowed. "D'ya s'pose Tommy will be there?"

"I don't—"

"He's gotta come. Can you nudge him for me? Sure you will. You're good at that. It'll be *amazing* to see Tommy…and you of course…and everyone. Gotta run. *Ciao.*"

Isa hung up the phone. Switching on the desk lamp, she caught her reflection in the window. "Shit, shit, shit!" How could she possibly let her business school chums see her like that—tired, defeated? "Six weeks to get lovely," she grumbled, sucking in her tummy, pushing out her chest and pinching crinkles to the edges of her face. She remembered another race with the calendar—a summons before blistering Lady Blatherwicke. *Life*, Isa pondered, *is merely a series of auditions, deadlines, and final acts.*

Six weeks flew by like an English summer. A starvation diet, gallons of green tea, weekly facials, and an afternoon of beauty salon machinations made Isa presentable. Weren't emergency funds intended for just such a crisis? She squeezed into a D&G red sweater dress, camouflaging bulges with a black linen jacket. Isa transformed herself into a Balenciaga-shod *trompe l'oeil.*

Had she gone too glam? Standing at the druggist's counter inside the Baker Street Underground, she encountered two gawking urchins. Did they think her a wax-figure fugitive from nearby Madame Tussauds? Isa was about to stick out her tongue at the little monsters when the girl, tugging her mother's sleeve, said, "She looks like a film star, Mum." The precious little boy nodded, his mouth dropped open. Beaming a smile for the little darlings, Isa threw the breath mints into her handbag with surging confidence.

She strode up Baker Street toward Regent's Park as if on a red carpet. Sunshine and a breeze steeped with the perfume of late spring blossoms filled her with delight. The sweet scent stirred memories of afternoons in the park. She often fled the stale dormitory, escaping across the ring road for long walks.

A gust of wind chilled the air and her mood. Her mind wandered to a secluded, darker section of the park. Had that ghastly bower, the site of her humiliating betrayal, been spared the Biblical plagues she cursed upon it?

The screeching brakes of a black cab returned Isa's focus to Baker Street. Flocks of pilgrims loitered in front of 221b. *Blind faith,* she thought, *is the foundation of all religions, even the cult of Sherlock Holmes.* The fact that the legendary sleuth was born in the pages of *The Strand* didn't deter camera-toting tourists drawn to a fictional address. She read that the current occupant of the glass and concrete office block, a building society, hired a secretary to answer letters posted to the master of deduction, a *Dear Santa* for desperate delusionals.

Perhaps she'd overlooked a potential lifeline. "Dear Mr. Holmes, help! I fear the nefarious Moriarty has purloined my career." *How silly.* Her life wasn't as bleak as that of a tormented Victorian heroine. She'd managed to keep herself fed, sheltered, and schooled in vocal technique—if only just barely. Thank heavens for Luca Caruso and his friends-of-Leech discount, or she'd dine exclusively from Sainsbury's tuna tins.

The *Volunteer* sign, depicting a man in tri-cornered hat, yellow stockings and musket, stirred nostalgia as it swayed above the pavement. The cozy pub had been the venue for many spirited debates among Isa's business school clique: America's trickle-down economics, Tories' tough-love labor policies, emerging markets, and the future of the EU. After a few pints and last-call whiskeys, conversation turned to loftier matters—football, American television, and English royalty. That routine was true for all of Isa's chums, except Willy Epson. For that zealous capitalist, every breathing moment inside or out of the classroom was a must-win competition.

"Isa!"

She heard her name as the door of the pub swung open. She recognized her old study buddy, Jamie Stuart. The wavy-haired Scotsman from Glasgow was great company. He had a stockpile of stories, jokes, and anecdotes from his overactive libido. Between charming tales told with a rugged accent and eyes self-promoted as *Loch Lomond blue,* Jamie never lacked an audience. *Birds,* as he called his female admirers, flocked to him, lured by a sexy kilt and tree trunk legs.

"Ya look braw, love—smashing," Jamie said, pulling Isa into a bear hug. "Ya just missed Willy," he added with a nod up the street.

Isa hadn't seen Willy Epson since that night at Amore a year and a half in the past. But he had followed through on his promise, sending her client leads. "Eva with him?"

Jamie ushered her into the pub. "Who?"

"His fiancée. South African, I think. Met her last year. Well, not really met, more like toasting breadsticks across a restaurant."

Isa followed Jamie to his table. "Eva's his wife…er…*was* his wife," he said. "New gal's a pretty little one. Canadian, Australian…some kinda English."

Isa raised her arm in a flourish. "Good ole Willy. For Queen, Empire… and sex."

"Don't forget pound sterling," Jamie said before downing the last of his ale. He grabbed two empty pint glasses, tapping a third, half full. "Brad's here." He nodded to the back of the bar. "In the loo."

"Brad?"

"Novak. You remember. American chap—outdoor type, square chin, face full of teeth." Jamie grinned like the Cheshire Cat.

"Sure, sure. We called him Cowboy."

Jamie winked. "That's the fellow. We joked about his penchant for denim and boots."

"And his disdain for detergent, razor, and comb," Isa said, recalling Brad's wild image.

Jamie rose from the table, holding the empty glasses. "What can I fetch ya, love?"

Isa asked for Chardonnay when a shout bellowed from behind her. "Is that Isa Fabrini?"

She recognized Brad's voice. At school he had an annoying habit of adding, 'huh' to every sentence and dropping his final 'g'—*how ya guys and gals doin', huh?*

Isa was amazed at the change. The tumbleweed had blossomed. Brad, a picture of John Kennedy, lifted her into a hug. Her cheek glided on cashmere, her nose filled with the scent of Armani cologne. "You look fantastic," she gasped as she brushed his jacket to remove red lint shed from her dress.

He winked. "You look pretty fabulous yourself."

During their chat, Isa tried not to gawk. The metamorphosis was incredible. The ranch hand had disappeared under broadcloth and fine wool. Perfect diction and a mid-Atlantic accent hid any trace of the rustic. Isa noticed a wedding band and asked about a wife as Jamie returned with drinks.

"You'll get a chance to meet Alexandra at the reunion." He looked around and lowered his voice. "She'd kill me for saying so—getting herself done up. You know, nails, face, roots." His voice dropped to a whisper. "And maybe some Botox if she can find it."

Jamie slapped Brad's shoulder. "Hope ya recognize her, Cowboy."

Brad's face changed, green eyes darted from Isa to Jamie. "Do me a favor, lose the Cowboy thing."

"But it's brilliant," Isa said. "Especially now that you look like a polo playboy."

Brad took a deep swig of his lager. "Alexandra hates that name. Calls it a political liability."

Isa disliked the woman at once. "Political? Are you in politics?"

Brad nodded, a sheepish little-boy head bob as if he'd just been caught eyeing his first girlie magazine. "Small time, really. A state senator."

Jamie flinched. He looked at Brad with newfound respect. "Not a wee nothin' of a state either. Booming tech sector—eighth largest world economy or some such. So says Willy the wizard. Got bundles of money invested over there, he does…and by extension I guess, so do I."

Brad blushed—a trace of the humble cowboy. "I'm just a junior senator, really. Alexandra's father says it could take years before I hit my stride."

Isa sipped her wine, studying Brad out of the corner of her eyes. "Alexandra's father?"

"State's powerhouse. He pulls—"

Words scrambled off of Jamie's tongue. "Governor? Your father-in-law's the bloody governor?"

Brad shook his head. "Nope, Speaker of the State House. But he pulls all the strings." The Cowboy surfaced. "Governor don't fart without askin' Alexandra's father. Pretty dang nifty, huh?"

Isa hadn't planned a grand entrance, but sandwiched between Jamie and Brad, she felt like a queen. The handsome trio marched, arms interlocked, toward the school. They passed another old haunt, Gandhi's Indian restaurant. As Isa lifted her nose, savoring the exotic smells, her empty stomach rumbled.

"Remember the hazing ritual?" Brad asked, prompting fits of laughter. They took exchange students to the restaurant, ordered the spiciest curries, then sat back and waited.

"Red as beets. Sweated like devils, they did," Jamie said.

"Almost as good as your haggis challenge," Brad added with a snort.

As the trio crossed Park Road, camaraderie had all but erased Isa's dread. Clatter of china and glassware rose above the chatter that grew from din to distinct voices. Strings played Handel. She tugged her escorts closer. *You can do this, Isa Fabrini.*

The sight of the school president's house transported her back a dozen years. She had begun her studies in terror. How would peers, most several years her junior, receive her? Christina called every night that first week from Buenos Aires. "Say the word, Isa. I'll fly over and horsewhip any stiff who hurts you with a shout of 'Remember the Malvinas'."

Isa laughed in reply, "The English? They're more concerned with portfolios and cricket than with women, the buggers." Isa, one of only a handful of women in the small, hundred-person class, settled in when she befriended the few students her age—Jamie, Willy, Cowboy—and Walter.

Passing beyond an iron fence and laurel hedges, Isa's enthusiasm surged. With formal colonnades and cupolas resembling whipped-cream dollops, Nash's stunning creation looked like a cross between a Georgian wedding cake and an Indian pavilion. Huge tents dominated the school's generous garden. The lawn buzzed with activity. Smart servers, dressed crisply in black and white, shuttled champagne and hors d'oeuvres among clusters of alumni and guests.

Isa gazed up to the third floor, her lodging for two years. Her park views rivaled those of the American Ambassador whose residence, Winfield House, sat just up the road. But the vista was icing on the cake. Inside the room, she shared dreams, insecurities, fears, desires, and most importantly, her heart with another human being for the first time in her life. He made her feel sexy, smart, and beautiful. In that small chamber she found tenderness, passion, and yes, true love with Walter Benchley.

Jamie tugged Isa's arm. "Isn't that one of the American exchange students?"

"That's Danny." She waved but the little New Yorker didn't see her. Even at that distance, Danny Chance looked like a refugee from a Long Island garden party—tanned, slick and perfect hair, blue blazer, crisp blue shirt, Topsiders, and a jaw that meant business.

"Better find Alexandra before she gets bored," Brad said, purging all traces of Cowboy. "Let's meet up later. Maybe dine together?" He headed toward a tent, before disappearing into the crowd. An open flap revealed tables set with china, crystal, and vases of spring flowers.

"*Amazing!* Miss Fabrini, you look *fabulous.*"

Isa turned toward the voice. Danny Chance navigated toward her, a gin and tonic in his hand. He pecked her cheek. "Sorry I couldn't swing by your place—power lunch then cocktails. Necessary evils to expense my airfare and hotel. You know that drill," he said with a wink before scanning the lawn. "You seen Tommy?"

"Sorry, no. We only just arrived. You remember Jamie?" Isa said, grabbing the Scotsman's arm.

As Danny extended his hand, gold cufflinks glistened in the late afternoon sun. "Sure, sure, good to see you again, Mr. Stuart." After sizing up Jamie, Danny again scanned the crowd. He addressed Isa out of the corner of his mouth. "You nudge Tommy like I asked?"

"Sent him a note."

Jamie stared down at Danny with a curious expression. He cocked his head. "Refresh my recollection. From where were ya on exchange, Danny?"

Annoyance flashed on Danny's face. "Wasn't here on exchange. And I prefer, Dan—"

Scratching his temple, Jamie interrupted. "Could swear we took you to Gandhi's. Ordered that—"

Danny groaned. "Stomach-scorching curry that landed me in the hospital."

Barely able to speak between laughs, Isa added, "Case of mistaken identity. Danny, er…Daniel left after our first year. Finished his studies in New York."

Jamie punched Danny's shoulder, splattering his drink. "Sorry. I lump you and that other American chap together. What's his—"

"Tommy," Isa said. "Tommy Evers. He truly was on exchange…from Chicago." Isa turned to Danny. "Easy mix-up—you two *were* inseparable."

Danny blushed. "You did tell Tommy, he *hadda* come?"

"Merely suggested it."

Danny sighed before motioning to a corner of the lawn with his drink. He turned to Isa. "Speaking of inseparable, I ran into Walter Benchley squabbling with Willy Epson. Something about money. Expected to find you cozying up to Walter."

"Walter and I didn't last beyond school," she said. Feeling her cheeks warm, she hated herself for reacting. Of course she didn't blame Danny. He didn't complete his studies with them. He wasn't aware of her meltdown.

Danny rubbed his hand down her shoulder. "Sorry—didn't know."

"Catch ya later," Jamie said, offering Isa a kiss on the cheek. "Got some unfinished business with a bonnie bird. Save me a seat for dinner."

As Jamie walked away, Tommy Evers, with a thick head of blond hair and a face still the ideal picture of an American farm boy, inched up behind Danny.

"Speak of the—" Isa began, but stopped when Tommy, smiling playfully, held a finger to his lips. From behind, he threw his arms around Danny. The New Yorker's eyes bulged and the glass fell from his hand, splashing gin at his feet.

"What the hell?" Danny bellowed, kicking the lime from his shoe.

"Dan, my man. Hoped you'd be here," Tommy said in a flat Midwestern accent.

Danny turned to face his captor. His face relaxed. "Mister Thomas Evers! What a shock. I'd no idea you'd be here." He drew Tommy into a hug, a look of contentment spreading across his face. "Amazing to see you, ole pal. You alone?"

"Fraid so. My girl's been to London before. She didn't wanna be a third wheel." The mention of a girlfriend seemed to deflate Danny. After hugging Isa, Tommy turned to Danny, eyebrows pulsing. "How 'bout you? Here with your girl?"

Isa grabbed their arms and pulled them close. "You're both here with me. I couldn't think of more divine escorts."

Tommy nodded. Big eyes and an open face gave him the look of a puppy. "Cool. Maybe we can hang out. I'm here for a few days."

Danny's face brightened. "Amazing! Me too."

"You boys are on your own," Isa said. "Got a big week ahead." The brooding image of Lady Blatherwicke rushed into her head. She'd been looking for an excuse to boot Isa from the chorus since she joined, twelve long months before. Isa credited Leech's backdoor dealings with Malcolm for her reprieve. Cruella DeVil, Isa figured, dreamt up the private recital as an excuse to cut the cord—she'd paid her debt to Leech. At the last practice several sopranos gossiped that the professional chorus had tapped Ivy. *How far she'd come—stripper pole to opera stage.* "Maybe dinner or drinks one night," Isa added. "I must practice all weekend." Truth was, Isa needed time alone to get her head around her performance. Success in Lady Blatherwicke's chorus was as much about mind control as it was tone, projection, and diction.

"Rehearse?" Both said in unison as a server appeared. Tommy took a glass of champagne from the tray and offered it to Isa.

She held up her palm. "Something stiffer, please."

Danny plucked his glass from the lawn. "I need a fresh drink. Get you something?"

"Vodka, make it two."

Danny nodded. "Not a peep till I get back."

Isa stole glimpses of Walter Benchley, but kept her distance. She directed the Americans to garden chairs under an apple tree in full bloom. She liked the pair of boys the moment they met in Business Ethics class. The professor presented the case of fruit-flavored *rubbers* for children. The Americans, unaware of the Brit slang for *erasers*, fell into giggling fits.

Isa loved their spontaneity; she'd seen the same in Cowboy. Americans, she sensed, embraced failure as a step toward success. She wished she had that perspective as she grappled with her opera dreams. Living in London, perhaps she'd become more like the English. They feared failure or anything that showed vulnerability. She blamed an elitist class structure, and public boarding schools—*Lord of the Flies* and all that wickedness.

Isa opened up to Tommy and Danny. "I'm on the verge of being booted from the chorus."

"There are other choruses," Tommy said with a sympathetic nod.

"None that leads to the Royal Opera."

"What's the issue?" Danny asked.

"Lady Blatherwicke. That ogre hates me. I can't do anything right."

Danny leaned in and whispered. "One word—*schmooze*."

"What?"

"Butter up the old bitch. Find out what makes her tick."

Isa shook her head. "This isn't New York. She's not wired that way."

Danny scoffed. "Everyone's wired that way."

Tommy nodded. "Danny's right. Everyone's got a soft spot. It's worth a shot."

Isa shook her head. She doubted tea and biscuits from Fortnum & Mason would thaw the icy chorus mistress. "Thanks, boys, but that plan won't work."

"Who needs Lady Blabberwit, anyway?" Tommy said with a twinkle in his eye.

Danny patted Tommy's knee. "I agree. Put on your own damn concert."

"Yeah!" Tommy said. "Ever hear of Florence Foster Jenkins?"

Isa shrugged. "Never."

"New York society woman," Tommy said. He and Isa looked at Danny as if they expected him to know every New Yorker, but he responded with a blank expression. Tommy continued, "Early 1900s. Booked Carnegie Hall—gave her own concert. Didn't give a hoot what anyone thought. Packed 'em in. Became a legend."

Danny eyed Tommy, a curious expression on his face. "You like opera?"

"Sure, I like lotsa music."

Isa watched Danny's mind race as his door of opportunity cracked open. "I'm with Tommy," Danny said. "Do the concert. Once you start talking it up, ole Lady Blatherwicke will see you in a new light. She'll kill for you to be in her la-di-da chorus."

"Got another idea," Tommy said, practically jumping off his chair. Danny and Isa leaned into him as he continued. "You got somethin' Bladderwicke doesn't." Isa's eyes prodded him to continue. "You're Italian."

"So I've been told."

"Do the concert in Italy," Tommy added. "It'll be a big draw."

"Amazing idea," Danny said. "Seal the deal with the ole bat using a little—"

Isa nodded, interrupting him, "I know...*schmooze!*"

The taxi raced along nearly empty London streets on the way back to Isa's flat. Her body struggled with the sleep-inducing effects of a liter of alcohol and her first full meal in weeks. But the party sparked her excitement and stoked her confidence. Wonderful people had reentered her life. Most importantly she had a plan if, or more likely *when*, Lady B gave her the boot. But questions nagged at her. *Who was this Jenkins woman? And do I, Isabella Fabrini, have the pluck to put on a concert?* She muttered something aloud.

"A wee less blabbin', love, and a bit more shaggin'."

Yes, Isa thought looking at the rugged Scotsman whose hands were busy under her bra, *Reunions are bloody brilliant!*

Chapter 7

The dark auditorium reverberated with noise. A percussion of thunderous applause accompanied the drumming of Isabella Fabrini's heart as she edged closer to the stage. The smell of fresh wax drew her eyes to the floor. Oak planks gleamed under the hot lights. Her fingers, knuckles white, clutched the red velvet curtain. She looked to the pit. The face of the white-haired conductor signaled concern for her: was she ill, scared, would she sing?

Spotlights bathing the orchestra cast a halo over the first row of seats. Faces flashed with anticipation. Friends and family applauded. Isa's mother clutched a rosary. Brad Novak, wearing a tuxedo and white cowboy hat, raised two fingers to his mouth and released a walloping whistle. Kilt-clad Jamie Stuart stomped his feet. Other familiar faces beamed: Gina, Danny, Tommy, Willy, Christina, and—

Were her eyes playing tricks? Walter Benchley, preening in pinstripes, sat with Ivy Vine, clad in sequined bustier and red miniskirt. Isa gasped; their hands clasped. "Bloody hell!" she grumbled. "The stripper's practically in his lap." Where were her biggest fans, Ana and Papa?

The baton's flourish got her attention, but the conductor mouthed something she couldn't make out. Isa's gaze wandered across the stage to a shock of platinum blonde hair. Her stomach soured, hands trembled. Lady Blatherwicke stood in the opposite wing—jaw clenched, head turning from side to side. A low-cut gown showed off her cleavage. Below the waist, the dress resembled the black, billowing robes of a judge. Isa's nose filled with the aroma of the other woman's perfume, a mix of cardamom and citrus that Isa grew to detest. The lips of her nemesis moved, repeating like a ship's distress signal: *Told you so...told you so...told you so!*

Fanning herself with a handkerchief, Isa patted her forehead. The skin was cold and clammy. Perspiration beaded her chest. She closed her eyes. *Please don't let me faint.* Escape fantasies hijacked her thoughts. *I could barricade myself in the dressing room or bolt out the stage door, climb into a taxi, and never look back.*

Her gaze arced from Lady Blatherwicke to the conductor whose face had turned bright red. Why hadn't she noticed how much the moon-faced maestro resembled Leech? He began to cough; sweat dripped from his jowls onto the musical score. With an urge to flee, Isa turned away from the stage. But a broad-bosomed woman blocked her getaway. Her heavy gown and dramatic pose recalled images of Dame Nellie Melba and Lillie Langtry.

"Let me pass," Isa cried. "I can't go on." She tried to move but the wax ensnared her feet like flypaper.

The other woman stood firm, arms folded across her chest. "Poppycock! You're a professional." She nodded toward the audience. "They've come to hear you sing."

"That's what terrifies me."

"Don't fret, my dear. This hall has marvelous acoustics. Provides cover for a multitude of sins." Her hand pressed her breast. "Of all performers, I should know."

"What if they hate me—tell me I can't sing? Or worse...laugh?"

The matronly woman inhaled, squared her shoulders, and lifted her chin. The seams of her lavender brocade gown strained. "Obey my credo."

Isa's mind raced. Surely the woman wouldn't throw her own vow back in her face. *No Sing, No Sleep* seemed trite, inadequate. Perhaps, she'd offer something more profound. Isa leaned forward; her stare invited the woman to proceed.

The mysterious matron spoke to the catwalk above Isa's head as if it were a crowded balcony. Ostrich plumes quivered in her curls. "People may say I can't sing, but no one can ever say I didn't sing."

Isa recognized those words. Her back stiffened; eyes grew wide with the epiphany. She wasn't standing in the wings of the San Benedetto Opera House. She gazed into the auditorium. It was Carnegie Hall. The woman wasn't attired in period costume from the wardrobe department. Before Isa stood *The Diva of Din—The Queen of the Sliding Scale.* The sudden realization cleansed the air. Instead of noxious floor polish and stale perfume, Isa delighted in the sweet aromas of the woman's gardenia wrist corsage and the basket of carnations hanging from her arm.

"It can't be. You are…"

The woman presented pudgy fingers encased in white, elbow-length satin gloves. "Yes, my dear, Florence Foster Jenkins." Every word rose from the depths of her diaphragm with dramatic vibrato.

Here stood a woman who knew how to breathe.

Isa closed her eyes and counted to ten. When she reopened them, the imposing figure hadn't vanished. With eyebrow raised, the woman glowered with the impassive face of an empress.

Isa stammered, "B-but how? Y-you're—"

The woman took Isa's hand, pressed it between gloved fingers. "Opera, my dear, dear Isabella, is shrouded in mystery. Of all people, you should know that."

Indeed, Madam Jenkins, as she liked to be addressed, was one of opera's most enigmatic personalities. Ever since Tommy mentioned her name at the reunion, Isa had gorged on her history. Isa found parallels to her own life. A kindred spirit, Madam Jenkins took up singing in her early forties, giving her first concert at the inspiring age of forty-four. She rose to great prominence despite dubious talent.

"You're simply brilliant," Isa blurted, unable to contain her excitement. "Selling out this very hall at the age of seventy-six. Your crowning glory." Her story gave Isa hope. She dismissed Madam Jenkins' death just one month after her triumph as a coincidence—at least she hoped that was the case. The woman's heavy makeup and white-powdered face crinkled under the stress of a broad closed-mouth smile. Isa came to her senses. "You're either a ghost or the consequence of too much vodka."

"Pshaw! Believe what you will—spirit, specter, phantom, or merely a dream. Labels are unimportant, and a wicked waste of breath."

"Why are you here?"

"To help, my dear. To guide you on your artistic journey." Undeterred by critics, Florence Foster Jenkins plowed ahead, clearing a unique place in the small, snooty world of New York's artistic elite. She founded and funded the noted Verdi Club, surrounding herself with loyal supporters for whom she gave an annual concert.

"Why are you so…" The woman's eyes, rimmed in black liner, darted; she searched for a word. "Discombobulated?"

"I don't want to fail."

Madam Jenkins lifted her chin. "Balderdash!"

Isa swallowed hard. Wasn't fear of failure the reason her nerves twisted into knots? Searching her mind, the answer came. She looked into Madam Jenkins' eyes. "I'm petrified of humiliation."

"Sounds like you're experienced in that regard. We all are. Successful people are ridiculed as readily as are failures. They simply don't surrender—end up laughing at their detractors."

Madam Jenkins shared a story that Isa had read in her biography. As a young woman, she found herself in a loveless marriage. Adding insult to injury, her husband, a medical doctor, infected her with syphilis. Her parents, like Isa's mother and sister, tried to crush her passion for singing. The obstacles of her chauvinistic world made Isa shudder. A modest inheritance from her father freed Madam Jenkins to pursue her truth. She became a trailblazer, shaping her destiny in an age when women didn't have the right to vote. Embarking upon a career required courage; achieving success demanded determination.

Madam Jenkins stared into Isa's eyes. "As for failure, have you faced any yet?"

Isa assumed the woman had no interest in her litany—a stalled career, unsatisfying flings, and a catastrophic romance with that bastard, Walter Benchley. Responding to her question, Isa shook her head. "In pursuit of music, no. I haven't failed…yet."

Madam Jenkins creased her brow and narrowed her eyes, an expression that reminded Isa of her papa whenever he caught her lamenting life's travails. "Lady Blatherwicke took you into her chorus. You survived one year under her yoke."

"But she hasn't rendered judgment on my recital. I could be out on my ear."

Madam Jenkins swatted at the air. "Inconsequential! Ask yourself why she's pushed you."

"She's a sadist."

"Perhaps she's done so to exorcise your bad habits—to unleash your talent."

Isa recalled her interactions with Lady Blatherwicke—taunts, jeers, bullying—torment worthy of an Olympic god. "No!" Isa scoffed, arms folded across her chest. "Benevolent tutelage never crossed my mind."

Madam Jenkins shifted her weight from one leg to the other and placed a hand on her hip. "Of course you may be right. Lady Blatherwicke could very well be a Captain Bligh of a woman—pompous, smug, irascible… *toxic*. Heaven knows I've dealt with my share. But then again, she may be the sculptress and unforgiving chisel you needed to shape your voice." Madam Jenkins lifted Isa's drooping chin. "Do tell, dear heart, despite her dubious tactics, what has this *nemesis* taught you?"

Isa had to think. She continued to attend practices, week after agonizing week. Passion drove resolve. Lady Blatherwicke's criticism made her stronger. She wanted to sing for Ana, Papa, even Leech. She yearned to show the old bitch she was wrong. Digging deeper into her mind, the answer came. A smile flashed victory. "The only person I need to please is *myself*."

Madam Jenkins closed her eyes. Satisfaction swept across her face as if she'd hit the elusive high C. "Yes!" she exclaimed, opening her eyes. "That's the secret. Precisely what drove my will to succeed at all costs."

"But your critics, the bad press—" Isa stopped abruptly, her hand flying to a warming cheek. "I'm so sorry. I—"

Madam Jenkins shrugged. "Blah, blah, blah. Never listened to them. Nothing more than bleating sheep—cowards—naysayers. How many critics ever took a stage, faced an audience, wrestled their fears, gambled with failure? Each must find her own way." She thrust a finger in Isa's face. "Nobody gives a flying fig about your success more than *you*. Remember that!"

"What about Ana, Papa?"

"We have our supporters—cheerleaders, advocates—"

"Who believe in me more than I do."

"And that, dear heart, is your fatal flaw—suffocation by self-doubt. Put on the blinders of success. When I took the stage, I became a different person—Mozart's Queen of the Night, Strauss's Adele. No one dared repeat my triumphant 'Clavelitos'." She lifted a carnation as a nostalgic gaze wandered to the stage.

"Clavelitos," meaning little carnations, was Madam Jenkins' favorite encore. As she sang, she threw carnations into the audience. In her exuberance, she often hurled the empty basket.

Her expression changed. With a look of stern resolve, she faced Isa, eyes fired with emotion. "Don't let *anyone* steal your triumph…most of all, yourself."

"Is it that easy? Lose myself on stage. Allow the role to consume me."

She laughed, one of those halting society laughs. "Not easy—an artist's life is *never* easy. Struggle sweetens applause. But *never* go to bed disappointed with your performance." Madam Jenkins filled her with awe. She made Isa's pursuit sound easy—a simple click of the ruby slippers.

Isa sighed. "What should I do?"

"Listen to those American boys. Stage a concert in San Benedetto. Keep it private—surround yourself with family, friends. Harvest sympathizers. Build and buttress your singing career from there."

"How can I recognize supporters?"

"False friends reveal themselves. Some will surprise you. Wash your hands of them." In dramatic fashion, her hands pantomimed her words. "Cast them to the black depths of oblivion."

Another round of booming applause roused Isa. She spun toward the stage. When she glanced back over her shoulder, Madam Jenkins was gone.

Isa awoke with a start. Lightning flashed through her flat; rain pelted the windows. As she pulled the covers under her chin, she smiled. She had the guidance for which she yearned.

Chapter 8

Daylight has a way of sorting things out—banishing demons, tempering anxieties, defrosting fantasies. Isa wasn't foolish. She knew that sticky cobwebs of worry and self-doubt remained. They merely hung in the shadows, waiting for nightfall to ensnare her again in blanket-kicking, sweat-soaked fits of restless slumber.

Sunshine streaming through her flat's tall windows awakened Isa's reason. She couldn't rely upon Madam Jenkins to shepherd, no, *prod* her toward her goal. At best, the nocturnal visitor represented a muse, a call to action. At worst, she was a mischievous fairy tricking Isa toward a Midsummer's nightmare. The truth probably lay somewhere in the middle—a mix of an overstimulated imagination and Cabernet from the local wine bar.

Hacking through the tendrils of fear was Isa's responsibility alone. *Each of us finds her own way,* Madam Jenkins had said. *Put on the blinders of success.*

Charing Cross Road was still the center of London's book trade. Isa made her way to Pudlow's not by choice, but by necessity. The centuries-old bookseller carried many of the materials for her consultancy. They knew her. More importantly, they hadn't yet closed her house account. Her credit was good.

Isa resisted the urge to dawdle. She pushed past the stacks of books at the door where she could lose herself for hours. After a nod and mouthed *hellos* to a couple of white-haired clerks, she moved to the business section. She scanned the familiar aisle, but marched forward. *Confidence, inner strength, blinders of success*—the words of Madam Jenkins, Leech, Ana, and others clicked in her head. If only the repetition could brand the words into her personality.

An overhead sign beckoned her: *Self Help, Self Improvement, Personal Development.* Isa wasn't alone. Promises of salvation from an assortment of maladies from A to Zed drew a disproportionate share of the shop's customers. She never guessed the market for such books had mushroomed. She hadn't expected to find much more than updated works by Dale Carnegie, Norman Vincent Peale, Napoleon Hill, Maxwell Maltz, and Tony Robbins.

She edged down the crowded aisle sideways. Did it matter where she plunged first? Volumes looked eerily similar—bright-colored covers with happy, attractive faces promised bright, happy, attractive lives for the mere cost of ten quid and a weekend's reading. Words: *Discover, Awaken, Release, Transform*—repeated, dust jacket after dust jacket.

"Good heavens! Where to begin," she said to herself, with a heavy sigh.

"Daunting, isn't it?" came an unexpected reply. A crouching figure at Isa's feet stood up, six or so books cradled in one arm. The woman brushed a hand down her trousers and tugged at the hem of a green wool jumper. "Been here over an hour. Still can't make up my mind. Much easier if I were a sex junkie," she said with a nod up the aisle. Her bright red halo of curls and thick brogue identified her as Irish. "Only two choices for those addicts. More fun too," she added with a squawking laugh and elbow nudge. The aisle's other seekers of self-help eyed the two women and inched away.

Isa nodded politely. However, she had no intention of exchanging pleasantries with the stranger. Had she been browsing Travel, Fiction, or Interior Design, she wouldn't have cared. But Isa didn't know what personality disorder ran beneath those still waters. *Best to use caution akin to avoiding handshakes at a communicable disease clinic.*

But the fiery woman with the round, freckled face persisted. "Watcha lookin' for, darlin'? I can help. Been up and down the aisle, twice. Three shelves on sexual repression, if that's your poison."

Christ! One peep from Isa and the redhead would snare her. In no time at all, she'd invite herself to tea. "Just looking," Isa whispered, taking a step backward.

The woman took a step forward. "Nonsense! Everyone's searchin' for somethin'. Take me." *No thank you!* The books in her hand, however, were curiosity magnets—peepholes into her personality. But before Isa could scan the covers, the woman's arms thrust upward. She rattled off the titles: *"Awake Your Sleeping Giant, Tear Down This Wall, Blinders of Success."*

"Wait!" Isa blurted. Had she heard correctly? "Let me see that one." With the glee of an evangelical pamphlet pusher, the woman pressed the book into Isa's hands. The sky-blue and grassy-green dust jacket showed a daisy-covered mountain ascended by handsome people fitted with horse blinders. Isa flipped the book over and read aloud, "Climb the highest tree…Sing from the mountaintop." She flinched. "Sing!" Surely this was a sign. Isa looked up, returned the woman's beaming smile and asked, "Got time for a cup of tea?"

The Irish woman introduced herself as Kate Maureen Mahoney from Dublin. Arms laden with book bags, the two made their way to a pub in the theater district—the offer of tea surrendering to the appeal of stronger beverages.

Kate nodded toward the Bloomsday Pub. "My home away from home, you might say, darlin'. Proprietor's a real charmer from Killarney—a looker too."

"Come to London often?"

Kate nodded. "Much as I hate to admit it. The Catholic Church has a near monopoly on mendin' souls…and psyches. Fresher ideas here." She winked. "Besides, California's a rather far and dear journey."

Once settled into a comfortable corner of the pub near the electric fireplace, Kate shared her story. One wine became two. By round three, Kate graduated to whiskey, liberally poured by the handsome publican. "Divorce made me redundant, ya might say, darlin'—outsourced by my husband I was, for, Fiona, bubble-butt, Gallagher."

Isa grimaced. "How awful."

Kate squawked. "No worries. Don't need a stinkin' man to complete me."

Isa pointed to the woman's bag of books. "What are you looking for?"

"Can't put a finger on it. Maybe that's the problem. Been outta the game so long, don't know what I don't know. Just gotta believe there's more out there."

Isa was impressed. "You seem to have taken the gut punch and moved on."

Kate sipped her whiskey. Her eyes focused on her companion, but Isa sensed the Dubliner looked inside herself for the answer. Her expression went from cheerful to dour. "'Twasn't always that way. First year, locked myself up like a leper—blinds drawn, lights off, phone off the hook."

Isa patted the woman's arm, recalling her own crippling depression after the Walter episode. Work provided her a path out. "Sorry. Must've been rough. Makes your current state that much more remarkable."

Kate's face lit up with a broad smile. "Owe it all to Lighthouse."

"Lighthouse?"

The Irish woman's light blue eyes sparked. "American program— California." She spoke as if the state represented paradise. "All about seein' how your past hinders your future." She must have read the skepticism in Isa's face. "I've seen that smirk. You're thinkin' snake charmers, faith healers, leprechauns. But it's not like that. I'm livin' proof it works. Said so yourself."

"Guess I shouldn't judge—"

She let out a squawk of sorts. "Meanin', darlin', that's exactly what you'll do." Her outstretched palm and raised eyebrows invited Isa to continue.

"It's just that..." Isa said with a shrug. "You probably had the strength to push through all the time. *You* were the miracle worker, not this... Lightswitch or whatever you call it."

Kate flashed an impish grin, the kind that seems exclusive to the Irish. Her fingers tapped the bag from Pudlow's. "Did ya *not* read the book covers? Did we *not* bump into each other in a self-help aisle? What part of *self* don't ya get? Of course we're our own solution. Just need a little goosin' from time to time, that's all."

Isa sat back and laughed. "A victim of my own cynical past."

"Lighthouse clears the clutter—allows you to help yourself." She squawked. "Got a brilliant flash. I'm here in London for a Lighthouse course. Starts tomorrow night. Come, see and judge for yourself."

Isa wagged a finger in her face. "Aha! Knew it. Clever scheme to infiltrate London's bookshops. Lighthouse sent you to lure floundering wayfarers from self-help aisles."

Kate's breathing stalled, her eyes bugged. After a few seconds, Isa burst into laughter, raising her glass in a toast.

Kate gaped at her. "Then you'll come?"

"Beats reading psychobabble."

Kate didn't take any chances. Three follow-up calls suggested to Isa that the trawler of self-help aisles didn't want her prized catch to drop off the hook. Kate had reason to be concerned. After the pub talk, waves of buyer's remorse buffeted Isa. How easily she could have slipped through Kate's net. But where would that have left her? Fishtailing alone through a murky sea of doubt and inaction.

What the hell? She was a big girl. She had nothing to be scared of. Or did she? Isa envisioned brainwashing sessions, turning up at Heathrow, head-shaved and wearing a salmon-colored tunic, busking for donations. A little insurance wouldn't hurt. She called a few trusted individuals.

"Fantastic, darling," cooed Ana. "Sounds delicious. I'd kill to be brainwashed."

"Brava, my pet," said Leech. "A true artiste embraces experimentation." Isa sensed he had stopped listening, bedazzled by the image of the salmon tunic.

Jamie Stuart offered his assurance. Through the phone, Isa heard him jot down the address and number, reading it back twice. "Ring me up as soon as ya arrive home, won't ya, love?" he urged. "Matter of fact, give me this Katie Maureen's number. You did say, a wee fair redhead?" Isa flashed her middle finger at the phone as she recited the phone number.

Isa did agree to a rendezvous with Kate before the course. Kate would be her guide and cattle prod. "Coffee!" Isa insisted. She wanted to keep her wits as she presented herself for mental dissection.

Isa suggested a café across from the British Museum, only a short walk to the Hotel Russell, the venue of the Lighthouse meeting. The simple Zen-like space offered tea, coffee, and organic sweets in a shop that sold books and *avant-garde* art. Service was slow but the coffee was good.

From her seat inside the café, Isa caught a glimpse of her red-curled acquaintance bobbing across the street, the black iron fence of the museum behind her.

"You've come. Fantastic!" Kate shouted from the shop's threshold, disturbing the shop's incense-infused serenity. Her face beamed as she made her way to the table.

Isa didn't share her new friend's joy. "You're absolutely sure they won't mind?"

Kate slid onto a chair. "Told you, darlin', guests are welcome. Best recruiting tool. Scotches skeptics."

"I don't have to commit or anything?"

Kate flashed a look of exasperation. "If you're frettin' so, don't give your real name."

Isa fancied the notion of transforming into Ivy Vine, exotic dancer, for the evening but dashed the idea. For all she knew, Ivy had blown that cover by having drunk the Lighthouse Kool-Aid. Instead, Isa extended her hand and spoke with exaggerated vibrato, "Florence Jenkins. Pleased to make your acquaintance."

Kate laughed. Her eyes suddenly grew wide. Her hands flew about. With rapid-fire frenzy, she straightened her turtleneck, smoothed her jacket, adjusted her curls, secured her earrings, and pushed up her bra. She leaned forward and whispered, "Philippe Blanchette." She nodded to the door but her eyes remained glued on Isa.

Isa craned her neck. "Who?"

"No! Don't look. He'll know we're talking about him."

"Well? We are."

"He's in the course, too. A dreamy Frenchman from Paris." She closed her eyes.

Isa took advantage of Kate's orgasmic sigh and turned in her seat. Philippe Blanchette wasn't her type but she could understand Kate's swoon—brown wavy hair, a six-foot athletic frame, and a taut, tanned face with thick scruff. He resembled a celebrity footballer.

As he ran his hand up and down the hostess's arm, he caught Isa's stare. He revealed his deal sealer—a gorgeous full-lipped smile. *Okay, maybe once,* Isa thought, transporting herself to his imaginary Paris boudoir or the back of a pretend motorcycle.

Kate gasped. "He saw us. What'll we do?"

Isa flinched, narrowing her eyes on Kate. "Not the best endorsement of Lighthouse's assertiveness program, are you?" Her companion didn't respond; her eyes glazed and her breathing labored. "Christ!" Isa added with a sigh. "Call him over. Hell, I'll do it."

Having recovered from her coma, Kate batted down Isa's rising hand. She lifted her own arm. With a toothy smile and sugared voice, she called, "Philippe, over here."

"'Allo, sweet Kate," he said, reaching their table.

He leaned down and kissed the flustered Irishwoman's cheeks. Isa didn't find his scent of musky cologne mixed with rain-drizzled leather entirely displeasing.

Kate motioned toward Isa. "My friend..." Her blue eyes raced with panic.

"*Isa*...Isa Fabrini," she said, forgetting her alias.

He grabbed Isa's palm. It disappeared between large hands. "My pleasure," he said with a head nod. "Philippe Blanchette." His eyes, the color of roasted chestnuts, lured Isa's gaze from his amazing mouth. "May I?" he asked glancing down to the empty seat.

"Yes!" Kate and Isa answered in unison. Isa pulled her bag from the chair and placed it at her feet.

"Isa's our guest tonight—bit nervous. Thinks we're a cult," Kate added with a wink.

Christ! Kate makes me sound like a sniveling ninny. Isa stiffened at the unexpected warmth of a hand, but relaxed and sat back into Philippe's circular back massage.

The Frenchman shook his head, his expression serious. "*Non*, not a cult. We're legitimate, bonafide what you call...sex traffickers."

Kate slapped the table and Philippe's pronounced Adam's apple pulsed. Isa blushed before sharing in the laughter. She sat forward, pulling away from his hand. "Frankly, I don't know what to expect."

"I remember my first time," Philippe said, drawing out the words. His accent made his dabble in double entendre quite effective. "You'll *love* it. I promise. But you must give it time, *oui*."

"How long have you been a Lighthouse...disciple?"

Kate giggled. "Again with the cult thing. We call ourselves *Seekers*."

Philippe shrugged. "Disciple, student, seeker—whatever. Been going three years. Saw results after six months."

"Results? What kind of results?"

Kate's hacking cough drew Isa's attention. The Irishwoman's creased forehead and headshake signaled concern. Isa got the message. "Sorry," she added, "didn't mean to pry."

Kate patted Isa's hand. "It's just that...you're still...an outsider of sorts, darlin'."

Philippe slapped his leather pants. "But all that changes tonight, *oui?*" He glanced at Isa but didn't wait for a response. "I don't mind sharing."

"Don't feel obligated on my account. I'm Italian, genetically coded to share—food, wine…neuroses. I forget others aren't wired that way."

Philippe laughed. "I was an addict…*am* an addict. Never cured, but under control."

"You credit Lighthouse?"

"*Bien sûr.* The program gave me courage. Tackled issues. Broke past cycles."

"Lighthouse did all that?"

He shook his head. "*Mais non.* Not by itself. My mind's a pincushion for psychiatrists and twelve-step programs."

The waiter arrived to take their order. Philippe flirted with him and the waiter flirted back. Isa cleared her throat and tapped her watch. "What time does the course begin?"

With a look to her wrist, Kate gasped. "You're right, Isa. We've been babbling away."

Philippe pressed the boy's arm and craned his eyes toward the nametag. "I'm guessing Geoff's a star. He'll have us served and on our way in no time. *Oui,* Geoff?"

Showing cosmic speed, Geoff served them coffee and complimentary scones before escorting them to the door. Isa had never been in and out of the shop so fast.

With a deep breath, Isa marched into Russell Square wedged between her companions. Above the square's trees loomed the Hotel Russell, a Victorian monolith of orange masonry and terracotta facing the color of milky tea. Young people she took to be students from the nearby University of London hurried along the pavements. She envied their exuberance, minds like sponges, and lives clean slates of endless possibilities.

Isa glanced at her walking partners. She'd known Kate less than a day, and Philippe barely an hour. Yet both shared tales of despair. Lighthouse gave them the will to help themselves. Would Isa find a beacon shining a channel forward or a false light that scuttled her dream on the rocks?

Following signs from the hotel's lobby, a vast temple of marble pillars and crystal chandeliers, Isa and her companions found the conference room. High ceilings with decorative crown molding and oak paneling gave the space a warm elegance. At the front of the room, rows of chairs faced a podium. At the back, in addition to a refreshment table with silver urns and biscuits, chairs formed four intimate circles.

"Good turnout tonight," Kate said, nodding to the thirty or so people already in the room. Most were dressed in business or smart casual attire.

Lighthouse doesn't shine its beam on the dinghy or rowboat crowd, Isa thought, considering the conference venue and clientele.

Philippe whispered in her ear, "You can always spot newbies. Anxious faces and rattling cups and saucers in shaky hands." Isa took heed, forcing her lips into a polite smile and clasping her hands together to steady her trembling fingers.

Kate motioned to a handsome man on the opposite side of the room. "That's High Beacon Ardmore." Breaking away from a small cluster, the group's leader made his way to the podium. Not a strand of thick, dark hair moved out of place nor did a perfect smile ever leave his face. Isa thought his well-tailored suit and crisp shirt looked incomplete without a tie, a feeble attempt at informality.

Several people started clapping, including Kate. "The Beacon, everyone," she and others murmured, shepherding those not yet seated into the rows of chairs.

After everyone settled and the room fell silent, Ardmore lifted his hands. "Welcome, Seekers and dear guests. Are you here to find your inner light?"

"Yes, Beacon," came the collective reply.

What have I gotten myself into? Isa thought as Ardmore continued to lead participants through a litany of questions and affirmations. Kate was the more zealous of her two companions. She shouted her responses while Philippe merely muttered his. The Frenchman, Isa saw, was preoccupied sizing up the newbies.

"Our feet are trapped by the cement of our past," Ardmore said. "This course will show you how to free yourself. Imagine floating toward your incredible potential."

Despite doubts, Isa couldn't argue with the program's objectives. Lighthouse promoted the tenets of self-actualization, the state of achieving one's true capabilities. Who wouldn't want to feel safe, content, accepted, loved, loving, and alive, living a fulfilling and creative life?

"Remember," Ardmore added, "deficiencies aren't our focus.

Lighthouse helps you grow into the exceptional human being each and every one of you fabulous people was always intended to be."

The room erupted in applause. In one ear, Kate sang the praises of Ardmore, "My spiritual hero." In the other, Philippe offered a more tempered reply, "Blah, blah, blah," he whispered. "But if you recruit ten Seekers, the annual retreat in Laguna Beach is free."

After the break, Ardmore split the group into four smaller ones led by a junior Beacon or someone called a Torch, a Beacon in training. Kate suggested their trio split up to encourage candor and mingling.

"Kate's a Torch," Philippe said as Kate took her place at the head of one circle.

"And you?" Isa asked.

"I can barely find my way in the dark. A common Seeker's fine for me."

Isa nodded; she could relate. She made her way to another circle. Her group leader was a junior Beacon, an amiable middle-aged woman named Sally from Putney. Fears of reentering the workforce after raising three children and finding herself divorced ferried Sally to Lighthouse a few years prior. Now she had a line of infant care products called Mother's Little Helpers slated for expansion into the North American market.

In the small group, Sally took Isa and the other Seekers through a series of visualization exercises. First, Sally wanted them to imagine their ideal states of being. "Think of yourself as an island," Sally said. "Be specific. What does it look like?" The man seated beside Isa replied, "Hawaii," drawing a few laughs and a look from Sally that suggested she'd heard the joke before. After sharing their ideal island worlds, Sally instructed them to visualize their current state, again as an island. *How about a sinking Pacific atoll?* Isa thought, with a silent chuckle. But once she applied herself to the exercise in earnest, Isa felt more focused, emboldened.

"This course helps you navigate from one shore to the other," Sally said. "We'll help you identify the obstacles that keep you anchored in your past."

Isa attended the first session as a guest, but she'd have to join for a chance to escape the sinking atoll. There was one certainty. Her commitment brought Kate one Seeker closer to Laguna Beach. Uncertain was whether Lighthouse could keep Isa on course to fulfill her dream? She was running out of options.

Chapter 9

London—One Year Later

Sometimes Isa needed to disappear. She didn't require a wide-brimmed hat, dark glasses, and a secluded café on the Cote d'Azur, or a thatched cottage in the Cotswolds. She could vanish within herself—to breathe, to sort, to navigate forward. Unfortunately, guideposts and mileage markers were often strangers on the path of self-reflection.

Isa survived the probationary recital. With a thud of her stick, Lady Blatherwicke pronounced, "Despite my professional judgment and artistic instinct, Miss Fabrini, you may remain." After an exaggerated cough from Malcolm at the piano, she added in a whisper, "You've shown improvement."

Banishment was Isa's own fault. Several weeks after the recital, Lady Blatherwicke caught her in a compromising position with a man in an empty rehearsal studio. "Miss Fabrini," she said, ignoring their half-nakedness as if the two were mere characters on stage. "I've questioned your passion and capacity to emote. I've doubted your ability to use your mouth to produce anything of value within this hallowed hall. This evening, you've proven me wrong. Brava!" she said with a clap of her hands. "However, you've stained the dignity of this institution. You will resign from the chorus and we'll put this unseemly episode behind us." From the tone, Isa wasn't sure whether the *unseemly episode* referred to fellatio or her singing. She told people that she resigned to focus on work and her concert—neither a lie.

In the months that followed, Isa didn't have time to dabble in people. She had to focus on retaining clients, paying her mortgage, absorbing

Leech's direction, and applying Lighthouse teachings—all while planning logistics and securing resources for a concert half a continent away. One person could coax her from the cocoon.

Doctor Christina Negroni flew to London for a symposium on mental health. The childhood friends hadn't seen each other since Christina's wedding a few years before in Buenos Aires. They arranged to meet at the Waldorf in the Aldwych, where Christina was staying.

The Argentine woman was always, as they say, *put together*. Marriage, as Isa discovered when the friends hugged in the lobby, didn't change that. Despite the rigors of a psychiatric practice, Christina looked marvelous; her petite frame filled out the coral-colored suit in the right places. Her hair, a lighter shade of blonde than Isa remembered, complemented dark Latin eyes and olive skin bronzed by the Argentine sun.

Christina suggested afternoon tea in the hotel's Palm Court where she made the mistake of asking Isa, "What's new?" The Argentinian finished three cups of tea while Isa's first one grew cold. Isa confessed to the indiscretion that got her bumped from the chorus. Isa knew Christina, like Ana, wouldn't judge.

However, Isa stretched the truth, calling the incident "a temporary lapse of judgment; a burst of passion with a bass section lead." How could she confess the entire story?

"I won't lie," Christina said. "While sex is healthy, I prefer your future escapades involve a solid relationship and a firm mattress, especially at your age." Her laugh put Isa at ease although the psychiatrist's subtle counsel wasn't lost.

Although her other news seemed rather anticlimactic, Isa rattled on about her singing and concert plans.

Christina laughed. "Isa, you need the eyes of a fly and the arms of an octopus—"

"And the resources of a Rothschild," Isa added with a crunch of a cucumber sandwich.

"You ask me, that Lady Blatherwicke woman did you a favor."

"Is that your personal or professional opinion?"

"Both!"

Christina waved off the server. After transferring hot water to the teapot, she let her gaze wander across the room as she stirred. The pianist had returned. The conservatory motif of glass, marble, and brass produced excellent acoustics. The friends paused to exchange smiles. The crisp notes of a familiar tango recalled youthful escapades—sneaking out of their houses to go dancing.

Christina thumped the tango's rhythm on her thigh. "Tea's so civilized."

The scent of orange pekoe reached Isa's nose. She lifted her cup with extended pinky. "Gotta hand it to the Brits. Lop off the head of this queen or that, subjugate the world, plunder antiquities…but mustn't mess with afternoon tea."

After lathering a scone with strawberry preserves and clotted cream, Christina set it back onto her plate. She refolded her napkin across her lap and looked at her friend. "Why are you doing this to yourself? Seems a bit much…even for you."

Isa sat back, dusting crumbs from her skirt. "I'm exhausted, I'll admit that. But I have purpose. Feel alive…first time in years."

"And this…renaissance," Christina said, sweeping her hand toward Isa, "has nothing to do with a man? And I don't mean your bass, Johnny One Note."

Isa cut her eyes to her friend like little daggers. *A man?* Her back stiffened. She was too angry with herself to discuss her latest fling. It was Philippe Blanchette and not the bass section lead, an overwrought father of seven, with whom Lady Blatherwicke caught her *in flagrante dilicto*. Lighthouse frowned upon such romances. *Romance? Who am I kidding? It was a hookup.* High Beacon Ardmore said that physical relationships among Seekers "undermined camaraderie, and complicated the bonding experience." Although Isa considered the title *Beacon* used to address her spiritual guide, asinine, she conceded his point even if she didn't adhere to his counsel.

Doctor Christina would surely prescribe analysis. The sex was reckless and amazing but Isa discovered that the hunky Frenchman with the addictive personality shared his sensuous lips, simmering eyes, and other appendages with two, maybe three, other Seekers. And that's all she knew about. Poor Kate Maureen Mahoney; she would have given her last bottle of whiskey for Philippe's French lessons.

"Have you heard about Telma?" Christina asked, attempting to lure a brooding Isa back into the conversation.

Isa bristled. The women had an unspoken agreement to never discuss

Christina's younger sister. They were too fond of each other to let anyone, especially Telma, ruin their friendship. To Christina's credit, she had adhered to that protocol despite a mix of Italian and Spanish blood that commanded a fierce loyalty to family.

Responding to Isa's flinch, Christina added, "Sorry to bring her up. Assumed you'd know. And if you didn't, you should."

Although Telma also lived in London, Isa couldn't remember the last time she ran into her. The last Isa heard, despite having a smart townhouse in Knightsbridge, Telma spent her time at a country home in Kent. Telma had the decency to avoid events sponsored by the business school. She ceded Isa her turf, fair exchange for Isa's ceding her Walter.

"I've no idea what you're talking about—really." Isa disguised her interest by craning her neck to scan the room. Celebrities often sat at tables obscured by palms. She recognized a BBC commentator and a government minister at separate tables.

Christina cleared her throat. "Then I'll just come right out and say it."

"I wish you would." When Isa turned to her friend, she found a serious expression.

"Telma and Walter have separated. Divorce is likely."

Isa's fingers tensed around the teacup handle as she struggled to maintain her composure. "I hadn't heard. People avoid mentioning either of them to me."

"I'm assuming you're pleased," Christina said, studying her friend.

Isa scoffed. "Whatever gave you that idea? It's been years."

"You were hurt, terribly hurt. What they did was despicable."

Isa's mind replayed the scene in Regent's Park—the passionate lovemaking in a secluded bower—Walter and Telma's surprised faces—the ring Isa tore from her finger.

"I hated Telma for years," Christina said with a sigh. "But she's my sister." Isa nodded, watching her friend over the rim of her teacup. "I've said it before…thank you for not making me choose loyalties. I've always admired your ability to compartmentalize relationships. So…"

"So boring, but mentally stable. Right, Madam Doctor?"

Without much prodding, Christina proceeded to share the story. Telma was having an affair with a much younger man named Fernando. She kept the romance a secret—until Walter found them cavorting in bed on an unannounced mid-week return to the country.

Isa lifted a salmon sandwich. "And they say Kent is dull. One never knows what one might find."

"Walter found Fernando," Christina said with a raised eyebrow.

The pianist covered their giggling fit with a jaunty rendition of "The Lambeth Walk."

With serving tongs in her hand, Christina motioned to the dessert tray. Isa pointed to a lemon tart. After Christina placed a slice of gateau on her own plate, her expression changed. She started to say something but stopped; her lips quivered.

"Just say it," Isa said, forking a crumble of tart into her mouth.

Christina shook her head and looked down at the table. "I don't know."

"Go ahead. What is it?"

"All right," she said returning Isa's gaze. "Remember, you asked." Christina inhaled deeply. "Do you still have any feelings for Walter?"

"Christ!"

"He's rich, still handsome. Been a gentleman with this whole Telma disaster. Wouldn't think any less of you if you did."

"Any woman with an ounce of self-respect would think less of me if I did." There was only one way to escape that thread of questions. Isa looked to the bottom of her teacup and then into Christina's eyes. "I've started seeing someone."

Christina sat up. She folded her hands on her lap and leaned forward. "Go on. I'm on pins and needles."

"He owns a restaurant, an upmarket place in Covent Garden." Isa knew the best way to lie was to latch onto something real, fix a picture in her head, and add details—not too many, and at least one fact too silly that it must be true. In reality, it wasn't so much a lie, more a stretched truth. She'd enjoyed many nice meals at Luca's restaurant, partaking of his artist discount. He even asked her out on a few occasions. Perhaps she might even say yes one day.

"Exciting!" Christina cooed. "What's his name? When can I meet him?"

Isa's hand flew to her cheek. It was hot. She shoved a cream puff in her mouth to buy time. As she chewed, she studied Christina. Her friend wore the expression Isa remembered from their teenage years. They'd sit on the bed, tease each other's hair, play American rock-n-roll, and gab for hours about boys. That flash of innocence drew a pang of guilt for fibbing to her now. But Walter was a dangerous subject, a slippery slope Isa wanted to avoid, especially with a licensed psychiatrist.

"His name's Luca Caruso—a veritable hunk. Well," Isa said drawing a picture of him in her head. "More distinguished than hunky. Very handsome."

Christina's eyes widened. "Italian! Your parents must be thrilled."

"Oh, I haven't told many people. Don't want to spoil things. You know how Angelina and Gina can be."

"Angelina?"

"My mother," Isa replied, watching her friend's face. "Now, don't look at me that way."

"What way?"

"With that professional gaze. You know, the one where you pretend so hard not to show emotion. I stopped calling her Mama years ago. Wouldn't dare tell her about Luca."

"This Luca better be good to you. Better be single." She waved a fork in Isa's face. "Better have a mattress."

After they stopped laughing, Christina added, "When do I get to meet him?"

"You don't." Seeing disappointment on her face, Isa added, "Not this time. He's in Italy." Her frown made Isa dig deeper into her well of deceit. "His mother's ill. Perhaps you'll meet at my concert?"

"Tell me about this concert. Where is it?"

"San Benedetto."

Christina reached in her purse and pulled out a calendar. "Not that I should forgive you for keeping Luca a secret." She broke her stern expression with a wink. "I'm there. And if Luca knows what's good for him, he'll be there too. When?"

"Next May—fourth Saturday."

She circled the dates with a pen. "Never been to your hometown. Never made it to Italy. Got your venue?"

"Every Italian town worth its weight in pasta has an opera house. Ours happens to be pretty special. Late nineteenth century. They say Caruso sang there—*the* Caruso, not *my* Caruso."

"Sounds charming."

"If I can pull it off. Got eleven months."

"That's not much time. Can I help? Financially?"

"No." Isa had already declined offers from Jamie, Tommy, and Danny. This was *her* dream—succeed or fail.

"You've never accepted anyone's assistance." She reached forward and pressed Isa's hand. "Let people help."

The pianist's flourish interrupted Isa's response. She recognized the opening bars of a Verdi number that the chorus practiced for weeks. The piece had been one of her favorites until Lady Blatherwicke pounded her stick on the floor and groaned, "Stop! Butchers! You're slaughtering my favorite choral piece." She made the chorus sing until they were exhausted and couldn't do anything right.

Isa turned toward the piano. She froze. At a table beside the piano, camouflaged by palm leaves and a large feathery hat, sat Lady Blatherwicke. The chorus mistress chatted away with girlish animation as her companion pressed her hand to his lips. Despite Isa's Lighthouse training, the sight of her nemesis made her nauseous.

As Isa discreetly pointed out the chorus mistress, she gasped. Lady B's companion emerged from the shadows of the palms, leaning forward to kiss her cheek. Isa recognized the thick wavy hair, chiseled jaw, and athletic face of Philippe Blanchette.

Chapter 10

San Benedetto—One Year Later

Whiskey made Isa's journey back in time painless and quick. Whoever said alcohol clouds judgment was either a liar or a drunk. The amber liquid gave her an honest answer as to how she arrived at the current predicament, locked inside a dressing room of the San Benedetto Opera House, hours before her debut in front of a hometown audience.

A series of kicks thumped the dressing room door. She opened her fist and eyed the pink pills. With a faint sigh, Isa juggled her palm sending the pills fluttering through fingers to the floor.

"Time's up, Isa. You promised. Let me in." Christina, her voice calm and nonjudgmental, kicked the door.

As she lay on the sofa, Isa glanced at the clock between the glowering faces of Renata Scotto and Madam Callas. Thirty minutes of the present had condensed four years of recent past. Credit belonged to the Jameson. Isa looked to her hand, the glass and its amber passenger—companion, confessor, nurse. One healthy swig remained. "*Carpe diem*," she said, tipping the contents into her waiting mouth. Her foot padded the floor searching for the bottle. An ever-so-slight tap reassured Isa of her benefactor's ample reserve. She rose to her feet, stumbling like a toddler with the first step.

Christina called through the door, "Can't hear you."

"One second." Reaching for the doorknob, her heart began to race—*the glass, the damn glass*. Isa's eyes darted around the room for a hiding place. She ditched her companion behind the vase that held Luca's bloody flowers. *Damn Luca. Of all people, why have you abandoned me when I need you most?* Liquor and love were about to hijack Isa's mind when Christina, louder this time, kicked the door.

"Com—ing…com—ing…com—ing." Isa sang the words in ascending octaves, mimicking a vocal exercise as she pulled open the door.

"Glad you haven't lost your voice," Christina said, striding to the center of the room. Her wake produced a whiff of perfume, whose citrusy fragrance buffered the intoxicating scent of the whiskey. A purposeful look on the Argentine woman's face signaled an intention to stay.

Isa peered out the open door. Figures hovered in the shadows. Leech snuffed out a cigarette with his aqua-colored slipper and fanned the bluish cloud that hung in the stale air. He and Kate nodded back at Isa with expectant smiles. Would she signal distress or the all clear? She had no intent of dispelling the mystery. Isa flashed and held a smile then plunged her lips into a frown. She repeated the sequence one more time before adopting the inscrutable expression of the Sphinx. Giggles gurgled in her throat when alarm flashed on their faces.

"You are the devil," Christina said.

"Lovely to see you too."

Despite the sarcasm, Isa couldn't hide her pleasure at seeing her old friend. Christina always meant comfort and protection. As children, a small yet scrappy Christina had threatened to beat up any kid in their Buenos Aires neighborhood who laughed at Isabella's accent or teased the recent immigrant for wearing her older sister's patched and mended clothes.

But Isa's current unsettled state preempted any thought of a tearful reunion. In one swift movement she spun around and slammed the door shut with her hip. Pressing back against the door, she closed her eyes and inhaled, thankful at last for Luca's floral proxy. The sweet perfume of freesia suppressed the dust, smoke, and ancient odors of the theater.

Isa focused on the two paper cups in her friend's hands. The bold aroma from the vented lids confirmed the contents. "Doctor Negroni to the rescue, I see."

After placing her offerings on the dressing table, Christina walked into Isa's open arms and kissed her cheek. "How are you holding up, *mi querida?*" Isa fell into her friend's familiar embrace. Tension eased its grip on her muscles. She didn't want to let go. "Everyone's panicked," Christina added.

Isa sighed. Responsibility pulled her from the comfort of her friend's arms. "Blast them all. Or am I being too harsh?"

Christina clapped her hands. "Thatta girl. Blast all of us."

"Huh?"

"Since you hatched this grand plan, you've talked about singing to satisfy one person—*you!*" Christina said, shaking Isa's shoulders. "I applaud your selfishness."

When spoken by Madam Jenkins or read from a self-help book, similar words inspired and motivated. But Christina's assertions made her sound self-centered, egotistical—a bitch. "W-well, I-I don't mean—"

Christina's palm shot up. "Tut, tut, tut. No apologies. Isabella Fabrini charts her own course. Blinders on."

Cocking her head, Isa studied her friend's face. Where were Christina's words leading her? Isa followed Christina's dark eyes as they scanned the room. Isa scuffed the floor with her toe until she felt the tiny pills. Then, with a backward kick, she exiled the little demons to a void beneath the sofa. The whiskey bottle was too big to conceal. Isa's eyes widened as Christina's gaze dropped to the floor. Was that a frown?

Isa's chin lifted. Her eyes met those of Scotto as Lucia di Lammermoor. The story of Donizetti's heroine whose fate is tragically manipulated emboldened her. "Don't begrudge me one little drink."

Christina scoffed. "Begrudge you? Ha!" She stepped forward and plucked the bottle from the floor. She looked around the room again as if searching for something. "There you are," she said, snatching the sole remaining glass tumbler off the dressing table. Holding it up to the light, she lifted the unused tumbler to her nose. She turned to Isa, a puzzled look on her face. "Don't tell me you've been drinking from the bottle."

Feeling her neck stiffen, Isa pointed to her glass's hideout. "Christ! I may be bloody selfish, but I'm no lush."

Christina ignored the outburst. Humming, she set the two glass tumblers on the dressing table side-by-side. "Bosom buddies, just like us," she said with a sweep of her palm. She raised the bottle to eye level. "Perfect! More than enough for a toast between friends." She poured out equal measures. "One for you, one for me."

Isa wrinkled her nose. Her legs a bit wobbly, she flopped backward onto the sofa. Christina thrust a glass into her hand. Eyeing the liquid with unease, Isa groaned. "I don't know."

"Nonsense. Bad luck to refuse a toast. Aren't theaters hotbeds of superstition? Besides, if you've decided not to perform, what's one or even two tiny sips?"

As if in a trance, Isa lifted the glass tumbler to her lips.

Christina scowled. "Tut, tut, tut. The toast, the toast."

Isa's cheeks warmed. "Oh! I forgot." With some effort, she wriggled into a sitting position and concentrated on keeping her eyes open.

Following her friend's lead, Isa hoisted her glass. Christina's fiery Latin eyes lasered on her. "To dear friends," Christina said. "May life always bring us fields of flowers in which to dance and tiny thorns to better appreciate the rose's bloom."

Her words registered slowly. Isa expected some subtle mind game, psycho hocus-pocus to goad her onto the stage, a sappy reference to singing. Instead, the toast inspired images of friendship and mirth. The dear friends clanked glasses and drank. However, the whiskey no longer excited Isa's palate. She held her stomach and groaned.

Christina sighed. "Ah!" She licked her lips and joined her friend on the sofa. "Okay, your turn."

"Turn?"

She jiggled her glass under Isa's nose. "For a toast, your toast."

Isa frowned. She didn't care if she looked like a pouty-faced brat.

Christina nudged her with a nod, batting her long lashes. "I flew all this way—second trip to Europe in six months."

"I don't have anything to say."

The Argentine woman raised her eyebrows. "Humor me. Dig inside yourself. Your heart's not as hard as you make it out to be. Come on. What inspires you?"

Isa closed her eyes—images of Luca, Leech, Ana, her papa, other friends. The face of Madam Jenkins and her voice of fearless passion flashed into her head. She raised her glass. The friends exchanged smiles. Isa cleared her throat. "Sing from the heart. Surround yourself with people who bring you music and love...such as you do for me, my dearest friend." Isa clanked glasses. "Cheers, *bella mia*."

Sniffling, Christina was barely able to take a sip. Isa grabbed her hand. As tears trickled from her friend's eyes, Isa's emotions surged. Her own sniffles became tears, then sobs. Brushing Isa's cheek, Christina rose and took the glass from her friend's hand, emptying the remainder of both glasses and the bottle into the sink. She grabbed a box of tissues from the dressing table and returned to her place beside Isa.

"Thatta girl," she cooed, pulling Isa's head to her shoulder. "Let it out."

Isa quaked with sobs. "I shouldn't…this is stupid—silly."

Christina caressed Isa's back. "Nonsense! Emotion's never silly. Might be the most brutally honest thing about us. Hell, without it, I'd be out of business. Therapists and tissue go together like—"

"Whiskey and regret," Isa mumbled.

"What did you say?"

"Whiskey and regret," Isa repeated louder.

Christina's breathing stalled. A quiet snicker turned into a giggle, then a full-blown laugh. She dabbed Isa's cheek with a tissue. "Remember?"

Isa nodded her reply, feeling the soft cashmere of her friend's jacket on her face. Of course she remembered even though she hadn't thought of the phrase in years. Her own sobs surrendered to light, hiccupping giggles.

The best friends were nineteen, between their first and second years at university. After embellishing their sexual exploits to impress the "in crowd," that summer Christina and Isa vowed to lose their virginity. They dreaded the prospect of next school term, facing the snooty gaggle of popular girls without actual experience. Romance novels, sex manuals, and Hollywood films took their made-up boasts only so far. Trolling the library, they spotted two guys deemed worthy of plucking their maidenhood.

Dabbing her eyes, Isa pulled away from Christina and looked up to her face. "Oh how we thought those grad students were so handsome— law students, sophisticates, *real men*."

Christina tapped Isa's nose. "Turned out to be little, snot-nosed boys."

The girls spent days coaching each other—developing scripts to navigate their deflowerers toward their destiny. For their double date, Christina and Isa picked out a swanky club in Recoleta, Buenos Aires' posh district. But the foursome was turned away when the girls' dates didn't have the cover charge.

"That dive bar in Palermo should have been our cue to run," Isa said.

"Oh God!" Christina shrieked, putting her hand to her mouth. "Remember the condoms, those damn condoms."

How could Isa forget? The night before their double date, the girls guzzled a bottle of wine. They needed to build courage for the trip to the druggist. After an hour circling the same aisle, they worked up the nerve. With Isa providing cover, Christina snatched condoms from the shelf. They hid the box between two fashion magazines.

"Christ," Isa said with a chuckle. "And who pops up at the cashier? Cute little—"

"Father Menendez," Christina snorted. "I'll never forget his purchase—Hershey bars, Crackerjack, and the biggest bottle of gin I ever saw in my life."

They never knew if Father Menendez smelled the Malbec wine on their breath, or saw their condom purchase. Perhaps the ancient priest chose to ignore their transgressions, putting his faith in the redemptive powers of confession and the memory-lapsing effects of gin.

Isa held her sides, flopping backward into the sofa cushions. "Some good they did."

Howling with laughter, Christina slapped Isa's knee. "Those boys would have mistaken those condoms for party balloons."

They never got that far. In a display of machismo, the girls' dates dared each other to a drinking game. After watching each of the boys throw back four double whiskeys, the girls abandoned their would-be conquerors, passed out at a table inside the dance club.

"How we sobbed in the taxi," Christina said.

"Blasted driver thought *we* were drunk."

"Honest mistake. We both reeked of whiskey drool."

Isa shrugged. "Remember his warning—"

"Delivered with shaking head and hellfire eyes in the rearview mirror."

Isa mimicked the driver's accusatory finger and evangelist tone. "*Chicas, escuchame!* You know where whiskey leads? I'll tell you, *ruin and regret.*"

From that night forward for many years, *whiskey and regret* entered the friends' vernacular as shorthand for sisterhood and foolhardy blunders. And just as they'd done that night in the Buenos Aires cab twenty years in the past, Christina and Isa embraced, collapsing into a ball of hysterical laughter.

After their uproar subsided, they heaved sighs. Isa was exhausted but no longer felt queasy or drunk.

Christina looked at her. "So, what are you going to do?"

"You know damn well what I'm going to do."

With a hand held to her cheek, Christina's tone mocked with exaggerated innocence, "I don't have the slightest idea what you could possibly mean."

"Now who's the devil? After a beauty nap, I'm going to do myself up like the Queen of Sheba. Tonight," she added, pointing to the door, "Isabella Fabrini conquers that stage. *My* audience will get the best bloody performance this theater has witnessed in years."

Frenzied pounding at the door interrupted Christina's response. Leech shouted, voice pitched high and tempo fast. "Isa, Isa, Isabella, my pet. *Fiasco!* Not a Leech fiasco, a veritable, *frigging fiasco.*"

Chapter 11

"Calm down, Leech. I'm supposed to be the basket case, remember?" Isa grabbed the braided epaulets of the voice teacher's pink Sergeant Pepper jacket, hoping her touch would ease his anxiety. She spoke slowly, trying to focus his eyes that ping-ponged from side to side. "Breathe. Breathe deeply." Student became teacher.

"Quick. Get him a seat," Christina cried.

As Isa inched him toward the sofa, a torrent of people streamed into the room. The scene was reminiscent of a Marx Brothers farce.

"So, so sorry, darlin'," Kate cried, her hands tugging at a halo of red curls.

Ana glided past the Dubliner. Pulling Isa from Leech's side, she drew her sister into an embrace and kissed her cheek. "It's not the end of the world."

Hearing a loud gasp at the door, Isa spun around to face the source. There stood Gina, her hands pressed to her cheeks. "You look ghastly! But at least you're not dead."

Isa shuddered, still trying to make sense of the chaos.

"Don't mind her. I'll muzzle the pit bull," Ana whispered before marching toward their older sister.

Throwing an arm around the floundering Leech, Christina tugged him to a seat. She fluffed cushions and positioned pillows before launching him onto the sofa. Sweat spread across his forehead. His lips quivered.

"He's fine. Bit overheated, that's all," Christina said, responding to the horror on Isa's face. She nodded to a pitcher of water on the dressing table, beside the empty Jameson and tumblers.

Damn! Isa thought, *Why had Christina drained the whiskey bottle?*

She resisted the urge to drop to the floor. A pathetic picture shot into her head—her on all fours, groping under the sofa for Ana's magic pills. The banter in the room grew deafening—the oxygen level plunged. Isa grabbed Luca's flowers off the dressing table and moved to the center of the chaos. As she glanced at the chattering faces, she felt the room sway. She closed her eyes but the clamor intensified. With both hands, she lifted the crystal vase over her head and let go. The smash produced the desired effect—sweet silence.

Her hands moved to her hips. "What the hell is going on?"

Terrified faces gave way to babble. Leech swooned, head tilted backward, palm to forehead. Christina scooped Isa's slippers from the floor and rushed to her side. "Put these on," she said. "Don't need bloody feet to add to this bloody drama."

Leech recovered. Lavender infused the air as he fluttered his handkerchief. "C-come here, my pet." His head continued to shake and his tiny feet, wrapped in satin, tapped the floor.

As Isa moved toward the sofa, the others closed in behind her. She commanded the spotlight, a starring role in her own opera. But this libretto's plot twist eluded her.

Somebody's arm shoved a glass toward the nearly prostrate voice teacher. After a flip of his head and a raised palm, Leech acquiesced. He accepted the water, lifting the offering to trembling lips. If someone hadn't snatched the glass from his quaking hand, it surely would have joined the crystal shards and freesias littering the floor. Isa's alarm grew until she looked to Christina who stood at his flank. Rolling her eyes, the Argentine moved her head from side to side. Her message—*this was the death scene of a drama queen.*

"Closer...closer," Leech rattled, tapping the sofa cushion.

Taking a seat beside him, Isa took his extended hand. "What is it, Leech? What's this fiasco?"

He looked at Isa with drooping eyes. "We're undone, simply undone, my pet."

Isa spoke in a hushed voice, squeezing his hand before drawing it to her bosom. "Dear, dear Leech, tell me."

"The piano, the piano..."

Given Leech's proclivity for drama, Isa anticipated his news. She'd rehearsed for days with the ancient instrument. "Are you here to tell me that the piano is out of tune? Well, so am I. Probably even flatter than the bloody piano." Her laugh was deep and sincere. Self-deprecating humor often broke the tension. She expected a chorus of snickers from her audience but only Christina shared in the amusement.

Leech's face went white. He pulled their interlocked fingers from Isa's breast to his lips. "No, no, no, Isabella. There's no piano."

"Dear Leech, we have a spare."

"But not a spare pianist. Signor Bertini has been rushed to the hospital."

Isa gasped. "Is he all right?"

Leech shrugged. "They don't know yet."

"Gall bladder or appendix." Isa recognized Gina's dour voice.

Isa pressed her forehead. "Poor Signor Bertini."

Leech's hands flew to his cheeks. "Bertini will live, but the concert. *Fiasco!*"

"Pish posh!" Isa said. "Not the end of the world." She gazed at Ana, reminded of her words. A toss of Isa's head dismissed Leech's hyperbole. "So I go from quintet to quartet. The other musicians must simply carry me. The show must go on." However, the others met her cheery optimism with anguished expressions.

Leech maintained a viselike grip, keeping Isa tethered to the cushion. "You only have a cello, my pet."

The full extent of the situation finally hit her—she pressed her stomach. She sank deeper into the sofa. Ana and Kate fanned her with concert programs plucked from a side table. Gina stood arms akimbo, a self-satisfied smirk on her face.

Leech shook a finger in Isa's face. "I warned you not to stage your debut in Italy."

"I don't understand," Christina said.

Leech released Isa hand to press his chest. "Italian villages teem with incest."

Cocking her head, Christina looked around the room with a bewildered expression. Isa grabbed her friend's hand and recited the musician roster, "Pianist, Signor Bertini; Violinist, Signora Bertini; flautist, Germana Bertini; viola, Giovanni Bertini. Got it?"

Leech, Ana, Gina, and Kate nodded solemnly.

"All whisked to hospital in the family Fiat," Kate added with a sigh, before stooping to pluck the scattered freesias from the floor.

Christina slumped her shoulders. "And the cellist?"

"Silverstein," Isa replied. Pulling her hair, she looked like Medusa. "I can't perform with only a cello."

Christina caressed the top of Isa's head. "Can anyone else step in, *querida*?"

Ana put her arm around Isa. "We can scour San Benedetto, darling."

The room fell silent as everyone tried to come up with a solution. Kate began to sweep up the broken glass. The Irishwoman squawked—all eyes turned to her. With hands and chin resting on the broom handle she spoke, "I've got it. Why not walk onto the stage, darlin'? Ask if there's a pianist in the house. Seen it work on airplanes—for doctors."

Gina offered a giant groan of disgust. "In that case, why not solicit for a sober soprano?"

"Hush!" Ana said grabbing hold of her oldest sister. "You're impossible."

Isa considered all the alternatives. Her voice simply didn't have the strength to sing *a cappella*. An inexperienced pianist would be even worse—they'd both be scavenging for the right notes. She sighed. "Even if we find someone, they wouldn't know my arrangements."

"Pity Papa's eyesight's not good," Ana said.

Gina motioned toward Leech. "What about *him*?"

Leech winced, lifting his arm with sheepish embarrassment.

"He's got no strength in that hand," Isa answered.

"I–I'm scheduled for surgery in two months," Leech stammered.

"Oh, the wonders of modern medicine—the joys of the National Health Service," Isa said, finding comfort in gallows humor.

"It's not merely my malady," he protested. "I haven't rehearsed these arrangements. Isabella's voice demands precision, not hunt and peck. Oh, my, my, my."

Isa felt a sudden urge to slap him before he descended into more hysterics. Christina read her friend's mind. Wedging herself between the two, she grabbed Isa's wrists. "Let's think," she said. "There must be a solution to *our* dilemma." A habit of assigning joint ownership to Isa's problems endeared Christina to her childhood friend.

"Always the Pollyanna," Gina snapped.

Ana clapped her hands. "I agree with Christina. Let's not surrender, just yet."

Having swept the floor clean, Kate moved to the open space in the middle of the room. Her hands glued to her sides, she kicked up her heels and bounced like a pogo stick. "I dance a mean jig."

"I feel sick," Leech moaned, drawing a glare from Kate's fiery Irish eyes.

Ana squealed with delight. "Kate's onto something. Papa's eyes might be shot, but he knows a few songs by heart. May not be your arrangements, but who cares? We can reunite the fabulous Fabrini sisters."

"Oh no! Count me out!" Gina's crossed arms hugged her torso so tightly, Isa thought she'd compress her lungs.

"Harrumph!" groaned Christina, jutting her chin toward Gina. "Count me in. I can recite Neruda and dazzle with a tango, accompanied by Silverstein." She thrust an arm forward and held the other to her waist. Reciting the tango beat—*slow, slow, quick, quick, slow*—she took two steps forward then spun around.

"Brava!" Isa shouted.

"That's the spirit, darlin'," Kate exclaimed, reprising her jig.

Isa put her arms around Ana. The laughter and mirth reminded her of their childhood, à la Papa Fabrini. "Certainly not the concert I envisioned, but it'll be bloody damn entertaining."

The collaborators pulled up chairs around the sofa to design a mishmash of a program. They sent Gina off to ask Papa Fabrini to prepare two or three piano pieces. Isa had to get her older sister out of the dressing room before somebody killed her.

Kate winked. "That hunky Jamie could parade around the stage in a kilt, for all I care, darlin's."

Leech winced. "Is this a concert or a carnival?" But despite moans and groans, the allure of performance was too much for him. Like a mother hen, he poked his nose over their huddled shoulders, offering advice on pacing and sequencing. "Silverstein will expect a solo," he said.

"Hell," Isa scoffed. "Silverstein can bloody well have the entire second act."

Isa scanned Leech's face, hoping to catch the glimmer of a smile. He continued to sweat profusely; his coloring never paled beyond medium rare. A few moments later, she didn't know what came over him when his eyes suddenly widened and a look of childish delight danced across his face.

A rapping at the door soon gave Isa the reason for Leech's miraculous recovery. As her eyes moved to the doorway, a husky voice announced, "*Bonsoir, mes amis.*"

"Philippe!" Kate screamed. The Irishwoman leapt to the door, throwing herself into his arms. The Frenchman's startled expression seemed at odds with the confidence of his leather and denim outfit.

Christina and Isa exchanged looks. Their smirks recalled tea at the Waldorf where they watched Philippe and Lady Blatherwicke paw each other behind potted palms. Their lips mouthed in silent unison—*whiskey and regret.* Isa rose to greet her fellow Lighthouse Seeker, the man Lady Blatherwicke credited with inspiring her finest oral performance before booting her from the chorus. Apparently, the chorus mistress sought similar inspiration.

Philippe glanced over Isa's shoulder at Ana. "Who is that divine creature?"

Isa cleared her throat, producing a cheek for the Frenchman's kiss. "*Enchantée* to see you too, Monsieur Blanchette."

As if lured by Philippe's stare, Ana came to her sister's side. "I'm Isa's sister."

He grabbed her hands, drawing her close and kissing her cheeks. "*Enchanté, Mademoiselle.* Beauty's synonymous with Fabrini." He bowed. "Philippe Blanchette."

From the hall came an exaggerated sigh. Isa's nose filled with the scent of that horrible and familiar perfume. Words repeated in her head. *Couldn't be, couldn't be.*

"*Mon Dieu!*" Philippe exclaimed. "I am so rude. My surprise awaits." With a roguish expression, he edged backward out of the room. Everyone stood silent, eyes riveted on the black void of the hallway.

Mumbles and whispers grew. Then, *she* appeared—Italian knit suit, satin opera cape and white gloves. Diamonds and emeralds bedazzled.

Christina whispered in Isa's ear, "What, no tiara or teacup poodle?"

Isa didn't respond. She didn't know what to say. She froze, surely she gasped. She stood with eyes wide and mouth open.

Philippe, hands on Lady Blatherwicke's shoulders, guided the chorus mistress into the room. Rushing forward, Leech looked as if he'd curtsy and kiss her ring.

The Frenchman turned to Isa, beaming like a schoolboy delighted with a tagalong puppy. "Gaby, I mean Lady Blatherwicke has come for your concert. If all goes well, she'll take you back into her chorus."

Thank God Ana and Christina buttressed her flanks or surely Isa would have fainted.

Philippe squeezed Isa's hand. "I know what you're going to say."

"You do?" came a chorus in reply.

"*Mais oui!* You're *honored* Lady Blatherwicke made the journey. *Pleased* she's reconsidering you for her chorus. And convinced she'll find the concert *magnifique.*"

Leech foundered; his knees buckled. Kate rushed to his aid, navigating him back to the sofa as he muttered, "Mother of all fiascos."

Drawing Lady Blatherwicke's attention to the empty Jameson bottle, Christina whispered, "Don't mind him. Merely a case of pre-concert jitters."

Lady Blatherwicke sneered. As her eyes scanned the room like a security camera, Philippe plucked a couple of programs from a table. Isa looked in horror but before she could grab them out of his hands, he spoke, "*Voilà,* a concert extraordinaire." He handed a program to Lady Blatherwicke who received it with a thumb and forefinger.

With a finger as his guide, Philippe read, "*La Bohème, Turandot, Nabucco—*"

Lady Blatherwicke sighed. "Italians. How predictable!"

The Frenchman patted her behind. "Lighten up, Gaby. We're in Italy. Hey, here's a Silverstein."

With a bewildered look, Lady Blatherwicke opened the program. "Mozart...hmm, Bellini's *La Sonnambula*. Points for difficulty—courageous." She peered down her nose. Isa remembered that sneer from Covent Garden.

"W-well. Um…" Isa stammered.

Lady Blatherwicke looked at her. "Something wrong?"

"N-no—"

"Everything's fantastic!" Ana exclaimed, stepping forward to take Lady Blatherwicke's hand. "Artist to artist, I guarantee, dear Lady, you won't soon forget this evening."

The chorus mistress glanced at Ana, a look of genuine fondness forming on her face. Isa wasn't surprised. Unpretentious, her younger sister's personality ebbed and flowed with the people in her presence. Everyone, regardless of age or position, found Ana charming.

"I'm your guide. First the hotel, then a divine tearoom. Better yet, grappa and a massage," Ana said with a wink.

Lady Blatherwicke's eyes wandered up to the clock. "Do we have time?"

"Practically four hours. In Italy, that's an extended workday."

With a flash of concern, Lady Blatherwicke looked to Philippe. Ana pounced. "Monsieur Blanchette won't mind—we *three* go together, *oui*?" The Frenchman could only nod at the offer. Toying like cat with rat, Ana would have Lady Blatherwicke pickled, poked, and spent before the spectacular-spectacular. *Brava, darling Gattina!*

"*Grazie mille,*" Lady Blatherwicke said in perfect Italian, unaware of what awaited her. "But we must wait for our companion."

Isa looked to a smirking Philippe. "Companion?"

With her arm slipped under Philippe's, Lady Blatherwicke responded, "Malcolm, of course. The three of us are quite inseparable."

Rallying from the sofa, Leech crowed with delight. "Malcolm?"

Isa clapped her hands. "Malcolm!"

Christina again scanned the faces. "Who's Malcolm?"

"The answer to my prayers." More than anyone, Malcolm knew the peaks and potholes of Isa's voice. His piano skills covered a multitude of her sins. Unable to hide her joy, Isa trilled, "The show will go on."

Chapter 12

"*Bellissima!* A goddess!" Clapping his hands, Papa Fabrini stood in the doorway of Isa's dressing room. "But alas, tonight I must share my *principessa*."

"Oh, Papa! Careful of my makeup."

Although gripped with fear, Isa's heart danced with delight. Her papa's joy enveloped her with happiness. As he stared at Isa with an ear-to-ear smile, Papa made her feel like a little girl basking in the praise of her bigger-than-life hero. But since she returned to San Benedetto to prepare for the concert, his health worried her. He seemed smaller, frailer. He brushed off her concerns by doing what he always did—singing an aria or sweeping her into a dance. What would she ever do without him?

Isa shuffled to the door in satin slippers, her gown rustling on the floor. A whiff of his sandalwood aftershave erased the years. She was her papa's little princess begging for an arm hoist. His eyes glistened with tears as Isa lifted his hand to her lips.

"There may be an audience, Papa, but tonight I sing for you."

Staring into her face, he clasped Isa's hands. The same hands had wrapped themselves around a sobbing child when neighborhood girls pushed Isa to the ground, tearing her dress and scraping her knees. The same hands guided her onto the plane with a gentle nudge when she left home for school in London…and they wiped away her tears the night Walter Benchley humiliated her.

But his grip had weakened. In the past, Isa was the one whose shaky hands sought refuge in her papa's firm grasp. Her hero's fingers now felt fragile, almost brittle. She didn't want to let go.

"Isabella, my sweet little girl, you make me so proud."

"Hope you still feel that way *after* the concert."

"*Principessa*, you fill me with pride tonight, yesterday, and *always*."

Tears welled in her eyes as she studied the kind face and crinkled eyes. She never doubted her father's love but she always thought her younger sister made him most proud. Wasn't Ana the daughter who embodied his dream—a life lived in the moment that embraced beauty, creativity, passion?

No doubt sensing her confusion, Papa Fabrini guided Isa to the sofa, their fingers still interlocked. "I love each of my daughters. Gina, I see your mother, pillar of strength. As I adore your mother, I can't help but love your older sister. And Ana," he said with a twinkle in his eyes and the hint of a grin. "Sweet Ana—half girl, half sprite. She belongs to me no more than a rose claims a bee or a tree holds the breeze that sets its leaves to song. But you, Isa, you have all that *and more*."

"I never felt good enough, no matter how much I tried. I'll never be you."

He tapped the tip of her nose. "Nonsense! You're a better me."

"Don't say that, Papa. You're perfect!"

Letting go of her hand, he wiped his eyes. "Yes, you always thought that. I saw it in your eyes. You got so angry when you couldn't leap as high, hold a note as long, or draw a flower as well as I."

The magical world he created for his family in Argentina flashed through her head. "I know I disappointed you."

He squeezed her hand, his grip suddenly stronger. "Isabella, you misunderstood. Your mother may be too practical for all our sakes," he said with a snicker. "But I float too high in the clouds for my own good." His lips quivered; his eyes clouded. His focus shifted from Isa's face to his hands, clasped tightly in his lap. "I felt like a failure—uprooting my family from our home, from our people. When each of you cried, my heart shredded into little pieces."

"B-but you were strong," Isa stammered. "You gave us a good life. Showed us adventure—taught us how to live."

He kissed her hand. "I'm a proud man. Couldn't let my three little girls see their papa as a failure." He described his bouts with sadness, especially in the first few years in Argentina, second-guessing his decision to move the family, unable to see a path forward. Isa's mother guarded his secret, telling the girls that their papa was too busy painting, sculpting, or reading to be disturbed. "If you saw me sad, felt my sorrow…No, I wanted you and your sisters to be happy—to see life as magical. I couldn't let you grow up feeling sad, thinking your lives were secondhand—that we weren't good enough for Italy."

Isa sniffled. "Oh, Papa!"

"We survived, though, didn't we?" The twinkle returned to his eyes. "Now, look at you—successful, educated, smart, beautiful—with friends all over the world. Gowns instead of hand-me-downs. And here you are, back in Italy. Gina couldn't put on this concert, neither could Ana or me. So my darling *principessa,* you see—you make me proud because you're a better me—feet anchored to the ground yet brave enough to poke your head above the clouds."

Isa wrapped her arms around his shoulders, inhaling his wonderful sandalwood scent. "Oh, Papa, I love you so much."

Mascara ran down Isa's face. But she didn't care that she looked more like Mephistopheles than she did Madama Butterfly. This moment was hers to relish.

"Thirty minutes, Miss Fabrini," Christina called from the dressing room sofa. "Always wanted to say that," she added with a girlish laugh.

Christina had stood in the hall until Papa Fabrini left to welcome, as he called them, his talented daughter's *adoring public.* Maria, a woman who introduced herself as Isa's mama's best friend and the best beautician in San Benedetto, waited beside her, fretting about the passing time.

"Almost finished," said the hairstylist. Since entering the dressing room an hour earlier, her hands busied themselves applying makeup and fussing with Isa's hair.

"No worries, Maria—good art and bad hair both take time," Isa said, with a wink at the woman in the mirror.

Maria frowned. "You got beautiful hair." With arms folded across her chest, she circled the chair. "*Bene, bene,* Isa. *Bellissima!* I wait here for your costume change." She kissed Isa's cheeks, wished her good luck, and scurried out the door just as Leech entered.

"Brilliant!" Leech bellowed as he dropped onto the sofa beside, Christina. "I'm simply brilliant."

Exchanging a smirk with Isa, Christina patted Leech's pudgy hand. "Of course you are, dear sweet Leech. But doesn't our diva look divine?"

Leech flinched. A blush rose in his cheeks as he turned from Christina to Isa, his hand fluttering. "Oh, yes, yes, yes, my pet. Delicious, simply delicious."

"How very kind of you to notice," Isa said with a snicker. "Now dazzle us with your brilliance."

"The stage's all set. It's wonderful, wonderful," he said, clapping his hands like a matinee maven. "Signor Bertini may be losing an appendix," Leech said with a wicked glint in his eye, "but we gain a distinct advantage over your old pianist…and that relic of a piano."

Preening on the couch, Leech looked like an elated Humpty Dumpty about to crack out of his shell with his *brilliant* news.

"Well, are you going to keep it a secret?"

"Thought you'd never ask, my pet. *Eye candy*; we gain eye candy."

Leech explained how the idea came to him after Malcolm arrived and agreed to serve as accompanist. Instead of using the orchestra pit and its upright piano, they rolled out the concert grand, relocating Malcolm and Silverstein from obscurity to center stage.

Leech fanned his face. "Screams professional recital. And, oh that Malcolm—the applause he'll draw. Silverstein's not hard on the eyes either," he added, batting mischievous blue eyes. "In a nerdy, bookish sort of way."

"Leech complaining about me again?" Malcolm asked, entering the dressing room.

Isa understood Christina's sigh of delight at the appearance of the substitute accompanist. Malcolm dazzled, his look best described as *sophisticated smart*—designer dinner jacket, black silk shirt with skinny tie, tight creased jeans, and branded leather loafers. A few hours of Italian sun bronzed his dimpled cheeks. The dark outfit and tan gave contrast to his brilliant smile.

With Malcolm sharing the stage, just who will be looking at me? Isa thought.

"Program's respectable," Malcolm said.

"And you're certain trimming to six arias is fine?" Isa asked.

"Of course. Under the circumstances, it's a triumph."

"What will Lady Blatherwicke think?"

Resting his hands on Isa's chair, he lowered his face to hers. "Don't mind her. Charming Ana has extinguished the dragon's mighty flame. If you merely stood on stage in silence, she'd call the performance inspired."

Leech wagged his finger. "Don't put any more ideas of not singing into Isabella's mischievous little head."

Ignoring Leech, Isa pressed her concern. "But you and Silverstein are okay with the program—sequencing, selections?"

"All…good." But something in Malcolm's voice suggested otherwise.

Leech moved to Malcolm's side. "We take a break right in the middle—after 'Tacea la Notte'…to rest your voice—"

"While praying the audience gets tipsy," Isa interrupted with a nervous chuckle.

"Free champagne at intermission is a stroke of genius," Malcolm said. "Ana's an enchantress."

"Downright diabolical and I love it." Isa said, turning to her friend on the sofa. "And so kind of darling, Christina to pay for it."

Leech pressed his temples. "Pray the bubbly works fast," he whimpered. "Act Two opens with 'Queen of the Night'."

Clearing his throat, Malcolm looked from Leech to Isa. "You're absolutely sure of the Strauss and Mozart? 'Queen of the Night' has its challenges."

"I must sing those arias," Isa said, staring into Malcolm's eyes. Since deciding to stage the concert, Isa played and replayed the nine known recordings of Florence Foster Jenkins. "Queen of the Night" and "Adele's Laughing Song" were among her muse's favorite repertoire of songs. "I wouldn't be here without Madam Jenkins."

Malcolm looked confused. "Who?"

"A kindred spirit."

Leech fluttered his hand, more hawk than butterfly. "Pshaw! Madam Jenkins! American!" He uttered her nationality as an indictment. "Neophyte, spotlight stealer. Had money to sing, but not the talent."

"She sold out Carnegie Hall."

"And promptly died one month later," he snapped with a sneer.

A wicked grin formed on Isa's lips as she turned to Leech. "Do you believe in reincarnation?"

Leech's face puckered. "What does that have to do with anything?"

"Positively uncanny how you channel my muse." Isabella studied Leech's face for several seconds before squealing with laughter. Playfulness felt good.

Leech's face turned red; his head bobbled. "I've warned you not to idolize that Jenkins woman. She was a demon."

Isa thrust her hand toward his face. "Tut, tut, tut. No arguing with the performer before her concert."

Brushing a wisp of lavender hair from his forehead, he threw his hands up in surrender. "Infuriating!"

Isa leaned forward and kissed his cheek. "Hush, my dear little Pygmalion. I'd be lost without you."

The kiss did the trick. Leech grabbed Isa's hand and pressed it to his lips. "Thank you, my pet. Now launch your unbridled exuberance onto that stage."

"Your encore will be wonderful," Malcolm said, pulling together his music. "I've heard your 'O Mio Babbino Caro'. You'll send the audience away with a smile."

"You're an adorable optimist," Isa said.

"How so?"

"You expect the encore to be à la Puccini."

He tilted his head. "Yes?"

"It very well may turn out to be *à la pomodoro*," Isa added with a laugh.

With a kiss to her cheek, Malcolm whispered in her ear, "No tomatoes for you, Isabella, only kisses and flower bouquets."

As Leech led Isa through some final warm-up exercises, she caught her reflection in the mirror. Using photos of Madam Callas, Maria had pulled back Isa's hair. For good luck, Isa's mother loaned her daughter a pearl and diamond pendant, a gift from Papa Fabrini on their twenty-fifth wedding anniversary. Isa's blue sequined bodice glimmered in the dressing room lights, and Isa recalled Ana's endorsement when they chose the evening's gowns. "You'll glitter and glam the audience, my darling sister."

Between exercises when Leech wasn't looking, Isa stole more glances of herself in the mirror. An incredible transformation—her dream was coming true. She swayed her hips; the chiffon folds of the full skirt rippled. She was Cinderella floating on a cloud. Only nerves and a performer's concentration kept her from giggling like the little girl who played dress-up in front of Mama Fabrini's wardrobe mirror.

After finishing warm-ups, Leech stood before her. "When the curtain opens, my pet, remember to—"

"I know, I know. Breathe!"

His chin rose; his chest puffed. "You listened." Then, with narrowed eyes and lowered voice he added, "After you master breathing, soak in the milieu. Let the audience absorb you. Steep in the mystery. Remember, my pet, performance is equal parts perception and reality. Malcolm's a pro. He'll follow your lead."

"You're a dear little man, Leech. Give me five minutes, please."

He kissed her cheek. Exuding a trail of lavender, he left the room.

Alone, Isa stood in the middle of the dressing room. With eyes closed, she concentrated on the performance. She pictured herself singing and acting the roles. A vision came to her of Madam Jenkins, costumed as the Queen of the Night—crown, scepter, and haunting makeup.

"That stage is your domain, dear heart. Seize it," the vision of Madam Jenkins said with customary vibrato.

"How?"

"Believe! Stake your dominion. Project absolute power. At that instant, the audience becomes your subjects, your vassals, your slaves."

After a tap at the door, Christina poked in her head. "Going to my seat. I'll be waiting here at intermission. So proud of you, darling."

Isa didn't have time to respond to another knock before Leech was in the middle of the room. Powered by an adrenaline high, he spoke rapidly, "Malcolm and Silverstein are set. They're on stage and in place. Are you ready, Isabella?"

Isa inhaled and closed her eyes. Her own rush of adrenaline saved her from shedding tears of stressful joy. She nodded to Leech, her eyes sparking. *"No sing, no sleep!"*

Extending his hand, Leech led her out the door. Halfway to the stage, Isa pulled away.

"Don't peek," Leech said in a stern tone. "It's bad form and worse luck."

Isa hesitated. But the rustling, whispering, and mumbling of the audience was too much to resist. She recognized that unique mixture of anticipation and excitement that filled any theater before a performance. Despite Leech's groan, Isa moved to the curtain and peered into the auditorium.

The sight stole her breath. Though like her, no longer a blushing maiden, the theater radiated with matronly dignity. The proud people of San Benedetto united in communal spirit to primp their prized theater for the curious eyes of out-of-town visitors. Men fixed broken seats, oiled doors, and replaced the bulbs that illuminated three tiers of gilded boxes. The century-old crystal chandelier glistened, suspended from the auditorium's ceiling—a blue sky dotted with puffy clouds and playful angels. The women of the town cleaned, dusted, and polished every square foot of the venerable old lady. Strolling through San Benedetto in the days before the concert, Isa filled with satisfaction. The pride and appreciation in the eyes of the people was, in part, her doing.

Family, friends, and townspeople filled every seat. The houselights dimmed before Isa had a chance to scan the faces. Leech's reproachful cough drew her attention back to the stage. She inhaled. The smell of summer flowers filled the air. Cowboy, Jamie, and Willy donated her arrangements, shocking the local florist who'd never received such a large order. Isa looked for Gina's contribution—a bouquet of red roses.

"They're too small," Gina griped when Isa suggested they place the arrangement on the piano. "They'll look cheap next to the garden of flowers from your *rich* friends." But Isa insisted, and there the lovely roses sat.

Stepping to center stage, Isa smiled at Malcolm and Silverstein. Leech's busy hands positioned her in front of the piano, inching her back then tugging her forward like a furniture mover. Malcolm, visible in her peripheral vision, assumed the conductor role. Silverstein and his cello sat slightly behind her left shoulder. Isa snickered, watching Leech kneel on the floor and fuss over her dress like a maid of honor.

"Beautiful, beautiful, my pet," he mumbled. Pushing himself up from the floor with a groan, he nodded to Malcolm and Silverstein before squeezing her shoulder and looking in her eyes. "You're a star!"

Isa swelled with joy and admiration as Leech, a colorful beach ball of a man, hustled off stage. She owed so much to him. He believed, pushed, molded her voice. She wasn't his best or even the most patient of pupils, but in their sessions he made her feel as if she were. He never surrendered. Isa would next see him after the curtain parted, with his little round head and wisps of lavender hair peering up from the pit.

Malcolm whispered, "Ready?"

Isa nodded. The pianist signaled to the stage manager. The sound of her breathing and the pounding of her heart gave way to thunderous applause as the curtain parted.

Chapter 13

Joy consumed Isa. She'd done it—survived the first act, her first solo recital, and she hadn't fainted or flubbed. And to Leech's good fortune, despite the somersaults in her stomach, she'd not thrown up—the pit from where he prompted would have been a bull's-eye.

An off-stage motor gurgled and grated, driving the pulleys that closed the red velvet curtain. Isa stood in character, hands clasped to her chest, head erect and eyes focused on an imaginary troubadour at the back of the dark auditorium. She basked in the applause until the curtains kissed with a soft thud. A final whoosh of air infused with dust and perfume, tickled her nose.

With the curtain closed, Leech would surely dash out for a cigarette or two…or three. The little voice teacher, very possibly, was more exhausted than she. Oh, how his face and hands had strained.

From the first note, his color crescendoed to crimson and never scaled back. He guided Isa through arias with pulsing eyebrows, puffing cheeks and eyes that fired and cooled depending upon the piece's tempo and mood. He saved the most grueling of workouts for lips and jaw. A wide mouth with animated lips coached Isa through "Adele's Laughing Song." For *Butterfly*, his floating hands and prayerful lips first calmed, then steered her into the role's passion, excitement, and anticipation. Leech navigated her through the act's final and most difficult aria, "Tacea la Notte," nudging her to deliver Leonora's surprise, wonderment, and joy.

Isa respected her voice teacher, even admired his talent. She was fond of him, to be sure. But during the first act, she saw, and more importantly, felt, his strength, passion and, yes, even love. Leech poured his heart and soul into *her* performance. Beneath the Pantone facade, and beyond the clownish pantomimes was a man of profound emotion, perhaps even a tortured soul. The riddle of Leech fascinated yet panged her with guilt. She knew so little about this precious man.

As applause quieted beyond the closed curtain, Malcolm rose from the piano bench, grabbed Isa's hand, and kissed her on the cheek. "Brava, Isabella!"

Fighting an urge to giggle, Isa caught her breath. "Did I do—"

Malcolm stopped her with a raised palm. "You were marvelous. Now, run along. Prepare for your next set." He nodded toward stage left. "I'll grab Leech. We'll come along shortly."

Isa had a million questions but they'd have to wait. Malcolm, a consummate professional, didn't want her to dwell on the past. She had to rest her voice, get her head around act two. He and Leech planned to regroup in her dressing room. They'd offer a pep talk of sorts—a dose of encouragement and a plan to survive the next half.

"*Querida,* you were fantastic."

Isa recognized Christina's voice behind her in the corridor. When Isa spun around just outside her dressing room, her childhood friend rested a hand on her shoulder.

Shaking her head, Isa heaved a sigh. "But I missed so many notes."

Christina shrugged. "Didn't notice; guessing no one did."

"Thank Malcolm for that. He's quite the magician."

"And adorable. I could hardly keep my eyes off him."

"Thanks a lot."

Christina scoffed. "Please! I fought every impulse not to telescope the program on his gorgeous dimples. I watched you *both*—like a spectator at a tennis match," she added with a chuckle. "Do you need anything?"

Isa glanced into her dressing room. Wearing a white smock, the hairstylist busied herself at the table, readying brushes, combs and makeup. "I'm good," Isa said with a wink to her friend. "Maria's prepped for surgery. Go! Have fun—mingle. Drink some of that fine champagne you paid for."

"Oh, that reminds me." From under her cashmere sweater, Christina produced a bottle. "Snatched one for you." As she handed the bottle to Isa, her smile melted into a frown. "For later, *after* the concert."

As Christina turned to go, Isa grabbed her arm. "I couldn't see the faces. Even if I could've, don't think I would've—no guts. Tell me, how'd they—"

Christina squeezed her shoulders. "Don't worry. Everyone's having a grand time. You're fabulous."

"And Papa, how's he enjoy—"

"He'd love his little princess if she flatted every note. He and your mother glowed with pride. Grabbed each other's hand from Adele's opening note to Leonora's final trill. Your father mouthed every word as if willing them into your head. So adorable."

"And Lady Blatherwicke?"

Christina rolled her eyes. "Why care about the old cow?"

"Her ch-chorus," Isa stammered. "Validation—stamp of approval—redemption of sorts."

Christina gasped, color rising in her cheeks. "How many times have I told you? You're fabulous. As for Lady Blatherwicke, couldn't see her. Her royal tipsy highness sat in a box behind me—propped up between Monsieur Testosterone and clever Ana."

Isa snickered. "Go! Be my eyes and ears and keep the champagne flowing."

"Like a raging river, *querida.*"

As Isa entered her dressing room, Maria avoided her eyes. The hairstylist looked everywhere but into Isa's face. She helped the performer out of her blue gown and into the red. Isa waited for a compliment or at the very least, a congratulations. Was she being presumptuous—silly? Malcolm and Christina stroked her fragile ego with praise. Even Silverstein flashed thumbs up as Isa headed off stage. Maria, however, went about her tasks in silence as if it were an average day in her salon.

"Come," Maria said, patting the chair. "Sit. Not much time."

Isa studied the stylist in the mirror. "Maria, you like the concert?"

The stylist's head leaned close to Isa's hair as if she had trouble unfastening the pins. "*Sì, sì,*" she mumbled, "but I don't know much about such things." A hint of pink haloed her heavily blushed cheeks.

"You get a good seat? Could you hear?"

Maria's head moved from side to side. "No seat. Listened from here. Needed to prepare things. Your mama and papa will be proud. Parents always are."

"But you liked—"

Isa stopped herself before breaking a cardinal rule—*never ask a question unless prepared for the answer.* Her confidence wasn't strong enough to deflect a lancing critique. Maria, Isa guessed, lived by her own cardinal rule. Humming a tune with hairpins pressed between lips rendered her unable to speak. The hairstylist tuned Isa out as effectively as if she cupped her ears and crooned like a child, *la, la, la, la, la, la...*

Isa studied her own reflection in the mirror. Maria transformed her into Mozart's haunting queen. Wild raven tresses replaced the smooth, sophisticated pullback. Thick mascara and under-liner extended for an inch beyond the corners of her eyes. *Is Madam Jenkins staring back at me?* At once inspired, Isa knew how her bold muse would respond to tepid endorsements like that offered by Maria. Isa's own lips, under a diva's dark eyes shadowed with violet and earthy hues, mouthed the words—*Art takes guts!*

As Maria worked, Isa reflected on the second act. With a nod to her muse, Isa reviewed "Queen of the Night." Many criticized Madam Jenkins for making a mockery of Mozart. Certainly her recording taxed the ears, but Isa admired the off-key diva's determination. She took no prisoners. The aria covered two octaves, a vocal minefield that always tripped Madam Jenkins...*and* showered her listeners with shrapnel.

A knock at the door jarred Isa out of character. She expected Malcolm and Leech although her voice teacher customarily barged into rooms without an invitation.

Isa's face lit up. She hadn't seen her younger sister since she shanghaied Lady Blatherwicke. Wearing a black sequined mesh dress with spaghetti straps, Ana radiated elegance. A silver necklace and wrist clasp shimmered against tanned skin. Her hair, normally smart but simple, was done up as if for a movie star walking the red carpet.

"Gattina, you're a knockout!"

"Credit the spa. But tonight's your night," Ana said, advancing into the room clapping her hands. "*Brava, cara sorella!* Fabulous!" She gave Isa a quick peck on the cheek to avoid mussing the star's makeup. Then she kissed the stylist whose hands flew about Isa's face with brushes and blush. "Pure genius, dear Maria," Ana said. "Isa dazzled in the first half. Now, she looks positively ghastly."

Maria giggled, batting the air with her hand.

Isa laughed. "Thanks!"

"All in the name of art, darling, all in the name of art." Ana picked up the champagne bottle from the dressing table and nodded toward the label. "Fantastic stuff—potent. Bottles uncorked, glasses poured—waiting to intoxicate."

"Thirty minutes isn't very long."

"Long enough. Lady Blatherwicke got a head start. I snuck two bottles into our box."

"Good girl."

"She's having a splendid time, by the way."

"After all that alcohol? I should hope so." Isa may have joked, but Lady Blatherwicke's reaction consumed her. But she didn't want to sound pathetic, especially after Christina's scolding. Instead, her curiosity took a circuitous route. "You mentioned the spa. Do tell."

"Lady Blatherwicke splurged—massage, facial, the works." Ana wiggled her fingers, showing off a French manicure. "She's really not all that bad, you know. Has you beat—got the boot from two choruses and one opera company."

Isa was intrigued but didn't have time for gossip. "No wonder she's an ogre."

Ana flashed a disproving look. "I'm not so sure, darling. She's overcome quite a bit. Hope I'm still high kicking at her age. And as much as you'll loathe me for saying it, my dear sister, Lady Gabriella Blatherwicke is a very likable person."

Isa groaned. "*Et tu, Brute?* And Philippe?"

Without responding, Ana returned the bottle to the table. She dropped her nose into Luca's freesias, salvaged by Kate, and spun around to face Isa. Assuming a coy expression, Ana toyed with her hair.

Isa glared at her sister. "Don't tell me you—"

Ana leaned forward, her face inches away from Isa. "What do you think, darling?"

Isa considered Maria's eavesdropping ears. But discretion was futile. Maria had more sources than the combined stringers of *The Times of London* and *La Repubblica*. Since she was the town's premier beautician, gossip flowed through her salon with the swiftness of a Roman aqueduct.

"Oh, Ana, you didn't?"

She shrugged. "I did."

Isa couldn't blame her…or him for that matter. Pairing them was akin to waving wine under the nose of an alcoholic. Philippe, she assumed, would bed half of San Benedetto before the weekend was over.

"Watch yourself."

Maria nodded but didn't speak. Her animated face did the communicating.

Ana's eyes twinkled with mischief. "I may love candy, but I never eat the whole box."

Maria's heavy breasts lifted as she waved a hairbrush in the air. "Frenchy's a sweet bonbon, all right. Poke with a finger, but best kept in the wrapper."

Isa's breathing stalled. Her eyes popped, so did Ana's. They looked at one another and then to Maria. The sisters burst into laughter as Leech trotted through the door followed by Malcolm. Isa caught their eyes in the mirror. "So much for a courtesy knock."

Leech tilted his head, his eyes blinked repeatedly but he didn't respond. Instead, his hand fluttered in front of him. "Marvelous, my pet, you were simply marvelous." Licorice-laced breath didn't camouflage the nicotine.

Malcolm turned to Ana. "From my vantage point, I'd say you're doing splendidly as well. Her Ladyship looks as serene as a puffy cherub on the opera house ceiling."

Ana acknowledged the compliment with a slight bow of her head. "A mightier task lay ahead. Gotta keep the champagne-infused Lady B from swan-diving out of the box." Ana glided from the room amidst a chorus of laughter.

After Maria secured Isa's crown, she withdrew in silence. Malcolm shut the door and Leech plopped onto the sofa. No doubt, his round bottom had made a permanent indentation in the seat cushion. Leech thumped the sofa, but Malcolm remained standing.

The handsome pianist glanced up at the clock. "We've got ten minutes."

Leech launched his butterfly fingers. "Stretch it to twenty. I need another cig." He turned to Isa. "Now, my pet. Sweep act one out of your pretty little head. Your voice still ripens."

"B-but," Isa stammered. "You said I was good, no?"

His forehead creased and his neck stiffened. "Yes, yes, fine, fine. Time for victory laps and arse slaps later. We've three arias yet to conquer. How do you feel? How's your voice?"

"I'm a bit nervous of the Queen's high Fs."

"You and me both. Mustn't be meek. Attack them with fury. Hit and run, hit and run. Keep moving."

Isa looked to Malcolm. "I'm counting on more of your magic. You're brilliant."

He sighed before offering a half smile. "We'll survive the Mozart. I'm a tad nervous about the Donizetti. It's a rather long piece—"

"Lots of leaps and runs," Leech interrupted.

Isa gulped. "Perhaps I should have gone with *Norma*?"

"Too late!" Leech snapped. "We've crossed the Rubicon. Just remember, it's not Lucia's mad scene." He stuck out his tongue, bugged his eyes, and bobbled his head.

Dear, sweet Leech. Isa could rely on him to make her laugh when she needed it most.

We conquer Donizetti and the Bellini will be a snap," he added. "But don't get ahead of yourself. Focus! Lucia demands stamina, not a sprint."

Malcolm nodded his agreement. "And of course, the encore."

Isa felt her muscles relax, recalling the pianist's earlier comments. After a satisfactory first act, Isa began to share Malcolm's confidence that her encore would send the audience streaming with smiles into the streets of San Benedetto.

"The encore?" Leech said, making a dismissive gesture with his hand. "Yes, easy breezy, Pucceenee!"

Isa laughed again but prayed Leech was right. They helped her drape the deep violet cape over her gown. Emboldened, Isa peacocked in the mirror. Her transformation to the Queen of the Night was complete. "To the stage," she said, thrusting her hand forward.

As the curtain parted for the second half, Isa felt more relaxed. She hoped the audience, spiked with champagne, felt the same. Applause awoke her adrenaline. She didn't really care whether they cheered for Maria's makeup, Malcolm's Hollywood smile, or her.

Isa signaled her readiness to Malcolm. She assaulted Mozart with the fury of an invading army. Following Leech's command, she missed one, two, maybe more high notes but kept marching forth. *Limit the vocal shrapnel,* she thought to herself. The audience rewarded her perseverance with a hearty round of applause. Leech looked ill, but he managed a smile while dabbing a beaded brow. The aria was a mad dash and Isa had crossed the finish line—a bit bruised perhaps, but a finish nonetheless.

Isa walked to the wing for a prearranged rendezvous with Maria to shed her royal trappings. Receiving the singer with an unexpected hug, Maria's expression conveyed sympathy as if she greeted her at a wake. "It's okay, Isa, it's okay."

What does that mean? Isa nodded in silence as Maria removed her cape and draped it over an arm. Still projecting empathy, she took the crown from Isa's head. A tear fell from her eye as she kissed Isa on the cheek. *Christ! The woman loathed my singing.*

Art takes guts, Isa repeated to herself as she shook off Maria's response. Filling her head with images of Lucia di Lammermoor, she reclaimed center stage. A burst of applause and cheers greeted her glittery, cleavage-popping gown. From the pit, Leech pulsed his eyebrows. "Boobies and scarlet," he had said when Isa first modeled the dress, "will harvest a bounty of *hurrahs.*"

"Regnava nel Silenzio," to Isa's joyful surprise, became her finest moment of the night. Perhaps she identified with Lucia, a tortured woman whose true love eluded her. Isa hit the highs, managed to conquer the final runs, and held the closing note. The audience responded with enthusiasm. Her confidence surged.

At last she found the courage to look down into the first row. Papa clutched his hands above his head like a champion fighter. Her mother bobbed her head, her hands clasped as if in prayer. Even Gina managed a smile. Leech beamed. From behind, Malcolm and Silverstein whispered *Bravas.* The black abyss before her rang out with cheers and cries of "Brava!" She detected a variety of accents. "Atta girl!" was unmistakably Cowboy. The New York taxi whistle belonged to no one but Danny Chance and the thunderous foot pounding had to come from Jamie's sturdy legs. Isa took another bow, swelling with delight at the sight of her parents blowing kisses to the stage.

If only the concert had ended at that glorious moment.

Chapter 14

Isa had rehearsed "Ah! Non Credea" plenty of times. At half the length of her prior piece, Amina's final aria from *La Sonnambula* should have been a breeze. In addition, the composer, Vincenzo Bellini, wrote the piece in the *bel canto* tradition, lyrical and lush. The opening started well…*Ah! Non credea mirarti, sì presto estinto, o fiore*—I did not believe you would fade so soon, oh flower. Leech sighed, looking relaxed for the first time all evening.

Then tragedy struck. Isa didn't see it coming. Like a bad tumble, her vocal pratfall started with a slight trip that knocked her concentration off balance. She missed a note. She regained her mental footing, but overcompensated. Her voice raced ahead of the music. Dear Malcolm did his best to catch up. He plunked notes here, then there, like someone trying to swat a nimble fly. Isa's voice cracked. She recovered. It cracked again. Then, the unthinkable—she opened her mouth—nothing. She stood, horrified, eyes darting, pulse racing, head growing light and numb. A performer's worst nightmare…but this was real.

The piano and cello kept circling. The music looped back like a carrousel, coaxing her to jump back on. The repetition continued like a broken record. Isa looked down at Leech. He waited, mouth frozen open on what should have been her next note. She bowed her head, a trembling hand rose to her cheek. She turned, falling forward. Her flailing hands reached for, and found the piano.

Someone shouted, "Curtain! Curtain, dammit!"

Malcolm and Silverstein rushed to Isa's side. With tender assurances, they assisted her to the dressing room. Maria stood, statue still. Hands pressed her cheeks, face devoid of all color. After Isa's escorts settled her onto the sofa, Maria recovered. The stylist poured Isa a glass of water. After dabbing her forehead with a cool, damp cloth, Maria kneeled on the floor, removed Isa's shoes, and massaged her feet.

"I'm so sorry," Isa muttered.

Isa closed her eyes. Her mind filled with images of the stage meltdown. She moaned. Would that single moment haunt her forever—faces frozen in shock and embarrassment—the thumping of her heart—the relentless music, at once deafening and distant? Was the vision merely a mirage or had Lady Blatherwicke stood with arm extended toward the stage and face gripped by fury? Isa groaned.

From the rush of air, Isa sensed several people flying into the room. Scents and voices identified Leech, Christina, and Kate. Isa opened her eyes to the hovering faces of concern.

She repeated, "Sorry, sorry, sorry."

Above the mutterings, words broke like a thunderclap, "Where's my daughter? Where's my little Isabella?" The voice belonged to Isa's mother, Angelina. "Let her breathe."

As the wall of bodies parted, Angelina approached the sofa. She caressed Maria's shoulder and whispered, "*Grazie, mia amica.*" The stylist kissed Angelina's hand and left the room.

"You heard her. Out!" The second and more menacing thunderclap belonged to Isa's older sister, Gina. Scampering feet and a door slam followed her rant.

"You, too, Gina. Leave us," Angelina said in a kind but firm voice.

A heavy sigh preceded the opening and closing of the door.

Taking a seat on the sofa, Isa's mother cradled her daughter's head in her bosom. "Hush, hush, Isabella."

"Oh, Mama. I froze. I panicked. I'm a failure at everything."

Angelina kissed the top of her daughter's head. "You were fabulous. Remember that. As long as I live, I'll never forget seeing you up that stage—talented, beautiful, bold."

"Why did I think I could sing? I should never have put on this bloody concert."

Angelina squeezed Isa's hand. "If I've learned one thing from your father in fifty years, it's that hiding in a cocoon is no life. No shadows for my dear Isabella. The spotlights were the rays of a thousand suns on my beautiful butterfly."

"But Mama, you always said—"

Her mother pressed fingers to Isa's lips. "Hush! Sometimes, your father's right. Never repeat that. I'll deny I said it."

"I love you, Mama."

"Love you too, little star."

After a minute or two finding comfort in the gentle rocking of her mother's arms, Isa asked, "Where's Papa?"

As her mother began to answer, the sound of singing seeped through the door. Mystified, mother and daughter stared into each other's eyes. Voices started soft then grew louder until the entire auditorium throbbed with the music of "Va Pensiero" from *Nabucco,* Italy's unofficial anthem. Above it all, Isa heard her papa's voice.

"Your father," Angelina cooed. Her eyes shone with affection.

Isa sat up. Her mother grabbed a box of tissues and the cold cream from the dressing table. With a few strong rubs, she erased the menacing queen from her daughter's eyes. After fixing Isa's hair and applying lipstick, Angelina helped Isa to her feet.

Outside the door, Gina stood legs apart, arms folded across her chest as music roared through the dark, empty corridor. Taking her cue from her mother, Gina burst into song. Too astounded to utter a note, Isa marched as if in a trance toward the light.

Isa froze. Had her eyes deceived her? Papa Fabrini, like the Pied Piper, had drawn everyone to the stage. Aisles held the overflow. Malcolm and Silverstein had reclaimed their instruments. Grabbing her mother's arm, Isa scanned the jubilant faces. She gasped. Beside her papa stood a beaming Lady Blatherwicke, her cane tapping out the tempo. The chorus mistress's voice, with its distinct vibrato, rose louder than all but that of Papa Fabrini.

Ana nudged her father. As he turned toward Isa and her mother, his face lit up with joy. He pushed through the crowd. After kissing his wife, he put an arm around Isa. Kissing his daughter's cheek, he whispered, "Verdi always delivers."

After a gentle squeeze to her husband's arm, Angelina grabbed Gina and dragged her onto the stage.

Isa pulled her papa close. "You're wonderful."

"Remember that *after* my request." Mischief danced in his eyes.

Her eyebrows rose. "Yes?"

"Sing once more. Your encore."

Isa sighed. "I can't." *What can he be thinking?* He'd just redeemed the concert. Now he wanted to sacrifice her again. Isa groaned. "No, no, Papa."

"Sing for me." His eyes scanned the stage. "Sing for your friends. Most importantly, sing for yourself."

She shook her head. "I can't, Papa. Please don't make me."

"I wouldn't ask if I wasn't sure you can do it." He stared at his daughter. The same look coaxed her back onto the hostile playground, nudged her toward a new life in London, urged her to forget Walter Benchley. Isa exhaled; her shoulders relaxed.

As the chorus ended, the opera house filled with a burst of cheers. Papa returned to the center of the stage. "Ladies and gentlemen, dear friends, family," he projected. "Our star shines again in the evening sky. Isabella has agreed to humor her old papa with one final song." The silent crowd followed Papa Fabrini's arm as he gestured toward Isa. Isa felt every eye on her face. After an awkward pause, the auditorium erupted in applause—several people shouted, "*Brava!*" Others, "Encore!"

People filed off the stage. Some reclaimed seats, many stood in the aisles. Isa's family, close friends, and Leech huddled in the wings. Isa nodded to Malcolm.

Where it came from, Isa didn't know. Madam Jenkins would have puffed out her chest with pride, sending the ostrich feathers fluttering in her hair. Isa gave her finest rendition of Lauretta's beloved aria from Puccini's *Gianni Schicchi. O mio babbino caro, mi piace è bello, bello...*—Oh, my dear papa, I love him, he is handsome, handsome...

Chapter 15

Verdi's chorus resuscitated the evening and Isa's triumphant encore eclipsed the full-fledged fiasco. The crowd chattered with joy, their mirth fed by the narrow escape from certain catastrophe. Malcolm's prediction came true—the audience streamed into the Italian night with music on their lips and smiles on their faces.

After the theater emptied, Gina and Ana volunteered to take the many bouquet tributes to the hotel restaurant—a small post-concert gathering for family.

Isa snatched back one of the bouquets. "For you, Mama."

"Don't give away your pretty flowers." Yet despite the urging, Angelina clutched the bouquet to her chest. Her grip tightened as her nose dropped into the fragrant red roses.

"Sorry, Papa, nothing for you."

Papa Fabrini squeezed her hand. "What does an old man need? This concert was heaven." He puffed out his chest. "You gave me the chance to sing on this stage—a dream since I was a boy."

Angelina poked him in the ribs. "*Bene!* Now, it's out of your system."

He laughed, but his sideways glance suggested thoughts of a return engagement. "Go!" he said, motioning Isa to the dressing room. "We wait—walk with you."

Isa's hands gestured toward the exit. "Shoo! I've got to change. I'll be along."

Angelina motioned to her other daughters. "Ana and Gina will walk with you, then."

But Isa had no desire to hold her sisters back. She wanted to bask in the moment for a while longer, alone. She didn't need to press hard. Gina hurried off eager to escape the musty air. Ana however, required a firm hand to guide her to the door.

"Gattina, please go. I'll be fine. Play hostess till I get there."

In Ana's eyes, Isa saw the understanding of a fellow artist, sensitivity to a desire to steep in the achievement. "Okay," Ana said. "But don't be too long. You're the star of the evening."

As Ana headed to the stage door exit, Isa called after her, "Keep your eye on Papa. Our new Pavarotti's liable to goad the restaurant into song—maybe even the whole town."

Only the stalwart Maria remained with her in the theater. She helped Isa exchange her gown for a smart dress. Isa didn't protest when the beautician insisted on transforming her hair and makeup from stage glitz to post-concert glam. Maria made Isa look as beautiful as she felt.

Isa handed Maria the unopened bottle of champagne and an envelope—her prearranged fee plus a small gratuity. "*Grazie mille.* Your Queen of the Night was sheer brilliance. Without you, the audience would've been left with only my singing."

A touch of pink colored Maria's cheeks. "Damn lucky to get, Isabella Fabrini. Your encore—it was…nice."

Maybe not the most glowing of compliments, but Maria's sincerity touched Isa. She helped the stylist load her car, a case filled with beauty aids and the costumes and accessories that Isa would fetch in a day or two. After waving good-bye from the street door, Isa returned to the dressing room for her coat.

What to do about Luca's freesias? Kate had done a fine job; one would never suspect the fragrant white blooms had lain scattered among shards of crystal on the dressing room floor. For Isa, the smashed vase and pre-concert chaos seemed a lifetime ago. She had pushed through, survived. People always said that great moments in one's life—tragedies or triumphs—changed the person. Did she feel any different? She shrugged. Soon she'd be back in London. An ordinary life out of the spotlight—work, worries, bills—awaited her return. *And Luca?* How would getting through the concert help her figure out what to do with him?

Isa stared at the florist's card. Luca's message confused her—*Sorry I can't be there for your triumph. Sing from the heart, my sweet, xx.* To her surprise, they'd come far as a couple—friends, lovers. Then again, she and Walter were nearly married. But did she really know Luca Caruso? Sometimes he was distant. Perhaps keeping something from her, a dark secret, another woman? She didn't know. He guarded his past and she, not wanting to spoil the relationship, didn't pry. *Perhaps I should have.* Now, Luca's skipping the concert sent another message. She could ask Leech again, but that path never got her anywhere. Leech loved Luca too much to gossip, offering only assurances of his old friend's generosity and impeccable character. "You couldn't do any better, my pet," Leech had said, "I'd marry him myself if he'd have me."

Isa looked at the card again. If Luca truly loved her, he would have come to San Benedetto. After the flowers arrived, she phoned him in London for an explanation. He was evasive, distant. When she pressed him for a reason, Luca offered a lame excuse about an important group booking at the restaurant. *Hell, he can't even lie well.*

Maybe she was too old, too set in her ways, to put her faith in another man. She considered the rubbish bin but instead placed the card in her handbag. Lifting the clusters of white blooms from their vase, she held them to her breast before rolling them in newspaper. Oddly enough and in a way she didn't understand, Luca's flowers comforted her.

"Foolishness," she mumbled as she walked to the door.

Her fingers fumbled for the light switch. She turned for one last look. Her eyes met the posters of Callas and Scotto. Experience fed a greater appreciation for their courage and stamina. "*Grazie mille*, dear ladies," she said as the room went black.

Isa flipped the toggles that bathed her in spotlights. The stage, *her stage*, was cleared of all but the grand piano, Silverstein's chair and his music stand. She moved her hand toward the lever that opened the curtain. But she kept the red velvet wall closed. She sought intimacy, not the grandeur of the opera house. Isa wanted to inhale the theater's scent, feel the lingering warmth of applause before the feeling vanished forever. She thought it unlikely that she'd ever again set foot on that stage, or for that matter, *any stage*. Had Florence Foster Jenkins wandered back onto the Carnegie Hall stage after her final concert? Isa moved toward the exit. "*Grazie et ciao*, Madam Jenkins."

The theater door shut with a thud. A breeze cooled the warm spring air and fluttered Isa's scarf. From the opera house, the restaurant was a ten-minute stroll through the center of a still busy San Benedetto. The town's spas attracted visitors, respectable numbers for a small village far from the trendier meccas of Tuscany and Umbria. Natural springs put San Benedetto on the map in the early nineteenth century and kept its name from fading from guidebooks. Although one wouldn't find Prada, Ferragamo, or a Four Seasons, offerings satisfied the tastes and wallets of middle-class tourists.

Isa strolled past the Terme, the ornate spa that had pampered clients for eighty years. The white, pink, and green granite building wed two styles, the mixed marriage a result of destiny. It was conceived as Art Nouveau, but the First World War delayed final design and construction until the Deco period.

Isa sighed at the prospect of a spa day. Christina booked them both mineral baths and massages for the following morning. Oh, how the best friends would gossip and giggle about the concert—just like old times.

Thank God and Papa for the encore or I'd be attending a wake, not a celebration. The thought buoyed Isa as she walked toward her rendezvous.

Ana first suggested a post-concert gathering. "Something intimate."

"No," Isa had insisted, protesting with words that in retrospect were prophetic. "I'll barely survive the concert."

But Ana, relentless as usual, pressed on. "Family, close friends. Christina's crossing the equator *and* an ocean for you. And of course, *your* Leech."

Yes, the colorful voice teacher from Soho had indeed become *her* Leech. His selfless devotion and frenetic energy would need refueling. Isa surrendered. "Okay, but nothing lavish."

Isa's mother and older sister proposed a small café known for its veal and pasta, but her papa and Ana insisted upon the Excelsior. "Fit for our diva," Papa Fabrini said. Like the Terme, the Excelsior was once called *Grand.* And also like the Terme, the hotel and its restaurant had a tenuous grip on grandeur, a struggle waged amidst a thinning reputation and thickening patches of plaster. Still, the food ranked among San Benedetto's best.

Isa waved to clusters of concertgoers sitting in small groups at cafés that dotted the pedestrian zone. She snuck up to a table of business school chums, five handsome men attired in dark suits. With one exception: her favorite Scotsman wore a dinner jacket over a kilt.

Tucking Luca's flowers under her arm, Isa used her silk scarf to cover Jamie's eyes. He jumped. Cowboy, Willy, and the American boys howled with laughter. "Guess who?"

"Do ya got all weekend, love? Too many birds know my penchant for blindfolds and handcuffs."

"Devil," Isa said, tapping the top of his head.

The quintet burst into applause as Isa returned the scarf to her neck. Begging them not to get up, she circled with a kiss for each. Singing a chorus of praise, their superlatives made her giddy.

"One helluva show, kiddo," Brad said with a slap to his thigh. "Damn proud of ya."

Jamie punched Brad's arm. "Cowboy can say that now. If Alexandra were here it'd be *a fine performance, dearest Isabella, very fine.*"

"How kind of you to say so," Isa replied, mimicking Eliza Doolittle's practiced pleasantries. "Where is Alexandra? And your—" She looked to Willy never sure where he fell in the matrimony cycle.

"*Wife,*" Willy responded with a smirk. "She ran back to the hotel with Alexandra. They wanted to freshen up before—"

"Meeting us here," Brad, said, finishing the sentence.

Isa turned to Danny and Tommy. "Got you two to thank. You gave me the idea for a concert at the reunion, remember?"

"Our idea, but your triumph," Tommy said, brushing blond hairs from his eyes.

Danny squeezed the back of Tommy's neck. "*My* idea. But, I don't mind sharing the credit...with *him.*" Tommy rolled his eyes while the other fellows teased Danny for his bluster.

"You looked stunning on stage," Tommy said.

"Loved the gowns and shoes, too. Amazing," Danny added.

Isa snickered as the other men cast curious expressions at Danny who gave wardrobe details only a fashionista could appreciate. Only Tommy nodded in time to the New Yorker's quick tempo.

Willy interrupted Danny's gushing litany. "All I saw, mate, were blue and red dresses and that queen thingamajig." Jamie and Brad hoisted their beers in a toast to Willy.

"And now this snappy number," Danny added, ignoring the gibe. Isa had changed into a sleeveless dress that fell to just above her knees. The cream-colored scarf had a subtle paisley in the same indigo-blue as her dress. "Twirl," Danny commanded with a spin of his finger. "Amazing."

The others voiced agreement. Brad and Danny got into a whistling competition.

Throwing her head back, Isa laughed. Their compliments helped her forget the concert mishap. "Down, wolves, this isn't the wild west."

"You're right," Jamie said, his eyes sparking with mischief. "Here in Italy gents appreciate a fine-looking lady in other ways." He reached around and pinched Isa's bottom.

She slapped his hand. "Perhaps I should sit down."

Brad motioned toward the Excelsior. "We'd ask you to join us, but we saw your sisters scurry to the hotel."

"Probably waiting on dinner for you," Tommy added.

Isa looked over her shoulder to the hotel. Her friends were right. "Will you be here later? Or perhaps breakfast in the morning." She didn't want to end the weekend without a visit. They all had come so far. Her head had been in a fog before the concert to play the gracious hostess.

"Come back later," Danny said. "We want to party with San Benedetto's very own Queen of the Night."

Isa clapped her hands. "Brilliant!"

Swept up in a spirit of camaraderie, Isa practically floated toward the hotel. Every ground floor window glowed, casting halos of warm light. The Excelsior, a decade younger than the Terme, was a cake box of a building. Chipped stucco betrayed fading health, although a pink hue suggested that the Grande Dame retained a glimmer of life.

The music of a small orchestra wafted outdoors on the same breeze that billowed white draperies in the windows. A celebration, perhaps a wedding, Isa thought, occupied the banquet hall. *Papa will sneak in to dance for sure—if he hasn't already done so.*

In the foyer, Isa found Christina sitting in a chair, eyes glued to the front door. Her chic Argentine friend jumped up, intertwined arms, and led Isa toward the restaurant.

"Don't be angry," Christina said, guiding Isa forward.

"Angry? About what?"

"You know we all love you. Your family, me…"

"Y-yes?" Isa grew suspicious. What was her friend getting at?

Chapter 16

Instead of turning right into the restaurant, Christina guided Isa to the left and into the Excelsior's banquet hall. Isa gasped. Christina's grip tightened—she wasn't going to let Isa escape.

"Remember. Everyone here loves you," Christina whispered.

The orchestra stopped in the middle of a swing era standard. After quizzical looks directed toward the bandstand, the couples stranded on the dance floor turned toward the door.

"Christ!" Isa muttered under her breath. Her protest drew a squeeze from Christina that nearly bruised her arm.

The hall fell silent. Everyone froze except for one gentleman in his best suit, Papa Fabrini. After slapping the orchestra's leader on the back, Isa's papa hurried toward his daughter. He paused when he reached the middle of the dance floor. With hands clapping above his head, he rotated in a circle. Following his lead, the room erupted with applause.

Grabbing her friend's coat and Luca's flowers, Christina pushed Isa forward. "Curtsy, bow, genuflect—or whatever the hell you divas do."

"I'm no diva," Isa said through gritted teeth as she bowed her head.

"Thatta girl. A diva by any other name."

Instinct took over. Isa blew kisses, exaggerating her arm movements.

"Easy does it, Bernhardt."

Papa Fabrini held out his arms. Isa met him on the dance floor, her nose greeted with a fresh dose of sandalwood cologne.

"Not a word," he whispered in her ear as they embraced. "You deserve this."

After unlocking arms, Papa Fabrini held fast to her hand. Isa shot him a piercing look. "Oh, Papa, you know how much I hate—"

"Tut, tut," he said, putting a finger to her lips. "Our little bird must rest her voice."

Isa's hands lifted in surrender. Guests mistook the Evita-like gesture as a plea for more applause. Cheers broke out a second time. Speaking loud, Isa tried to silence the clamor, "Thank you, *grazie, merci, danke.*"

Despite her embarrassment, Isa calmed. Her parents stood on the edge of the dance floor beaming with pride in front of family and friends. She couldn't deflate their joy. Was she absurd to think of the party as the wedding reception she denied them? As for Ana, Isa seldom got angry at the blithe spirit. Gazing over her papa's shoulder, Isa grinned as her younger sister flitted from table to table, churning laughter in her wake.

After a signal from Papa Fabrini, the orchestra started to play. Isa recognized the waltz. Papa scooped her into his arms and whisked her around the dance floor. As they completed a spin, Isa saw her business school buddies. Danny announced their arrival with a two-fingered taxi whistle. The five, laughing and making funny faces, looked like schoolboys pleased at having fooled her. Willy's and Brad's wives, two sculpted beauties, joined them.

As the music waned, Papa Fabrini scissor-stepped Isa to a table filled with the family and friends with whom Isa had expected to be dining *alone*. "You rats," Isa said, wagging a finger. "Paybacks are hell." Despite her words, Isa enjoyed the attention and applause. But what pleased her most was seeing people she loved come together in celebration.

Taking a seat between Christina and Ana, Isa machine-gunned both with questions. The party, she learned confirming a suspicion, was Ana's brainchild. Needing no excuse for fun, her papa endorsed the idea. Ana contacted Christina who welcomed the invitation to help. The collaborators then ensnared Jamie. A windfall courtesy of Willy's financial wizardry oiled the rusty hinges of the frugal Scotsman's wallet. While pleased that her parents didn't shoulder financial burden, Isa was distressed that friends had been strong-armed. *Isa Fabrini doesn't accept charity.*

In spite of her misgivings, Isa devoured the five-course meal and dessert. The food was wonderful. Gina, however, whined about the "chewy veal" and her mother complained that the pasta was "rubbery and bland and must have come from a box."

Leech excused himself for a cigarette every ten minutes to escape Isa's aunt, a widow who developed a reputation as a flirt among San Benedetto seniors. Sparkling wine made the aunt's eyes bat and hands wander. Leech looked flustered as he deflected the woman's advances using the only Italian he knew—snippets from opera roles.

Leech harvested Figaro's lines like a drunken farmer zigzagging through fields. The ancient aunt tried to pull him onto the dance floor. He, like Mozart's comic valet, feigned a twisted ankle. "You're faking," she responded. "I see it in your face." Leech tapped Figaro's wit. "*Mente il ceffo, io gia non mento.*"—well then, my face is lying, not me. After dinner, he excused himself with "*la turba m'aspetta*"—the crowd awaits me—before limping from the table.

Bravo, Leech! Isa thought, pleased that her aunt wasn't an avid fan of opera.

"Party's lovely, darlin'." In a high-spirited brogue, Kate slid onto Leech's vacated chair as Isa sipped her coffee. A full-skirted, green tartan plaid with velvet bodice complemented red curls. "Still tryin' to get that broodin' hulk of a Scotsman to dance."

"Jamie merely needs time to warm up."

"Any warmer he'll combust. He's toured the dance floor with half the women here."

As Isa laughed, a woman approached the table. Although shorter and a few years older than Kate, she didn't have to speak to tag her nationality. Dressed in Irish plaid, she wore the Emerald Isle on her face—round, freckled, and rosy with impish crinkles around the eyes. Her ginger-colored hair was a couple of shades lighter than Kate's.

Kate grabbed the woman's hand, pulling her close. "My best mate, Brigid Clancy."

Isa smiled at the giddy newcomer. "Glad you could come."

Brigid giggled, releasing a mix of whiskey and wine into the air. "Pleasure's all mine, darlin'. Havin' the time of my life."

"First time in Italy?"

Brigid's eyebrows pulsed; small round blue eyes twinkled. "First time outta Ireland."

"Hope you enjoy yourself."

"Haven't been mugged or molested yet. But the holiday's still young."

Kate cleared her throat. Her expression careened between amusement and embarrassment. "What B-Brigid m-means," she stammered, "is that we're thrilled to visit your beautiful country."

Brigid rolled her eyes in rebuttal. Squaring her shoulders, she pushed out her chest. "He's in."

"Who?" Isa asked.

"That hottie in the kilt, this one's been pining after," Brigid said, elbowing Kate.

Kate's cheeks reddened. Her gaze wandered to her feet; her fingers picked at the pleats of her skirt. Brigid whacked Kate in the arm. "Now don't go playin' the blushin' maiden on me. He's all yours, dance after next."

"How'd you manage that?"

Brigid's face lit up, her eyes dancing with mischief. If female leprechauns existed, surely one now stood before them. She pointed across the room. Isa recognized a cousin, a very attractive twentysomething from Rome.

"Had that Etruscan goddess ask your Scotty to save a dance. The ole bait and switch." Brigid cackled; she shimmied, grinding her hip into Kate's side. "Your chance to grab the brass ring, Katie Maureen Mahoney."

"I'll grab somethin', that's for sure." Kate doubled over in laughter. "Prayin' for a sultry, sexy tango."

Curling her fingers like a cat, Brigid roared like a lion. Kate excused herself to powder her nose. "*Cheesin' the trap*, ya mean," Brigid said, howling with laughter.

Dropping onto the vacated chair, Brigid snatched up Leech's half-full wineglass. After a swirl, she took a generous gulp. With twinkling eyes, she motioned to the dance floor. "Ringside seat, darlin'."

Isa nodded to the dancers. "How about you?"

Holding up her left hand, Brigid shrugged. "Married."

"Never hurts to look."

The Irishwoman pulsed her eyebrows. "Never said I wouldn't. But too many bleedin' Englishmen—the rotten bastards. Love to steal a peek under Scotty's kilt myself or even pinch a few of those firm little Italian bums."

As the party rocked and rolled toward midnight, Isa made her way from table to table. Her script was generally the same: gratitude for attending, answers about local sites and activities, and inquiries about further holiday plans. Compliments jumbled praise for the town, the opera house, the music, the costumes, the veal, the wine…and only then, her singing. People viewed the concert as an all-inclusive holiday—*Isabella's Italian Adventure*—with Isa as hostess, entertainer, and tour guide.

Halfway through her gratitude tour around the room, Isa sat down at a table of cousins.

"Isabella, you've made your parents so happy. The wedding you never had," said Cousin Teresa.

"Much happier than the wedding your parents wish you *never* had." Isa delivered her comeback with a smirk, dressing up her barb as a joke. Teresa's parents subsidized their daughter, her chronically unemployed husband, and five sniveling brats.

Isa turned her attention to another couple, thanking them for coming all the way from Oklahoma.

"Pleasure's all ours, Cousin Isa. We'd never have reconnected with relatives if your concert hadn't given us an excuse to come to Italy."

"Hope you enjoyed the experience."

The Oklahoma cousin bobbed his head. "Excellent. Everything's excellent, the opera house, music, the meal, everything—*excellent.*"

"Be sure to tell Mama and Gina that the veal and pasta were *excellent.*"

His wife, a plain woman with a thick Oklahoma accent, nodded before assuming an odd expression. Isa followed her stare across the room. "That man, your voice teacher, is a bit of a f—"

"*Flamboyant* chap," Isa interrupted, uncomfortable with the woman's tone. "*Fabulous* teacher. *Fantastic* person. Couldn't have done this concert without him."

"Oh," the woman said as if sucking a lemon.

"I'm sure I can get him to ask you to dance. Light on his feet as you can imagine."

The woman's face went white; her head shook from side to side. "I d-don't dance."

"Sorry to hear that. At the very least, I'll have him introduce himself. Colorful man—miracle worker for the drab and dowdy."

Isa needed some air before greeting the remainder of the guests. Walking toward the terrace, she caught sight of a leather billfold. She crouched down to pluck it up just as the orchestra ended a spirited number. She recognized the American accents. Glancing up, she saw the heads of Tommy and Danny above the back of the sofa. As she searched the wallet, she couldn't help but eavesdrop.

"Gosh, honored you told me, I mean it, Danny. Couldn't have been easy for you."

"So you're okay with it? You're not…freaked out." Danny's tone teetered between relief and anxiety.

"Yeah! No! I mean of course I'm okay with it. Truth is, I kinda had an inkling."

Danny gasped. "You did? I don't see how. But, you never said anything."

"If you wanted me to know, you'd tell me—like you just did."

"Please, don't tell anyone."

"I wouldn't do that. You're my friend."

"How 'bout you, Tommy?"

"Me?" Tommy paused for several seconds. "Still…figuring things out. But I'm happy for you, Danny."

Isa stood up to see Tommy reach over and hug the New Yorker. Danny sighed. As their heads met, Danny's eyes moved to the side. He spotted Isa; his eyes widened. He pushed Tommy away and jumped to his feet. "I-I didn't see you," he stammered, now red-faced.

"Just got here. Found this on my way out for air." Holding up the billfold, Isa nodded toward the French doors. At the sight of the wallet, both men reached for their pockets. "It's Willy's," Isa said. "Bursting with banknotes."

"Figures," replied Tommy.

Something else in the wallet had caught her eye—business cards from London's preeminent solicitors—specialists in criminal defense. She kept that information to herself.

"You boys enjoying yourselves?" Isa called them *boys* because they were several years her junior. They also had youthful airs about them, especially when they got together.

"Lots of great people—from lots of places. You've got lots of great friends," Tommy said, sounding awestruck as he scanned the room with wide eyes.

Danny shook off his unease. He ran his hands down his suit jacket. "Love your family, especially your dad. Adorable man."

"I should introduce you to my voice teacher. You'll like him."

Tommy nudged his friend. "He's more interested in meeting them," Tommy said, pointing out Malcolm and Philippe. "Right, Danny?"

Danny's eyes grew wide; color rose in his cheeks. "Don't go there."

Amen! Danny may have been from Manhattan, but Philippe wasn't for amateurs.

Tommy's eyes darted from Danny to Isa to the dance floor. "And those two," he said, pointing to Brigid and Kate. "We want to meet them, most of all."

Of course! The tame American boys would temper the Irish firecrackers—keep them all out of trouble.

By night's end, Isa spoke to every guest except one—Lady Blatherwicke. Leech and Ana refused to discuss the chorus mistress, deflecting the subject each time Isa brought her up.

"Don't give her another thought," Leech said, flitting his hand.

"Tomorrow," Ana said poking the table. "Worry about Lady B *tomorrow.*"

Isa downed two more glasses of wine before she worked up the courage to confront her very own *queen of the night.* Taking a deep breath, Isa turned toward the sofa where the chorus mistress held court. Isa wasn't surprised to see Tommy and Danny and the Dubliners at her side. Isa rehearsed her words in her head.

But someone grabbed her hand. "Last dance, Isa."

Isa couldn't turn down Jamie. He was a major bankroller of the dinner. Besides, she didn't mind the reprieve from facing her demon. "Saved by the man in the kilt."

"You're the savior," he said, shaking his head. "That wild Irish minx."

"Kate?"

He shuddered. "Nay! The other one—little ginger lass—more dangerous. Been dodgin' her prying little fingers all night."

Isa grabbed him close. They held onto each other, howling with laughter.

When the music stopped, Isa intended to find Lady Blatherwicke. But she was too late. Arm-in-arm, the chorus mistress and Malcolm left the room.

That night as Isa lie in bed, a smile formed on her face. She remembered her vow—*No sing, no sleep.* Even after the adrenaline high of her performance subsided, slumber still evaded her. She tossed and turned, struggling over the question of Luca.

Isa had indeed sung, but she was too bewildered to sleep.

Chapter 17

Isa barely finished her lemon brioche when the buzzer sounded. "That'll be Christina," she said, swallowing the last of her cappuccino and dabbing her mouth. She looked toward the mantle but flower-filled vases, water glasses, and jelly jars arranged on her mother's ubiquitous lace doilies obscured the clock. With the many concert tributes, her parents' vintage flat looked and smelled like a florist shop. There wasn't a surface in the dining and living rooms without some arrangement.

Angelina glanced at her pendant, a timepiece that Papa Fabrini called a coach's stopwatch. "Only half two," she said. "You got time. Invite her up for coffee."

Despite no makeup and hair pushed under a black sports cap, Christina looked glamorous in body-hugging jeans and oversized pink sweater as she stepped into the flat. Her eyes scanned the walls. She stood transfixed.

Isa giggled. Everyone who saw the flat for the first time had the same reaction—rooms filled with artwork—paintings, sketches, sculpture. "Welcome to the Fabrini gallery. Papa says art inspires. Mama says it collects dust."

"Sit, sit, sit," Angelina shouted from the dining room as she put coffee, breads and fresh fruit on the polished wood table.

"You sure we have time?"

Isa nodded. "The Terme's only a fifteen-minute walk."

Christina rubbed her temples, taking a chair between Gina and Isa. "I could use some coffee. Got such a headache."

Isa laughed. "Me too—whiskey and regret."

Christina managed a pained chuckle. She nodded to the center of the round table. "Certain flowers are created more equal than others, I see."

Gina looked up from her ham sandwich. Angelina took a seat at the table and stared at Isa. When Isa first entered the dining room, she was surprised to find the roses she gave her mother banished to the sideboard. Instead, Luca's blooms held center stage. But she hadn't said a word; nor had Gina or Angelina. As usual among the family, it took an outsider, Christina, to broach the subject.

"Figured those flowers were special," Angelina said. "That's why I put them there."

"Please!" Isa said.

"You held onto those," her mother replied. "Remember the third-grade boy who gave you chocolate? Kept it by your bedside till it grew mold."

Isa felt her cheeks warm as the three women stared at her. She remembered Luca's card now tucked away in her purse. How foolish to keep his card and the bloody flowers. She had hoped their relationship was more than sex. Luca seemed genuine, interested in her—the kind of man she thought she wanted—kind, smart, strong. But if Luca really loved her, nothing could have kept him from her concert. *The biggest moment of my life, and he wasn't there.*

"They're no more special than those damn carnations," Isa said, pointing to the top of her papa's upright piano.

Gina clicked her teeth and assumed the bratty tone Isa remembered from childhood. "Someone's getting testy. So when do we get to meet Signor Freesia, your Luca?"

Isa scowled at her older sister. How did Gina know who sent them?

"I read the card in your dressing room," Gina said, her tone oozing with self-satisfaction. "Like to ask Romeo what he's got in mind."

"You'll never get the chance." Isa jumped out of her chair, grabbed the freesias off the table, disappeared through the swinging door, and dropped them into the kitchen rubbish bin. "Better question—who gave me these?" She said, reappearing and lifting yellow roses from the sideboard. "Whoever it was cared enough to attend my concert," she added, placing the vase in the center of the table. "Let's go."

Christina and Isa hurried into the Terme for their massage appointments. The cackling laughter of the Dubliners echoed in the cavernous marble vestibule.

"Sound of trouble," Christina whispered.

Kate and Brigid met them at the reception desk. The ginger leprechaun pulsed her eyebrows and nudged Kate in the side. "What Katie couldn't coax outta Scotty or Frenchy, she came nigh on gettin' from the masseur."

"And you?" Isa asked.

Brigid held up her hand. "As I said last night, darlin', married." A devilish twinkle returned to her eyes. "Doesn't mean I didn't have fun… just can't kiss-n-tell."

"Francesco has magic fingers," Kate said with a sigh. "Worth every euro."

Before they left, Isa informed the redheads of the plans for a casual dinner later that evening in the hills above San Benedetto. The town's planting festival coincided with the concert. "Good food, music, and cheap wine."

The faces of the two Irishwomen lit up. They spoke in unison, "Count us in."

"By the way," Kate said grabbing Isa's arm, "you probably saw that we cozied up to that Lady Blatherwicke woman last night."

"Hope you had a good time," Isa responded trying to conceal her annoyance.

"She's a blarney-spewin' b—Brit," Brigid blurted. "Those lovely American boys were smitten with her though."

Kate looked around the hall; her voice dropped to a whisper. "I discovered her hotel. Put in a wake-up call—*five a.m. sharp, young man,*" Kate said, mimicking Lady Blatherwicke's upper-class vibrato.

Isa giggled. "You didn't?"

"Also ordered her a cab for six and another for seven."

Brigid squealed so loud that Isa thought she'd wet her pants. "Old cow couldn't have had any sleep."

As Christina and Isa started up the grand staircase, the sound of pattering feet made her turn. Looking up, Kate spoke in a hushed voice, "Philippe nested elsewhere last night. Tell you later."

The town's festival was something out of a travel brochure. Strings of white lights swayed in the warm breeze that carried the mouth-watering fragrances of country cooking. A small band attracted a number of couples to a makeshift dance floor on the side of a mountain. Spectators in their Sunday clothes sat on blankets atop the small knolls surrounding the dancers. Tables with red and white checkered cloths lined a hillside path, their candles glittering in the twilight like fireflies. Jovial neighbors and friends washed down platters of cured meats and cheeses, homemade pastas, and other local specialties with inexpensive but good wine. A number of Isa's concertgoers found their way to the celebration.

Ana commanded the dance floor in a short, yellow summer shift, keeping company with the Dubliners and the American boys. Christina needed a nap and time to pack. She agreed to stop by Isa's parents' flat to bring them to the festival. Leech and Isa found themselves alone at a table, sharing a bottle of local wine.

"Christ!"

"What's wrong?" Leech asked.

"Is there no escape?" Bent over the table, Isa's eyes motioned in the direction of the food tent where stood a yawning Lady Blatherwicke with young Malcolm on her arm.

"She can't harm you. Hasn't the concert taught you anything?"

The sight of her tormentor swept away Isa's self-esteem. She recalled her agonizing struggle to reinvent herself, earn respect as a serious singer. With the concert behind her—more tragedy than triumph—she had to face reality. "I'm a delusional idiot, fooling myself into thinking I could sing." *Not to mention my silly illusions about Luca.*

Leech topped off their glasses. "Listen! You staged a concert, an *incredible* performance. More important, you *did* sing."

Isa shook her head. "Why do I feel like a failure?"

Leech looked angry. "Haven't you been listening to people?"

"Sure, everybody's so polite. What did you expect them to say? You can't hit a frigging note to save your life."

"Isa, my pet. Perception is reality. This experience transcends even your singing. The music is not in the notes but in the silence between."

Isa laughed. "Last night Figaro, today Mozart."

Blushing, Leech fluttered his hand. "This weekend's been magic. The entire town, your friends, everyone—buzzing about like star-crossed lovers in a Shakespearean fantasy. You, my pet, are responsible. You're a genius."

Isa responded with rolled eyes and a headshake.

"Stop that!" he said. "Your biggest problem is and always has been your inability to believe in yourself. I hate myself for suggesting it, but listen to that Jenkins woman."

Isa's eyes narrowed on Leech, never a fan of her muse. "I can't wait."

"People may say you can't sing, but no one can ever say you didn't sing." He beamed like a little boy.

"You are an angel," Isa said, pulling him into an embrace and kissing him until he turned crimson.

Isa looked over Leech's shoulder. Malcolm acknowledged her with a smile. After he whispered into his companion's ear, Lady B also looked in Isa's direction.

"Was that a sneer?" Isa muttered.

Leech grabbed her arm. "Calm down. Here they come."

"Why must you always kowtow to that woman?"

"I owe her a great deal. By demanding perfection, she's made me a better teacher. And like it or not, dear Isabella, you wouldn't have had the will to mount that stage or courage to sing without her. Lady Blatherwicke doesn't want or need singers to like her. She stirred your passion. Why didn't you surrender? Because you wanted to prove you could sing—yes, yes to yourself for sure. But also to show her."

Isa pulled away. "That may be true. But face it, Leech. I'm finished—one and done."

"She's also your guest," he said, standing up to greet the pair.

Malcolm leaned down and kissed Isa's cheek. The pianist pressed her hand. "Lovely party, Isa, lovely. Thank you so much."

Lady Blatherwicke cleared her throat. She stood rigid. Isa rose, rehearsing an arsenal of vitriol in her head.

"Miss Fabrini," she said in that horrific tone that scratched Isa's spine. "I know you had hopes of rejoining my chorus."

Leech gasped. Isa prayed he wouldn't hyperventilate.

"Yes, I did," Isa said matter-of-factly.

"After this weekend, I still have my doubts."

Here it comes, Isa thought as she loaded her verbal cannon.

Leech started to speak, "B-but Lady Blatherwicke—"

The chorus mistress turned to him, but her tone was pleasant. "Please wait until I've finished." Then she reached out and took Isa's hand. "Miss Fabrini, I'm impressed."

"You are?"

"This weekend has been enchanting. Not many people, and I dare say nobody in my chorus, could produce an event like this. Most singers would have fallen into fits of tears if they'd lost four-fifths of their orchestra. But you—"

"Thank you." Isa felt buoyed.

"You're not much of an opera singer, my dear. Perhaps the talent shall surface one day. Miss Fabrini, you may not yet be professional caliber, but you are a performer, a charming, talented performer."

"I am?"

The chorus mistress's hand swept through the air, motioning to all of the festival activities. "I recommend you mine this charming hillside and quaint little San Benedetto for gold. Don't let this concert be your last." Malcolm coughed, prodding Lady Blatherwicke to add, "I'd like you to speak to my chorus about your experience. A valuable lesson—artistic passion, creativity, and all that."

"And singing?"

"Continue with Leech. What he's done with you is remarkable." Leech whimpered like a puppy. "And I will see you once a month." Malcolm coughed again. "Free, of course. I take on charity cases for the Royal Arts Council. The chorus isn't out of the question."

Leech's face went white at the mention of *charity case*. His hands clasped together as if in prayer and he looked to Isa with eyes pleading for her to be kind.

Taking a deep breath, Isa jumped up from her chair. "I accept!"

The exchange with Lady Blatherwicke put Isa into a joyous mood. She ate and drank well, and danced with anyone who asked. Words echoed in her ears—*best holiday ever, amazing vacation, wonderful weekend...please, please do this again.*

"I'm exhausted, but I don't care," Isa said, dropping onto a chair at the table full of friends. She threw back her head and laughed.

"Isn't that your sister?" Tommy asked.

Isa turned to see Gina running up the hill. She stopped at the tombola booth where someone pointed in Isa's direction. Isa waved to her with a broad smile. Even dour Gina couldn't spoil her exuberance.

"Thank God. Hoped I'd find you." Gina's face signaled distress, her tone urgent.

"What is it? What's wrong?"

"Hospital," Gina cried, still panting. "We must get to hospital."

Part II
Telma's Redemption

Chapter 18

London—Two Years Later

"*P*rosecco!" Telma shouted, repeating the order for a fourth time. "Don't you speak English?"

She'd only herself to blame—forgetting her vow to avoid the Harrods Food Hall for any juicy rendezvous. The babel of voices and clatter of dishes echoed off tiled floors, glass cases, and porcelain columns. Wait staff consisted of Commonwealth castoffs for whom English was merely a concept. Then there were the Yanks, tagged by toothy grins of perfect teeth and bobbing heads, peppering conversations with a "Hi, how ya doin'," here, and a "Have a nice day," there. Dressing them up in vintage boater hats didn't fool anyone.

Telma suffered the tribe of clueless bunglers as she waited for her ex-husband. She knew better than to think that Walter would have had the decency to arrive first. His poor sense of timing knocked over that first domino: an inopportune return home to discover Telma in bed with Ernesto—no, Fernando. The divorce was easy—a crossword equivalent of a three-letter word for house pet beginning with the letter *C*. The annulment, however, was another matter altogether.

If sex scandals and medieval doctrine didn't strangle the Catholic Church, Byzantine bureaucracy would. The meeting in Rome was Telma's last hope to part the sea of red tape to free her to marry again. She was not beneath throwing a tantrum in Saint Peter's: *Let this divorcée go!*

She grabbed two stools set around one corner of the counter. She wanted to see her ex-husband's face when he heard the request. Just how deep a shade of purple he'd turn she didn't know.

When Walter entered the Harrods Food Hall, she waved him over. He got to her side just as a mop-headed beach boy returned with sparkling wine. *Piss-poor timing.* Telma had hoped to down a couple of glasses to inoculate herself against her former husband's irritating pomposity.

"Sorry I'm late. Taxi driver got in a tangled mess crossing through Westminster. Some military parade or protest—very bothersome." As Walter became more steeped in the posh life of privilege, his boyish charm gave way to peevish entitlement. Telma was used to his petty annoyances and excuses.

Telma flashed an exaggerated pout. "Poor boy."

She proffered a cheek for his methodical peck administered by cold, chapped lips. Walter swiveled onto the stool, ruffling a trove of green and gold shopping bags at his feet. With expressions of distress on round, bronzed faces, the trio of women seated next to Walter rescued their treasures. Telma smiled as the women giggled amongst themselves in Spanish about the handsome but rude Englishman.

"Have you ordered?"

Telma motioned to the bottle. "Only the wine."

As Walter wiggled more securely onto his perch, his cologne hit her nose. The bold scent of vanilla and tobacco disguised a heavy pipe habit. *Alcoholics,* Telma thought, *would kill for popular after-shave aromas reeking of whiskey or gin.*

"Shall I order then?"

Telma's hand swept above the granite counter. "Be my guest. You're happiest when you're in control."

His shoulders slumped. "Let's not start, Telma. I hoped we might enjoy a *civil* lunch. *Pleasant,* I knew, was too much to expect." He made an effort to stand. "Shall we continue this conversation in my solicitor's office?"

Always the martyr. She squelched an instinct to attack. "Please sit down."

Behave, Telma, behave. After all, she needed Walter's help—her big ask yet to come. She knew that as far as her ex-husband was concerned, divorce gave him his freedom—liberty bought for a hefty sum. Telma was the one who needed an annulment; her future mother-in-law insisted upon it. The old crone waved her latest will and threatening testament in Telma's feckless fiancé's face like a battle mace. Poor Graham—frightened little mama's boy. In an island full of Protestants, Telma had to hook a Catholic millionaire. *Next time, I insist upon a dead mama.*

"I'll play nice, Walter. I promise."

"How decent of you."

Walter ordered a dozen assorted oysters and a platter that included lobster, crab and other fruits of the sea. He flirted with the server—too adorable in a short skirt, long bangs and thick Italian accent—another female smitten by her ex-husband's deep voice and broad shoulders. Walter leveraged that natural charm into a lucrative career in banking. Visionary superiors assigned him to the commercial division where he smooth-talked tycoons and grieving widows into investing billions.

Telma caressed the arm of his suit jacket. "Lunch is my treat."

Oh no, not the smirk. She'd seen that smug look before, a reminder why cheating on him had been so easy. Walter, no doubt expected her to add a catty remark about his greediness. How often had he called her snipes about his money-grubbing insincere? He'd laugh, that horrible mocking cackle, before adding a jibe, "You poor, poor dear—the miseries you endure as Mrs. Walter Benchley disposing of my ill-gotten gains on Sloane Street, Fifth Avenue, and the Via Condotti. A Sloane Ranger on God's crusade!"

Walter couldn't fathom the truth. Spending binges were Telma's reward for insufferable garden parties and afternoon teas in ancient drawing rooms that reeked of pretension and old people. Chamber music and pipe tobacco replaced jazz clubs and the occasional joint. Victorian wallpaper and chintz curtains had more personality than her husband's moldy friends. Walter scoffed when she accused him of sacrificing his originality and freedom for a seven-figure bank account. The broad, white lines of Walter's chalk-striped Savile Row suits reminded her of a prisoner's uniform. Yet, she was the one who grew increasingly imprisoned by their marriage and monotonous life. Telma used to laugh at the irony. Until she cried.

"All set for your trip?" With his hand, Walter brushed back the fine brown hair from his forehead. That's when she noticed the platinum band. He still wore his wedding ring.

"I'm sorry, what did you say?" she asked, shifting her focus from his fingers to his face.

"I asked if you're all set for Rome."

"Yes, flight's on Thursday—leaving a week early."

He rolled his eyes. "Making a splendid holiday out of it, I see. Well, imagine you view the trip as a celebration of sorts—final chapter of our miserable marriage."

"The marriage ended years ago. Last year's divorce was merely a formality."

"And still that didn't satisfy you. You needed to erase everything—redact our life together as if it never happened. How tidy of you and your church."

"Stop the drama, please." Her patience was stretching thin.

He inhaled, clenched his jaw. She detected something more than anger. Sadness? Certainly not! More likely regret born of arrogance. He didn't necessarily mind her string of lovers—saved him time and effort. *No, Walter,* she thought, *couldn't stomach the idea of being cheated—infidelity on par with corporate fraud, insider trading, and tanking share prices.*

After downing most of his wine, he stared at Telma. He hadn't yet acquired the saggy eyes like others his age or the paunchy middle, that badge of honor worn by English gentlemen when they hit fifty. His oval face with warm, brown eyes, strong chin, and commanding nose was still quite handsome.

"Divorce is one thing," he said, "but this annulment hocus-pocus obliterates everything."

Telma reached over to pat his arm. "How touching."

He recoiled. "An insult, that's what it is!"

"An annulment doesn't mean the marriage never happened—only that it was...*invalid.*"

"Absurd! People don't live together as husband and wife for ten years and then call it *invalid.*"

"Why are you making such a fuss? A revoked license doesn't void the surgeon's hysterectomy."

Walter wrinkled his nose; his eyes crinkled. "Small comfort."

"Now, don't take offense. I'm only going through with this charade to marry Graham. Thought you'd be thrilled to rid yourself of the alimony."

"The silver lining, to be sure."

Telma played the alimony card strategically. She needed to soften Walter, remind him of the financial benefit before she castrated him. "But that big, bad alimony won't go away without a tiny, little favor."

Walter sighed. "Dare I ask?"

She caressed his hand and smiled. "No one will ever know…"

"Yes?"

"The Judicial Vicar says it makes for a stronger case…and, um…"

"Blurt it out, for Christ's sake."

Telma filled his glass and handed it to him. "Walter, dear, remember the alimony." She inhaled, forcing a smile. She spoke slowly, calmly. "I need—er, I'm asking you to swear that you're impotent and have been since we married."

His face puffed like a crimson marshmallow. His mouth emitted that mocking cackle of a laugh that made her skin crawl. "You've got balls, my dear. I wanted a family. You were the one who insisted that children would ruin our marriage and your figure. You insisted we marry in the Catholic Church. Cuckolding me wasn't enough—now I'm to be a bloody eunuch." He grabbed his glass, emptying the wine. His eyes turned cold as they narrowed on her. "If you want brutal honesty, you—" He stopped, turned away, eyes closed.

Telma's bristled; her back stiffened. "Brutal honesty?"

He gazed at her, a look of surrender on his face. "Doesn't matter. Not anymore."

"I'm sorry, Walter. It's the only way. Then it's all over," she added, clinking his glass.

"Is Graham accompanying you? That why you're traveling early?" Walter's fingers tensed so much so that Telma wondered whether they would snap the wineglass stem.

Telma pretended to study the bubbles in her wine flute. *What to say?* She hadn't intended to tell him—not then—not until after. Didn't want him trying to talk her out of it. But she didn't feel like telling any more lies—not then. She turned to him. "Graham's not coming. I'm going to see Isa."

His expression hardened. "Isabella Fabrini! You must be joking. Rub salt in her wounds. Perhaps a measure of penance so you can enter the Vatican with a clear conscience?"

Telma shook her head. "I want—no, I *need* to thank Isa. For all she did for my sister, Christina."

"That was two years ago!"

"Perhaps I haven't had the courage until now. Maybe Rome and all this religious crap stirred my conscience." Telma didn't know why she felt compelled to see the woman whose fiancé she'd stolen—embarrassing her in front of peers and family.

"Could have saved yourself the trouble. Isa lives in Bayswater as far as I know."

"She'll be in Italy, an anniversary of sorts. The stars are aligned."

Walter's neck straightened. "Of course, the bloody opera. Jamie mentioned it to me."

"Yes, Isa's concert."

"More to the point, Isa's *folly*. The money she wastes on that damn thing. I have it on good authority that she's broke...and the singing, well..." He puckered his face as if he'd swallowed a spoiled oyster.

"Must you always think of money? It's Isa's first solo performance since my sister's..." *Do not cry, do not cry.* "She's dedicating the concert to Christina."

"So, you're going to honor your sister?"

"Might call it a pilgrimage. That weekend in San Benedetto was Christina's last. She had a splendid time, I was told. I didn't have a chance to say good-bye."

"More contrition?" Walter's brow furrowed. She felt him scrutinizing her as if she were a museum piece. "I'm seeing a new side of Telma Benchley."

"*Rossi!*" She regretted the word the second it left her lips. How foolish to remind him that she'd retaken her maiden name in anticipation of the annulment.

"How lucky for you. Triple redemption for the mere cost of a cheap Italian holiday. Shut the door on our marriage, your sister, and Isabella Fabrini. Heaven awaits, *Miss* Telma Rossi."

She sighed, willing herself to maintain composure. "Perhaps you've found me out, Walter. Truth is, I never properly thanked Isa or her family for all they did. They were with Christina when she died."

Anger vanished from Walter's face. He not only respected his former sister-in-law, he loved her. Everyone did. "I'd almost forgotten that all happened at Isa's concert."

"Overshadowed Isa's triumph, I'm afraid. The aneurism came out of nowhere. Christina's body was on a plane back to Buenos Aires before her family had the chance to travel to Italy."

"Surprised me that Isa didn't attend the funeral. Christina's husband made it quite clear he'd cover her expenses."

Telma let Walter's obsession with money slide. She had it on good authority that Isa was heartbroken, blaming herself for not being able to save Christina. "Gina represented the Fabrini family."

Walter inched closer to Telma, a boyish grin on his face. "Tell me, what did Isa say when you told her you were coming? Must have been quite the shocker."

"Isa doesn't know," Telma said, dropping her eyes. "It's a surprise."

Chapter 19

Italy—One Week Later

"Damn, damn, damn!" Telma muttered aloud onboard the train. Her brain was on overload as she imagined how she might announce her arrival in San Benedetto.

Dearest Isabella, what priceless childhood memories we have of Buenos Aires. I hope to relive those cherished moments at your concert—if you'll have me.

No, no, no—sappy shit with tones of pathetic groveling.

Dear Isabella, I find myself in Italy on your concert weekend—how serendipitous. Let's toast to our shared past in San Benedetto!

Oh Christ—now I've become one of Walter's shallow friends.

Dear Isa, fate binds us together—we share a former lover. Let's swap stories at your concert.

Devilishly delicious! But dangerous. I made Walter her ex.

Isa, I'm in Italy—coming to your concert. Dedicated to Christina, isn't it? Couldn't miss it.

Telma closed her eyes to avoid contact with the passenger beside her who had turned at the sound of her outburst. He was a hunk—brown, wavy hair, chiseled jaw, and lips to which she'd freely surrender her mouth and any other body part. If the annulment hadn't preoccupied her, she might have seen fit to slip into the loo for a Eurail quickie. But Christ, she'd been in Italy barely four hours. She didn't need another stain on her conscience—*or was it her soul*—when she entered the Vatican. *Piss-poor timing.*

With her head tilted back and mind on pause from a playback of hypothetical greetings, Telma grew drowsy with the train's rocking motion. Pressures of the impending interview in Rome, and her reunion with Isabella Fabrini had screwed up her sleep for weeks. Makeup camouflaged her dark, puffy eyes.

Telma had flown British Airways from London to Milan. If Mussolini were alive, she might have trusted Alitalia to transport her closer to San Benedetto. She transferred from Malpensa to Italian Rail, praying that the socialists hadn't obliterated the fascist legacy of trains running on time. She killed two hours thumbing through fashion magazines, scanning the first page of a novel, and crafting the note to Isa, all while avoiding the advances of the musky-scented passenger beside her. Relief swept over her as the train chugged into Bologna.

She traveled enough to avoid judging a city by the neighborhoods that abutted rail lines—seedy apartment blocks, public housing estates, and riffraff. What sane person would choose to live near the constant noise of rattles and whistles? And consider the gypsies, beggars, pickpockets, and purse-snatchers who flocked to stations like pigeons.

Telma looked beyond the blight—red-tiled roofs and ancient towers gave the city appeal. She only knew one nugget of Bologna trivia—a university touted as the world's oldest. And universities always attracted good bars, great music, and randy boys.

After rejecting a liaison with her seatmate for the third time since the train lurched to a stop, Telma disembarked to search for her connection. Pulling luggage and pushing through hordes of tourists, she cursed herself for rejecting her fiancé's offer to accompany her. Graham could have carted her suitcases and plowed through the crowd.

She recalled the advice of a fitness friend in London who warned of scavengers who preyed on confused tourists. Telma's observations confirmed the warning—darting eyes, hesitant steps, and frantic fingering of guidebooks and timetables cued the opportunists. Marauders pawed at the luggage of ditherers. Earnest smiles gave the baggage pirates airs of confidence as if their actions were sanctioned protocol. "Before you know it," Telma's girlfriend had warned, panting from her Stairmaster, "they've carted your luggage onboard and demand ransom—that is, if they don't rob you blind." *No thank you.* Telma's fingers formed death grips on her Vuitton roller-board and matching overnight sack in which she hid her Fendi handbag.

A clacking departure board confirmed her onward travel to San Benedetto on the Venice–Rome train. Parched, she had fifty minutes before the scheduled departure. Long lines of scruffy tourists with screaming brats gave her a perfect excuse to detour away from the café. She'd grab a quick drink instead. With another two hours of monotonous countryside ahead, she saw benefit in a foggy head.

Dark spaces with muffled jazz and a hint of stale beer were the international standard for cocktail lounges. The bar was an oasis from the station's hot, sun-drenched public areas. Not a modest maiden, Telma was comfortable sitting alone at a bar and ordering something stiffer than Chardonnay.

"Double vodka with a twist," she called to the bartender as she slid onto an empty stool between two broad-shouldered men.

The scent of musky cologne lured her gaze to the left before her brain processed the sensory warning. Her eyes met his—dark pools the color of chestnuts. Gorgeous lips framed a perfect smile. Alarm bells rang in her head—those lips were as lethal as a claw-tooth bear trap. Too late—she'd been spotted and snared. His face was even more captivating than the profile at which she'd snuck glimpses on the train journey from Milan.

"*Bonjour* again, *madame*," he said, "Trains, I see, make you thirsty too." He jiggled a tumbler, infusing the air with a peaty smell of whiskey.

"Not as thirsty as you," she said, nodding toward two empty glasses lined up in front of him. "Or as quick."

He leaned his head back and gave a throaty laugh. "We all have our little devils—indulge those that give heavenly pleasure."

The bartender deposited Telma's drink on the bar. She checked her watch before taking a generous swig. "I don't have much time."

The Frenchman's smile turned into a smirk, an eyebrow rose. His look told her that he took her response as both an invitation and a challenge. Perhaps it was.

"I'm Philippe," he said. He let go of his drink and extended an arm sheathed in the butterscotch leather jacket she had admired on the train.

"Telma," she replied, accepting his large, warm hand. "No *h*."

"Telma," he repeated back, holding fast his grasp. "Lovely name. Italian? No, Spanish, *sí*? Fits the accent."

"Argentinean—father Italian, mother Spanish, but I'm all South American."

His face moved closer; his voice dropped to a whisper. "Foolish to confess such a thing when I'm surrounded by beautiful Italian women." He paused, scanned the room, then continued in a softer and sexier voice, "I'm simply wild about South American señoritas—so striking, sophisticated...fiery."

Telma reclaimed her hand and grabbed her drink. "Really?"

"You don't believe me." Even his mock pout was sexy.

"Why should I?"

His hand moved from the bar to her knee. She didn't resist. "Dismiss criticism as lies," he said, "but always, *always* believe compliments."

She tried but couldn't stifle a giggle. "Your personal philosophy?"

His laugh was deep, velvety. "*Mais oui!* Power of positive thinking, *non?*" His fingers applied gentle pressure to her leg.

"Ask me, smacks of denial. Self-serving at that." From experience, humor was the best foreplay. The Frenchman's confidence added to his allure. But Telma wondered whether alcohol and playfulness masked a frightened little boy.

As she glanced at her watch, Philippe's hand glided from her knee, up her inner thigh to the hem of her skirt where it stopped. Fingers teased, inching up, then down and up again. Philippe leaned closer. Soft, supple leather rubbed her bare arm. His head turned; he nibbled her ear. The hand slid upward, reaching its velvet goal. She sighed, or was it a moan?

In solidarity with South American señoritas, Telma validated Philippe's assessment. Her hand moved to his crotch. The denim was warm, smooth, and bulging with the Frenchman's self-confidence. *Mais oui!* she thought, *the power of positive thinking*.

The train was crowded—the amount of luggage obscene. First class on Italian Rail meant nothing more than a complimentary beverage, a tooth-cracking cookie, and travel companions who shared respect for deodorant. As she'd discovered on the Milan–Bologna segment, an advanced reservation with seat assignment was a wise decision.

Telma became mildly annoyed to find the seat beside her occupied. But unlike Philippe, this one seemed harmless. She had noticed the short man at the station. His distress amused her. He swatted away gypsies drawn to him by predatory instinct. His clothes branded him as American: creased short pants, bleached white sneakers, and a pastel polo shirt with designer logo. Sunglasses, dangling from a chain, rested on his chest.

After fussing with his luggage, adjusting and readjusting his pieces, the American sat down only to get up and rearrange everything again. Between intermittent mumbles, he huffed, sighed, groaned, and grumbled. Telma pretended not to notice his glares, directed at her with increasing intensity. *What the... Does he expect me to lift his damn suitcase?* Telma buried her head in an Italian fashion magazine purchased at the station. No matter that she didn't understand the captions—the faces, figures, and clothing were divine.

Curiosity returned her attention to the American. From a black Tumi bag, he pulled several Italian travel guides, a notebook, and a trashy pulp romance whisked between the pink folds of *The Financial Times. Too late, mate.* She already saw the book's cover—two bare-chested hunks, one with a flowing blond mane and the other with dark hair, cropped military style. With this passenger, there'd certainly not be a repeat of her cocktail lounge interlude.

Telma pushed the fussy American and the sexy Frenchman from her mind to refocus on the message to Isa. She pulled a pen and notepad from her purse. Several minutes passed of unproductive scribbling. She scratched out her last draft, tearing the paper. "Damn it all to hell!" The intensity of her voice surprised her—her seatmate deserved an explanation. She motioned to the notepad. "Not very good with words."

The American squirreled away his book between newspaper pages. "Maybe I can help," he replied, producing his notebook. "I jot down everything in a journal."

Telma eyed the spiral book with dread. *One of those people. Lucky me, minutiae from a closet case.* She glanced at his poised hand. *What will he write about me?* "I'll probably just wing it," she replied. "Usually works best for me."

What followed was inevitable—usually was, with Americans. One word and they were best chums, setting sail on a course to bare their souls. He inhaled and Telma braced.

"First time in Italy?" he asked. She pegged his accent as East Coast, likely New York.

She nodded. "Hard to believe, since I've lived in Europe for fifteen years."

The American twisted in his seat, turning slightly to face her. *Here it comes.* "Oh! Where are you from—originally, I mean?"

"Buenos Aires. Argentina," she added, knowing Americans' geographic challenges. "Have you been?"

He shook his head. "No, but it's on my list."

"I'm guessing you're from New York."

He narrowed his eyes. "Amazing! How'd you know?"

"Lucky guess. What brings you to Italy—holiday…perhaps a little romance?" Her eyes wandered to the bulge in the newspaper.

"Romance? Wh-what, me?" He leaned close, whispering, "Hopefully."

His caution informed Telma that he was the kind of fellow who liked to ask but not answer questions. She clapped her hands. "Wonderful! Italy intoxicates with romance. I'm sure you'll find a nice woman—or man."

He blushed, stammering his reply. "We-we'll see. I-I don't know. I'm not—"

She tapped his knee without fear of unintended consequences. "This is Europe. We're not so uptight about such things. Americans are Puritans." She shook his newspaper; the gay romance fell to his lap. The man clutched his chest.

Had she gone too far? Would he hyperventilate, pass out? She recalled her first-aid training at the convent school. To avoid shock, calm the person—talk slowly—touch them—make a personal connection.

She extended her arm in greeting. But the man kept clawing the polo logo over his heart.

"Telma," she said, grabbing his hand. "No *h*."

With eyes glazed, his head tilted. "Huh?"

"My name…it's Telma, not Thelma. I'm from Buenos Aires, but I live in London." He still looked apoplectic. In lieu of slapping his face, she squeezed his hand. "And you, Mister New York, what's your name?"

He blinked; his breathing slowed. "Daniel, Daniel Chance."

"Well, Daniel. What would you say if I told you I just enjoyed a quickie in the station loo with the sexiest stranger I've ever met? And I do mean hot—French. What's more, I'm going to Rome to get an annulment so my fiancé and I can marry in the church."

She watched the American process her confession. His creased forehead and narrowed eyes signaled confusion and doubt. They gave way to wide eyes and an open mouth. The slow nodding of Telma's head accompanied by an earnest smile seemed to hypnotize him.

Daniel sighed; his shoulders relaxed. He sat back, smiled. "Really? Amazing! And I thought New Yorkers were progressive."

"My point, Daniel, in telling you is to show that sex isn't something to be ashamed of." Did she believe that? Didn't matter. Her story worked. Daniel Chance's tight little ass relaxed—he sank three inches into the vinyl seat cushion.

Betraying a grin, he spoke, "Well, there is someone—a special...guy. I'll see him tonight, and all weekend. Our friend's having a big bash."

"Fabulous! So this is a romantic getaway—a sexcapade."

Daniel turned away; he stared at the seat in front of him. Telma waited—no need to rush his confession. His chest heaved. When he looked at her again, she detected a tear. She reached in her purse for a tissue. He wiped his eyes. "He doesn't know. I've had a crush on him since we were in school together...never told him."

She caressed Daniel's arm. To her surprise, he clasped their hands together.

"Never told him you were gay or about the crush?"

"About the crush, of course. I came out to him—exactly two years ago—here in Italy. I thought, well, maybe, my coming out would make it easier for him."

"So you know he's gay although he never told you. Is that gay radar?"

Daniel chuckled. "Gaydar—that's what it's called. But it's more than that. Tommy Evers is adorable. He's almost forty, still single—no girlfriend."

She looked into his eyes. "Have you considered asking him?"

"Oh no! Couldn't do that—goes against gay etiquette. But he's never denied it. He likes the same things I do. We think alike. We're so damn compatible."

Telma was fond of sincere Daniel. "You like this guy—this Tommy—a lot."

He looked down as he spoke. "Afraid I do."

"Well, Daniel, here's what we're going to do. You help me craft my message and I help you get Tommy into the sack. We leverage our strengths. Deal?"

"Deal!" he replied, shaking her hand. "Telma, you're amazing! I've never opened up to someone like this, especially someone I just met. I'm only out to a handful of people. Want to keep it that way…at least for a while. I'd die if anyone knew what I told you."

"It's easier to talk to strangers—safer, no strings. I never would have confessed to my naughty behavior back in Bologna to someone I knew or thought I'd ever see again."

Daniel nodded, his face beaming. "Hitchcock made a movie about that—*Strangers on a Train*. Tommy loves old movies too."

"That a gay thing?"

Daniel nodded. "Yes, but not exclusively. What I mean is, all gays like old movies but not all old movie fans are gay."

"Got it. But we don't have much time. I'm not going with you all the way to Rome."

He stiffened. "Neither am I. I thought you were going to Rome."

"I am, but not until Monday."

"I'm getting off at San Benedetto," he said. "How about you?"

She stared at him—*no, couldn't be.* "San Benedetto," she replied. "And who's this friend of yours and Tommy's?"

"Oh, she's from London too—" Daniel stopped; his face went white. "Oh my God, the friend…the note…it's not…"

Telma nodded. "Yes, Daniel, the station slut and the gay pulp romance fan with a crush on Tommy Evers are both attending Isabella Fabrini's concert."

Chapter 20

Telma formed her first impression of San Benedetto from the window of the taxi shared with Danny Chance. Even though the New Yorker kept reminding her that his name was Daniel, she preferred the boyish Danny hidden beneath the uptight facade.

The sight of a bustling high street surprised her, although the store offerings were dubious: cheese, synthetic fabrics, more cheese, dried meats, and plastic trinkets. She saw enough gelato shops to fatten a continent of starving children. Despite Danny's assurances of a fashionable quarter, Telma had her doubts.

Danny got out of the taxi with her. His hotel, he explained, was just a few hundred meters away. She wondered if that was a ploy to avoid getting stuck with the entire fare. He was as precise as a chartered accountant as he divided the extra charges. "Your Fendi equals my Tumi. Your large case matches my Samsonite. That leaves you up a mid-size Vuitton." She couldn't help but laugh. *Dare I ask if the U.S. Mint presses quarters between his tight little ass cheeks?* But Telma was in Isa territory—behind enemy lines. She needed every ally. Besides, she liked Danny. Wanted to loosen him up a bit, perhaps shake a few pence from his buttocks.

Danny's eyes widened; he practically gasped when Telma pulled out a fifty-euro note and paid the entire fare. "Walter's money," she said. "Before that gravy train runs out of steam."

The two agreed to meet for drinks later. Telma planned to forget her money.

"*Sì*, signora, I ensure you it's our *bestest* room." The reception clerk was pretty, but flashes of officious indifference combined with clothes of clashing colors and patterns tagged the girl as some brand of Eastern European.

"Can someone help me with my luggage?"

"We got no porter," the girl said, eyeing Telma's bags from across the counter. "And handyman, he at lunch." Dark, unemotional eyes moved on a path from Telma's luggage to the elevator while a stone face shut down any additional plea for assistance.

Good Lord! Why had they torn down the blasted Iron Curtain? Telma assumed the handyman's lunch would last at least two hours. She leaned forward and glared into the young communista's face. If the girl could pull a plow or milk a cow for mother Russia, Telma saw no reason why she couldn't carry bags to the room. She smacked ten euros onto the counter, grabbed her key, and marched to the elevator. Regardless of one's economic ideology, money always got results.

As hotels in rustic Italian towns went, San Benedetto's Hotel Central was adequate. Telma's priorities were cleanliness, comfort, and convenience. She didn't expect to find more than one—two out of three a miracle. She chose the hotel based on its proximity to the Terme. She credited the spa for keeping the town alive—an example of artificial life support.

The nicest feature of the room, the hotel's *bestest*, was a large balcony—the premium worth every cent. It provided fresh air and a chance to keep Telma's back turned to the shabby quarters, gaze onto the town, and wish she were staying someplace else.

From that vantage point, she was forced to admit that the town wasn't without charm. A mix of locals, tourists, and shopkeepers appeared adequately groomed, and of average or slightly above average means. Green and pink mosaics on the Terme's facade reflected the mid-afternoon sun. Glistening water jets rose from the piazza's fountain.

Standing on the balcony, Telma found herself overcome by wistfulness. Her sister spent her last weekend alive in that town. A gentle breeze fanned the scent of jasmine. The sweet fragrance reminded Telma of the terrace garden of her family's cramped flat in Buenos Aires. Her father fretted over those plants as if they covered acres of land of the family farm left behind in Italy. Telma's father, like Isa's, emigrated from Italy for the promise of riches. He found misfortune, settling for a modest income and a small flat. Seemed he only had enough love in him for one child.

Christina was the fair-haired one, inheriting the high cheekbones and striking good looks of her Italian lineage. Telma, on the other hand, got the round face, stubby nose, and dark complexion of their mother's Spanish side. Until London's best plastic surgeon made her a modern beauty. Christina also had brains and drive. Like his love, their father only had enough savings for one university education. With a six-year head start, Christina got the nod. Thankfully, the practice of committing dowry-less daughters to the convent had ended. Telma would have caused the holy sisters to flee the cloister, screaming the Pater Noster.

She couldn't blame their father. By the time Telma reached university age, his business was gone. He survived on a string of menial jobs. Her older sister was a saint. Two years out of university and working two jobs to save for medical school, she slipped Telma money to finance an education. A two-year deferment of Christina's dream headed toward an indefinite delay. Although she tried to disguise the angst, the pressure was killing Christina. Her stalled aspirations were taking a toll on their father. So Telma hatched a plan, flunking out of her first term at university. It wasn't as easy as she thought. Professors said she had natural intelligence and an inquisitive nature. Their attempts to help forced Telma to change tactics. Her transformation into a bitch, a self-absorbed caustic witch, worked like a charm. The school suspended her before she reduced a fourth professor to tears.

A valuable lesson, too—possibly, the most practical skill anyone ever learned in the first year of university. Telma had a knack for pissing off people. And, she discovered she very much enjoyed it. Anyone can be likable—those insipid Miss Congeniality types—but sweetness and dimpled smiles only go so far. A degree as a royal bitch carried her further in life and bestowed greater rewards than had she studied finance or law.

Telma's legs welcomed the stretch after the long train journey. After walking to the Terme to confirm spa treatments for the following morning, she window-shopped before stopping for a drink at an outdoor café. Many of the women she saw looked like Isa, or at least her memory of Isa. Was that her riding through town on a bicycle? To be safe, Telma raised the menu over her face as if she were in a campy spy film from the sixties.

It was six o'clock before Telma wandered back to the hotel and retrieved her key from the young communista with whom she was already on snarling terms.

"Oh dear! Graham," she muttered, sitting on the bed to remove her shoes. She'd completely forgotten about her fiancé. She'd promised to call the moment she checked in.

"Yes, my sweet, arrived safely," she said into the telephone. Graham's mother grumbled in the background. "Yes, rung up just as soon as I arrived…um…train was late…very late. You know the Italians…It's darling the way you worry about me…I'm a big girl…Yes, I'll call tomorrow. Love you too…Please give your mother a big—" She disconnected in the middle of her sentence—let Graham fill in the blank. His sentiment would be more endearing than the *kick in the arse* she wished upon the meddling hag.

Telma fell backward onto the bed and closed her eyes. She only needed to play nice for a few more months—complete the annulment, become Graham's wife…then find a green pasture for Mama. While odds of winning the annulment increased, she had less confidence in Graham's ability to divorce his mother, the dowager Duchess of Mordor.

After a nap, Telma asked the desk clerk for directions to the Tazza d'Oro, the café bar where Danny suggested they meet.

"Out front door, then fifteen meters to right," the girl snapped in her Eastern European accent. "If you like, I call taxi."

Telma winked in reply before turning to the door. She liked the girl's spunk. A little friendly sparring would keep her bitchiness sharp for the rendezvous with Isa.

Danny had told Telma that the café became a meeting point for many who attended Isa's first concert. "It's not much," he had said, "probably not what you're used to, but it's fun." She guessed that her designer wardrobe gave Danny the impression she was an upper-class snob. Danny's fashion IQ surprised her. None of her ex-husband's London banker friends could have correctly identified her scarf as Hermes, skirt as Prada, or shoes as Louboutin.

Cackles, squawks and shrieks of laughter guided Telma to the outdoor café. She spotted Danny sitting at a table with two red-headed women, some years older than he. From the hair and round, white faces she guessed they were Scottish, maybe Irish. Danny waved her over with the flailing arms of a drowning swimmer.

"Telma, you made it. Amazing!"

"Always love a good party. Heard the hoots and hollers from my hotel room," Telma said with a thumb hitched over her shoulder. "That's my balcony."

The smaller woman shrieked with laughter, rattling the ice of a tall drink. "Better watch our words, darlin's, this one could be a spy," she said, pulsing her eyebrows. "And you know how naughty we can be."

Danny coughed, more to restore order than to clear his throat. He stood up, kissed Telma's cheek, and hugged her like an old friend. "May I introduce Kate Maureen Mahoney and Brigid Clancy, otherwise known as the darlings from Dublin?"

Kate giggled. "We've been called plenty worse."

"Most of which can't be uttered in polite company," added the little imp of a woman named Brigid with a slap to her knee.

"I can only imagine," Danny said as he helped Telma with her chair.

"How do ya know Isa?" Kate asked, before taking a sip of whiskey.

Telma glanced at Danny who knew the whole sordid story. His innocent expression made her doubt that he'd shared the gossip. "We grew up together."

The server arrived. Telma asked for a double vodka with lemon. The others ordered another round, quite possibly their third...or fourth.

"Buenos Aires, right? Where you grew up." said Brigid. "You've come a long way."

Danny replied, "Telma lives in London now. I'm sure you both remember her sister, Christina, Isa's beautiful friend, from last time."

Recollection of the tragic death swept grins from the Dubliners' faces. Reaching across the table, Kate squeezed her hand. "Of course—pretty Christina. She helped talk Isa off the ledge and onto the stage. Wonderful girl. So sorry for your loss."

Caressing Telma's shoulder, Brigid's face emoted compassion. "Such a lovely woman. My condolences. Came as quite a shock for all of us."

"Especially Isa," added Kate. "Poor darlin' slid into depression."

"Not even your double, double toil, and Lighthouse trouble could help." Brigid's tone matched the sarcasm of her words.

Some women among Telma's social circle had sampled the self-awareness program offered by Lighthouse. Though a few swore by its effectiveness at boosting self-esteem and confidence, others called it a cult. Although intrigued by seminars in exotic places, Telma cringed at the prospect of mingling with gaggles of neurotic people. Her own neuroses were already a handful. Kate, she gathered from the conversation, was a Lighthouse elder—something dreadful called a Beacon—whereas Isa merely dabbled in courses.

Kate bit her lip as Brigid turned back to Telma. "Well, I'm sure Isa's thrilled you're here to cheer her on this year, darlin'."

Telma glanced at Danny before responding, "Actually, bit of a surprise. She doesn't know I'm here yet. We grew apart after I married."

Kate gasped; whiskey squirted from her mouth. Her eyes went wide and she gaped at Telma as if she were a two-headed ghoul. *Clever girl— she'd connected the sordid dots.*

Brigid turned toward her friend with wrinkled nose. "What's wrong with you? Better not get sick or that Blatherwicke woman will boot you from Isa's chorus."

Kate's face lost its color; eyes darted. "I'm fine, fine," she said, forcing a smile. She leaned into Brigid and whispered, "Tell ya later."

Telma took a deep breath. A cozy Italian café that served alcohol was a fine place to start the redemption process. If the story was going to be told, she'd do the telling. She assumed a smile and nonchalant air as if she were about to discuss the weather. Telma turned to Brigid, the only one still in the dark. "You've heard the story about Isa's fiancé?"

Gulping her cocktail, Brigid bobbed her head. "Who hasn't? Poor Isa. Ambushed two weeks before the wedding. At her graduation—in front of friends and family. Shameless bitch!" Telma presumed the kick to her shin was intended for Brigid who kept rattling away, "That were me, the bloody bodies of that bitch and bastard—*English* as you'd expect—would still be buried in Regent's Park."

Danny went white; Kate clutched her throat. Telma waited for Brigid to take another swig before speaking up. "I rather fancy Regent's Park as a final resting place but don't think the authorities would approve." With head cocked, Brigid's blue eyes fixed on her. Telma extended a hand. "I'm the shameless bitch. Pleased to make your acquaintance."

"Now, now," Danny said. "That all happened a long time ago."

Telma turned to him. "You're awfully sweet, Danny. But Brigid's right. I was a bitch—still am. No excusing my behavior. Walter and I betrayed Isa."

"You seeking forgiveness then?" Kate's manner and tone suggested relief that the admission brought the subject into the open.

"Don't know what I'm looking for. Too late for forgiveness, I imagine."

Danny cast her an earnest look. "It's never too late."

Telma patted his hand. "Dear, sweet Danny. Spoken like a good little Christian boy. Human nature's more complex than scripture stories."

He bristled. "What do you mean?"

"Now, don't be hurt. Didn't mean it as criticism. I don't expect Isa to forgive me and please don't think I'm wringing my hands unable to forgive myself. I was never wired that way. Life's a forward march…at least for survivors. Eyes on the horizon till you cross the finish line."

"That's awfully harsh."

Kate spoke, "Life's harsh, Danny. Telma's right on that point. Lighthouse says as much. We're trapped by our past."

Brigid squawked, slapping her knee. "Well, I'll be. The mighty Lighthouse Beacon finds common ground with the home-wrecker." She leaned toward Telma, eyebrows pulsing. "No offense, darlin'. I think I'm gonna like you."

"B-but, you c-can't throw morals aside," Danny stammered struggling with the logic. "Can't charge ahead without regard to others. Isa was hurt."

Again Kate spoke, "But in a way, she was saved. Walter cheated with Telma. Tells me he'd cheat again. I'm not condoning her behavior. Not my place to condone *or* condemn."

"What about Isa?" Danny asked.

"I stand by my friend. Guide her forward," Kate said, sitting up and nodding briskly. "I brought her to Lighthouse. Like to think I helped her grow, push ahead, put on the concert."

"And Telma?" With a confused look, Danny glanced from Telma back to Kate. "What about her?"

"I accept her for who she is. If she's come to seek some peace with Isa, I support that." She held up her refreshed whiskey and clanked glasses with Telma. "But if she hurts our Isa, I'll scratch out those big brown eyes." Kate cackled, Brigid squawked, and Telma threw back her head in laughter.

Telma raised her glass a second time. "I'll drink to that."

Danny Chance looked like he wanted to throw up.

They spent the next few hours talking, sharing stories about their pasts. The darlings of Dublin weren't shy when it came to laughter or liquor. The others regaled Telma with memories of Isa's first concert, including Christina wherever they could. For those magical hours, Telma pretended that Christina was still alive—sisters sharing San Benedetto and concert weekend, together.

Telma realized at once that Isa's concert captivated her three drinking buddies. They spoke in awe of that weekend two years ago. With animated faces and nostalgic tones, they went on, gushing about the music, fascinating concertgoers and newfound friends.

"Wouldn't miss this concert for all the whiskey in Dublin," Kate said.

"'Tis magic, indeed," Brigid added, before turning toward her friend and speaking with a scolding tone. "But don't let fairy dust blind ya into dancin' with the devil."

Telma exchanged confused looks with Danny. "Who's that?" he asked.

Kate tried, but failed to fake a smile. "Nothin', nothin'."

"Don't tell us your fancyin' a Brit is nothin'! It's dangerous…damned unpatriotic." Alcohol fueled Brigid's fury. "Cozyin' up to the enemy." She railed on despite Kate's protests, explaining that a Londoner in the chorus had caught Kate's fancy.

"Well, better get to bed," Telma said, seeking to avoid the tussle. Liquor, man-trouble and redheads always proved an explosive combination. "Got an early up for the spa."

"I'll walk you to your hotel," Danny said, also seeming eager for an escape.

Telma grabbed her purse and started to stand, but froze. With a gasp, she fell back onto the chair.

"You okay?" Danny asked. The Dubliners turned to her as well.

Telma nodded, fingering through her purse as cover. How could she tell them that she just saw the stranger with whom she had a quickie in the Bologna train station? Worse, the sexy Frenchman walked into another café arm-in-arm with Isa.

That weekend, Isabella Fabrini wasn't the only one in for surprises.

Chapter 21

Dark sunglasses hid Telma's puffy eyes, and a scarf covered her unwashed hair. Breakfast ended thirty minutes before, but ten euros slipped to the cleanup girl produced a large coffee, brioche, and a vase of roses on a sunny table in the empty dining room. Although a few of the other early arrivals like Danny and the Dubliners were already in San Benedetto, Telma assumed most of the out-of-town concertgoers would check in later that Friday afternoon or early Saturday. By then, she hoped to be glowing with the shimmering skin, taut muscles, and vitality promised by the Terme's glossy brochure.

Nursing a perfect cappuccino, Telma turned her thoughts to the prior night. The trio of Danny and the darlings from Dublin were great fun despite their incessant drooling over concert weekend. They were awed by Isa's achievements. But even Telma had to admit that their tones suggested more, something special that transcended the music. Was it revelry, an *esprit de corps?* Cult worship? All three jumped at the chance to join the San Benedetto chorus, a feature Isa added to her concert that year. Their first rehearsal occurred prior to the rendezvous at the Tazza d'Oro. Although they spoke of Lady Gabriella Blatherwicke, the chorus mistress imported from London, with fear, Telma sensed her three drinking companions respected the woman's talent. Isa's ability to attract someone of Lady B's caliber to assist with the concert impressed Telma.

Telma smiled recalling the prior night's conversation.

"Can ya believe it," Brigid said with mock sarcasm. "Flew all the way to Italy to be a Hebrew slave."

Kate cackled. "You're just miffed about the costume."

Brigid shrieked with laughter. "Costume? It's a bleedin' rubbish sack."

"But your legs are knockouts under the plastic hem," Danny said before making the sound of a New Yorker whistling for a taxi.

Raising the hem of her skirt, Brigid elevated her leg. "Not too shabby, huh, darlin's?" she said with a shimmy in her café chair.

Their excitement was contagious. Telma was surprised to find herself eager to attend the concert, to be part of the carnival weekend. But she had limits—she'd never become another fawning groupie of Isabella Fabrini.

Then there was Danny's unrequited love. "You simply must confront Tommy," Telma told the New Yorker on their walk back to her hotel. "Don't be shy. Blame your lust on the Italian moon, *la bella luna*." She wasn't convinced she'd bolstered his courage, suggesting he use his journaling skills. "Put your love in writing. Speak from the heart," Telma had said with a pat to his chest. "Add erotic details. Draw pictures. Always worked for me."

Without looking up from the registration book, the young communista bade Telma a good morning as she descended the steps from the breakfast room.

"*Buongiorno*," Telma replied, dropping her key on the counter. "Off to the Terme."

"*Sì, perfetto.* They work wonders—some even say…miracles."

"Pity," Telma scoffed. "With such a resource, shame you haven't taken advantage." The girl's pursed lips couldn't hide her satisfaction. *This might just be the beginning of a beautiful friendship*, Telma thought, turning toward the exit.

Hello! Before Telma stood a most distinguished man—the classic tall, dark stranger with broad shoulders, wavy hair peppered with gray, and eyes crinkled at the corners. She didn't see a ring as he held open the door.

"*Buongiorno, signora*," he said in a deep voice. Telma tipped her head and smiled, pausing on the doorstep long enough to hear him give his name to the young communista, "Luca Caruso."

The dismal hostel passing itself off as a hotel held promise after all.

Walking across the threshold of the Terme felt like stepping into a different world—opulence mixed with the exotic—a marble palace worthy of Kublai Khan. A domed skylight topped a two-story vestibule. White smocked attendants welcomed guests at a desk behind which stood cases filled with the spa's signature brand of balms, oils, towels, and robes. After checking Telma in, the receptionist directed her to the upper floor.

Murals of Roman gods painted in classical style dominated the walls above the granite staircase. At the top of the stairs, corridors with barrel-vaulted ceilings and marble floors inlaid with green and pink mosaics led to the treatment rooms.

After Telma slipped into a disposable thong, slippers and a plush white robe, an attendant directed her to a room decorated with palm trees, wicker furniture, and ceiling fans. French doors lined each end of the cavernous waiting room, called the Reflection Lounge.

Telma poured a glass of water from a pitcher filled with cucumber slices and basil leaves before settling onto a chaise longue to await her mineral bath. Her eyes drooped, falling victim to lilting music of lute, lyre, and mandolin and the scent of jasmine wafting through the open windows. She surrendered to sleep.

Did she dream of sexy Philippe Blanchette, or had lust merely triggered the fantasy? Seeing him again stoked her passion. Was he more dangerous than she imagined? How did he know Isa? Would he reveal Telma's indiscretion? Isa could use that information to sabotage the annulment—sweet revenge for having lost Walter. Telma's own capacity for spite sparked her paranoia.

Muffled whispers roused Telma. The voices became sharper, more distinct. Two women chatted behind her, unaware of, or unconcerned with, her presence. The language was English, one accent American, the other something different.

"Italy's wildly cool, don't you think?" The voice was that of the younger woman.

The American woman sighed. "If one had time to enjoy it." Her simmering tone suggested urgent need of the spa's stress-relieving treatments.

"Well, I think it's absolutely fab. Italians know how to live—food, wine, passion…then work."

The American clicked her tongue. "Explains the fall of the Roman Empire, doesn't it?"

"Ouch!"

"Wouldn't be so damn stressed if we didn't have an election to win in November. We should be on the campaign trail instead of all this frolicking in Italy." The older woman's voice seethed with frustration.

"But your hubby insists on supporting Isa. Brad's so sweet."

The American scoffed. "Compassion and loyalty are fatal flaws for a politician. Victory goes to the best fundraiser, Vicki, not to the best man or woman."

"Sounds dreadful—nasty business."

"Campaigns are. Got to develop a stomach for them. Better to go on offense—shoot first, seek forgiveness later. Once you learn the game, it's a piece of cake—even fun. I love the challenge of slinging dirt while keeping my hands clean."

The woman was a viper. From the first mention of Brad, Telma figured out the American was Alexandra Novak—the rodeo queen behind the cowboy. Walter frequently spoke of his business school chums, including Cowboy. Telma never attended Walter's school functions. Her action wasn't selfless. The men were generally polite but the women, especially the wives, were ruthless. They forgave Walter, but Telma forever wore a scarlet letter.

Walter once returned from a business trip to America with a magazine. Inside, Telma found an article about the Novaks, some piece obviously intended to humanize the Ken and Barbie pair before an election. Photos showed the happy couple at home with their all-American kids and floppy-eared dog—maybe it was the other way around—sunshine, smiles, and shag carpeting. Telma's favorite picture featured Alexandra as a happy homemaker preparing a birthday dinner for Brad. The photographer struck the perfect balance, portraying his subject as a confident woman and loyal housewife. Dubbing the shot "cleavage with apron," Telma laughed, imagining the consequences of an errant splatter of grease.

Reclining in a wicker chair, Telma delighted in eavesdropping on unfiltered Alexandra. Walter always said she wore the chaps in that family. Telma guessed that she and Vicki would careen between bouts as best friends and bitterest enemies.

"Willy says Brad's got no worries. He'll be governor, probably even president. Says your father has the election all buttoned up."

Alexandra laughed. "No sure bets in politics."

"Willy only bets on sure things."

Telma laughed to herself. Five or six wives and an endless string of mistresses repudiated Willy's winning streak. Unlike the quaint mnemonic device schoolchildren learned to recall the fates of Henry VIII's six queens—divorced, beheaded, died, divorced, beheaded, survived—the outcome of Willy's marriages were simple: divorced, divorced, divorced.

So this was the latest Mrs. Epson. Walter mentioned that Willy had fallen head over heels with a grad student he met on a business trip to New Zealand. How long before cheerful Vicki figured out the common denominator in Willy's troubled relationships?

Alexandra mustered a well-honed tone of humility. "Didn't mean to be so flip. Brad and I are thankful for Willy's generosity. He's simply the best of friends. Oh, and you too, dear. Simply marvelous." *Here's a woman who knows how to raise money.* "We're both grateful to Willy—not only for the campaign support but also for his fabulous investment advice."

"You and Brad aren't the only ones enjoying Willy's bounty. Jamie Stuart bought a second home in France. He's buying a Ferrari before heading back to London."

"Shame Isa didn't have money to invest," Alexandra said. "She's barely getting by—may have to sell her flat. Don't know how she affords this concert. Then there's Walter Benchley."

"Ingrate, Willy says. They barely speak anymore. And after all Willy did."

"Don't be so harsh on Walter. He's been distracted with that bitch of an ex-wife. Probably bled him dry."

Telma kept still; her fingernails dug into the wicker. Willy burned through lots of Walter's money. House of cards, Walter called it. "If he's tricked others," Walter said, "prison may be the safest place for Willy Epson." Walter rebuffed any suggestion that he register a formal complaint. Although Walter cited school chum loyalty, Telma assumed that embarrassment of being hoodwinked kept him silent.

Telma was happy that the Terme operated like the rest of Italy—unapologetically late. She enjoyed her seat—perhaps even more than the anticipated mineral bath. Juicy gossip and useful information soaked into her pores before warm springs purged them of toxins.

"I recognize him," Alexandra whispered as Telma sensed someone enter the lounge. "Met him at the last concert—American. Exchange student, I think, at school with Brad and Isa. What's his name? Danny? Tommy?"

At the mention of the names, Telma glanced at the entrance. Standing at the water pitcher was a tall, fair-haired man with boyish good looks. She guessed this was Tommy. His companion wasn't Danny. Olive skin radiated against the spa's brilliant white robe. Thick, dark hair and large brown eyes contrasted with the fair-featured Tommy. Something about the way the attractive couple toyed with each other told Telma this was no platonic friendship. Her heart sank. Perhaps Danny could recycle his erotic love note.

"Tommy?" Alexandra said as the men approached her.

"Alexandra, right? Brad's wife," the American said.

"Good memory, yes. This is Vicki—she's married to Willy."

Tommy stared at the younger woman before stammering, "N-nice to meet you. I—"

"I know, I know, sweetie—hard to keep track of the Mrs. Epsons. I'm the newest model—still have my factory tags." Vicki spoke in a way that disarmed awkwardness.

"Glad to meet you," Tommy said in a Midwestern accent. "This is Miguel Rivera."

The handsome Latin man extended his hand. "Pleasure to meet you ladies." His voice could have been Tommy's—the same accent, tone, and cadence.

"And you are?" Alexandra asked. Based on Danny's speculation, Telma wondered whether Tommy would be honest. Or, would he try to pass Miguel off as a buddy, omitting the fact that they shared the same bed?

"Miguel's my partner," Tommy responded without hesitation.

"Partner!" Alexandra exclaimed.

Partner! Telma thought, *Not even boyfriend.* The news would crush Danny. He wanted Tommy gay, but gay with him.

"You coy little devil," Alexandra said. "Kept your handsome Latin boyfriend hidden at the last concert. Made us all guess why you didn't have a date."

"We met a month *after* the last concert," Miguel said.

"Somebody I danced with at the last concert connected Miguel and me in Chicago," Tommy said. "You might say that Isa brought us together."

Telma rolled her eyes to the ceiling. *Oh, joy, yet another miracle to canonize the woman. Saint Isa.*

"Speaking of Isa, has anyone seen her?" Miguel asked. "I must thank her." With that, he put his arm around Tommy and kissed his cheek.

"Imagine we won't see her till tonight," Alexandra replied.

"Either of you singing in the chorus?" Tommy asked.

"I am. Unless the funny little man named Leech or the drill sergeant kick me out," Vicki said with a giggle. "We rehearsed yesterday. Got another this afternoon and one tomorrow before the concert. We're all scrambling to learn Italian and inking the words on our hands."

"Silly to come all this way to Italy and be cooped up in an opera house," Alexandra said.

"Agreed," said Tommy. "But Danny's singing as are the Dubliners."

Telma closed her eyes to envision Kate and Brigid vamp about the stage as sultry gypsies. She felt someone hover over her. Musky-scented cologne overpowered the sweet breeze. She opened her eyes expecting a man. But, her fantasy-filled dream tricked her senses. Standing before her was a pretty young woman dressed in white. "I'm your masseuse, madame."

"But I requested a man."

"Okay, okay. I fix. But first, I take you for mineral bath," she said, bending down to help Telma from the chaise. That's when Telma saw *him*. Standing behind the masseuse was Philippe, his bronzed, muscular chest visible under the spa's white robe.

"*Scusi.* Token of my appreciation," the Frenchman said, handing forty euros to the masseuse.

The woman seemed flustered. "*Grazie.* Glad you liked the treatment." She put the money into a pocket and fished out a card. "Should you need anything…day or night."

Philippe glanced down; his eyes widened. "Bologna!"

"How kind of you to remember." As Telma rose, every face in the room turned toward her. She pulled Philippe into an embrace. "Telma, No h," she whispered into his ear. Then turning to her gawking audience, she announced, "Otherwise known as the former Mrs. Walter Benchley."

Chapter 22

Lowering herself into the oversized tub, Telma laughed recalling the shocked expressions. Who was more startled—Philippe or Alexandra? Vicki and Miguel were too distanced from her scandalous tryst with Walter to really care. Tommy's surprise faded quickly. If Isa owned his allegiance, he hid any trace of animosity. Tommy, a wholesome Midwesterner, approached with a smile and hug, mentioning that he and Walter were friends in business school. The sweetheart even remembered to offer condolences on the loss of her sister. Tommy's kindness combined with boy-next-door looks showed Telma why Danny was smitten. The masseuse handed Telma off to the bath attendant, mumbling in Italian— probably a dig about the crazy foreigners.

A cough and the smell of cigarettes brought Telma back to her porcelain refuge. A pretty yet overly efficient attendant hovered over her. Between the girl's broken English and Telma's limited Italian, they managed to communicate.

The girl rested a pillow behind Telma's head. "Get yourself relax."

The high-ceilinged room of black and white tile looked more like a clinic than a day spa. Candles, soft music, and a vase of wildflowers softened the mood, giving the chamber an air of pampered indulgence.

"Rejuvenation, relaxation, or stimulation?" the girl asked, practiced in her routine. Telma's silence prompted her to add, pointing to a jar of bath salts, "The bath? What type you prefer?"

"Relaxation." Telma had enough stimulation for one morning and rejuvenation was best left to the experts—plastic surgeons.

The girl moved to the foot of the tub where copper piping looked like an apparatus from Frankenstein's laboratory. "Water," she said as if from a script, "come from thermal springs. Go way back to ancients."

Rust-brown liquid gushed from the spigot. The attendant placed a thermometer into the tub. The warm water with an odor of sulfur and salt turned hot.

The girl added bath salts to the steaming tub. "Water okay?"

"For boiling lobster."

The girl cocked her head, baffled.

Telma nodded. "*Sì, sì—bene, bene.*"

The girl inserted a tension bar across the tub to keep Telma from floating to the surface. Once the tub filled, air jets gurgled and fanned the rising vapors. Telma felt like the main course at a cannibal buffet. The girl giggled throughout her demonstration, pretending to dunk a sachet in the water before rubbing the air above her bare arm. Feigning a look of contentment, she lifted it to her nose and sighed. Telma nodded her understanding.

The girl slid a reading rack toward Telma. "Magazines, if want."

Lights dimmed; the door creaked closed. Sun filtered into the room through white lace curtains while hints of jasmine floated in through an open window. Telma relished the solitude. Once the sachet hit the water, lavender mixed with the bergamot and vanilla from the bath salts—relaxation overdose. Dancing shadows cast by courtyard trees hypnotized her into a drowsy trance.

Telma sighed. For the first time in weeks, tension melted away. Her mind drifted on a wave of calm. But the interlude was brief. Her mission rocked the serenity. Spas were a fool's paradise. Cold, unrelenting reality awaited her outside the warm, soothing waters of the granite temple.

She had yet to face Isa and her family—hadn't seen them in years except for Gina. At Christina's funeral, Gina was warm. Well, as warm as she ever was—cordial to Telma's father and civil, almost polite to Telma. Gina, Telma knew, wasn't altogether unhappy that she'd plucked Walter Benchley from Isa's life. Did Walter set off warning bells or did sisterly rivalry keep Gina from wanting to see Isa happy? Where Gina stood two years later, friend or foe, would remain a mystery. Isa's older sister didn't make the trip to San Benedetto. "Some lame excuse," Kate said over drinks the prior night at the Tazza d'Oro. "Ask me," the Dubliner added, "Gina's plain selfish. Hates to see Isa get applause." *Hmm*, Telma wondered, *the enemy of my enemy is...*

Isa's staunchest supporter had always been her younger sister. Would Ana slap Telma's face or excuse the betrayal as the consequence of a free-spirited life? Walter told her that Ana had become more philosophical since her successful bout with cancer.

Telma recalled the long-ago meeting with Ana in London. The meet up took place mere days after Walter and Isa's marriage plans imploded because of the incident in Regent's Park. Furious with her sister's lapse of judgment and morals with Isa's fiancé, Christina aborted their holiday, securing return tickets to Buenos Aires. But Telma refused to return home with her. Ana rang up Telma at her hotel. She seethed through the receiver, "You owe our family the courtesy of a face-to-face meeting."

Telma couldn't help herself; she suggested Regent's Park. After a long pause and restraint, Ana said she preferred an artsy coffee house in Camden Town. They compromised, settling for the open-air craft market of St. James Church on Piccadilly Street. In recent years, fully established as Mrs. Walter Benchley, Telma often passed the market on her way to the Ritz Hotel, Fortnum & Mason, and the Royal Academy of Arts. But, she never forgot that afternoon reckoning with Ana.

Arriving early, Telma strolled through the church market admiring the handiwork. The church, a Wren creation and one of the architect's favorites, wore scars of the Second World War. She admired the way London patched itself together, plastering over wounds and marching forward. The results weren't always pretty, but they were functional.

When Telma happened upon children's toys—puppets, quilted animals, dolls—she paused. She plucked up a doll, caressing its soft fair hair before holding the little milkmaid to her chest. She always wanted a big family like the Fabrinis, and was heartbroken when the doctor told her she couldn't. Perhaps that was the first lie to Walter—telling him she didn't want children. She'd spent her entire life feeling inferior. She didn't want Walter, the first man who showed an ounce of interest, seeing her as damaged. She couldn't risk his abandoning her.

After returning the doll, and retreating to the food stall for coffee and a slice of spice cake, Telma settled onto an iron chair in the courtyard. Her eyes wandered to a placard: "Caravan Drop In." According to the sign, crisis counseling and emotional support were available in the green caravan parked in the courtyard. She snickered. Had fate guided her to this place? Would she require the caravan's services after Ana finished with her—first aid for mind and body?

The happy faces and voices of the market faded into the background as Telma anticipated the meeting. Ana was right about her debt. Growing up in Buenos Aires, the Fabrinis treated Christina and her as extensions of their family. Papa Fabrini viewed life as an endless Sunday of parades and picnics. If pity motivated him to welcome the sisters into his celebration, he never showed it.

As a child, Telma envied the Fabrini sisters. Their papa never allowed himself to be consumed by work like her own father. Papa Fabrini delighted in his family—never missing a birthday or holiday—any excuse to sing and laugh. Maybe Telma envied them most because the sisters still had a mother—a smothering personality, but a doting caregiver nonetheless.

Mama Fabrini was sensitive to Telma and her sister, even kind. But no matter how hard Telma tried, she couldn't cross the boundary of love Mama Fabrini reserved for her own daughters. It took Telma many years to stop trying and many more to stop hurting.

Telma learned early that life was harsh. Her mother died bringing her into the world. Her poor father did his very best with a six-year-old and a newborn—neither a boy. He worked hard to make a go of his floundering business. Telma wondered whether he drowned himself in work to escape the daughters who confounded him. Telma often heard him crying alone at the kitchen table when he thought his girls were asleep.

Her father managed with the help of a tight-knit Italian community and occasional visits by family from Italy and Spain. Surviving on hand-me-downs from Christina and the Fabrinis, Telma felt guilty wishing for new things her father couldn't afford. Christina was her savior. Although a child herself, she mothered Telma the best she could. In turn, Christina found comfort in her friendship with Isa and the love of the Fabrini family. Gina was eight years older than Telma, Christina and Isa, six, Ana four. As the baby of the brood, Telma was happy to have four big "sisters"—until she wasn't.

The sound of a purse falling onto the table roused her. "Grabbing a tea," Ana said by way of introduction. "Watch my bag."

Ana didn't return the smile Telma's mental journey to the past plastered on her face.

Setting down a cup of tea, Ana took a seat at the table and scowled. "This isn't a doll."

"What?"

"We're adults now, Telma. This isn't child's play. You stole Isa's fiancé."

Telma remembered. She was three, maybe four. Isa had received a new doll for her birthday. Telma never saw anything so beautiful. The doll, dressed in a yellow, polka-dot dress with shiny black shoes and pink barrettes in her hair, looked like Christina. Sneaking the doll home, Telma hid it under her bed pretending it was her baby sister. Christina and Isa found her cuddling and singing a lullaby to the doll. Ripping the doll from Telma's arms, Isa cried, "Thief! You're nothing but a thief." Telma's father spanked her. A week later, Papa Fabrini presented her with a doll, smaller but just as pretty and new smelling as Isa's. Telma's father objected but Christina and Papa Fabrini wore him down. "She needs a big sister," Papa Fabrini said, handing the doll to Telma with a wink, "to sing her sweet lullabies."

Ana sniffled, dabbing her nose with a tissue. She waited for the church bell to stop chiming the hour. "How could you, Telma? Isa's been like a sister to you. We've all been. Stealing Walter was despicable."

Telma looked at her. She wasn't about to quibble whether she took Walter or he pursued her. She saw the indictment in Ana's eyes—Telma was a thief. "You're forgetting the fact that Walter loves me."

"I don't believe that for one second. He loves Isa."

"Maybe you should ask him."

"I'm asking you not to see him any more. No good can come of it."

What she said after that didn't matter. Telma heard that she wasn't good enough. She wasn't educated like Isa. Telma didn't deserve a rich, handsome husband or a secure future. No, she was still the little ragamuffin who should be satisfied with handouts and hand-me-downs. At that instant, Telma made up her mind to take Walter. Love would come later…or not at all.

The green caravan was for amateurs, weaklings who didn't have the guts to grab what they wanted from life. That wasn't Telma Rossi.

The bath accomplished its objective. The hot, pulsing water drained Telma of stress and the herbal sachet left her skin soft and mind clear.

She imagined how wonderful she'd feel after the deep tissue massage. The doorknob rattled and the door creaked open.

"*Grazie mille,*" she said, craning her neck toward the door. "The bath was absolutely de—" She stopped; her heart raced.

Standing in the doorway was Isabella Fabrini.

Chapter 23

Déjà vu! In a split second, Telma's memory snatched her from the warm, bubbling comfort of the Terme's mineral bath. She was back in London—a June evening long ago.

She and her sister traveled to London to attend Isa's graduation. They kept the visit a secret, aided by Ana who delighted in surprise and spontaneity. Christina wanted to make the most of Telma's first trip to Europe. Before London, they spent a week in France and afterward they planned to tour Spain and Italy to see family before returning to Argentina.

Christina was thirty-two, the same age as Isa. Telma's twenty-sixth birthday coincided with Isa's graduation. "Let Isa have her day," her sister said. "You won't mind celebrating a day or two later."

What could Telma say? The trip was Christina's birthday gift to her. As a psychiatrist in Buenos Aires' leading hospital, Christina earned a good living. A private practice catering to a wealthy clientele courted her with a huge signing bonus. Although Christina never said so, Telma wondered whether the extravagant European tour sprang from a sense of guilt. In a way, Christina's success came at her younger sister's expense. Telma was merely an assistant clerk in a bank, and eked out an existence by sharing expenses with their father. But the motive didn't matter. Telma intended to party before returning to her dismal life.

Ana met the sisters when they got out of the cab at the business school. She ushered them into a sprawling garden. For Telma, the graduation eve reception droned on with the drabness of a quilted tea cozy. They spotted Isa across the lawn. She wore a dress of vibrant scarlet with lips the same color. She looked stunning—confident, successful, and loved. Everything Telma wasn't. Isa stood with her family and a dashing man later introduced as her boyfriend. She squealed with joy when she spotted her childhood friends, falling into a frenzy of hugs and kisses. After pulling Christina aside, Isa paraded her around. She introduced her to friends as "My best friend from Argentina, practically another sister. She's not only gorgeous but also a highly successful doctor." A tidal wave of tailored suits and designer dresses swallowed the best friends.

Telma stood alone at the party's fringe and sipped vodka as she studied the faces of *the anointed ones*. Did any of them appreciate their good fortune? Or were hubris and self-absorption prerequisites for graduation and success? These were the *grosses têtes,* the big heads Gertrude Stein wrote about. These people made the rules they expected others to follow.

"Looks as if we've both been abandoned," said a voice from behind her.

Turning, Telma saw the man introduced as Isa's boyfriend. She shrugged, toasting his whiskey with her glass. "It's only vexing when the liquor runs dry," she said, drawing his chuckle. "It's Walter, right?"

He nodded, stepping closer. "Yes, Benchley. And you're Telma Noaitch."

She creased her forehead. *Had he heard me wrong?* "Rossi, Telma *Rossi.*"

He blushed. "Sorry. Feeble English humor. I meant your name. It's not Th…Thelma. No *h*—Telma…oh, blast it all. Miss Rossi it is."

He was adorable when he got flustered—less *grosse tête*, more human. His heart-shaped face lit up; brown eyes sparkled. "Here," he said grabbing her glass, "let me refresh these…then let's walk, shall we? How 'bout I show you a slice of London, Miss Rossi?" He must have seen concern in her face as she gazed toward the Fabrinis. "No worries. I'll have you back before your carriage turns into a pumpkin."

As Walter walked to the bar, Telma caught herself giggling like a schoolgirl. The veil lifted from her senses. Her ears tuned into a joyous allegro of the string quartet and her nose delighted in the perfume of rose and lilac. Laughter no longer repulsed. The idea of a stroll with Walter excited her. Was she wrong to feel that way? Isa, as far as Telma knew, hadn't staked a permanent claim. In Paris, her sister Christina attracted the stares and advances of good-looking men. Telma was left at a café table for one to thumb through guidebooks, Gertrude Stein, and nurse her *vin blanc.*

Walter seemed conflicted, anxious. "I should be ecstatic," he said, "but my good news is bloody wasted." Telma detected sadness among the alcohol and anger. He looked away and talked about the weather—her cue not to pry.

They strolled through the garden, passed the president's house, and exited through an iron gate. Walter motioned across the road as he led them into the crosswalk. "Regent's Park—appropriated from the Catholics by Henry the Eighth."

"I admire a man with vision."

Suddenly, Telma's body jerked backward as a red Jaguar sped across their path. Her hand flew upward, releasing the drink glass that crashed to the pavement and shattered. Vodka splattered her nylons. She stumbled. Her back came to rest against Walter's chest. Walter's fingers pressed into her skin; his arm folded across her body like a shoulder harness.

"Careful!" he shouted. "Pedestrians are magnets for London drivers—tourists a bonus."

Telma's eyes glanced at Walter's other hand, still grasping the whiskey. His index finger pointed to the ground. Stenciled onto the pavement in large white letters was the warning—*Look Right*. That incident should have served as caution for what lay ahead.

With a deep breath and gentle boost from Walter, Telma steadied herself. "Hell with Henry the Eighth. Give me a man with good reflexes and strong arms." She looked into the confident eyes of her white knight. "Thank heavens!" she exclaimed, "Isa'd never forgive me for upstaging her celebration."

They both laughed as they completed the crossing, but Telma's body still trembled from the near miss. Walter paused at the park entrance. "Here," he said, pushing his glass toward her. "Take a sip." She shook her head; she hated whiskey. "Go on," he said. "Do you good." As he pressed the glass to her lips, his other hand caressed her back. She let the cool liquid enter her mouth. Her tongue tingled with the first drizzle. She pulled back but Walter's hand pushed her forward. She took his whiskey willingly until he pulled the glass away. "That's my girl."

Walter finished his drink with one gulp and placed the glass on the edge of an empty park bench. "You should be safe on the walking paths, but just in case." He looped her arm through his. "My hostly duty."

Telma loved the attention. At first, she attributed the Englishman's attentiveness to her being a childhood friend of Isa. But his concern mixed with her fertile imagination led her to embrace other possibilities. Telma let the spark of desire ignite her seasoned kindling.

They stopped on a bridge overlooking a pond. White swans and chattering ducks glided below. Walter told her that he'd landed his dream job at one of the City's most prestigious banks. The call came as he dressed for the evening's reception.

"How wonderful!" Turning to face him, Telma squeezed his shoulders and lifted herself onto tiptoes to kiss his cheek. "I bet Isa's on cloud nine."

His smile faded; his gaze moved from her face to the pond below. "She doesn't know."

"What?"

"Couldn't be bothered—she's too damn busy with her family, now with your sister." She detected the hurt of a little boy in his tone. His lip quivered. Telma couldn't believe Isa's insensitivity. No doubt sensing her surprise, Walter added, "It's a lot of things, really."

Telma stood, silent. She didn't want to give the impression she was eager to snoop into their private matters. She hadn't seen Isa in years and only just met this man. Her hand slid along the railing until it touched his. She too gazed into the pond; their faces reflected in the rippled water.

"She's walling herself up," he finally said. "She gets like this when things don't go as planned. Isa must face every crisis alone, solve everything by herself."

Telma was astounded. Isa had everything—a great education including a degree from one of Europe's top business schools, and now the handsome, sensitive, and intelligent man beside her. "Isa's got a future!" Telma's exclamation was as much an assessment of Isa's good fortune as a lament for her own lonely, dead-end life.

"She can't see the rainbow through the storm. She's graduating without a job."

Walter's explanation seemed rather weak. Even Isa must consider the lack of a job merely a temporary setback. But Telma kept quiet. The truth usually followed once the gate opened. She studied his reflection. His face winced.

"It's her bloody independent streak," he said. "She's terrified of humiliation and dependency. She won't let anyone help her. We haven't had sex in months."

Telma felt sorry for him. Englishmen, she'd heard, obsessed about sex but seldom talked about it except by way of bawdy jokes. How to respond to his confession?

Walter guided her deeper into the park. Appearing to be on autopilot, he led her past the pond then down a path. Playing fields stretched out on wide lawns to one side while thickets of trees huddled in the shadows on the other. Lilacs and dogwoods presented spring's last blooms. Walter veered onto the grass. A smile cast over his shoulder beckoned her to follow. He pulled her through an opening in a hedge where she found herself in a lush and secluded bower.

"What is this place?"

"Fantastic, isn't it? Isa and I happened upon it by accident. We spent many afternoons studying and making..." His words trailed off, eyes focused on a spot on the grass.

Telma took his hand. "I've known Isa all my life. This...closing herself off...it's just her way. I'm sure it'll pass."

"Fine way to show it." His hand grasped hers tighter. "Why isn't she here with me? Why must it be *you*? A woman I—"

Telma's face must have betrayed the sting of his words. Stopping in mid-sentence, he faced her and grabbed both of her hands. "I'm so sorry, dear girl. I didn't mean that. I'm just upset." He lifted her hand to his lips and kissed it.

She wasn't going to let him see her cry. She spent enough of her life crying. "It's okay, really it is. I understand, really I do."

After guiding her to the bower's only bench, he whispered, "Another one of Isa's weaknesses."

She slid closer to better hear him. "What?"

"Understanding...or rather, lack thereof. She expects everyone to tick like her. And when they don't...You get the picture." His breath carried traces of whiskey.

"Maybe we should go," Telma said. Her outstretched palm collected droplets with increasing intensity.

Walter looked up to the sky. "Just a bit of a spit. Plenty of blue. You'll get used to London."

He pulled his arms out of his suit jacket and held the makeshift umbrella over their heads. They scooted closer together, Telma's head resting in the crook of his shoulder. His wool trousers and muscular calves pressed against her legs. She quivered at the smell of his aftershave. His face was close enough for her to see the dark stubble on his strong jaw. *How could Isa be so cruel?*

Within moments, the drizzle stopped and they were on the ground. Walter laid out his suit jacket on which she reclined. *How chivalrous.* Around her, a lush green carpet with a scent freshened by the rain extended to the bower's edge. She couldn't believe what was happening. If it were fantasy, she didn't want to awaken. A happy birthday, indeed!

Walter was on top, penetrating her. One hand cradled her head while his other reached under her blouse, caressing her breasts. She couldn't take her eyes off of his face—handsome, strong...determined. Sweat beaded his forehead; his eyes were closed. *Is he pretending that I'm Isa? Does it matter?*

Telma felt the presence. Her heart started to race. She'd never done anything like that. This was stiff, staid London. Would they face arrest? Would her picture be plastered in newspapers? Even more important, would her new protector abandon her in the face of scandal?

Telma looked past Walter's head. Her eyes adjusted to splotches of red and black—scarlet silk covered by black linen—red lipstick—black mascara—red fingernails—black raven hair—red umbrella.

"You bitch!" the interloper's voice screamed.

Walter's eyes opened wide; he gasped. He pulled off of Telma as she pushed him away. On his feet, he zipped up his pants and pulled at the suit jacket that wasn't there. Telma wanted to roll over, bury her head in the satin lining of his jacket, and will herself invisible. Instead, she wiggled in the grass—adjusting her undergarments, pulling at the hem of her skirt, and kicking the space around her feet for shoes.

"You filthy, ungrateful bitch!" Isa repeated with increased intensity. She flew toward Telma. Walter stepped between the two women, receiving a hard slap to the face. "You bastard. On the very spot where you proposed."

Proposed! The word boomed in Telma's ears like a thunderclap. Walter turned, eyes scanning her expression. The horror on Telma's face gave him his answer. But Isa's growls demanded his attention. He held her wrists as fingers twitched and twisted in eye-gouging, skin-scratching menace. Telma saw the ring—diamond and sapphire—turned upside-down to guard a surprise announcement.

Isa bellowed, "You goddamn bitch!"

"Calm down, Isabella, calm down," Walter repeated. "It's not Telma's fault."

Then Isa laughed, a horrible mad shriek. Was it contempt or pity Telma saw in her face? "Wait! I want to remember this scene. My fiancé screwing a troll with a grass-stained arse."

And with those words, Telma's surging shame fizzled like a sputtering firework.

The loud ringing of a telephone somewhere outside the bathing room reminded Telma of the open door. Isa, guarding the threshold like a sentry, showed no sign of restoring her privacy. Arms crisscrossed Telma's chest to cover bare breasts. She kept her eyes focused on the door—she wasn't about to turn her back on Isa.

"Close the door so I can stand up and get my robe."

"Age has brought modesty, I see. There was a time when you didn't care who saw your naughty bits."

Isa stepped into the room and shoved the door with the same forceful whack she had used to slap Walter in Regent's Park. The door closed, rattling the jars and fixtures of the porcelain and chrome room. The force blew out the candles, sending up a trail of gray, pungent smoke. Telma lifted herself out of the bathwater. Breezes from the ceiling fan and open window chilled her skin. The bold citrus of Isa's perfume and the subtle scent of fear banished the soothing aromas of her refuge.

Telma grabbed her robe and dabbed her skin. Isa's back remained planted against the door. Telma waited. *Let her show her hand*. If experience were a reliable predictor, Isa wouldn't keep her mouth shut. Telma didn't have to wait long.

"Why are you here?"

Telma's hand swept the air toward the tub. "For the waters, of course. What else draws anyone to San Benedetto?"

Isa scoffed. Teeth clenched. Furrows formed at the edges of her mouth. Arms quivered at her sides. "Don't tangle with me!"

Telma stretched, adjusting her spine. She sighed. "I know, I know," she said with a yawn. "You're older, larger, and meaner than me—a veritable armada of one."

"I'm also a bigger bitch."

Telma clapped her hands. "Brava! The truth at last."

Telma sat on the edge of the tub. Bathrooms had too many sharp edges and hard surfaces to host a safe brawl or catfight. Her sitting diffused the tension. Isa's shoulders relaxed—a lioness reassessing her prey after the initial surprise and chest puffery.

"Actually," Telma said, "I came to thank you for taking good care of Christina."

Isa's expression remained hard. "All right, you've said it—now leave."

Telma laughed. She didn't mean to, but all of a sudden an image of an American Western popped into her head—*this town ain't big enough for the two of us.* "Hold on, pardner, you can't get rid of me so fast."

"How can I say it any clearer? These are not your friends, your family. You're not welcome here."

I'm not good enough! That was the moment Telma decided to stay…for far more than the waters and offering a proper thank you.

Chapter 24

Telma descended the Terme's marble stairs with the nimble step of a fairy queen. Whether the result of a miracle or merely a mirage, the spa peeled away layers of exhaustion. The facial produced a fresh, almost iridescent, glow. And the massage, *oh,* the massage—the masseur pressed, kneaded, and rubbed every inch of her body save one—an experience more satisfying than most sex. How many people craved a cigarette after their session...or began an affair with the masseur or masseuse? *What the hell!* Next time she'd try her luck with a nimble-fingered woman.

The treatments put her in a state of bliss, a whole-body anesthetic that made Isa's ambush dissolve into a fog. Their confrontation seemed days, not hours, before. Telma could look at the incident objectively. Her initial fear—Isa frying her in the tub with a toss of the electric fan or holding her head underwater—seemed laughable in retrospect. If she weren't the target, Telma could have applauded Isa's bravura.

By design, they hadn't cast eyes on each other in years—not an easy feat. They lived in the same city with several mutual connections including Christina and school chums Isa shared with Walter. The portrait of Isa that Telma carried in her head remained frozen; only the vibrant hues of the mental canvas dulled with time. To Telma, Isa was forever tempestuous—a prickly, cornered animal who bristled her quills at the slightest provocation. The decade-old image was a snapshot of rage and fury unleashed in Regent's Park.

Telma relished stories that told how the years had been unkind to her nemesis. She harvested gossip with the cautious step of a minesweeper. She trod gently, hoping curiosity didn't explode in her face. She exercised extreme caution with her sister, never testing the borders of Christina's allegiance. Others disclosed shards of information, allowing Telma to create a mosaic of Isa's life. Jamie Stuart proved particularly vulnerable to her clandestine trawling missions.

Telma didn't need a picture to tell her that Isa suffered a blow discovering Walter and her desecrating the sacred ground of her marriage proposal. But reconnaissance informed her that the episode left an indelible scar. Fury fed bitterness that created intimacy issues. For several years, Isa squirreled herself away like a cloistered nun. Self-imposed chastity gave way to a flurry of one-night stands and brief romances. As with most converts, Isa embraced her new sexual doctrine with zeal. Those invited into her solitary cell were damaged or, more often, unavailable, physically and emotionally. According to sources, Isa didn't flee the corporate world as much as she was kicked to the curb. Her Swedish boss's wife issued her husband an ultimatum—his mistress or his scrotum.

Isa grappled for any ledge to lift her from failure and depression. A rocky consultancy and the quixotic quest to climb the opera stage at forty were two examples. Guilt for her role in Isa's downward spiral never haunted Telma's sleep. Walter had been a safety hook that dangled above both their heads. Isa may have grabbed hold first, but Telma had the firmer grip. Telma had fewer paths out of the abyss than did Isa. Desperation often spurred super-human strength. How was Telma to know Isa would dangle from the safety rope for years?

As for the concert, Christina considered Isa's plan therapeutic. While never expressing doubt at Isa's ability to train her middle-aged vocal cords, Christina framed the ambitious foray in clinical terms as a harmless way to deal with insecurity and mortality. Opera was Isa's version of a middle-aged man's fascination with sports cars and twentysomethings. In contrast, Telma viewed Isa's pursuit as pure folly, a narcissistic variation of the soapbox crazy who delivers messianic messages with a bullhorn.

But the woman who intruded upon Telma's bath and ordered her out of San Benedetto wasn't her frozen portrait of Isa. The change wasn't clear at first. Ambush, barked commands, and history clouded her perspective. But as the steamy rage dissipated, Isa's transformation came into focus.

To Telma's naked eye, Isa looked pretty much the same: raven hair and dark eyes, strong cheekbones and chin, wide mouth and plump lips. *Time hasn't been unkind*, Telma thought. *That is, for a woman past forty.* Had they not been rivals, Telma might have complimented Isa's appearance.

Plastic surgery wasn't the answer. She'd know. But what drew her stare and kept it riveted?

Confidence! Isa tapped into a well of self-assurance that rejuvenated her appearance. Squared shoulders, the tilt of her head, and deliberate movements exuded strength, sureness, poise, and something else... satisfaction, joy. Was this altered state a by-product of the concert? The change mesmerized Telma—a riddle that required investigation. And yet another reason to impose herself into the weekend. If Isa's new foundation had weaknesses, Telma wanted to find them. *The smallest crack, with just the right pressure, can grow into a great fissure.*

Telma wanted to make a big splash, cannonball into the middle of the concert. But Isa had the marked advantage—makeup, costumes, lighting, and accompanists. Most importantly, she had the stage, a legitimate platform that commanded an audience. Telma was merely an interloper. She'd need every conceivable resource to keep from becoming a mediocre sideshow. Why shouldn't Isa have a little competition? Italy, contrary to free-market skeptics, was still a capitalist country.

Had Danny spoken the truth about a fashionable high street with upmarket stores? A new dress would boost her confidence—a low neckline and high slit would bolster her fan base. No one ever upstaged a widow by wearing a black choke-neck gown. Contrast was required if she was to offer *their* audience a provocative counterpoint. *Telma Rossi will out-diva the diva.*

With her plan set, Telma strolled with confidence from the Terme toward her hotel.

"Telma? That you, love?"

She recognized the voice—a Glasgow accent with a deep, husky tone. She turned. "Jamie Stuart, my favorite lusty Scotsman."

He squatted slightly, grabbed her waist, and lifted her off the ground. "No tellin' what sensuous creature awaits a man in Italy."

She adored Jamie, one of Walter's few friends for whom she cared. He was neither stuffy nor pretentious despite making a small fortune investing with Willy Epson. Regardless of his opinion about her indiscretion with Walter, he never made her feel ashamed. In Jamie's world, the man was still the hunter. "None of my business, love," he said early in her marriage. "There's already a chorus of hypocrites condemning you to hell—why add to the clamor?" He never mentioned the subject to her again. What, if anything, he said to Walter remained a secret. Jamie was a sweetheart to Telma.

"How 'bout a little lunch?" he said, returning her to the ground. "Though surely I'll see you at tonight's wee do."

Telma couldn't contain her delight. Jamie just handed her an engraved invitation to Isa's weekend. Grabbing his hand, she blurted, "Fantastic! Wondered which lucky man would escort me to the party." Details were irrelevant; Jamie was her guide. "Tell you what. I've got a little shopping and some calls to make. How about drinks at three...no, make it four? Still gives us time before the *wee do*."

"Plenty of time. You know the Italians—nothin' gets goin' before nine. Now scurry your cute little arse so you don't keep me. A man grows mighty impatient waiting for a lovely lady." Reaching around her waist, he swatted her behind.

She felt his eyes on her as she continued toward the hotel. The whistle was undeniably his. Not only had Telma found an escort, but Jamie, whether a willing confidant or not, might also shed light on the mystery of Isa's transformation.

As Telma stepped into the hotel lobby, the young communista averted her eyes to the registration ledger.

"Sensible," Telma said, pausing long enough for the girl to look up. "A frock of gray floral—a fashion choice that'll take you well into old age."

The girl's expression remained stonelike. "*Sì*, nothing more pathetic than old woman pretending she still young." Her dark eyes scanned Telma from head to toe before she creased her forehead. "Tsk, tsk. What a shame. Guests usually return from Terme looking better than before they go."

With raised chin, Telma pushed out her chest. "Hard to improve upon perfection."

The girl shrugged. "Pity you no try." She handed over the room key with a playful twinkle in her eyes.

Telma took the key and winked. "By the way, I need a salon appointment for tomorrow morning. You know—hair, fingers, toes. I know it's a leap of faith, but San Benedetto must have at least one decent shop."

The mischievous expression returned. Telma braced for a snide retort— perhaps a comment about lost causes or a recommendation for an auto body shop. Instead, the girl merely said, "No worries, signora. Leave it to me."

Up in her room, Telma tried ringing up her fiancé. The mobile went directly to his voicemail so she rang up his home phone instead. The second time she got Graham's mother, but as was her custom, Telma hung up when she answered. They played little games with each other. The old crone would understand the signal and tell Graham that his fiancée had phoned. That ploy saved them both the loathsome task of speaking to one another. Telma fulfilled her responsibility—committing to ring up Graham, not actually talking to him.

Telma changed into something more suitable for shopping and headed back out. As she stepped into the hall, a man exited his room. She recognized him as the, tall broad-shouldered guest who checked in when she left for the spa. *What was his name? Something operatic?* It didn't matter. Telma watched out of the corner of her eye as he locked his door. She inserted her key into the lock. She jiggled the key back and forth making lots of noise but no effort to turn it.

"Blast it!" she shouted in the man's direction. "Damn, damn, damn!"

Footsteps stopped their retreat then started again toward her. As her peripheral vision charted his approach, she toyed with the lock, muttering frustration.

"May I help you?" The voice was kind.

Telma detected a slight Italian accent, but otherwise his English was excellent. She stood up and turned. Taller than she recalled, he had a handsome face: olive skin, brown eyes that crinkled at the corners, a square jaw, and a prominent Roman nose. His full head of wavy hair had touches of gray at the temples. His look and demeanor defied placing his age with any degree of certainty. A rich, mature voice provided the only clue. He was nearer fifty than forty.

"Hate to be such a nuisance," she said, exaggerating her distress. "I'm just a mess with these things."

"Allow me."

Telma stepped aside, feigning surprise when he secured the lock with one swift turn. He smiled as he handed her the key.

"Telma Rossi," she said, grabbing his hand before he retracted it.

"Luca Caruso," he responded with a gentle handshake. She confirmed her initial reconnaissance—no wedding band.

"Lovely hotel," she said.

"For a small town, *sì*."

"How rude I am. You stop to help, and now I'm keeping you." But she made no effort to release his hand.

"No worries. Glad to assist." He bowed his head and started to turn away, but Telma grasped his hand even tighter.

"Luca. You don't mind if I call you Luca?" A smile was his reply. "I'm here by myself. Trying to find the high street, the fashionable one. Do you know where it is?"

"My first time in San Benedetto," he replied as if in apology. "But, I passed some nicer stores on my drive into town."

"I couldn't ask you to walk me there. It's just that…well, I don't speak Italian, and as you just saw," she said, motioning to the lock, "I'm rather… helpless. I'd be eternally grateful…that is, if your wife doesn't mind."

"I'm not married…here alone also. I'd be happy to walk you, but—"

She squeezed his hand, stopping the refusal. "Then it's settled."

He slid out of her grasp. "I must get to the opera house. Unfortunately, it's the opposite direction. My apologies."

"Opera house? Are you singing?"

He shook his head. "Merely a friend of the performer."

"How nice. Just a friend?"

Ignoring her innuendo, he simply asked, "You here for the concert?"

"If I can get a seat."

"I'll leave a ticket for you at the box office—Telma Rossi, yes? *Ciao*." He nodded and turned.

Telma stared at his retreating figure—broad shoulders, long strides, strong legs, and a firm bum. Luca Caruso wasn't only someone she needed to know—he was a man she'd thoroughly enjoy getting to know.

Chapter 25

Sipping Chardonnay at the Tazza d'Oro, Telma caught herself plunging out of character. She didn't quite know what to think. San Benedetto had cast a spell on her. While certainly not Cannes, Monte Carlo, or Mykonos, the town purred with a pleasing harmony. Visitors couldn't hopscotch among celebrity-frequented venues—none existed. Instead, simple moments delighted—gelato in the park, banter with friends, a drink in a sun-dappled café. Concert weekend exhibited all the charm and drama of a fairy-tale wedding.

She didn't mind that Jamie was late. The wine was chilled and awnings gave protection against the hot afternoon sun. The close-by gardens of the Terme laced the breeze with hints of honeysuckle and the twitter of songbirds. Had she been in San Benedetto only one day? Time stretched like molten glass, distorting minutes into unrecognizable units. Hours bent to accommodate a schedule that in London caused stress ulcers.

The Tazza d'Oro stood at the intersection of two lanes. One path led to the spa, the other to the stores and cafés of a pedestrian zone. The vantage point gave Telma unobstructed views of her hotel and the Terme. From an outdoor table, one tapped into town gossip simply by gazing at passersby.

Alexandra Novak paraded past with husband, Brad, who looked more like a dutiful mule than maverick cowboy. Telma didn't pick up much of their bickering except for words that seethed from the perky blonde's mouth like an emperor's declaration. "Daddy says…Daddy wants…Daddy will get." Brad brayed something in reply before Alexandra spun in her Roman sandals to face him. "Think! Once you're governor, congressional vacancies are fucking golden." Had Caesar ever been as eloquent? Telma felt sorry for Brad—saddled with a conniving bitch who turned him into a gelding. He no longer had the balls to buck.

The sight of Kate Maureen Mahoney and Brigid Clancy brought a smile to Telma's face. The Dubliners seemed to breathe happy gas. Interactions with the pair pitched like a raft over white-water rapids. They carried on an animated conversation, hooting and hollering as they peacock-strutted from the Terme. Telma waved them over.

They surprised her with their refusal of a late afternoon nip. Brigid was willing; she dropped onto a chair and sighed. "Feel more battered than pampered," she whined. "Masseuse punched and pummeled me with the might of a West Country boxer."

Kate remained standing. "Did ya hear, darling? Ivy's cancelled."

"Who?"

"Another soprano," Brigid said. "After the last mess, Isa wasn't taking any chances. Added a second soloist as well as the chorus."

Kate nodded, a look of concern on her face. "But now Ivy's gone up and cancelled. Somethin' about an understudy's understudy. A shot at a starring role in London."

"With Ivy *kaput,* darlin' you're now lookin' at the last line of defense between Isa and a nervous breakdown." Brigid laughed, rolling her shoulders.

Kate scowled, gesturing to Brigid. "Up! No time to dawdle. Gotta get ready for tonight."

Whimpering, Brigid held up thumb and forefinger. "Aw, just a thimbleful?"

Kate shook her head. "No! Cement requires less time to set than our makeup and hairdos." She fluffed her deflated halo of red curls. "Barely 'nough time as 'tis to squeeze into our party finery."

Turning to Telma, Brigid flashed an impish grin; eyes crinkled into tiny slits. "Quite right, quite right. We're trussed with more belts and bindings than a Donegal virgin."

"Come on!" Kate exclaimed, tugging the imp's sleeve. With leprechaun in tow, she hollered back to Telma, "Later, darlin'. We'll save ya a seat."

As they trudged away, Brigid cried one last plea, "How 'bout a wee one in a takeaway cup?"

Telma snickered. Would they have the willpower to make it back to their hotel without stopping for a nip? She spotted Danny Chance scurrying into the Terme. From the way he bounded up the marble steps with his head high and a confident smile, she assumed Danny still held out hope of a Tommy conquest. A massage, however, was probably his only hope for a happy ending.

The young waiter, who enjoyed flirting as much as Telma did, took her request for a second Chardonnay. She returned to sentry duty, soaking in the town, imagining stories about tourists and locals alike. Perhaps the young, giggling couple who pawed each other were honeymooners. Maybe the suave playboy type in sunglasses, red pants, and a shoulder-draped sweater was the town gigolo. She spotted two smartly dressed women. They strolled arm-in-arm, stepping in unison, faces lit with laughter.

Sentiment stirred. Perhaps she and Christina were happy sisters once. But Telma didn't remember those feelings. Isa was more like a sister to Christina. Memories flooded her mind. She saw Christina and Isa as school chums running hand-in-hand through Buenos Aires. Then, as giggling boy-crazy teenagers, and finally locking arms in joyful reunion at Isa's graduation. That blasted evening with Walter that drove a wedge between the sisters forever. With Christina's death, they'd never reconcile to delight in the joys of sisterhood.

If Telma was jealous of their relationship, she never admitted her feelings to anyone...including herself. As a child, she grumbled that Isa already had a perfect family that included two sisters. Why did she have to take her only sister and hoard her like a prized doll? As she grew up, Telma observed women who journeyed through life with a best friend, sometimes a sister. She never had that kind of a relationship. She probably wouldn't have enjoyed one if she had. Telma found women cold, petty, and possessive—the same traits, no doubt, they saw in her.

Telma dabbed away tears for Christina and forced herself back to concocting stories. An older man with hair in color and style more suitable for a camel preened like a rooster. His companion might have been mistaken for a granddaughter except for her micro-mini skirt, stiletto heels, and cleavage that advertised *for hire*. Yes, people flocked to San Benedetto for many things besides gelato, sun-dappled cafés, and the therapeutic waters.

She glanced down at the table. How long had a fresh Chardonnay been sitting there? Sensing the waiter, she turned to thank him. "*Scusi,* I must have zoned out—" She stopped. Her eyes traveled past strong calves, up weathered denim to muscular thighs and the impressive bulge she recognized from Bologna. The deep-throated laugh and musky cologne were familiar.

"Hello, Philippe," she said as her gaze reached his eyes, those chestnut-colored pools that made her chest quiver.

"May I?" Not waiting for a reply, he kicked back the empty chair, placed his beer on the table, and sat. They leaned into each other and he kissed her cheeks.

Having already exchanged small talk that morning at the spa, Telma dispensed with pleasantries. "Have you told Isa about us?"

His neck stiffened. "*Mais non.*" He described seeing Isa inside the Terme after his encounter with Telma in the lounge. "I've seen that look before. You don't talk to a charging lion. Did *you* say anything about us?"

Telma scoffed. "What would I say? Italian Rail has wonderful loos for shagging. Sorry, Philippe, no matter how hard I tried, I couldn't work that detail into our conversation."

He shrugged. "It's okay if you had, I guess. Isa and I aren't...really involved...romantically."

His words left wiggle room. "Define *really.*"

Philippe sat higher in his chair; a smirk formed on his lips and his eyes focused on Telma's. She'd seen that look before—uniquely male. He mistook her catty snooping into Isa's private life as interest in him. "Simmer down, Don Juan," she said. "I'm not going to scratch her eyes out over you. I'm just...*curious.*" A playful laugh informed her that he wasn't convinced. *Fine!* He'd share more if he thought his story fanned her jealousy.

He swigged his beer before speaking, "Sure we're fuck buddies, now and then. We each have needs—nothing more—no emotional shit."

Philippe's story veered from his history with Isa to pheromones, primal urges, and the program for wayward souls called Lighthouse about which Kate and Brigid argued the prior night. Telma looked over his shoulder. Luca Caruso, a most-interesting man, plodded toward her hotel, his head down, shoulders slumped. His confident swagger had vanished. He carried a cellophane bouquet of flowers. Instead of holding them like a tribute, he dangled them from one hand like a rotting fish.

"Telma...Telma," Philippe said, repeating her name. She turned to him but his eyes wandered to where her gaze had been. They both watched Luca disappear into the hotel. "Poor, crazy fool." Philippe spoke, his tone lacking empathy.

"Know him?" she asked, studying his face.

"*Mais oui.* And by your stare and dreamy joyride, I'd say you do too... or want to."

A blowjob in Bologna and the man thinks he knows me. Perhaps he does. Telma hoped her warming cheeks went unnoticed. "He's merely my neighbor. Has the room next to mine."

Philippe smirked. "Fat lady with a moustache has the room next to me—don't see me swooning over her."

Telma raised her eyebrows. "The weekend's young."

"*Touché.*"

She nodded toward the hotel. "Well, I confess I do find Signor Caruso *interesting.*"

"If only Isa did. That's the poor bastard's problem." Philippe took a gulp of beer. "Was a time, she was, as you say, smitten with him. Back and forth, back and forth."

Telma wouldn't have to wait for Jamie. Philippe could be squeezed for juicy gossip. She grabbed her wine and sat back. "What are you waiting for? Fill me in...every sordid, passionate, erotic detail."

For the randy Frenchman, sex was a contact sport. He spoke about it like most Englishmen talked about cricket and automobiles. Luca, she learned, owned chic restaurants in Covent Garden and Bayswater. He met Isa as she embarked upon her singing folly. With Isa walled off after Christina's death, Luca couldn't find a path to reconcile for months. "Today, he's a lovesick Romeo," Philippe summarized with a shrug.

"And Isa?"

He scoffed. "*Une femme.* Doesn't know what she wants—silly fool. Last concert, she was distraught he didn't show. This time, treats him like *merde.* And in between, it's kiss, fight, kiss, fight. For *moi,* too much trouble—move on."

Hours before when she met Luca, he brushed her aside because of high expectations for a rendezvous with Isa. From the downcast expression worn on his return, Luca was primed for consolation. Nothing would drive Isa into fits quicker than to see Telma drawing in her friends...and lovers. At best, Telma would drive her rival mad with envy; at worst she'd be the catalyst that brought Isa and Luca Caruso together—redemption of sorts. *Jealousy is as old as opera, and oh, what fun!*

Telma peppered Philippe with questions. After revealing more of Luca's unrequited love, he identified characters in Isa's real-life opera: her flamboyant mentor, Leech; the indomitable dragon, Lady Blatherwicke; and the handsome and quietly influential accompanist, Malcolm. Philippe filled in details about Isa's missing co-star—former stripper and current darling of Covent Garden, Irene "Ivy" Vine.

"The most colorful characters are off stage," he added with a wink. Before excusing himself, Philippe squeezed her hand. "Do sit with me at the concert."

Despite joy with yet another concert invite, Telma was noncommittal. "By the way," she added in a casual tone, "feel free to tell Isa that you're dying to get me in the sack." *Why not hit Isa with every piece of ammunition I have? A shock and awe campaign to wipe her out before she knows what hit her.*

"You little minx. Or better yet, piranha," Philippe said before walking away.

The young communista strolled to Telma's table and waved a piece of paper in her face. "From a man," she said coyly. "Phoned hotel—knew you'd be here."

As she reached for the note, the girl pulled it to her chest. Telma groaned. "Money?"

"*Sì*, the signor, he say you give me five euro for my trouble."

"Oh, for heaven's sake," Telma grumbled, grabbing her purse. After fishing out the ransom, the girl read the note to her. Jamie was detained—a crisis involving Willy Epson. He'd pick Telma up at nine.

"Wait!" Telma shouted to the retreating communista. The girl trudged back and stood over the table, arms crossed. "Sit!" Telma snapped. "Five euros should buy me five minutes." Ignoring the girl's exaggerated huff and puff, Telma fumbled in her purse for pen and paper. She scribbled a note. "Give this to Signor Caruso."

The girl glared; hands remained in her lap.

Telma sighed. "Please, *per favore*." The girl remained still. "Oh, for Christ's sake!" Telma reached into her purse for another five euros and slid the banknote across the table.

Snatching up the note and money, the girl spoke in a sugary voice, "*Grazie, signora.* My pleasure."

Telma called after her, "Feel free to correct my grammar."

The girl's fingers brushed under her chin—universal for *screw you*—before she waved Telma's handwritten note in the air. As the girl disappeared into the hotel, Telma was ever more convinced she'd found a new drinking buddy.

Not ten minutes later, Luca Caruso hurried out the hotel's front door and turned toward the Tazza d'Oro. He'd abandoned his jacket but the dress slacks and cuff-linked shirt were the same he wore earlier. Dabbing a tissue into the Chardonnay, Telma pressed it to her eye and stared down at the table.

"How can I help, Miss Rossi?" He sounded winded when he reached her side.

Telma motioned him to the empty chair without looking up. The waiter scurried over but Luca attempted to shoo him away.

"Please," she said, looking at him for the first time and affecting a sad expression. "Won't you stay for one? I hate to drink alone. I'm just so…" She stopped to sniffle.

Telma saw surrender in his dark eyes as he turned to the waiter. "Campari and soda with a twist, *per favore.*"

Telma produced a weak, pathetic smile. "*Grazie,* Signor Caruso."

"Luca, please." He sat down in the empty chair.

She patted his hand. "Call me Telma. I insist."

"Your message sounded desperate. How can I help?"

"Forever the white knight—always rushing to my aid. It's just that I'm alone—weepy." Telma dabbed her eyes hoping he wouldn't notice the wine's aroma.

"I don't mean to pry."

"No, no, please. I wanted you to come. Ask anything."

"What happened? Why are you crying?" His deep, melodic voice was rich with concern.

"My sister died."

He gasped; his hand reached for hers. "So very sorry. What a shock. And you alone in a strange town. Was it sudden, unexpected?"

"No, no. Nothing like that."

"Thank heavens. But it's still hard. Did you only just get word?"

Telma shook her head. "She died two years ago."

"Oh!" He straightened up.

Telma acted fast. She pressed her chest. "Happened right here in San Benedetto. I came as a pilgrimage. Never had the chance to say good-bye…didn't expect the emotion to hit so hard." She squeezed his hand and waited—the moment of truth. He didn't pull away. Instead, his other hand caressed her shoulder.

He shook his head. "Grief can bubble to the surface like a dormant volcano. I'm very sorry. What can I do?"

"Just being here—someone I can talk to. You don't mind?"

"Certainly not. Truth is, your note was a godsend. I needed fresh air… and a drink. In a way, you rescued me."

She leaned over and kissed his cheek. "I'm so glad. You're such a kind man. But I sense that comes at a cost."

"A cost?"

"People take advantage of kindness. Assume it's a bottomless well." A quiet nod told Telma she hit her mark. "You seem like a man who gives much and gets little in return."

Luca's shoulders relaxed; his eyes warmed with gratitude. He sighed as his drink arrived.

Telma smiled. He was hers.

Chapter 26

"Dazzlin'!"

Besides his hearty exclamation, Jamie greeted Telma with handclaps and whistles as she stepped out from the elevator and into the lobby of her hotel. With lifted palm, he halted their embrace before spinning an inverted index finger. She whirled around on command, spinning on the balls of new, cherry-red sandals. The spaghetti-strap dress proved too short for a full flourish, but its black silk hem lifted as she made the turn. She checked her hair in the hall mirror to make sure the French twist hadn't come undone.

Jamie's chest, well defined under an open-buttoned shirt, heaved as he inhaled. "Mmm. Smellin' as good as ya look, lassie."

With a hand on her hip, Telma shifted her weight from one leg to the other. "Chanel gets all the credit."

"Fuck Chanel! Your mum and dad gave the world a goddess."

"A plastic surgeon in Mayfair gets some credit." Telma threw her arms around his shoulders, kissing him on the lips until his cheeks reddened.

Telma glanced around the lobby. "Hope I didn't keep you waiting."

"No worries, love." His eyes moved from Telma to the young communista who stood behind the counter, partially hidden by a vase of summer flowers. "Gave me time for a lovely chat with pretty little Svetlana." *So that's her name.*

"Enlightening, I'm sure." Taking a few steps, Telma peered into the lounge—white laminate, acrylic glass, and red leather. *No wonder this horrid little room is always empty.*

"Shall we?" Jamie said, bending his elbow as an invitation to tuck in her arm.

She batted him away. "Must wait for both my boys."

"*Boys!* You say, *boys?*" Jamie exclaimed, eyebrows pulsing. "Guessin' you're not meanin' me and my one-eyed trouser mouse."

Stifling a laugh, Telma lifted her chin to affect a regal tone. "If you hadn't stood me up this afternoon, I'd be all yours. Now, you must share."

He seethed. "Best not mention this blasted afternoon just yet. Who's this bloody trespasser?"

As his question simmered in the air, Telma opened her clutch purse and retrieved the compact and "Scarlet Nights" lipstick. Did Jamie know Luca? She'd find out soon enough. In the meantime, she let Jamie stew.

"A dashing Italian," she finally said, resting her purse on the counter and opening the mirror and lipstick tube. "Sweetheart and a gentleman. Spent hours together this afternoon. Gave him a shoulder to cry on."

"Bet ya did."

She ignored the sarcasm. After applying lipstick, Telma looked from the mirror to the young communista. "Svetlana, has Signor Caruso come down yet?"

The girl nodded; a trace of a smirk formed on her lips. "*Sì*, signora."

Telma glanced out the front door and window. "Well," she said, turning toward the girl. "Where is he?"

The girl's eyes became animated. "Signor Caruso apologizes. He won't be joining you this evening—another engagement."

Telma's heart raced. Her lipstick tube and makeup mirror clattered onto the counter. She leaned forward on both hands. "When did he leave?"

The girl turned from Telma to the vase; her fingers pulled and tucked lupines and hydrangeas. "Twenty…thirty minutes ago—he needed a florist."

So, Luca ran back to Isa the first chance he got.

Jamie roared with laughter; he slapped the counter. "Looks like you're stuck with me and the trouser mouse."

Maintaining a stoneface, Telma looked from his toothy-grin down to his crotch. She quoted Robert Burns. "And, a wee, sleekit, cow'rin, tim'rous beastie, it is."

Telma decided not to let the dashing Italian's timidity and retreat back to Isa ruin her evening. With a hunky Scotsman on her arm and a slinky dress, she'd command a grand entrance with or without Luca

Caruso. A boisterous contingent anticipated her arrival—the Dubliners and the gays from America.

Telma always attracted gay men—something about being a strong woman, she'd been told. Telma Rossi stood on the pedestal alongside Princess Diana, Evita, and Madonna. While her fiancé's own fascination with gay icons gave her pause, Graham's millions pressed the fast-forward button toward matrimony. They could sort out his sexuality and Judy Garland record collection later.

Jamie and Telma walked arm-in-arm through the bustling town center. Friday night revelers filled the pedestrian zone. Cafés and restaurants buzzed with activity. Jamie and Telma, as was their custom, teased each other.

Telma glanced at Jamie's pants. "Depriving the world of your gorgeous legs, are you?"

"Savin' the kilt for tomorrow night, love. Don't want to spoil the birds," he said with a growl. "Besides, couldn't stomach the competition. Your wee, sexy number leaves nothin' to the imagination." He dropped his arm, reached behind, and cupped her ass.

Jamie didn't have to tell her they were close. Around the corner, cackles, chatter, and the clatter of glass heralded a festive atmosphere. Clutching Jamie's hand as they passed the closed grates of a fine jewelry store, Telma took a deep breath. Appetite-stirring aromas—garlic, onions, roasted meats, vegetables—teased her nose.

Her mind flew to fantasy. Her entrance triggering a hush; eyes turned in panic. Silence thickens until lightning clears the charged air. Thunderclaps boom, heralding the arrival of Isa who rises from the heart of the crowd, a green and black gown flapped by a furious wind. With fiery eyes under Medusa locks, Isa thrusts forth an accusatory finger and bellows with fiendish vibrato, *Death to she, who dares defy my banishment decree.*

With Jamie tugging her arm, Telma dismissed the vision with a laugh. She prepared for the showdown. While her clutch purse didn't contain pepper spray, her mind carried an arsenal of invectives to debilitate.

The restaurant was one of many on the swanky street. Most offered *al fresco* dining in large seating areas segregated by latticed corrals and colorful canopies strung with white lights. Manicured flowerbeds sweetened the air and ornamental trees softened the clamor. The sound of an accordion and strings infused the night air with romance.

The voices of Kate and Brigid rose above the rest. Their shrieks of laughter hit octaves to stoke a soprano's envy. As Telma and Jamie entered the terrace, the Dubliners' faces shone like winter moons under shocks of red hair. Jamie nodded toward Brigid, words trembling from his lips. "Aye, there's that ginger lass. The she-devil stalked me somethin' awful at the last concert. Wanderin' hands and twitchy fingers."

Telma snickered, pleased that Jamie found himself on the cheeky end of an ass-grab. Tommy Evers and Miguel sat at the Dubliners' table along with a little man who looked as if he'd been dipped in a bath of Easter egg dye.

"That's Leech," Jamie said. "Odd little bird, but as loyal to Isa as water is to whiskey."

The business school contingent preened with pretension at a far table. The Novaks looked too perfect with white-toothed smiles and upmarket haircuts. Square-jawed and tanned, Brad bantered with a politician's confidence. Silky-haired Alexandra, in dress of blue floral and red linen jacket, looked like a campaign prop—patriotic red, blonde, and blue. They caressed, nodded, and laughed giving every outward sign of marital bliss. Assessing the battlefield, Telma doubted whether Alexandra would assist Isa in a skirmish. The icy bitch preferred to scheme behind the frontline in order to keep her flawless claws unsoiled.

At the same table, Vicki Epson sat in blissful ignorance, looking happy and radiant. The understated elegance of her cream-colored shift came, Telma guessed, at great cost from a top designer in Rome or Paris. Her husband Willy, with sleeked-back hair and black silk shirt, reminded Telma of a shoe salesman. A creased face and puffy eyes made him appear every bit his age, twice that of his wife. Vicki smiled when she saw them, offering a half wave before elbowing her husband. Willy looked first to Telma, then to Jamie. She sensed the Scotsman bristle. Willy picked up his wineglass and returned, a bit more agitated, to the conversation at his table.

"Bastard's lucky to have his manly bits," Jamie muttered.

Telma grabbed his hand and led him from confrontation to the merrier mood of the Dubliners and gays. She scanned the terrace for Isa and her family. Every table brimmed with boisterous people. Philippe worked the crowd like a hawk, swooping from one innocent target to another. For whom would he reserve his talons? And where was Isa? She got sketchy answers in response to questions about their hostess' whereabouts. Some didn't know. Some pointed to chairs she had since vacated. Others claimed she was in the toilet. Still others said she went home in a rage, angered by Ivy's cancellation.

Leech looked up from his conversation. Wisps of lavender hair, the consistency of cotton candy, covered a cue-ball head. "I sent the diva home with takeaway." The odd little man wore peach-colored Capri pants and a turquoise silk tunic gathered at the waist with a gold-looped belt.

Tommy shouted from the other end of the table. "The show must go on."

Leech nodded, his expression quite serious. "Don't want a repeat of last time. The night air's too raw for her fragile voice."

"We're mere slaves and gypsies," Brigid cackled, hoisting a glass of wine. "We can carouse and cavort till we're hoarse—probably better for the audience if we were."

The table erupted in laughter as it did every few seconds. When the exuberance lulled, Kate spoke. "Pity, you just missed Isa. Her gentleman friend escorted her and Ana."

"Gentleman friend?" Jamie asked.

"Ya know, darlin', the fella who fancies her," Kate responded.

Brigid's eyes disappeared behind tiny slits as she bobbed her head. "Everyone knows that the poor fool's been bitten by the love-bug… everyone, that is, 'cept Isa herself."

"Ya mean ole pasta pusher, Luca," Jamie said.

Kate nodded. "That's the one, lovesick Luca Caruso."

"*Caruso!*" Jamie exclaimed. "You're tellin' me he's Signor Luca *Caruso?*"

Jamie didn't see the faces at the table react with quizzical looks to his bellow. Apparently he never knew Luca's surname. With eyes blazing, he tugged Telma close and whispered in her ear, "Ya wee devil. You're playin' with fire."

Telma replied with a smirk before dipping onto the empty chair between Leech and Brigid. Jamie moved toward an empty seat.

"No!" Kate shouted, wagging a finger at him. "That one's taken."

"For our fearless leader," Brigid added with a purr. "Gaby's takin' a pee—" Her shriek stopped her in mid-sentence. With a pained expression, she reached down and rubbed her shin.

"Mind yourself!" Kate said with a scowl from across the table.

Brigid mumbled expletives before blurting, "Lady Blatherwicke's takin' a piss. That better? Blasted English and their bloody, la-di-da titles."

As they howled with laughter, Tommy and Miguel rose from the table to greet Telma. Both said they were happy she decided to come. When Telma asked about Danny, Tommy whispered in her ear that he'd tell her later.

The merry atmosphere dampened when news circulated that Papa Fabrini was in hospital, a mere precaution they said. Isa's cousin from Oklahoma delivered a welcome toast on behalf of the family. He ended his speech with words of encouragement dictated by Papa Fabrini from his hospital bed. "I prefer Italian opera but let me paraphrase a Russian—*sing and dance this magical weekend and forget about our dignity.*" Teary-eyed, the crowd erupted with whoops and cheers before settling in for dinner.

The food was simple: platters of artichokes, olives, salamis, and cheeses followed by ravioli, lemon chicken, fish in a sauce of white wine and capers, and mixed salad. Wine was plentiful and laughter continued late into the night.

Those who signed up for the chorus were especially giddy. Most had never sung before in public. Three rehearsals holed up in the opera house had bonded the giggling Pavarottis and Sutherlands with an *esprit de corps.* They didn't complain about the hot, stuffy opera house or the hours of repetitive drills under the dragon lady's imposing stick. Instead, they spoke of Leech, Lady Blatherwicke, Malcolm, and Isa with reverence—masters and magicians who readied them for debuts on an authentic Italian opera house stage. In another place or time, Telma might have dismissed the exuberance as amateur-hour boasts, but on this special evening, their delight was infectious.

The mood reminded her of the *joie de vivre* captured by Renoir in his painting of a boating party at an outdoor café. When she was a lonely child, the piece mesmerized her. She sat for hours clutching the library's art book in her hands. How easy it was to disappear into the gaiety, wishing for a joyous life filled with friends.

That night at the restaurant, Telma tasted morsels of that *joie de vivre.* But something rang false. Did she belong? Isa's banishment decree left a bitter taste. But with the diva at home nursing her voice, and her immediate family with Papa Fabrini at hospital, Telma enjoyed a temporary stay of her sentence…at least for one night.

As the evening wore on, she noticed a subtle shift in Jamie. The usually exuberant Scotsman became sullen. After throwing back several glasses of wine, he turned to whiskey. The way he glowered at Willy scared her. She would have gladly cheered, even wagered on a good old barroom brawl, but Jamie's grimace signaled more murder than mayhem. Telma took advantage of Kate's departure for the toilet to insert herself beside the Scotsman. Squeezing Jamie's arm, she drew his stare away from Willy. "You still owe me five euros."

"What?"

"Your darling Svetlana said you promised five euros to deliver your message this afternoon. Pay up!" Telma said, holding out a palm. "One way or another."

He whistled into the air. "Why that crafty fox! All I said was, we'd both be mighty appreciative. Said nothin' about money." His tone turned somber. "But sorry to disappoint you, love. Can't get ale from a dry barrel."

She pushed her chair back from the table and brought her head closer to his. "What's going on?" she whispered. "What's happened with Willy?"

He sighed. "It's bad, very bad. Shouldn't be dumpin' my problems on you, love, 'specially tonight. But you've heard I invested heavily with Willy?"

"Yes! And spending like a fool—a big flat in London, holiday home in France, and a new Ferrari awaiting you when you leave San Benedetto."

He groaned. "I'm a damned fool. There's no Ferrari in my future, only a one-way bus ride to the poor house," he grumbled. "Foolish, stupid, greedy."

"Can I help? Can Walter?" she asked, guessing Jamie was too proud to take money from friends.

He squeezed her hand. "Thanks, love. But I can't take charity." With head bowed, he looked as if he could cry. She'd never seen him so distressed. She put her arm around him. He attempted a smile that collapsed into a frown. "Wish I were the only victim, the only one snared by my stupidity."

"What do you mean?"

He shook his head and pursed his lips. Internal struggle played out in his eyes. Would he keep his secret or share the burden?

"Tell me what's wrong. I insist."

His chest heaved with a heavy sigh. "The bloody concert. I'm the underwriter. Now that I'm broke, Isa won't be able to pay the theater fees or the musicians."

"Perhaps Brad or Willy could—"

Jamie groaned, interrupting her. "Bastard Willy's as tapped out as I am and Brad's been pressin' the flesh for campaign donations."

"There must be something you can do…perhaps a collection?" As Telma spoke, Jamie's face flushed; his shoulders slumped. Even she understood that such an announcement would be an embarrassing admission for Jamie, a blow to his big heart and ego. She kissed him, branding his cheek with Scarlet Nights.

"Gotta break the news to Isa," he said, "that the show won't go on!"

Chapter 27

Telma rolled out of bed, rubbing her throbbing temples. What possessed her to think she could drink all night? The gays drank for fun, the Dubliners out of habit, and Jamie, she guessed, to numb his brain before he told Isa about losing the concert funds.

Telma didn't take advantage of her one chance to escape the hangover. After dinner, she excused herself to ring up Walter and Graham only to get her fiancé's blasted mother again. Then, instead of tucking herself into bed, pleasure trumped reason. She hurried back to the party that had moved on to the first in a string of bars.

A bloody church clock chimed six times somewhere outside the hotel window as she threw on jeans and a cotton jumper. *Whoever heard of an Italian business opening at sunrise?* The young communista, no doubt, tapped into a sadistic vein when she secured the ungodly early salon appointment. Only middle-class housewives, insomniacs, and working fools got hair done before lunch.

"Sorry, signora," Svetlana had said in response to Telma's groan. "Booking had to be early. Owner has special engagement rest of day. She open special... just for you."

"Hurray!" Telma responded, stifling the urge to scream, *Oh fuck*.

San Benedetto greeted Telma with another cloudless morning. Light that inspired the world's greatest artists graced her with a celestial blue Raphael sky. Stucco facades of rose, peach, and apricot hues glimmered in the dawn. The drowsy town freed songbirds to rehearse in peace and flowering trees to sweeten the air without assault from carbon-belching engines. For all that natural beauty, Telma wanted nothing more than aspirin, sunglasses, and caffeine.

In her quest for the perfect cappuccino, she stumbled upon the weekend market, a hodge-podge of caravans and makeshift stalls crowded onto the high street. A shabby trailer with drawn blinds advertised a psychic. Besides the sleeping gypsy and eager vendors, Telma counted only a handful of customers, surely transients or midnight laborers. She snaked through offerings of tawdry crafts, soaps, jewelry, sweets, and savories. Peddlers of cheese and cured meats were everywhere; locals exalted prosciutto and Parmesan as deities. Her nose picked up a scent that led her to a handsome pair of Dutch brothers who specialized in crepes, waffles, and, as she learned, weak, tepid latte.

Continuing through the empty streets, she cursed Svetlana, the salon's accommodating owner, and anyone else for that matter who popped into her pounding head. She was entrusting her hair to a stylist in a provincial outpost like San Benedetto. She prayed the spa attracted a clientele that elevated the sophistication of local services. Svetlana assured her of the salon's reputation as the *bestest* in town. Locals and returning visitors, Svetlana alleged, sought out the owner who agreed to the early Saturday appointment. The testimonial provided small comfort—Telma resigned herself to emerge from the salon looking like a peasant or prostitute.

The shop with the pretentious name, Salon Venus de Milo, looked adequate from the outside. Inside, Telma found a gaudy showcase of chrome, glass, and a rainbow of leathers—a failed experiment in modern chic. Telma laughed at the irony; had Venus retained her limbs, she would have fled the salon with her arms flailing in the air. One consolation—the shop was tidy.

"*Benvenuto. Signora Rossi, sì?*" The small woman who greeted her had excessive eye makeup, perfect circles of rouge, and pitch-black hair adorned with a magenta-colored scarf.

In her foggy mental state, Telma's native tongue surfaced

"*Mi scusi, signora.* No Spanish…little bit English." She held her hands to her chest and bobbed her head.

Telma nodded. "*Perfetto. Mi, piccolo Italiano,* but English, *sì,* yes."

"Open just for you," the woman said as Telma glanced around the empty shop. She guided her to the styling chair. "Svetlana say… *un'emergenza.* Say you pay extra."

Telma sighed as she pondered the young communista's economic manifesto—rob from the bitch and give to the poor. Instead of protesting, she nodded and smiled. No good came from arguing with a woman who held Telma's fate, not to mention hair, fingers, and toes, in her hands.

After the woman spun her around to face the mirror, Telma cringed. Without a full night's sleep or makeup, she looked ghastly. She might have explained the reason for her condition if only she had the energy or language skills. Besides, the woman's overindulgence in perfume on top of the acrid salon odors aggravated Telma's headache.

"What you want? Bit of cleanup around edges?"

"No, I'm hoping for something striking…*differente, bellissima.*"

Raising an eyebrow, the woman studied Telma's face in the mirror. Fingers pulsed through her hair. "You no Penelope Cruz," she said. "But good structure—high cheek bones, full lips, okay nose."

In scrutinizing the face, the professional beautician probably guessed that the fine features were products of surgery. No matter. She'd soon discover scars from several facelifts.

She pointed to posters of hairstyle models on the salon's walls. "Anything you like?"

As Telma scanned the shop, framed photographs on the wall next to the mirror drew her eyes. Isa's image gazed back at her—photos from the concert. Two were stage shots of Isa in full costume and makeup. The effect looked surprisingly professional for an amateur production. Perhaps Telma had underestimated Isa. A third photo contained an autograph in thick black marker—*Per Maria, con amore e grazie, Isa.* In that picture, most likely from the post-concert dinner, the diva looked positively stunning in an indigo-colored gown with hair done up like a film star. Isa's broad smile radiated confidence and joy. The same things she saw in Isa's face at the Terme.

Telma choked up. In addition to images of Isa's family and Leech, a photo also featured her sister. Gazing adoringly at Isa, Christina looked stunning…and happy. That picture captured the last night of her sister's life. No one could deny Christina's natural beauty, her kinship with the Fabrinis…or her fierce devotion to Isa. Telma considered her own life—a mere shadow to Christina's vibrancy. Yet somehow, Telma's short time in San Benedetto had already bathed her in comforting light.

The stylist caught her staring at the photo. "You want to look like that…like Isa the diva?"

Telma flinched. "No!" As beautiful as Isa looked, Telma wanted to be the antithesis of Isabella Fabrini. She motioned toward the autograph. "You Maria?"

"*Sì, sì,* I'm Maria."

"Well, dear Maria, I want something different…opposite. *Capisce?*"

"*Sì, sì.* Trust me, okay?"

Do I have a choice? Was the grin on Maria's face a sign of mischief or creative genius? Svetlana's words, *leave everything to me,* popped into her head. But Telma merely nodded as the stylist grabbed a shawl from the coat hook and covered the mirror. "We have fun. You no peek," she said, hands punctuating the air for emphasis.

Maria's enthusiasm surged, no doubt excited by the challenge and artistic license. Local clients, Telma guessed, weren't daring. She observed that the mature women of the town wanted the dark, full-haired look of Sophia Loren in her prime. Those in their middle years favored a narrow range of conservative cuts and colors while young women sported modern styles and bold shades that looked like cheap, do-it-yourself jobs.

Maria prodded Telma from styling chair to washbasin and dryer with intermittent stops back to the chair in what seemed like random sequencing. Telma hoped there was method to her madness. "Okay with color? Okay with cut? Okay with highlights?" Maria rattled off questions in Italian and broken English without waiting for a reply. Telma merely nodded, smiled…and prayed.

From the dryer where a timid young thing polished Telma's toes and fingernails as she recovered from her hangover, Maria moved her to the chair for final styling. In that captive seat, Telma was cowed into submission by the clack of scissors, as Maria conducted her interrogation.

"Where from?"

"London."

"Married?"

"Engaged," Telma answered, waving Graham's large diamond.

"You no happy with him?"

Telma flinched. "No, I mean yes. I'm happy, very happy with my fiancé."

Maria's eyebrows rose. "If you say so. Bigger the ring, smaller the … expectation."

Before Telma knew it, she confessed her mission to Rome to seek an annulment, Graham's insipidness, and her frustration with his domineering mother. Maria listened to her story without comment, adding strategic sighs, groans, gasps, and chuckles to keep her going—a skilled psychologist...and hairdresser.

"Make sure you happy," she said after Telma finished the story. "*Domani,* tomorrow may not come." A piercing look from Maria's dark eyes emphasized the point before she changed the subject. "Svetlana say you go to concert, no?"

"Wouldn't miss it."

"*Sì, sì,*" Maria said. "I know Isa since she little girl...since before her father move family to Argentina. She good girl, good daughter, but now she thinks she's a big star."

"And the singing, it's good?"

Maria's expression said one thing, her words quite another. "*Bene, bene,* fine, fine."

"You're such a good friend," Telma said. "I heard the concert was... adequate, or better put...*amateur.*" The wheels of criticism needed greasing.

"*Sì, sì,* amateur. Means not good enough to get paid?" After Telma nodded, Maria continued, "I know only little music but," she said, bringing her mouth closer and whispering, "Isa's singing...it hurt my ears."

"Such a good friend! You may think that, but you'd never say such a thing to Isa. Am I right?"

"*Sì, sì, signora.* I think singing not good, but not tell anyone...anyone who'd repeat to Isa, I mean."

Telma affected a sympathetic expression. "A true friend—*una buona amica.*" She pointed to the photos of Isa. "Your masterpiece speaks to your loyalty. You love Isa, despite her lack of..."

Maria sighed; a look of contentment on her face. "*Grazie, signora. Capisce...*you understand, you understand." The acknowledgment was all Maria needed to unlock her treasure trove of gossip. As she pulled, pushed, and tucked Telma's hair with scissors, comb, and fingers, her mouth roared with the horsepower of a Lamborghini. She served up, and Telma devoured, every morsel of backstage intrigue of Isa's not-so-grand debut two years earlier.

With tears in her eyes, Maria spoke of Isa's father with saintly reverence. Crossing herself, she described his sudden trip to hospital the prior day. She called it a weak heart but didn't know his condition. "Isa's mama, tell me that Isa's papa, make everyone swear concert not stopped. Say he only get sicker if Isa no enjoy herself. She must sing with all her heart…so much so that he hear her at hospital." She dabbed her eyes.

Maria told how Papa Fabrini rescued the imploding first concert. "A miracle!" she bellowed in Telma's ear. Gazing up to the plaster-popcorn ceiling, she recounted Isa's return to the stage that night. "Only one explanation for such beautiful notes…a miracle."

Telma pressed her heart, feigning empathy with a sigh. "Too little, too late. Utter catastrophe. Poor, poor thing."

"*Sì, sì.* Felt so sorry for poor girl and her parents, dear people. Audience showed pity…applauded," she said with a shrug. "For months, people talked, called concert success." Her face took on a sympathetic expression as her tone became somber. "But, think praise had more to do with that poor girl's death—tragic." She pointed to the photograph. "Beautiful woman…beautiful spirit. Isa's dearest friend. Christina…her name, I think. Doctor from Buenos Aires."

Maria described how Christina saved the concert…encouraging Isa, holding her hand, donating money. "And then, brain clot. Isa go into fit of depression. Stayed in San Benedetto months before go back London. Stop singing for long time."

Telma recalled her reaction to Christina's death. Had she shed one tear before flying home for the funeral? Even then, were her tears genuine or merely a reaction to the sobs of her father and scores of distraught mourners? While she lived, her older sister outpaced Telma in life, love, and accomplishment. With an untimely death, Christina pulled away and sprinted across the finish line, proclaimed a saint by all who knew her. What was the point of still running when Telma had already lost the race?

The sound of scissors snipping near her ears brought Telma's mind back to the salon as Maria spoke. "Tonight, our big star returns. I'll be at opera house all afternoon and night."

"There'd be no concert without you, Maria. People in the shadows never get applause." Telma clapped her hands.

The stylist's rouged cheeks blushed redder. "*Grazie, signora.* Gotta make Isa look gorgeous. Shame other singer cancel. Had funny name… Ivy Vine. Soprano, professional, paid performer. Could have carried the show."

"Cancelled!" Telma exclaimed, pretending not to know the story. "Bet Isa's panicked, and on top of her father's health. Wouldn't be surprised if she turned to liquor and pills."

Maria's hand flew to her mouth. "*Mio Dio*. Poor Isa."

For the next half hour, Maria snipped, tucked, combed, smoothed, puffed, and gossiped. As the shop came alive with other stylists and customers, she said, "We booked with chorus ladies all morning...before last rehearsal."

"Concert's good for the locals?"

"*Sì, sì*. My girls busy all afternoon doing hair for women going to concert. Hotels, restaurants all busy too. Singing bad for ears, but good for business," she added with a hearty laugh.

Maria took a step backward to scrutinize her work. Telma studied her face for a clue. Lips pursed and forehead creased giving Telma pause. Despite Maria's magnificent creations for Isa's first concert, she was nervous.

The stylist's hands flew to her cheeks. "*Mio Dio! Mio Dio!*"

Chatter in the salon ceased; eyes turned to them. Telma's stomach soured; she held her breath. *My God, my God* wasn't a welcome reaction from plastic surgeons, first-time lovers, or beauticians.

"What's wrong?" Telma's gaze moved to the shrouded mirror. Did she want to see?

Maria clapped her hands with a beaming her smile. "*Bellissima!*" The other clients nodded in agreement. "*Mi scusi*," she added. "For one moment, I get shocked."

Shocked! Another terrifying word from a beautician.

"You twin of Isa's friend, doctor who died." She pulled the shawl from the mirror.

Telma gasped. Staring back at her was Christina—the pretty, fair-haired daughter with the striking contrast of dark Latin features and blonde hair. Telma hadn't realized how the plastic surgeons had molded her into the image of her sister. Was that her subconscious wish? Maria's bold transformation from brunette to blonde made it clear. The stylist pulled the photo from the wall and paraded it around the shop before pushing it into Telma's face. "Like you, *sì*?"

Before Telma could respond, the shop's front door swung open, rattling wall sconces, and shaking framed photos, jars, and bottles. Her peripheral vision caught the shadow of a brawny man.

"You're bloody wonderful, absolutely wonderful." She recognized the thick Scottish accent. When Maria moved from her side, Telma saw an animated Jamie Stuart. "Svetlana said I'd find you here. You're bloody wonderful, absolutely won—" He stopped—his eyes widened, and his head tilted.

"Christ! Am I that dreadful?"

He stammered, "Y-you're bloody g-gorgeous, lassie. Ya look just like—"

"I know…Christina," she said, interrupting him. "Maria showed me." She had not wanted to reveal her connection to Isa in that incubator of gossip. "Stop gawking." She spoke to Jamie but could have been addressing the entire salon. The clacking hens fell mute as they ogled the hunky Scotsman whose jeans and T-shirt bulged in the right places.

"Ya coy little minx. Opera house and restaurant rang me up. Got paid up…in full…*from London*. Everything's covered including the musicians." He hugged Maria, before leaning down and giving Telma a passionate kiss. "There's more where that came from, Miss Bloody Wonderful Anonymous."

Telma remained stonefaced. "Whatever are you talking about?"

Chapter 28

Why had I done it? Why did I call Walter and demand that he salvage Isa's concert?

Telma recalled their prior night's conversation, after she rushed from the pre-concert dinner still digesting Jamie's stunning confession. Unlike Graham with whom she still hadn't connected since arriving in Italy two days prior, her ex-husband answered on the first ring. Telma didn't have to push hard. The same guilt that nipped at her conscience from time to time haunted Walter. No doubt, his was a more severe case. He was, after all, the fiancé, lover, friend who broke Isa's heart. Maybe he viewed the bailout as penance, a down payment on his own redemption.

He groaned over the phone at Telma's insistence on anonymity for the charitable act. "You don't have to make a splash," he said, "but couldn't you, with utmost discretion, disclose our generosity? Let it slip out, like a weather report, or time of day."

Walter insisted upon spotlights and applause. Exceptions included questionable business deals and scandalous affairs. His church, the ballet, symphonies, art galleries, and other recipients of his charity understood his childish need for public affirmation. Telma blamed the obsession on a harsh father, a strict Presbyterian minister who favored the strap over praise and affection. Walter P. Benchley didn't attend Saint Martin's on a regular basis—he didn't have to. His private pew sat through every service with a shiny brass plaque proudly promoting the piety of its absent benefactor.

Walter donated just enough, not a single pound more, to ensure that his name appeared as a top-tier donor among program acknowledgments. He didn't enjoy cultural performances, attending only when he perceived a benefit such as an opportunity to hobnob with his bank's board and wealthy clients. Often, he slipped away at intermission after having mined all the benefit.

Telma scoffed into the phone, "A Good Samaritan? Heavens, no. A goody-two-shoes who takes in strays and opens her wallet for the slightest sob story? That's not me!"

Walter didn't go down without a fight. He tapped into the sarcasm that threaded the narrative of their marriage. His voice seethed into her ear. "For you, dear Telma, it's a question of authenticity. You've lived your life as a bitch. Kindness and sentimentality give you hives. Be honest, you want an opportunity to watch Isa sweat, and most likely fail, from the shadows of a box seat."

Telma didn't argue. She got her way. He agreed to sponsor the concert. He'd be pleased that Jamie, refusing to believe her denials at the hair salon, figured out Walter's part in the bailout.

But the question kept nagging her—why did *she* do it? She didn't even know herself. Certainly, Jamie's embarrassing predicament moved her, and the excitement of new friends singing in the chorus made her happy. Could she stand by and see their dreams squashed? As for bloody Isa, why did Telma care whether she sang or not? Walter was right; part of her wanted to see Isa flop—fall on her ass again. But Isa's fate was intertwined with that of her friends, people Telma liked...people who seemed to like her back. She didn't want to see them hurt. And selfishly, she was having too much bloody fun to let the weekend collapse. *Renoir's boating party must not sink.*

And possibly, Telma could parlay her benevolent gesture into goodwill with the Vatican official conducting the annulment interview. She fast-forwarded to the inquisition set for the following week. "Good deeds?" she'd exclaim, parroting the priest. "Why yes, your Holy Eminence. Since you ask, as a matter of fact, I aided an enemy. Bailed her bloody ass out of a tub of fucking hot water, I did." That morsel of charitable work should not only grease the annulment, but also reward her with a first-class suite in Paradise.

After the salon appointment and swearing Jamie to secrecy, Telma strolled back to the hotel. If jeans and cotton jumper garnered that many admirers, evening wear would make blonde Telma a knockout.

Danny Chance left an urgent message seeking a rendezvous at the Tazza d'Oro. She didn't have the heart to stand up the broken-hearted boy. His message repeated the word *Please*, a dozen times.

"Thank you, thank you, thank you for coming," Danny blurted, standing up from his seat at an outdoor table. He ogled her. "My God, you look amazing."

The peach-colored sundress was yet another purchase from the prior day's shopping spree. She twisted on the balls of her sandals, moving a hand to her hip. "This old thing?"

"Yes, no…I mean certainly." Danny blushed as he kissed her cheek. "Y-your hair, it's s-stunning, so s-sexy." He attempted to roar his approval but the high-pitched purr sounded less lion, more pussycat.

"You suggesting that going blonde will get me shagged?" she asked as they sat.

His eyebrow lifted. "Blonde, brunette, or bald, you don't have a problem in that area. But now you're a luscious do-over."

She cocked her head. "Do-over?"

He grinned. "Think *haute cuisine*. Leftovers are boring. But turn that boiled lobster into ravioli with truffle sauce or transform roasted quail into crepes with beurre blanc and it's a whole new ball game—an amazing do-over. Ooh-la-la."

"Despite the comparison to a doggy bag, I'll take that as a compliment."

He laughed. "If I were straight, I'd do you. That any better?"

She squeezed his hand. "Why Danny, you flatter me."

The waiter appeared. Danny asked for a prosciutto and cheese panini from the special board and an Italian beer. Telma ordered the caprese salad and a Pinot Grigio.

"They do say blonds have more fun." He tousled his hair. "Think it might work for me?" His face flashed a glint of humor, but his tone held a subtle hint of defeat. Tommy, Danny's favorite blond, told her the prior night that he revealed his new love.

"Missed you last night," Telma said as a way to dip her toes into the deep well of Danny's angst.

"Heart wasn't in it." He took a large gulp of beer.

"Sorry to hear. Love troubles?"

He looked at her with sad eyes. "Tommy introduced me to Miguel."

She pressed his hand. "I hope Tommy was kind."

Danny sighed. "Better he was an asshole. I could've walked away… comforted that I avoided romance with a shit heel. But Tommy's a real sweetheart. Always has been. Nothing like guys back home—heartless. In New York, size matters…apartment, stock portfolio, and penis."

Danny described his meeting with Tommy. Their conversation took place over drinks at the very table at which they now sat. "He came alone. Wasn't shy like the other times I tried to get him to open up. Came out to me before the cocktails arrived. His tongue twisted to get the words out." His heart leapt at Tommy's confession. He'd waited to hear his friend admit being gay since the two attended business school. "I was glued to Tommy's words. Would his acceptance open the door I fantasized about? Just as I had us moving into a love nest in Tribeca with matching pugs, a gorgeous boy appears. Before I could gasp at his good looks, he plants a kiss on Tommy's lips. And that's how I met Miguel."

Telma pictured the scene—wholesome Tommy baring his soul unaware of his friend's crush. An innocent confession lures Danny into a warm, gentle current of hope and passion. Then Miguel appears, and like a riptide pushes Danny hopelessly away from his dream. Her empathy for Danny surprised her.

"Don't know what's worse, the hot new boyfriend or the fact that Tommy went from gay newbie to partnered over one gin and tonic. I pined for that boy for more than a decade, for Christ's sake."

As he spoke, Telma spied Tommy and Miguel in the distance, over Danny's shoulder. Broad grins reflected the playful spirit of new love. She was happy for them, but didn't have the heart to tell Danny. She was relieved when they disappeared around a corner.

"Maybe I'll have to settle. Not everyone gets true love. I could be a gigolo."

She squelched an urge to laugh, snickering only after Danny did. For a split second she wondered if he were serious. "Pays well, but murder on the back," she said.

Who was she to judge? Wasn't she a gigolo…or worse? Gigolo, such a nice word compared to slut, hooker, or whore. Men always had an easier time of it; the word *gigolo* wasn't only lyrical, it sounded like a respectable profession complete with pension plan and health care.

She considered her situation. She was marrying Graham for his money, plain and simple. They had no spark, no sizzle. Sex with him was like diving into a bowl of leftover spaghetti—cold, clammy, colorless. But Graham satisfied her need for security, for being loved even if she didn't have the capacity to love another human being. The warranties on her surgeries wouldn't last forever. Sooner or later, the Grahams, Jamies, and even the Philippes of the world would swagger past without even a second glance. Sure, she could always find a gigolo but the lows after that kind of sex, those deplorable moments of self-loathing and regret, would only increase. Mirrors wouldn't lie—the passion merely a purchased commodity.

"Don't give up, Danny. You're smart, successful, and still young. Men have it so easy."

"Straight men do. In gay years, I'm an old dog."

Unfortunately, Telma couldn't sit and sing inspirational hymns to coax Danny from his funk. She had an urgent errand.

In preparing for her own debut at the San Benedetto Opera House, Telma selected her costume wisely. Her transformation into a blonde Venus required a last-minute adjustment. She had planned to wear a gown of deep purple accented with black lace. Isa, she knew, detested purple, preferring blues, reds, and greens. Concert photos on Maria's wall confirmed her suspicions. Those deep, bold colors complemented Isa's Italian complexion and thick, dark hair. Although thick stage makeup enhanced Isa's still striking features, the diva wasn't getting any younger. Vivid colors drew attention away from the flaws of a mature woman.

But her new look, courtesy of Maria, inspired her. She remembered that the boutique where she found the purple gown had another, better suited to the new her. She made the exchange and hurried back to the hotel.

She stared into the mirror, floored by her resemblance to her sister. Christina, however, would have chosen a simpler dress, something suited for a garden party. Pastels, her palette of choice, were too tame for Telma. She needed a more daring shade, black too cliché. Instead, she chose the color most likely to surprise—one Isa shunned.

The gown gathered above the hips and billowed to the floor. A sequined bodice accented her trim waist and large bosom. The style, including a revealing slit, was wickedly delicious, something worn to simmer a scandalous affair. She studied her cleavage with the proud gaze of a parent. The strapless top pushed the girls to attention. The adopted twins were just as plump and perky as the day she brought them home from the hospital.

People wouldn't see her as a cheap copy of the diva, but rather as an authentic alternative, the anti-Isa. She intended to make a grand entrance, a competing light that shone more brilliant than the star. Flocking moths would singe their wings.

"Stunning, *signora*." The young communista sounded sincere.

"Thank you," Telma said, pressing her chest. "And let me say how nice that shade of yellow suits you." She cringed the second the words escaped. Niceties left a taste as sour as vinegar. Had their perfect relationship, based on mistrust and ridicule, devolved into banal banter? Wit rescued her. "But, you should consider spending a bit of your extortion money on that bird's nest of a hairdo. Shame to let a halfway decent dress go to waste."

Svetlana didn't flinch. "Have a nice evening, *signora*," she said with a sugary smile. "We still charge for the room even if you bed elsewhere."

Telma heaved a sigh of relief. Their relationship survived.

Nestled in the Apennine foothills, San Benedetto cooled in the evening. Drifting on gentle breezes, the scent of oleander, jasmine, and honeysuckle carried away the crude odors produced by the blistering sun. Telma declined offers of an escort. The distance to the opera house was only three blocks, a quick stroll through the pedestrian zone and fashionable high street. Concertgoers dressed up in dinner jackets and glittery gowns fluttered about like fireflies among the casually dressed locals and tourists enjoying Saturday night in high season. Restaurants and bars brimmed with customers.

Across the sea of outdoor cafés, Telma spotted the Novaks hurrying to the opera house, dressed for an inaugural ball. Brad's tuxedo was crisp and traditional. Telma recognized the peach-colored satin gown worn by Alexandra as a piece from the new collection of a Paris designer. She laughed. Alexandra better wear her European wardrobe while she could. Once she got on the American campaign trail, she'd be stuck in Macy's polyester and Sears Roebuck twill.

Catching her eye, Brad smiled and waved. His ever-vigilant handler-wife followed his gaze. She sneered, locked arms with her husband, and pulled him to her side. *Listen, bitch,* Telma thought, *if I wanted to, I'd lasso your cowboy.* She bet Brad was the type of man who enjoyed spurs and a riding crop. He was probably tired of Alexandra's formulaic approach to sex—an ice cream sundae, served up in response to a calendar alert. Once Brad got past the cherry, whipped cream, and sprinkles, what did he have? Vanilla, bland and frigid. Unless consumed quickly, his treat melted into a warm, sticky puddle of unappealing ooze. *Strange bedfellows indeed.*

Willy Epson sulked behind. She thought he'd have been too embarrassed to get near the concert that his financial chicanery nearly sabotaged. He weaseled into a bar. Telma turned a corner and found herself in the piazza of the opera house. The structure's square facade featured apricot-colored stucco with white plaster decorations that looked to her like wedding cake trim. Large gaslights hung from a columned portico, flickering over the theater's three arched doors.

Amid camera flashes, beautiful people posed for photos. Concert posters featured a child's rendering of Isa in a red gown singing to a colorful, comic-strip inspired audience. Telma took the shorter, plumper caricature in black to be the missing Ivy Vine. The posters captured the evening's lighthearted atmosphere.

Telma was relieved to spot Tommy, Miguel, and Jamie chatting near a column. Tommy and Miguel wore matching tuxedos while Jamie looked dandy in a green plaid kilt with dinner jacket. The trio would insulate her from barbs she expected from Isa's family and allies. Isa's mother and father, she assumed, would be at hospital. When she sent flowers earlier in the day, she learned that Papa Fabrini's condition was still serious. The chatty florist, Maria's cousin, was only too eager to share the medical conditions of every patient in San Benedetto Hospital.

Ana entered the square from a side street. She looked radiant despite several piercings and a shoulder tattoo of the South African flag. A pencil skirt of cream-colored linen and a simple, white, sleeveless blouse showcased natural beauty. Her companions were a tall man in a lime-green tuxedo and a short woman with cropped hair, the same green as her escort's dinner jacket. The man's sneakers and eyeglasses matched yellow spiked hair. The pair might have been rock stars, artists, or just more of Ana's eccentric bunch of groupies. Telma adored the mixed crowd.

She ducked down a narrow alleyway that ran adjacent to the opera house. She didn't want to risk a scene before the concert. She didn't fear bodily harm—she had a physical advantage, plastic parts that didn't break or bruise. No, she couldn't risk having Ana bar her from the theater. Better to save fireworks till after the show. Telma followed a couple of women dressed in burlap sacks down the alleyway. Choristers no doubt dressed up as Hebrew slaves for the number Brigid spoke about. She entered the stage door behind them. A fiendish idea popped into her head. *Perhaps I should crash the chorus?*

Excitement inside the dim theater was palpable. In a corner of the cluttered backstage, Leech groveled before the spunky grande dame with a stick, Lady Blatherwicke. The pair shepherded the amateur chorus whose faces reflected a combination of worry and joy. Some chatted away nervously but the vast majority studied little pieces of paper that she assumed were words for their numbers. Telma recognized Brigid, Kate, and Vicki Epson and many others from the prior night's party. Danny waved.

In the opposite corner, the orchestra, betrayed by their instruments, huddled under a single light bulb that dangled from the ceiling. Several bore a strong family resemblance. All eyes of the rag-tag band focused on Malcolm, the dapper metrosexual who shadowed Lady Blatherwicke the prior night. His trim-cut dinner jacket, slim jeans, and black, silk T-shirt would distract any member of the chorus…man or woman.

Loud voices drew her attention to a closed door. She tiptoed across dusty planks, past stacked chairs, a worn settee, a fraying Chinese screen, and a splintered table piled high with costumes and tattered music scores. Garbled mumbles alternated between English and Italian before someone spoke. She recognized Isa's voice.

"Stick to English. Haven't we already provided enough gossip fodder for all of San Benedetto?"

Telma remembered Maria the hairstylist who lurked about somewhere in the shadows. Even the town's newspaper tapped her for stories. Telma moved to the door.

"Dearest, give us a chance." She recognized Luca's voice, his tone sincere, sad.

"I don't need a man. Tried that once. Failed."

"That's ancient history. We had a good thing. After your concert, after Christina's death, I came to Italy. Brought you back to London, back to life. You made me happy. I thought I did the same for you."

"Now who's talking history? Yes, I'm eternally grateful that you rescued me. Yes, I was happy. But that's over—finished—curtain down. You disappeared."

"To open up another damn restaurant. For us. So you wouldn't have to work, so you could sing."

"I'm not a charity case. I can take care of myself."

"Doesn't have to be that way. I love you. What about last night?"

"Wonderful, fantastic, fabulous. Is that what you want to hear? Did wonders for my stress level. That's called makeup sex, by the way."

"I've forgotten any other kind," Luca said, his tone becoming sarcastic.

"That should tell you something."

"But Isa…please, don't lock me out of your life."

"My father's in hospital, Ivy cancelled, and I'm about to go on stage. We all know what happened last time. Oh no, we don't—you didn't show up."

"I've told you how sorry I am. But I'm here now. Success or fail, I love you."

"What about your little…rendezvous at the Tazza d'Oro yesterday afternoon with a certain bitch."

At last, the real reason behind Isa's rage, Telma thought. So Isa's spies had reported back about Telma's afternoon session of wine and sympathy with Luca. *Marvelous! I couldn't have planned it better myself.*

"That's absurd." Anger mounted in Luca's voice. "I had no idea who she was."

"Leave me alone. Go back to your restaurants. Go back to that *bitch*."

"Tonight, my sweet, that title belongs to another."

The door pulled open with force, banging the wall behind it. Luca stormed out, still looking over his shoulder at Isa's back. After he tumbled into Telma's arms, their eyes met. She felt his heart race through the tuxedo. He tried to pull away but she wrapped him in her arms and kissed his lips. His heart still pounded, but calmed to a more regular beat. He surrendered; his urge to push past her subsided. He sighed.

"Meet me later?" Telma whispered into his ear.

Their next kiss was his lead and response before he made his way out the stagedoor.

Isa turned. Tears gave way to confusion and stammering, "C-Christina."

Then her eyes fired with the rage that Telma last saw in Regent's Park. Isa lifted her arms. Her fingers clenched the empty air in front of her. "You!"

Telma took a deep breath, walked into the dressing room, and shut the door behind her.

Chapter 29

I sa stood frozen except for her quivering lips and heaving chest. Her sequined gown of midnight-blue looked almost black in the dim light of two lamps whose fringed shades had tears like old nylons.

The stale air and stifling heat of the corridor gave way to perfume and floral scents kept fresh by a portable air conditioner whose labored breathing mimicked Isa's. Bouquets crowded the dressing table. Telma wondered which tribute was Luca's: the ostentatious funereal spray, a passionate cliché of red roses, or the simple white freesias.

Telma thought the room tired, past its prime…by more than a couple of decades. If the wall clock with the cracked face tracked years, the date displayed would certainly be mid-twentieth century. On either side of the aging timepiece with an amputated second hand hung two faded posters of opera divas.

Telma didn't recall the name of one woman, but she recognized Maria Callas. Why hadn't she seen the resemblance before? Isabella Fabrini's face and eyes were rounder than that of the tempestuous Callas, but the mouths, noses, and brilliant black hair were nearly identical. The opera legend's severe expression mirrored Isa's icy glare. Both Madam Callas and her living incarnation appeared on the verge of eruption—full lips primed to spew forth curses.

"Don't look so surprised. The national rugby team in all its naked brilliance couldn't keep me away. Your concert is the talk of the town…the tiny, bucolic, unsophisticated, easily impressed hamlet of San Benedetto."

Isa's scowl lasered on Telma. "Childish insults amuse no one but yourself. I told you to leave. You're not welcome here."

"I want to support you, fill a seat that would otherwise go empty."

Isa sneered. "What's with the ridiculous makeover? Are you mocking your poor sister or me?"

Isa shifted her weight with a slight pivot, just enough to allow Telma a glimpse of her reflection in the mirror. The blonde makeover and form-fitting gown gave her a regal air. If rage hadn't blinded her, Isa couldn't criticize the interloper's appearance. As much as Telma hated to admit the fact, Isa looked stunning. But so did she—the new look was a stroke of genius. Telma didn't take the bait.

"Darling, I know you're worried. Free concerts always draw riff-raff. I promise to behave."

"Behave? The word isn't in your vocabulary. You can't help yourself, Telma. You're hard-wired to hurt those around you."

Telma clapped her hands. "Brava! Ever the diva. But even the best voices need a little nudge to lift them above the mundane—like a porno fluffer who *elevates* the actor before his big closeup. Consider me your fluffer. Let me arouse you to sing from the depths of your soul." Isa's tongue clicked in disgust, but she kept silent. "You'll thank me later, after a second or even third curtain call." A clacking sound drew Telma's gaze upward. A ceiling fan limped around its orbit, one blade missing. "That is," Telma added, "if the curtain works."

Isa's forehead wrinkled. Her dark eyes seemed to look inside themselves as she processed Telma's words. Then all at once, her shoulders slumped; her arms dropped to her sides. She began to laugh, almost hysterical spasms.

"Careful. Don't waste that fury. Save it for the stage and your adoring fans."

Without speaking, Isa walked to the sofa and sat. Tension faded into the calm after a storm. Telma considered their circumstances, so much altered from that long-ago afternoon in Regent's Park. Both lives bore traces of time and worry. They survived while other souls like Christina's hadn't the stamina or good fortune.

In middle age, one began to recognize fellow survivors, even appreciate those once overlooked or branded as foe. Telma assumed the bonding process accelerated into old age—contemporaries dropping like flies, bridge partners and drinking mates harder to find. Reconciliation by default, a thinning flock limping toward a common fate.

Isa patted the sofa. "Come. Sit." Telma eyed the threadbare cushion with concern. "Don't worry," Isa added, "poisoned springs won't lance your bum. I'm not that clever."

Telma moved to the dressing table, checked herself in the mirror, and sat down beside Isa, stirring a cloud of dust. Fuzz balls launched from the floor beneath the sofa.

Isa laughed. "Not exactly Covent Garden or Carnegie Hall, is it?"

Telma snickered. "I'd say. But it has a certain charm, and it's all yours for the night."

She shrugged. "The last years haven't been kind." *Is she referring to the theater or herself?* Walter, Jamie, and others told her about Isa's struggles. "With cash," Isa added, "a troop of monkeys performing Andrew Lloyd Webber could claim that stage."

"Don't minimize your triumph. It's tiresome. Not many people follow their dream, let alone turn it into reality. Christina was very proud of you."

At the mention of the name, Isa looked to her slippered feet. Whatever Telma thought of the woman, Isabella Fabrini loved Christina. And with Telma's transformed appearance, Isa couldn't help but be reminded of her dear late friend.

"Funny," Isa said, "before my first concert, your sister sat precisely where you're sitting." Then with a tone and expression that veered between joy and sadness, she described the story that Kate Mahoney and others had already shared—Christina's talking her off the metaphorical ledge. Isa lost herself in the past.

Telma had seen other grieving people do the same, almost as if the recollection of a departed loved one—reliving a moment in time— breathed life into the lost soul. Hadn't Telma found herself doing as much that first night at the Tazza d'Oro, when the Dubliners and Danny shared stories about Christina?

Isa looked toward the door. "Christina prodded me onto that stage. Without her, there'd have been no concert. I'd have snuck out of town, a disgrace to my family and a failure in my own eyes. I miss her terribly."

"My sister was a marvelous person. She truly loved you, more than…"

Reaching across the sofa, Isa grabbed Telma's hand. Her touch, unexpected, jolted her with an electric charge. "She loved you too. She told me so."

The rattling of the doorknob followed loud successive knocks. The door flung open with a whoosh of air. Telma jumped to her feet but Isa remained seated, unfazed by the disturbance. She'd either taken a happy pill or entered that state of mind performers and athletes called *the zone*. Isa seemed seasoned, trained to overcome stage fright. She wouldn't see a repeat of the paralysis that threatened her debut. *Or would she?*

In a flash, Philippe was through the door. An invisible cloud accompanied him with his signature scent of musk and manliness. The rugged face bore a deep tan and sexy scruff. Windblown curls made him appear to have only just dismounted a motorcycle. Yet his crisp tuxedo, platinum cufflinks, and bold swagger made him look as if he only just dismounted a movie star. When his luscious eyes moved from Isa to Telma, he flinched before flashing a brilliant smile.

"*Quelle surprise!*" he said. "Good to see you two getting along." Then his smile vanished, eyes darted between the two women. "You are getting along? I didn't hear shouts or shattered glass."

Isa rose and stood at Telma's side. "We've been enjoying a civilized chat. And after last time, Leech banished bottles and crystal."

He clapped his hands; his smile beamed. "Then you're pals, *bonnes amies, oui?*"

Before Telma could answer, Isa spoke. "Let's say we've found common ground. A truce if you will…for the night."

Telma nodded her agreement. "Some truces," she said, "bring peace, while others…" Her hands broke an imaginary stick in half.

"The French, dear ladies, have much experience with treaties. Not all good."

"But even more experience with surrender," Telma said.

"Love, dear ladies, love inspires the French, not war. This Frenchman surrenders to your charms." Philippe kissed both women.

Telma turned to Isa. "Then, you're not the slightest surprised we know each other." She tucked her arm under Philippe's, feeling both the fine wool of his designer jacket and the warmth of his well-toned torso.

Isa scoffed. "Nothing surprises me about the two of you," she said, tucking in under Philippe's other arm. "So much alike." She pinched Philippe's hand until it turned purple. "Birds of a feather…"

Was Isa privy to their sordid sexcapade? Sabotaging the annulment and even her marriage were still worries. Telma pinched Philippe's other hand as signal for discretion. "Then, you know how we met?"

Isa waved her other hand in the air. "No matter. For all I know, you've been screwing each other's brains out in the opera house." Philippe's quiet chuckle and shared glance with Isa suggested more juicy gossip for Telma to squeeze. "My concert, I've been told," Isa added with a suggestive laugh, "brings people together. A beautiful thing, whatever the form or substance."

So, Isa didn't care if Philippe and she hooked up. Telma needed to be cautious. Their détente was still fresh. *Can I trust Isa with such damaging information?*

"Dear ladies," Philippe said, "fooling about with two women at once is usually quite stimulating. But, I've felt less shackled by the Paris gendarmerie." Gently, he freed himself from their clutches. "And they never resorted to torture," he added, rubbing patches of skin marked with crimson and purple.

Isa let out a devilish laugh. "I forgot. You prefer to play the shackler, not the shackled."

"Offer stands, chérie," he replied in a sensuous tone. "An open invitation of fun and games for *both* of you...alone or *ensemble.*"

Isa patted his chest. "Another time perhaps. It's been lovely chatting, but I must get ready. Maria will be here any moment for final touches and then there's Leech and Malcolm with last-minute instructions and the pep talk. After last time, I'm surprised they've let me out of their sights."

Philippe kissed her cheeks. "I only stopped by to wish you the best of luck. *Bonne chance!*"

As Telma retrieved her handbag from the floor, Isa said, "You two make a smart couple. Sit together during the concert."

Telma assumed that suggestion was self-serving. She and Philippe, as Isa must have guessed, were more dangerous apart than together.

A grin spread across Philippe's handsome face. "*Oui. D'accord*, agreed."

His presence intoxicated. The objects of his desire were blind to the danger with which they flirted. Philippe's raw sex appeal lured Telma like a Venus flytrap. She ignored her instincts or maybe switched them off on purpose. *What harm could come from playing footsie in the theater?* Luca waited for a post-concert rendezvous. Despite Telma's friendly session with Isa, Luca promised a rapturous encore that she didn't dare miss. With a gracious smile, Telma offered her hand to the Frenchman.

He pressed her hand between large, supple palms. "Fantastic. I reserved a private box. Velvet seats, *bonne* view of the stage, and discretion."

Isa wagged her finger. "Behave!"

Philippe's chestnut-brown eyes danced. "Won't do anything we wouldn't do on stage."

"Precisely what I'm afraid of," Isa said.

Telma hadn't decided whether she could trust Isa. And Philippe had shown himself a shameless cad. But could she trust herself?

An even larger question remained. Telma determined to put Isa to the test. Wouldn't take long for Isa to discover Telma's offering. Standing among the dressing table bouquets—Irish whiskey, its cap placed to the side to let the bottle breathe and beckon.

Chapter 30

Philippe whisked Telma from Isa's dressing room like a hawk with its prey. One couldn't be in his presence without feeling the magnetic pull of raw sexuality. He was a formidable predator—charismatic yet cunning. Telma assumed her sister, a trained psychiatrist, had figured him out. How many concert guests and locals had Philippe already charmed out of their pants and panties?

Backstage, chaos reigned as technicians and helpers scurried about finishing tasks. When she and Philippe stepped onto the stage, Telma gasped. The doors from the lobby were closed and the curtain remained open. Her eyes widened at the sight of the empty hall. Despite dust, cobwebs, and peeling paint around its edges, the theater was magnificent—a fairy-tale opera house fit for a princess.

Philippe rubbed her shoulder. *"Très jolie, n'est-ce pas?"*

"I'll say." Telma understood the town's pride. The theater was as much a diva as Isa. While neither grand nor in its prime, the opera house exuded charm and commanded respect. Antique lamps gave the hall a soft glow that masked imperfections. She moved to the edge of the stage. Even in that light, certain details stood out. Gold-leaf accents decorated the three levels of boxes while celestial murals and crystal chandeliers drew her gaze to the ceiling. Telma stood in silent awe until voices broke her concentration.

In the orchestra pit below, Leech and Malcolm gathered notes and music scores. Probably for the pep talk Isa mentioned. They were too deep in conversation to notice the eavesdroppers. Under the lights, Leech's formal attire glowed in Technicolor brilliance: a jacket of scarlet red with lapels and dress trousers in hot pink. A vertical stripe, the same red as the jacket, accented the pants. In place of a bow tie, a lime-green scarf fastened with garnet brooch snaked down the front of a pink polka-dot shirt.

"Pray lightning doesn't strike twice," Leech said.

"Ana promised no pills or liquor," Malcolm replied, "but the poor thing's been shuttling back and forth to hospital. She's there now. The last summons was urgent."

"A ticking fiasco. Ivy's cancelling was one thing. Surprised how well Isa took that, professional courtesy and all."

"Shows how much she's matured...as a person and performer," Malcolm said.

Leech sighed. "But Papa Fabrini, bless his heart, holds the key. A nasty turn and our darling diva does another swan dive. Why must opera be packed with drama?"

Malcolm chuckled. "Lady B did a sweep of Isa's dressing room an hour ago. Says all's well."

"Pray it ends well," Leech interjected, dabbing his sweating forehead with a handkerchief the same bright green as his scarf.

"Don't forget the chorus." Malcolm nodded to the stage, the side opposite of where Telma stood with Philippe. Lady Blatherwicke, with the air of a taskmaster, lined up her recruits for inspection.

Leech groaned. "There's not a drug potent enough to let me forget our tone-deaf glee club. Except perhaps hemlock."

Malcolm scowled. "Be kind. The show will go on with or without our star. The chorus can carry a tune. They have passion."

"Chorus? May as well call a hotdog *haute cuisine*. Holy Mother of God," Leech cried, looking to the ceiling as he crossed himself upside-down and backward.

Malcolm's laugh echoed through the orchestra pit. "Lady B says we'll be surprised."

Leech scoffed. "This won't be a Cinderella story. The pumpkin remains a pumpkin. When the curtain opens, our little darlings in burlap will stammer their Italian and sing off key."

"You're impossible. They're charming. They add a certain... authenticity."

Leech's head shook. "Pray one tumbles into the pit for a bit of comic relief. That's authenticity!"

Lady Blatherwicke's voice boomed from across the stage. "Doors open in ten minutes. Curtain rises in thirty. Get into character. You can do this. You will do this." She pounded her stick on the wooden planks and led the chorus in a series of vocal warm-up exercises. Three dozen men, women, and children looked like frightened rabbits as they sang the scales.

Grabbing her hand, Philippe whisked Telma down a set of stairs. As they hurried up the aisle, final preparations were in full swing. Italian boys, smartly dressed as ushers, huddled at the back of the theater. Their hands fidgeted with bow ties and programs. Young women, dressed in black and white catering smocks, received coaching on proper technique for opening and pouring champagne. The lighting crew, who commandeered one of the upper boxes, tested lights in a last-minute drill. Best of all, a troop of brawny firemen filed through the hall conducting final inspections of emergency doors, sand buckets, and fire extinguishers.

When Telma had first decided to come to San Benedetto, she viewed the concert as an exercise in self-absorption—Isa's attempt to grab the spotlight. But over the course of the weekend, she had an epiphany. The concert breathed life into people, the town, and the old theater. In addition to connecting people from around the world, Isa put the town to work and brought renewed pride to the people of her birthplace.

No sooner had Philippe pulled Telma up a set of stairs and into a box than he started to probe. "I won't be mussed," she said, batting down his hands. He sulked, dropping down onto the velvet bench with a sigh. Warm brown eyes pleaded with her. How could she resist giving the pouty-faced boy the playthings he craved? "All right," she said, sitting down beside him. "I'll allow groping…as long as it's mutual."

His expression lightened. "I promise not to wrinkle your satin." His hand maneuvered through the slit of her dress. Philippe took a break from ear nibbling. He whispered, "Take me to your room after the concert."

"My hotel?"

"Mine's not so—"

"Vacant."

"Comfortable," he said with a sly snicker.

"What about the party?" she asked. "Heard the post-concert bash isn't to be missed."

"Okay, okay. A quick drink, dinner, but then…"

"We'll see." But Telma had no intention of spending the night with Philippe. Luca was her target. She intended to send him a note at intermission suggesting a midnight rendezvous at the Tazza d'Oro. In the meantime, she strung along her seducer. She'd ditch him at the party where his appetite would surely wander to other alcohol-laced prey.

Telma extracted his hand from her panties. "Hold that thought." She collected her clutch purse. "Have to see a man about a light."

Philippe tilted his head. After a few seconds he nodded vigorously. "Oh, *oui*—out the door. Gents *à droite*, ladies *à gauche*."

By the time Telma returned to the box, the doors of the auditorium opened to the herd of Isa's supporters. The theater came alive with the chatter of many languages and the scents of perfume, aftershave, bath salts, and hairspray. From her vantage point at the back of the hall, Telma watched the parade of gowns, dinner jackets, summer dresses, and linen blazers make their way down the aisles. Outside the box came the sound of trudging feet and muffled voices as people climbed stairs and funneled through corridors to find reserved seats. Three levels of boxes filled with handsome people decked out in fancy clothes, done-up hair, and glittery jewels.

The dimming of the houselights hushed the voices. On the main floor, people settled into their seats and focused on the curtain. Those in boxes edged back from velvet rails and turned toward the stage. Two spotlights broke the darkness, bathing the stage in light and illuminating the red velvet curtain. Thunderous applause greeted Leech and Lady Blatherwicke as they stepped from the wings into the light. Even from that distance, Telma saw sweat beads glisten on the funny little man's forehead. Lady Blatherwicke was the picture of poise. Whereas Leech dazzled with bold colors, the chorus mistress cast an aura of grace with a palette of muted pastels. Her periwinkle-blue gown and diamonds evoked simple elegance. She looked at least two decades younger than her eighty years.

Telma turned to Philippe. "Great plastic surgeon."

He winked. "Not everything is *plastique*."

Leech bowed and Lady Blatherwicke curtsied to the audience. Malcolm rose from the piano to guide the grande dame down the stairs while Leech descended into the conductor's pit. The orchestra composed of the family Bertini, Silverstein, and a few others for insurance took its cue from Malcolm. Signor Bertini at the second piano, she assumed, insured against a repeat of the first concert's fiasco. The overture began. Telma recognized snippets from operas and arias listed in the program.

As the music waned, the curtain parted. Isa stood in the center of the stage, radiant in the midnight-blue gown Telma had seen in the dressing room. A second spotlight lit up three seats in the first row, empty except for bouquets of roses, red, pink, yellow.

"For her parents and Ana," Telma whispered to Philippe.

Isa quieted the applause with hand gestures. "Good evening," she spoke first in Italian then repeated in English. "Thank you for coming. I'm proud to share the stage with some of my dearest friends. I wish to dedicate tonight's concert to two people. First my dearest friend in the world, Christina." The audience applauded and Telma teared up. "And to the man who inspired me. He can't be with us," she said fighting tears, "but he made me promise to sing. For all those who know Papa, actually less promise, more arm twisting." The comment drew laughter. "So, dear Christina and Papa, I sing for you." As the hall erupted with applause, Isa blew a kiss to the empty seats.

The concert was splendid. Unlisted pieces filled holes in the program left by Ivy's solos.

"Singing's much better than I expected," Telma whispered.

"*Oui,* not so bad this time. Isa's improved, much improved."

Danny, Brigid, and Kate looked adorable as Hebrew slaves in burlap sacks. Vicki Epson wore a designer slave ensemble complete with snakeskin sandals and matching belt. Didn't every Hebrew slave own a strand of south sea pearls with matching earrings?

The curtain closed for intermission. Telma stood, whispering to Philippe, "Here goes."

On cue as the audience filed up the aisles to the lobby, the lighting man bathed Telma in spotlight. Her sparkling gown of white bedazzled. As she instructed, the houselights remained dimmed. She feigned surprise, first covering her face, then shaking her head and offering coy giggles. She waved as if from the balcony of Buckingham Palace. The hall erupted in a burst of applause.

"You devil," Philippe said, shrinking into the shadows.

"Told you I had to see a man about a light. A perfect gentleman too, especially after I slipped him a hundred euros."

T.D. ARKENBERG

Philippe groaned. From below Brad Novak let out a two-fingered whistle. Dear Alexandra, lips puckered and eyes angry, slapped him on the shoulder.

"She's just jealous," Telma whispered to Philippe through a fake smile. "Bet she steals the idea for Brad's campaign."

Tommy and Miguel both waved.

"Fabulous!" Tommy shouted upward. "Love the blonde you."

"Muy bonita Chica," Miguel added. "Stunning."

Jamie marched up the aisle in a kilt, trailed by a group of women ogling his legs. He looked up and flashed a smile. "Ya look mighty gorgeous, love," he bellowed, offering a salute. "Hope you're gettin' your money's worth?" he added with a wink.

Telma wagged a finger. "Hush!" she scolded before blowing him a kiss.

She slapped Philippe's hand as it glided up her inner thigh. "Let's go hobnob with my adoring fans."

Isa's face was the last the audience saw prior to curtain close, but Telma's face was the one they would remember when they sipped champagne and chatted during intermission. Perhaps Telma couldn't share the stage, but she certainly stole the spotlight.

The second half of the concert began with the orchestra's playing a short Rossini piece. When the curtain parted, revealing Isabella Fabrini, Telma clapped her hands with enthusiasm. "Perfect, simply perfect," she said. "The symbolism's divine." Isa's glittery black gown provided stark contrast to her own white satin. The chorus surrounded her. The music's tempo slowed. But instead of singing the opening line, Isa's mouth fell open. "She missed her cue," Telma said, drawing leers from people in the next box. At last, the embarrassing moment she desired had arrived. But why then—after the triumph of the first half? Had Isa run out of steam? Did she simply forget the words? Perhaps whiskey, guzzled during intermission, kicked in? Whatever the cause, Telma didn't care. The lion had entered the arena.

Leech's frantic hand gestures suggested fear. The heads of Malcolm and Lady Blatherwicke came together, lips clicking like telegraph keys. The music stopped and started as if trying to prod Isa into song.

"Mon Dieu," Philippe groaned. "Lightning can strike twice." Isa remained

— 230 —

frozen. The audience rustled; whispers grew louder. "You really are the devil. Be still," he said, responding to Telma's sighs of pleasure. "People will think we're having sex."

She laughed at the irony, but couldn't keep her eyes off the stage. What would happen next? The chorus broke out of character. They encircled Isa who began to cry. The spotlight moved from the stage. Its beacon illuminated the back of the theater. All eyes followed the light. Looking down, Telma gasped. Ana and Mama Fabrini stood in the open doorway. Was it bad news? As they stepped forward, a fragile Papa Fabrini appeared. Flanked by the two women and flashing a smile, he inched down the aisle.

Telma felt a lump in her throat. The audience jumped to its feet to give Papa Fabrini a standing ovation. Telma teared up. Even from the box, she saw pride and joy in the old man's face. Hurrying from the stage, Isa met the trio halfway down the aisle. The family hugged and kissed in a reunion that brought tears to all. Applause drowned out their voices, but Telma understood that Papa Fabrini wanted Isa on stage. A shaking finger pointed to the chorus before he clasped his hands together in a prizefighter's victory grip.

That gesture transported Telma to childhood at a gymnastics competition. Her father had to work so Papa Fabrini took her. She finished third. As she stood on the pedestal to receive the bronze medal, she looked to the bleachers. On his feet and beaming, Papa Fabrini gripped his hands like a prizefighter as if she'd won the gold.

Seeing him in the opera house, fragile yet still spirited, Telma sobbed.

Isa returned to the stage, blowing her father a kiss. "I love you, Papa."

"Love you too, *principessa*," he called back with surprising strength. "But none of these lovely people came to hear you speak. Sing!"

Chapter 31

"Not great, certainly not brilliant. I'll concede good, maybe even very good."

"But, Telma, a ten-minute standing ovation," Philippe said as they gathered their things and exited the box. "Can't deny that or the dozens of bouquets."

"A smidge of praise, maybe. As for the flowers, overkill. Most of the love fest was mere pity. A waltzing squirrel could get a standing ovation if he produced Papa Fabrini."

"Can't fool me. I watched you. Heavy sighs, lip quivers, tears. During the Mozart, you sat on the edge of your seat, arms draped over the railing, head swaying. Your hands turned red clapping until you caught me smile at you. *Non,* can't fool *moi,* Telma Rossi. You're as soft as cashmere and as adorable as a kitten. You loved the concert."

"Bah!" she exclaimed, slapping his shoulder playfully.

She'd never admit that the concert came off better than she ever expected. If she weren't her enemy, Telma might have been happy for… and yes, even proud of Isa. But when she made up her mind to dislike someone, Telma found it impossible to view that person through any other lens. She liked her friends conditionally, but disliked her enemies absolutely. To admit that Isa conquered her fears to reinvent herself, had the skill to produce an elaborate concert, and the appeal to attract a global audience, undermined Telma's absolute dislike. If she allowed one crack in her philosophy, where would it lead—pleasantries, civilities, and other rituals of polite society—that made her shudder.

The jubilation released at curtain close continued outside the theater.

Concertgoers intoxicated by champagne and song congregated in the piazza. The crowd shared hugs, kisses, and cigarettes before scattering through the narrow streets that led to the post-concert party. Colorful clothes, amber flickers of lanterns, and a full moon gave the cobblestoned streets of San Benedetto a carnival atmosphere.

After exchanging pleasantries with a few of the more distinguished guests, Brad and Alexandra scooped up Vicki Epson and beelined to the outdoor café where Willy sat out the concert. Even from that distance, Telma knew that the tall drink rattling in trembling hands wasn't his first, not by a long shot. Jamie snarled in Willy's direction but Telma grabbed his arm. "Don't tangle with a drunk."

Leech and Blatherwicke stepped out of the theater with heads held high, pimping for applause. The crowd accommodated, continuing as Malcolm and the rest of the musicians, toting instruments, filed into the square.

Isa's immediate family lingered inside the lobby. A car pulled to the door into which Mama and Papa Fabrini and Ana entered. The extended family of cousins from Italy and America congregated under the building's portico.

Locking arms with Philippe and Jamie, Telma led the merry trio away. Directly behind came Kate and Brigid. The pair made no secret of their fancies for the sexy Frenchman and Scot who darted away from their brazen pursuers like frightened deer. In consolation, the Dubliners grabbed Danny Chance.

"The thorn between two roses," Kate said with girlish giggle.

"Amazing," Danny replied. "Better the saint between the sinners, or the—"

"Squeak between the cheeks," shrieked Brigid, complete with mouth farts. The Dubliners howled with laughter.

Danny groaned. "Oh dear Lord, help me."

Directly behind them, Tommy and Miguel strolled shoulder-to-shoulder. "Anyone see the firemen?" Tommy asked.

Kate, Brigid, and Danny answered as if they were still in the chorus. "Yes, yes, yes."

"Amazing specimens of Italian manhood," added Danny.

Telma was surprised at Danny's candor. Perhaps the tightly wound New Yorker had also fallen under the spell of concert weekend.

"Lovely, just lovely firemen," cooed Brigid.

"Thought you'd collapse on stage and demand resuscitation," Kate said.

Telma gazed over her shoulder to Brigid's face, grinning like a jack-o'-lantern. "Surprised you didn't," she said to the impish woman. "You're a shameless hussy."

Brigid squawked with laughter. "Kate's referring to Danny Boy here, not me. I'm too old and married for such foolery. I simply pinched the best lookin' one in his pretty arse." Brigid's eyes twinkled with leprechaun mischief as her eyebrows pulsed up and down. Danny groaned and turned crimson.

The hoots and hollers of the little group echoed through narrow alleyways. Songs, stories, and laughter carried them along to their destination. The tide of camaraderie pulled Telma in. She felt lighthearted, happy to be communing with such carefree spirits. She'd not only crashed Renoir's boating party, she was in its glorious center.

"Here we are—" Jamie stopped in mid-sentence.

"Must be a mistake," Philippe said.

The party of eight stood side by side. In front of them sat a hulking structure alone in the shadows. Although just off the pedestrian zone, Telma hadn't noticed the deserted building. Weeds sprouted up between pavers that meandered through a neglected garden to the shuttered door. Vines sprouted from cracked stucco, advancing across a faded facade. She deciphered *Hotel Excelsior* on the tarnished nameplate. Leafy ivy, as if an agent of the tourist board, claimed two of the hotel's three brass stars. An abandoned hotel, dark and drained of life, was sad, almost sinister.

"Someone didn't pay the light bill," Kate said.

Jamie looked at Telma, his expression a mix of guilt and shame.

"Where is everyone?" asked Miguel.

"Gotta be the wrong place," said Tommy.

"I assumed the party would be at the same hotel as last time," added Danny.

As if on cue, a small group of fellow concertgoers, recognizable by their fancy dress, walked up behind them. "Excelsior shut down not long after the last concert," said a man speaking English with an Italian accent.

"Party's at the Villa Europa," added his female companion in perfect English.

Telma tapped her forehead. "That's right. That's the name I heard." Catching herself, she whispered to Jamie, "The place I had Walter wire the money."

Another man in the new group put his hand on Jamie's shoulder. "Follow us."

After a round of introductions, the two groups of revelers melded and made their way toward the party. The Villa Europa was more impressive than the Excelsior, even in the latter's best days. The old world hotel sat in a fashionable district, just off the high street that housed fancy boutiques. A long driveway cut through a pristine lawn dotted with meticulously pruned shrubbery. Gas lamps lit up the garden while knee-high lanterns guided foot traffic up a stone path to the entrance. Guests accessed the yellow hotel under a two-story portico from which hung a large lantern. Black iron flower boxes below ground-floor windows held red geraniums while stone planters contained gardenia trees shaped into globes. In contrast to the darkened Excelsior, lights blazed through glazed windows that glistened from a recent washing.

"I should've stayed here, although I'd miss the young communista," Telma said.

"Impossible, love," answered Jamie. "Booked up months ago. The Novaks and Epsons are here as well as some of Isa's wealthier relatives."

"La di da di da," sang Brigid.

"Looks mighty posh. We couldn't afford an hour in this place," said Kate.

"Hourly?" Danny said with sly laughter in his tone. "Those the kind of places you ladies are used to?"

"Aar!" Brigid whined, elbowing him in the ribs. Danny groaned for the third time.

Jamie steered Telma through the front door. "Let's grab ourselves a fine table."

The sound of an orchestra guided the group past a walnut-paneled bar where they lost Jamie and the Dubliners.

Philippe and Telma made their way to the large banquet room that took up an entire wing of the hotel's ground floor. They stood at the doorway, a few steps above the dance floor. The party was in full swing although Isa hadn't yet made her grand entrance. As far as Telma could see, the Fabrinis weren't in the room. A bursting scent of perfume preceded the grabbing of Telma's arm. Turning, she found herself face-to-face with Ana.

"Why are you two just standing here?" Ana asked. "Come. Join the party. Dance."

Philippe leaned down to kiss her cheek, looking at Telma as Ana whispered in his ear.

Laughing, Ana addressed them both. "I must mingle. Enjoy yourselves."

Telma's neck stiffened. As she watched Ana flit down the staircase and disappear into the crowd, she wondered, *What the hell happened to her?* That wasn't the greeting she had expected. Did concert weekend turn everyone into lunatics?

She turned to Philippe whose eyes lingered on Ana. "What did she say?" Telma asked.

"She's free tomorrow," Philippe replied. "So, tonight, she says, I'm all yours."

Chapter 32

Telma ducked out of the party shortly before midnight. It wasn't as easy as she thought ditching Philippe. Throughout the evening, whenever she found herself out of his company, someone, including Ana, threw them back together. At last, Telma found a willing accomplice in Brigid, who she discovered sulking alone in the bar. Kate had angered her by cozying up to the Englishman Brigid loathed. Anxious to return to the party, Brigid eagerly waylaid the randy Frenchman with a tango. Her torrid interpretation, pulling a white-knuckled Philippe into a dip, gave Telma cover to escape.

Confident that Luca awaited her at the Tazza d'Oro, Telma hurried back to the center of town. He wouldn't let her drink alone, especially at that hour. She hadn't made up her mind how far to take the handsome Italian for a joyride. An uncontrollable urge to sting Isa clouded her reason. Sure, she deserved some of the blame, but Isa's nuclear reaction in Regent's Park left scars. The pampered diva drove a wedge between Christina and Telma for which she never answered.

Perhaps Telma's dislike went deeper, wounds from childhood where she watched Isa stroll through life as Papa Fabrini's *principessa* while nobody paid attention to her. The thought of a fling with Luca appealed to her. He wasn't the usual class of man with whom she sought relief from boredom. He was too nice, and too much a gentleman to hurt…too deeply.

Still undecided on Luca's fate, Telma approached the bustling Tazza d'Oro. She recognized several of the café's customers as concertgoers who either skipped the party or weren't invited in the first place. Many recognized her with a smattering of applause as if she'd been on stage instead of merely in the spotlight. Whispers tagged her as a "film star" or "stage actress." She loved the attention but grew agitated when she didn't see Luca. Did he have cold feet? Had he run back to Isa? As she turned to leave, a big-haired woman rose from a table, announcing in a thick Texas drawl the need to use the little gal's room. That's when Telma spotted him. Luca sat in a corner, still in the formal attire he wore when he bolted out of Isa's dressing room. Had he got her note or had he been drinking at that table all evening?

He didn't see her until she reached his table. Rolling glassy eyes upward, he tried to stand but his knees buckled. Wearing a crooked grin, he managed a wobbly wave and a slurred hello that answered her question. When she leaned over to kiss his cheek, she smelled alcohol. He reeked of it. His hands cupped a nearly empty glass.

"Good concert?" he asked. "Isa sing well?"

Telma sat beside him. "All good. Everyone sang well, especially the chorus."

"And Isa, she sang well? Tell me she sang well. Brava, Isabella Fabrini."

"You should have stayed." Not interested in discussing Isa, Telma deflected the question.

"No, no, no. Isa didn't want me there. Isa doesn't want me around— end of story. Made that clear tonight. Has always made that crystal clear. I've been too stupid to see…maybe didn't want to see."

Telma squeezed his hand. "You underestimate yourself, Luca. You're a gem. I've told you that before."

He sighed. "She doesn't want me. Doesn't love me." His voice grew louder. "Isa, Isa, Isa."

As Telma considered how much Luca adored Isa, a waiter approached the table.

Luca hoisted his glass. "Grappa, another grappa."

"Let's go back to the hotel."

"No! Another grappa," Luca said even louder.

"It's late. We can have a nightcap at the hotel." She turned to the waiter. "Just the check. *Il conto, per favore.*" Telma pulled money from her clutch purse.

Luca made an attempt to swat her hand but missed. "No, no, no. Lady no pay. Lady never pay." His hands thrust into his trouser pockets. When he pulled them out, metal clanked to the ground. Coins circled at Telma feet. "No billfold," he cried. "I've been robbed."

Telma noticed a wallet bulge in Luca's jacket but pushed her money into the waiter's hand. After helping lift Luca to his feet, the waiter, with some coaxing and ten euros, agreed to help walk her tipsy date home. At the hotel's front door, mere meters from the café, the young waiter hurried off, anxious no doubt to supplement his tip with Luca's fallen coins.

Telma pulled Luca into the lobby. "Come on, lover boy, let me get you to bed." She propped him in a corner and scurried around the empty reception desk. She pulled her key from its slot but Luca's key was missing. She probed adjoining cubbyholes, but no luck. Luca saw her distress and giggled. "Key's right here," he said patting his pockets. "Oh my, here's my billfold," he snickered, flipping open his jacket flap.

He mustered the strength to use the elevator without much assistance. When they reached their floor, he began to sing, *Nessun dorma! Nessun dorma! Tu pure, o Principessa.*

"Sh!" she said. "None shall sleep if you keep that up."

"Don't you like?" he asked, before relaunching into song, *Nella tua fredda stanza…*

"*Sì*, I like. But not now, Pavarotti."

"Caruso!" he blurted, blowing alcohol-laced breath into her face. Luca had a strong, rich voice.

Had he ever sung opera? Isa could have benefited from his talent. After they reached the door to his room, she stood him against the wall. She extended her palm. "Your key? *La chiave, signor.*"

Flashing a silly grin, he lifted his arms and mumbled, "Search me."

"If you weren't drunk, I'd do more than fish for your key," she replied, reaching into his trouser pockets. After checking his trousers and jacket twice, she surrendered.

"Don't stop, I'm just warming up," Luca cooed with mischievous eyes.

A glance at the growing bulge in his trousers informed her he wasn't kidding. The reason for the missing room key came to her. The key probably fell out of his pocket at the café with the coins.

"Okay, lover boy, it's your lucky night. I'm taking you home." She would set him down in her room, and run back to the café for the key. When she opened the door, Luca protested, "Never the lady's room, never."

"Sh!" she said, holding a finger to his lips. "Don't get any ideas. This is only temporary."

Wagging a finger in her face, he stumbled forward. Telma caught him in mid-tumble but not before he spit up on her gown. "White does have its drawbacks," she muttered. She moved Luca deeper into her room. He could sleep in her bed and she'd take his after she retrieved the key.

From experience, Telma knew drunks made horrible lovers. But a little thrill could still be hers as a curious Florence Nightingale. What harm was there in merely undressing her would-be lover? The hardest trick was keeping Luca on his feet. She used her body to prop him up, his strong chest resting against her forehead. She pulled off his jacket, then the suspenders. As she removed his tie and unbuttoned his shirt, he kicked off his shoes. When she pulled the shirt from his arms, he caught a second wind. In a matter of seconds, he took off his remaining clothes. He stood naked, wearing only his socks and a silly grin.

"Tsk, tsk. True what they warn about alcohol," she said, eyeing his large but flaccid penis. She sighed. Even in that condition, he looked more like a man than did her fiancé, Graham. Then like an axed tree, Luca fell backward onto the bed and passed out.

Telma decided to change before retrieving the key. Her adoring fans at the café didn't want to see her in a drool-stained gown. She disrobed down to her panties when Luca's hand knocked the phone from the nightstand. In a panic, Telma rushed to the bedside. The last thing she wanted was the young communista running up to the room. Telma stood over Luca's naked prone body when she heard the door swing open behind her.

"You slut!" Recognizing the voice, Telma's heart pounded. "Mother was right about you."

Her body began to shake. She folded her arms across her breasts as she turned to face her accuser. Red-faced and trembling, Graham stood in the doorway. Before Telma had a chance to recover, Isa's voice echoed in the hall behind him. "Sorry, Graham. Not entirely her fault. Women are putty in the hands of that Frenchman." Isa pushed Graham into the room. She stood in triumph; chin up, head held high—quite a contrast to the jilted lover in Regent's Park. She glared, a sneer on her face. In her hand, Telma's Trojan horse, the full bottle of whiskey.

As Telma stood there, Isa's evil scheme crystallized in her head. No wonder she and Ana were so friendly. Granted, it didn't take much effort, but they pushed Philippe and her together. She understood why her calls to Graham in England went unanswered.

Her fiancé and Isa, shoulder-to-shoulder, stared in silence as if waiting for Telma to respond. Did they expect a fiery rebuke? Maybe a tearful plea for mercy? Instead, she took a deep breath and inched to her right. She didn't have to wait long. Isa's eyes widened; her lips and fingers twitched. The whiskey bottle crashed to the floor.

"Philippe, where's Philippe? I-I arranged—" she cried, gasping for breath.

And so Isabella Fabrini, skewered on her own sword, played her best dramatic role of the evening. That night, though, none but Luca slept.

Part III
Luca's Liberation

Chapter 33

London—Eighteen Months Later

"They here?" Luca Caruso wheezed after sprinting to his restaurant from the Covent Garden Underground. He guessed the answer. Of course they'd arrived. Although his guests' chosen professions afflicted them with tardiness, ninety minutes stretched beyond even their acceptable window.

"Yes, Signor Caruso. Your friends are here. I sent over a bottle of wine and starters with your compliments…and apologies."

Still catching his breath, he gave the pretty young woman a hug. "You're a star."

The woman blushed. Elizabeth Hyland had worked at the restaurant for three years, one of the few seasoned employees who hadn't jumped ship. Flaxen hair, clear blue eyes, and a creamy complexion miscast her as hostess of Amore. But what she lacked in Mediterranean looks she made up for with great efficiency, even spoiling Luca with her nurturing. Elizabeth didn't share her personal life. Although Luca had no patience for staff gossip, talk suggested that Elizabeth plodded through a string of relationships with what his most senior waiter called, ne'er-do-wells. Another rumor had her fleeing to London from an abusive boyfriend in Bristol. Whatever the young woman's past, Luca admired her professionalism and charm. She was good for business.

Elizabeth slipped two pieces of paper into Luca's hand.

"Tell them I'll be right down," he said before dashing up the stairs.

Pressing his pounding chest, Luca groaned at the dark upstairs dining room, yet another sign of waning fortunes. After flicking on the light to his paneled office, he gazed at the desk stacked with invoices. The tidy piles that Elizabeth sorted by past-due date caused his delay. Bankers never rushed when it came to credit line increases. He poured himself a drink, shaking his head over his predicament. A new restaurant was about to open down the street while another offering Italian tapas debuted to rave reviews in the Covent Garden piazza. Boutique eateries, designer chefs, and nouvelle cuisine were pushing aside the old guard. Food had turned into high fashion with global companies fronting the money. In no time, trendy eateries would fill the area, poaching what remained of his customers and staff.

A Sydney conglomerate was making inquiries—and no wonder. Luca's three locations would give the Aussies an instant foothold in the London market. Were they saviors or merely vultures waiting to swoop down on a gasping carcass? Whatever the motive, the Aussie scenario was preferable to Willy Epson's scheme to pluck him from ruin. Or was it? If Luca's inner voice screamed to slam the door on Willy and his unsavory associates, why did the plan linger in his thoughts?

Taking off his shirt, Luca held it to his nose. The cotton fabric reeked of cigarettes and alcohol. He hated himself for returning to filthy nicotine—so much so, that he drowned his guilt with gin. Or, was gin what led him back to cigarettes? Aftershave and breath mints covered his tracks. He squeezed into a crisp white shirt, hoping the blazer hid the missing button and stretched fabric. Shiny black Maglis replaced scuffed loafers.

He checked the mirror—tired eyes, red splotches, and puffiness, by-products of too much liquor and rich food. Weeks of skipping the health club had turned into months.

Downstairs, Luca glanced around the main dining room. Elizabeth had things under control. The half-empty room hummed with amiable banter. Instead of craning their necks in search of missing food and tardy servers, customers chatted away at tables. On the rare nights the restaurant booked full, service strained with inexperienced servers and an understaffed kitchen.

"All good tonight, Signor Caruso," said one waiter, hurrying past Luca with a tray of drinks.

Senior staff, he knew, put on brave faces although fear fed kitchen chatter. How much longer could he stave off a mass exodus? Luca nodded to a few regular customers before a colorful dream coat, radiating neon brilliance, drew his eyes to a corner table. He snuck up behind his old friend. Lavender strands, last holdouts of a once-proud mop, circled the round head in desperation.

"Leech, you still embrace the rainbow," Luca said, pressing his friend's shoulders.

Turning his pudgy neck slightly, the voice teacher patted Luca's hand. "I consider that a compliment, *bello*. Italians have an eye for fashion."

Luca grabbed his friend's hand and shook it vigorously before turning to Malcolm. The musician was on his feet, looking fit in skinny black trousers. They embraced.

"Leech has solved fashion's oldest dilemma," Malcolm said with boyish grin. "Drapes himself in every color imaginable. Something's bound to match."

"Mere envy, my lad, mere envy," Leech replied with faux indignation. He reached over and tugged on Malcolm's shirt. "Pink jacquard was my idea. If not for me, the lad would still dress like a funeral wreath."

With the finesse of a runway model, Malcolm flashed the lining of his black silk waistcoat. He revealed a scarlet paisley print.

Leech rubbed his hands together. "Well played, lad, well played."

"What am I, chopped liver?" said the third diner in their party.

Luca made his way around the table, bent down, and kissed the woman. "Good to see you, Irene."

"Save formality for the opera house, handsome."

Luca chuckled. How many times had she reminded him that among friends, she was simply Ivy? The singer's uncanny ability to switch between her stage personae amazed him. Matinee mavens from Mayfair would twist their pearls into knots if they knew that the Marguerite or Emilia trilling across the Royal Opera stage began her career as a burlesque queen. As a stripper, Ivy Vine wasn't only her stage name—a leafy green boa served as her signature striptease prop.

"You look lovely, *Ivy*," Luca said, studying her appearance. A scarf of red and white brightened a dove-gray sweater. Wispy bangs softened a full face. "What's different?"

A slight pink blushed her cheek. "My hair. Just had it done," she replied, pushing strands behind an ear. "Called a flirty bob."

"Adore flirty Bobs," said Leech with a playful laugh, "and flirty Shanes, Ewans…"

Luca grinned. An evening of good humor would do him good. "Sorry to be late," he said, "but Elizabeth said she took care of you." As he sat, he scanned the table. The Nero d'Avola was spent, but his friends' glasses were full.

Leech pulsed his eyebrows toward the empty starter plates piled before him. "You'll not hear a peep of complaint from me, nary a peep."

Following Ivy's lead, Malcolm and Leech raised glasses in a toast to their host.

"Lizzy's a peach," bubbled Ivy.

"We lacked for nothing," added Malcolm, "except your good company."

Although thankful for their kind words, Luca sighed. "My new restaurant's a drain."

"So Elizabeth told us," Leech said. "Hear you've been killing yourself. Staff's worried about you, she said. All work, no play, and no razor from the look of things."

Luca's hand rose to his chin; his stubble scratched like sandpaper.

Ivy squeezed his arm. "Don't mind him, handsome. I adore rough and tumble."

"You and me both," said Malcolm. "I say, why not add a manager?"

Luca avoided an urge to point out the empty tables and chide his friends to open their eyes. He couldn't afford another hire. He wished Elizabeth hadn't mentioned his workload. But he couldn't scold her. His short fuse was as guilty as deep-pocketed competitors for the exit of good staff. The thought of losing her made him shudder. He'd already made apologies for his brutish behavior more times than he cared to remember. Why she stayed was a mystery to him.

Luca shrugged, attempting a smile. "Restaurant openings are brutal. Can't really trust anyone else. Afraid it all falls on my shoulders."

A rational businessman, he told himself, *would have cancelled expansion plans.* The two current locations were floundering. Perhaps he was as delusional as the unhappy couple whose cure for marital woe consisted of tossing a new baby into the toxic mix. *Fools.* Pride kept him from shutting his restaurants and pulling the plug on the third. Or was it fear—fear of adding to his litany of failures, fear that he was too old and broken to start over?

"New place is on the South Bank, right?" asked Ivy.

Luca nodded. "The area's hot. Killer views of Tower Bridge."

"Killer rents, too, I imagine," Malcolm said.

The pianist was right. With the London Eye to the west and Tower Bridge to the east, the once seedy side of the Thames had undergone a renaissance that saw a new Globe Theatre, the Tate Modern, and a steadied Millennium Bridge join the National Theatre complex. Investors and speculators flooded the area. It took money, as is said, to make money.

"Thinking of closing this location?" asked Leech.

Piercing eyes informed Luca that this was less a question, more a suggestion. Leech had been a regular since the restaurant opened. No doubt he remembered the glory days when one didn't dine at Amore without a reservation and weekends booked months in advance. Now, however, economy-minded tourists replaced the chic set.

"Not my plan," Luca said, still trying to smile. "Hoping South Bank draws new customers to the brand. Success breeds success."

Malcolm and Ivy smiled, nodding tepid agreement to the glib prophecy. But Leech turned somber as he gulped wine, probably considering the more likely outcome—*failure begets failure*. Restaurants seldom pulled out of a tailspin, diners growing fewer and fewer, kept away by the specter of a crashing business. Despair risked spoiling the evening—Luca had to change the tone.

"If group packages and loyal dining programs don't fill the place," Luca said, drawing nervous chuckles, "I can always sell." He lowered his voice to avoid rattling staff. "An Australian syndicate's interested."

Leech perked up. The entire mood of the table lifted.

"Bloody fabulous," cooed Ivy.

"Fantastic," added Malcolm. "You can retire to a life of country squire."

Leech eyed Luca with concern. "Wonderful news, *bello*. But what would you do?"

"Count my money," Luca said to hearty laughter. "Let's cross that bridge…" he added as much for their benefit as his own. The Aussies' intentions remained unclear. Empty restaurants didn't command price premiums.

Leech tapped the tablecloth. "I've got it. You could sing opera."

Luca scowled. That page from his past was closed. Had he made a mistake in sharing with Leech the tragedy that ended his career?

"Speaking of singing," Ivy said. "The opera's been cancelled."

Luca flinched. "*Otello?* Cancelled?"

The group of friends had arranged the dinner around their rehearsal schedule for the Royal Opera's new production. Productions brought Luca hungry customers. A dark opera house would send him over the financial cliff. The mood chilled; Malcolm and Leech froze. All eyes looked to Ivy whose cheeks ripened to a full blush.

"Oh, oh, oh," Ivy stammered. "Sorry, friggin' forgot."

"Forgot? Forgot what?" Luca asked.

Leech cleared his throat, rolling his eyes at Ivy. "She meant Isa's opera, er, her concert. You know, the San Benedetto spectacular."

Luca felt the scrutiny on his warming face. "News to me. Isa and I aren't exactly on speaking terms."

Malcolm and Ivy glanced down to their laps as if suddenly finding their napkins fascinating. Only Leech maintained eye contact.

Luca snapped his fingers. "Where's the bloody waiter? David! David!" he shouted, flagging over a cherub-faced young man. "Gin martini for me, more wine for my guests. And clear away these filthy plates."

Ivy looked up from her lap. "Sorry. We intended to have a cheery gab and now I've put you in a pisser of a mood. Here," she said pulling something from her purse, "Ticket for *Otello*, opening night, main floor center. Forget I said anything about Isa."

Luca smoothed the tablecloth, embarrassed with his outburst. He'd apologize to David later. He thought he'd packed away all the old feelings for his former lover. "No worries. I'm fine. Isa and I weren't meant to be, that's all. Happy to hear she's still singing. Shall we order?"

"Aren't you curious?" Leech asked.

Luca dropped his face into the menu that he knew by heart. "About what?"

"Why Isa cancelled, *bello*." Leech's tone suggested suspicion that Luca was playing coy.

Luca reread the main-dish descriptions for the fifth time. "Could be money, health, her voice. Any number of things."

"She's doing remarkably well…financially," replied Malcolm.

"Her health…at least physically is quite fab," added Ivy.

"And her singing hasn't been better." Leech's tone was that of a proud teacher.

"Splendid!" Luca tried to hide his annoyance with Isa's near-perfect state of affairs.

"It's her father, my dear Luca," said Leech. "Seriously ill. No hope."

"The sweet man has lasted longer than doctors expected," added Ivy.

Leech nodded. "It's a stroke, very bad. Isa and her sisters are in San Benedetto. A vigil of sorts."

"Poor man," Luca said. "Soul of the Fabrinis. Poor Isa—" He stopped himself. He felt great sorrow. But what right had he to single out Isa for sympathy? Their bond was broken. Showering his former lover with special pity smacked of insincerity. "My heart goes out to all the Fabrinis."

Leech coughed. Whether a result of chain smoking or a prearranged cue, Luca didn't know. Ivy and Malcolm excused themselves for the toilets.

Leech waited for David to deposit their drinks and clear the dishes before tapping the table. "My dear Luca, call her."

"Isa? Call Isa?"

He stared into Luca's eyes. "Yes, Isa. It's been ages."

"Precisely. Nearly eighteen months and she hasn't rung up to apologize."

Leech shook his head. "You're both miserable."

Luca's back stiffened. "I'm perfectly fine," he said in a huff. "And we only just heard that Isa's perfect as well. 'Remarkably well' were Malcolm's words. Ivy said, *fab.*' I have that correct, no?"

Leech eyed Luca over steepled hands. "You and Isa are very dear to me. I want to see you both happy."

"She should have considered that before rushing to judgment about Telma Rossi and me."

Leech narrowed his eyes. "She found you in that woman's bed."

Luca scoffed. "She wouldn't listen to reason. Broke up Telma's engagement."

"What can I say?" Leech said with a shrug. "Nudity turns people into lunatics."

"Thanks, Leech, but it's over. We're through."

"Think about it, *bello*. Despite smiles and cheery words, you're teetering on the abyss. You need Isa and she needs you."

Fear and guilt! Do-gooders always invoked fear and guilt. Those twin demons already haunted Luca because of his business. His liver and lungs couldn't endure much more *fear and guilt*. Now Leech stoked the same emotions with the plight of the woman he loved, or thought he loved.

Leech downed a half glass of wine before he spoke again. "Luca, I saw your expression when I mentioned your singing. Aha," he added, pointing at his friend's glowering face, "there's that scowl again."

"I've locked that part of my past away. You know my reasons."

"Yes, *bello*, I know why. Doesn't make me any less sorry for you."

"Don't pity me."

"You're right. You carry that burden well enough on your own."

Luca wanted to ask Leech what he understood of burdens, knew of pain, but he knew all too well that everyone had demons. Hurt, loss, and despair were as much a part of the human condition as were birth and death.

Leech looked from Luca to the tablecloth. His hand quaked. "A fine show I put on for the world. The comical Leech, a Technicolor caricature. You wouldn't have recognized your ole pal in his twenties." He described a first love, a flamboyant boy, who attracted him for everything he wasn't or couldn't be. "As much as Edwin adorned himself in glitter and sequins, I was the drab boy that no one minded…or wanted for that matter, until Edwin."

"I don't believe that."

"As much as you think my vibrant exterior hides layers of fading color, you couldn't be further from the truth. Scratch the surface I'm a boring battleship gray. Color is my refuge. Edwin showed me that it was okay to be different, to find men attractive and to love them. And I loved Edwin." His eyes moistened.

"You've never mentioned him."

"Over in a flash, *bello*." Leech's expression signaled that his mind had traveled back in time "Edwin wore ridicule as a badge of honor. The more they mocked, the more colorful he became. They hated that. *They*, those cruel people who prey on unique souls like Edwin. His refusal to cower in the face of their bullying infuriated them. When he saw the power of his cheekiness, Edwin didn't stop. No, *they* stopped him with their fists. Beat him to a bloody pulp in a rat-infested alley. A threat to their manhood, I suppose. Barbarians always snuff out the light they don't understand."

Luca squeezed his friend's hand. "That's when you decided to put on your colorful mantle. A tribute of sorts to your lover."

Leech's gaze drifted over Luca's shoulder. "No! That came years later. I mourned in agonizing silence. Still too much the coward to admit I was different."

"Understandable in light of Edwin's tragic death."

"Absurd, that's what it was," he said, looking Luca full in the face. His blue eyes fired. "Other cruel bullies—and there are *always* others—found me behind wire rim glasses and Marks & Spencer wool. Edwin's brave life flashed before my eyes. I decided that hiding was pointless. I became the fabulous butterfly that now flutters before you—as much for sweet Edwin as for myself."

"And just maybe for a legion of Leeches and Edwins hiding in the gray shadows." Luca thought that he'd never forget the look of pride on Leech's face. Both dabbed their eyes.

"So you see, Luca, there's no sense keeping your past a secret. They will find you—and sometimes *they* are the unrelenting voices of your own conscience."

Later, Luca bid farewell to his friends and made his way up to the office, where he poured out a cognac. Leech gave him much to consider. Luca's fondness for the colorful man deepened with his brave confession. He took a deep breath and thrust his hands into his trouser pockets. Feeling a piece of paper, he remembered the unread messages. Fishing out the slips, he flattened them on the table to reveal Elizabeth's neat handwriting. *Mr. Epson rang up. Says you're all set. Got the man for the job.* The next message trumped the first. *Telma Rossi stopped by. Needs to see you.*

Chapter 34

"Damn it all to hell," Luca grumbled. Standing in front of the dressing mirror in his Holland Park flat, he pinched a finger attempting to fasten the shirt's collar button.

He had remembered alterations for the dinner jacket and trousers but the need for a new, larger shirt slipped his mind. The tailor's generosity flustered him. He refused to take any money to let out the suit. "Let people help, Luca," the tailor had said. "It's not charity. You've fed half the tradesmen of Covent Garden at one time or another. Consider it a return on your investment."

Luca fastened the bow tie, pulling tight to secure the unbuttoned collar. He grumbled at his reflection. "If you hadn't given away so much free spaghetti, you wouldn't be in this bloody mess." Fingers grappled with the cummerbund. "Maybe if you'd given away more, you'd be able to squeeze into your damn clothes."

A premiere at the Royal Opera was a rare treat, a luxury for his constricted budget. "Kind of Ivy to think of me," he said aloud, sitting on the bed and sliding into shoes. Was the free ticket a friendly gesture or simply another return on investment for the free meals he'd given her as a struggling dancer? He shook his head. Motives didn't matter. That night he intended to enjoy himself, pleased that the tailor's magic transformed him from overstuffed sausage to debonair gentleman. At least for one night he could pretend to be a commercial prince, one of London's successful entrepreneurs.

He walked the two short blocks to Holland Park Avenue, thankful that the late February precipitation was mere drizzle and not sleet or snow. Headlights lit up the wet pavement; tires swooshed through puddles spraying the curb with water. The air retained the raw, steely smell of winter rain. The fresh, crisp scent of spring showers was still weeks away. He flagged down a black cab, catching the driver just after he deposited a fare at the Hilton Hotel.

As the cab slogged through central London's dense Friday traffic, Luca stared out the window. Water-splattered glass, the rhythm of windshield wipers, and an army of light particles created by the prism of rain brought to mind another cab ride, another rainy night ferried to an opera house.

It was Milan, twenty years in the past. Winter rain with a harsh, metallic odor came in torrents, carried into the city on Alpine winds.

The argument was stupid really, but Luca remembered every detail as if it were yesterday. An exhibit at their daughter's school, a silly little art project. Amelia's teacher delayed his wife, Giovanna, to discuss programs for gifted students. Giovanna and Amelia arrived home to find Luca pacing the entry hall.

"You've made me late," he bellowed as they scurried in the door. He met their kisses with a sneer. "Let's go."

Giovanna protested. "Good Lord, no! We can't go to your premiere looking like street urchins. I won't be seen at La Scala dressed like this. And your little Picasso…" she added, raising their daughter's paint-smudged hand. Amelia hopped forward.

"No! Not tonight," Luca shouted, staggering backward. Stung by the hurt on her angelic face, he added, "Poppie can't get dirty…my little doll." But the damage was done. Amelia sniffled back tears. *Why didn't I kiss the top of her precious head? Why didn't I scoop her up in my arms?*

Giovanna pushed him toward the door. "Go then, Signor Opera Star."

"Honey, I can't be late." A softened tone was an attempt to apologize for his short temper. "It's my big break…our chance at a good future."

He'd paid his dues for several years singing in the chorus, working a second job in a cousin's restaurant to pay for voice lessons. He understood his good fortune. Many singers waited, and still never got a chance to solo. He was surprised when the opera company called him to audition for the role of Dottore Grenvil in *La Traviata*. When he got the part, he was flabbergasted. Anxiety showed itself in bursts of anger. He was scared of failing, afraid he'd never get a second chance. The chorus didn't pay well.

Luca felt inadequate as a provider for his family. He and Giovanna wanted to give their daughter more opportunities. Amelia was a precocious eight-year-old who showed signs of artistic genius. Brilliance demanded money to blossom.

"Go! Take the damn car," Giovanna said, still pushing his arm.

"Too late." He didn't have time to park and make it to the theater. He needed to wrap his head around the role, not lose it tangling with Milanese drivers.

"Fine, grab a cab. I'll follow with Amelia in another."

He seethed, counting to five as he felt his forehead vein throb. "Take the car," he said, calming to a simmer. "I don't pay for it to sit in the garage." They could barely afford one cab fare from the suburbs into the city—then a return trip home.

"You know I hate to drive into the city, especially in this weather."

His grimace stopped her protest. As he bolted out the door and into the pouring rain, his wife called after him from the front door. "See you at the theater. Break a leg."

Was she wishing him good luck or cursing him to suffer an actual fracture for being such an ass?

Luca didn't find out until after the performance, a triumph based on the praise lavished upon him by fellow cast members as well as the audience's response to his curtain call. The reviews were glowing. But they were meaningless in the throes of grief. As other cast members received friends and family backstage after the performance, Luca received two members of the Milan police force. They informed him that Amelia and Giovanna died when their car was broadsided by another vehicle whose driver explained that he didn't see the red light through the rain.

"Ya did say the Royal Opera House? Well, here we are." Turning from the front seat, the taxi driver raised his voice.

"Sorry, sorry, yes, yes," Luca stammered. The present reclaimed his conscious and he reached for his wallet.

Stepping out at the curb, Luca found himself awash in glamor. While lacking the spectacle of the season opening gala, premieres were still posh affairs. Bentleys and Mercedes snaked down Bow Street. Barristers, bankers, solicitors, and celebrities were among the horde of polished people parading toward the theater, a white neoclassical treasure with a six-columned portico above a ground floor base. He scanned the crowd, tempered in conspicuous splendor by umbrellas and raincoats. A few brave souls bolted from cabs, zigzagging through the bustling pavement to the doors.

"Can't be," Luca muttered, focusing on a figure by the door nearest his approach. He'd have to pass her to enter. He didn't want to see that woman and he certainly didn't want her to see him.

He glued himself to a herd of young professionals trudging toward a farther, less crowded entrance. They huddled, melded together by the rain. The men in designer tuxedos held umbrellas for fashion-plate perfect wives and girlfriends. Luca kept the urban wolf pack between himself and the unwelcome specter. The clump inched forward in stops and starts. A braggart hijacked the group's conversation. Like most boasters, he revealed his overblown history telling a self-serving tale of a storied career in investment banking. He halted the group for his banal climax—some insipid lament about the curses of too much money. Luca resisted an urge to throttle him.

The snail-paced advance soaked Luca, who had no umbrella. But he couldn't race ahead to risk her spotting him. When the woman turned her neck, her face caught the light. Luca felt a mix of nausea and dread. The woman was indeed Telma Rossi.

The dark hair was back. The face wasn't as taut or as fresh as he recalled, a sign perhaps that she neared the end of a nip-and-tuck cycle. But the eyes were the same—dark, purposeful, and, if one looked closely, marked by a dash of fear. Who was she waiting for—another trust fund mama's boy or an octogenarian millionaire? Perhaps, the evening was less business, more pleasure and she waited for a gigolo.

Like a vacuum, the herd to which he clung sucked him into the foyer. He shrank into a corner from where he scanned the entrances. *Who is that woman's current prey? Pitiable fool.* But Telma entered alone. Had her escort already slipped in or did he linger outside? Perhaps he got wise and stood her up? Luca willed the temptress toward the balcony, the grand tier, or even the stalls circle, anywhere but the orchestra stalls.

Fate can't be so cruel as to give her a seat in my row?

She disappeared into the ladies' toilet, giving Luca a chance to sneak into the auditorium. He found his row, seventh from the orchestra pit, and made his way to his seat. After nervous glances at the doors, he settled in and inspected the program. Ivy's picture and name—a flattering black and white headshot of Irene Vine as Emilia, wife of Iago and maid to Desdemona—produced a smile. Career highlights didn't mention her stripper past. Malcolm's name appeared as pianist and Leech grabbed an honorary mention among the assistant voice coaches.

A commotion came from just over Luca's shoulder. The loud voice broke his concentration. "Of course you don't mind swapping. I've got two seats just a couple of rows back." The tone suggested a command, not a request. Fate laughed at him. The voice was a familiar blend of Argentine and English accents. He turned toward the noise, but people blocked his view. He didn't make out what else she said, but people stood in his row and shifted to let in the seat swapper.

"Luca Caruso," Telma said, squeezing his arm, almost pulling him up from his seat. He guessed that was his cue to rise.

He kissed her cheek. "What a surprise. It's been—"

"Too long, you brute," she interrupted, slapping his hand before they sat. "And you haven't returned my phone calls. Hell, I even dropped by your restaurant. Brushed away by that storm trooper of a hostess."

"Elizabeth? She's a dear."

"Whatever." Telma's hand backswept through the air. "Can't imagine how she got a job in public contact. Practically tossed me out the door."

"I'll speak to her." *Yes, next time Telma Rossi doesn't make it across the threshold.*

"From the look of things, you can't afford to turn away…"

His neck stiffened. "What?"

She froze except for dark eyes that darted about as if revving up her mind. "Nothing. Only…well, you know…in business competitive forces…"

Luca's chest heaved. If typhoon Telma planned to ruin his one evening of escape, she had better move to the highest balcony before he launched her arse up there with a swift kick. He took a deep breath, counting to five. "Such a coincidence."

She fidgeted in her seat. "What is?"

"Your being here. It *is* a coincidence."

She cozied closer, rubbing shoulders. The smell of perfume, the same oriental blend he recalled from San Benedetto, reached his nose. "Sort of."

At last, the truth—somehow she'd planned their *chance* meeting.

Was Ivy an accomplice? Luca's voice rose with annoyance. "I suspected as much. What do you want?"

She caressed his arm with short, soft strokes. "Down, boy. I'm not that fiendishly clever. What I meant was, well…I saw you outside in the foyer... in the corner. You looked like a frightened little boy. I just knew then that I had to sit next to you." She told him how she stood in the aisle, waiting for patrons with tickets in his row. Her actual seats were a few rows back. She confessed to playing the role of a grieving widow who always sat in the same row with her dearly departed husband. "An Olivier Award performance," she said with girlish giggle. "You were so absorbed in the program, you didn't even notice."

Luca laughed, a robust bellow rising from the depths of his abdomen that drew glares from the well-heeled crowd. "Shameless, but genuine. That's what you are." Her confession put him at ease. This was no premeditated ambush, merely a tactical maneuver. She saw her opportunity and seized it. He patted her arm. "Do tell, why have you been harassing me?"

"You make me sound like a stalker or worse, a bill collector. I—"

The matronly woman seated in front whose hair resembled the graying helmet of the Queen, shushed them. The conductor had appeared and the orchestra began the overture.

Telma leaned over and whispered in his ear, "The green-eyed monster. How fiendishly poetic."

Luca cringed, closing his eyes. He hadn't thought of it before. Telma was right. Verdi's *Otello* set to music, Shakespeare's masterpiece of jealousy and the tragic folly of blind rage, was indeed a fitting soundtrack. While not of the same dramatic excess, the green-eyed monster clawed at the lives of Isa, Telma, and him. Was fate preparing him for a new adventure?

"Let's chat at intermission," Telma said, ignoring both Luca's brooding scowl and the shushing blue hair. "Treat me to a champagne cocktail and I'll tell you about an Argentine acquaintance who's very interested in your South Bank site."

Luca groaned as he turned toward her. His face warmed and he prepared to unleash a fury of curses. Telma held a finger to her lips. "Shush, now. All I'm asking is you think about it. He'll pay handsomely. He doesn't understand *no*."

Luca looked past Telma and saw a familiar face several rows back and to the side—Isa's Scottish friend, Jamie. Did Luca detect a judgmental sneer in the man's face? The curtain opened; Luca was hemmed in. His chest pounded. Perspiration beaded his forehead. He'd never felt more trapped in his life…on all fronts. His choices were few—fight, surrender—or escape.

Chapter 35

"You're finished."
Even though Luca's own thoughts echoed with similar words, they sounded harsher when spoken by someone else. "Wasn't this supposed to be a pep talk?"

"Can't help you, Luca, till you get your head out of your arse."

As Willy Epson talked, his brooding associate stared silently over a coffee cup. Steel-gray eyes studied the shelf above Luca's head yet the stranger didn't seem the type interested in antique coffee grinders or presses. Instead, the slight man in a crisp blue suit processed everything… and everyone. Willy introduced the man as Jay, or perhaps it was simply J—Luca never knew. No surname was offered and the man's viselike grip and menacing sneer deterred clarification. He looked the type who, if choosing to speak, asked but never answered questions.

Willy selected the meeting point, a popular coffee shop in Monmouth Street on the other side of Covent Garden from Luca's restaurant. The area known as Seven Dials owed its name to the convergence of seven streets and the large sundial marking the intersection. Originally designed as a fashionable quarter, nineteenth-century crooks turned the place into a notorious center of crime. Was the irony lost on Willy or planned? In recent years, Seven Dials transformed into shabby chic, attracting moneyed young people to boutiques and bars.

The shop chosen for the rendezvous was tiny but drew long queues for its baked goods and takeaway coffee. Customers hovered, hoping to snare a seat in one of the half-dozen or so booths at the back. Communal dining may have been encouraged, but J's repelling leers secured the trio's privacy.

Willy surprised him when he suggested such a public place. "Gotta show the world we got nothing to hide," he replied to Luca's concern. *How cliché. Those who professed they'd nothing to hide were always the most guilty.*

"Best cappuccino in London," Willy said, holding a large cup before him. "Still roast the coffee in the basement. Told the owners they won't get ahead that way. Gotta think big. Take risk." After another sip, Willy lowered his cup. The delighted expression of coffee aficionado transformed into stone-faced deal maker. "Say the word, Luca. J springs into action."

Luca couldn't believe he was talking about arson as casually as if it were a latte or a macchiato. Willy's version of financial restructuring outside the hostile reach of bankruptcy court had the cash-strapped restaurant owner torching the Covent Garden location, flipping South Bank to a high bidder and walking away from the Bayswater lease. "You'll be comfortable," Willy said when he first proposed the plan weeks before. "Take your money and move on, carefree. Others do it. Hell, arson's not that different from derivatives—lots of smoke, no assets, and oodles of cash." He had a way of making criminal activity sound respectable, and respectable pursuits sound criminal. The same logic, no doubt, helped City and Wall Street bankers sleep at night.

Lucia looked across the table to J. The menacing man still glared at the wall. Luca assumed he hadn't lost a pinkie, half an index finger, or the top of an ear butchering meat. "So when would you do it, burn down the restaurant?"

J didn't respond. He merely sipped his coffee and turned his eyes toward Willy who smiled a grotesque jack-o'-lantern grin. "I said we should be visible," Willy seethed through gritted teeth. "Didn't say to broadcast our plan on BBC. J doesn't *do* anything. That clear, Luca?" He nodded. "Good. Like me, J has…associates."

Luca's hands covered his eyes then slid down his face before steepling under his chin. "I need time."

J returned his gaze to the wall, a smirk detected on thin gray lips. Willy squeezed Luca's arm. "Bury your head in the sand, Luca, and you may as well dig the whole grave. Time's running out. You know that, Luca."

Willy's repeated use of his name stung, verbal pokes to the chest. Truth was, he knew time was running out. The bank was mere weeks away from cutting off his credit, the lifeline needed to complete the South Bank expansion and to fund continuing operations. Sufficient money remained to pay staff, cover lease payments on the Bayswater and South Bank locations, and meet the Covent Garden mortgage for three, maybe four months. Luca hesitated pulling the trigger on his business. If he eked through the February and March doldrums, might he survive until tourists returned in April? But foolish optimism wasn't a strategy.

He took a deep breath. "I'll let you know."

J cleared his throat, drawing curious stares from Willy and Luca. In a voice more ominous because of its unexpected high pitch, he spoke, "Your funeral."

The best cappuccino in London left a bitter aftertaste. Exiting the coffee shop, Luca walked in the direction away from his restaurant, first shuffling, then hurrying along the pavement. He needed to distance himself from the dirty business. A colorful sign, warm amber lights, and a pleasant hum of cordial voices beckoned him. He walked through the doors into the malty fog of the Bloomsday Pub. His energy surged; troubles lifted from his shoulders on angel's wings.

"Whiskey and pint of stout," he said to the publican, a ruddy-faced Irishman.

Once he paid, Luca and his liquid comforters found a quiet corner near the electric fireplace. After a sip of whiskey, he set down the glass and rubbed his hands along his shoulders to numb the chill. Willy's plan, although unpalatable, solved the entire problem and left him money—enough to resettle. The Australians demanded all three locations. But their terms weren't as favorable. Yes, their deal erased all debt and liabilities, but it left him with nothing except the taint of failure and the dismal prospect of starting over. And Telma? She kept calling, slowly raising the bid for the prime South Bank real estate. Taken alone, her offer did nothing to alleviate the mountain of debt and operating deficits of his other two locations. But, paired with Willy's plan…

"Well, look who we've got here."

The voice stirred him—Irish—not unusual for the Bloomsday Pub—but familiar. Pint in hand, he looked up. Standing before him in a green jumper was a round, white face haloed by red curls. *Brigid or Kate?*

"Nay, don't get up, darlin'," she said. "Ya can show yourself a gentleman by buyin' this fair lady a drink. The usual, Sean," she shouted across the crowded room to the smiling publican. "Home away from home," she said, sliding onto the padded bench next to him. In the process of removing hat and scarf, her oversized sack toppled, spilling books onto the table and floor. Luca snatched up his whiskey and stout in the nick of time. "Sorry, darlin'," she said with girlish giggle. "Might be cheaper to pay a blasted psychiatrist. Self-help's robbin' me blind and achin' Katie Maureen Mahoney's weary bones," she added, rubbing her forearm.

"Kate," Luca exclaimed, thankful for the prompt. He shoved the books back into her bag.

She furrowed her brow at his outburst but continued speaking, "Haven't seen ya since San Benedetto. All suffered dry mouth and droopy eyes that Sunday as we waved our good-byes, didn't we?"

He assumed a sheepish grin, uncomfortable with the revisit of that horrible day. Maybe she'd forgotten, or at the very least, valued discretion. Luca nodded. "All of us partied mighty hard."

Kate cackled, wagging a finger in his face. "Some more than others."

He gulped; his face warmed. His thoughts raced back to San Benedetto, a year and a half in the past.

He didn't remember much of that Sunday, the morning after Isa's concert. He awoke naked in an unfamiliar bed, his head pounding and his mouth tasting like a sour bar rag. His eyes adjusted slowly to the dark; the only light came from a vertical sliver of sunshine where the curtains met. He scanned his surroundings for clues but the room was practically ransacked—closet and drawers opened and emptied. He picked up the phone and dialed the operator.

"Signora Rossi?" He recognized Svetlana's voice. "Oh, *scusi, scusi,*" she added hastily. "Signor Caruso. Forgive me. I forget. Signora Rossi, she check out early."

"What's the time?"

"11:30, Signor Caruso. Breakfast over but I can send up coffee... and aspirin."

"Bene, bene. Grazie," Luca said and hung up.

Of course, Telma's room. Memories clicked through his mind like flickering images of a skipping cinema reel. He lifted himself out of bed, clutching his throbbing head. The stench of stale whiskey drew his eyes to the floor as he pulled open the drapes. A wet spot stained the rug. A few glass shards on the carpet caught the sun. Nearer the bed, a second stain stirred recollections of his drinking binge. His stomach churned with nausea and hunger.

He saw two pieces of paper on the pillow. The top note, carefully folded, was neatly addressed with his full name. The second slip, also on hotel stationery and scratched in red lipstick, didn't need a signature to tell him that Isa was its author. While the tones were markedly different, both notes relayed similar messages—*good-bye* and *get lost.*

Isa's lipstick tube remained on the nightstand. A broken tip and scarlet shavings offered insight into the fury of her farewell. He heaved a heavy sigh; he felt his muscles tighten. Surrendering to despair, he'd allowed himself to react irrationally. Rather than recognizing Isa's anger as a symptom of fear and vulnerability, he sought refuge in alcohol and revenge, the latter achieved by embracing Telma.

"Isa, dear Isa," Luca muttered aloud, holding her note in one hand and his head in the other. "You have every right to be furious."

Telma's note detailed every embarrassing moment. Fresh carpet stains and his horrible physical state corroborated her testimony. When Svetlana brought the coffee, aspirins, and his room key, she explained that Telma booked an early train to Rome and flew back to London.

"Cancelled her annulment interview," Svetlana added with raised eyebrow.

After showering, shaving, and trying to push puffiness from his face with cold water, Luca ran to the flat of Isa's parents. He planned to drop to his knees and apologize for acting like an idiot. Then, if Isa didn't knock him unconscious, he'd confess his love. She had to listen, to believe him, to forgive him…to love him. He was lost without her.

But Isa wouldn't see him. From an upper window, she screamed down to the street, "Go! I don't need you. Don't need any man. Get the hell out of my life."

She slammed the window. He held his head in his hands. Tears welled in his eyes when the front door opened. Papa Fabrini stood at the threshold on Ana's arm. He beckoned. Luca deserved the stern glare of Isa's younger sister before her father sent her back upstairs. Papa Fabrini and he sat in the building's lobby, the older man on a straight-back chair, he on the radiator.

"Listen, my boy. Isabella doesn't want to see you."

"I have to see her. Tell her how much I need her, how much I love her."

He shook his head. "She won't listen. Maybe she should, maybe she shouldn't. I don't know. But she won't hear what you have to say. Give her time."

"But I need to beg her forgiveness."

Mama Fabrini's gruff voice came from somewhere above. "Find a priest. Ask him for forgiveness."

Papa Fabrini rolled his eyes and dropped his voice to a whisper. He looked genuinely pained at Luca's grief. "Sorry, my boy, truly I am. My daughter's a sensitive creature. Maybe all women are. Prides herself on strength, independence."

"Damn her independent streak!" *I hate it...and admire it.* He sighed. The great satisfaction and, yes, even pride that Isa took in self-sufficiency made her tumbles into emotional waters that much harder for her to tread. But foibles and all, that was the Isa he loved.

Papa Fabrini patted Luca's arm. "You're nice, sincere. But, you're a man and we men think too much with what's inside our pants."

"B-but I didn't do anything."

A mischievous grin formed on his face. "Not me you have to convince, or even her," he said, thumbing toward Mama Fabrini's voice. "Hold off on your wanderings until after the ring."

"But I'm not—"

He held up his palm. "Okay, okay. Let's assume you're innocent. My principessa's heart also breaks. Wounds don't heal with words."

"When can I see her?"

He shrugged. "That's up to Isa."

"Can't you help?"

"Dear boy, I'm sympathetic, but not crazy. I live behind enemy lines. I've got three women upstairs and a fourth in Buenos Aires. Wife and daughters who don't trust me simply because I'm a man."

How Luca wanted to push past him, bolt up the stairs past Mama Fabrini to the flat, break down the door if necessary. But Papa Fabrini's heart wasn't strong. Luca didn't press. He left San Benedetto and flew to London without seeing Isa. Weeks went by before she returned his phone calls, and only then to make arrangements to collect her things from his flat.

"Listen, darlin', if you'd rather be alone." Kate's brogue and the clanking of the electric fireplace brought his mind back to the pub.

"No, no. Mind wandered, that's all. Been doing that a lot lately."

Kate sat up, twinkle in her eyes and color in her cheeks. She dug around in her bag. "Here," she said. "Take these. She placed two colorful paperbacks on the table with the prescriptive titles: *Leash Your Inner Voice* and *Hocus, Pocus, Focus: A Primer on Mind Control.* "'Twas fate that brought me here."

Over the course of two hours and three or four whiskeys, Kate caught Luca up with her activities and those of several others who bonded during Isa's concert weekends.

After a landslide election, Brad and Alexandra Novak moved into the governor's mansion. Kate didn't know the details, but rumors of a scandal with a pool boy and an FBI probe involving wiretaps cast a cloud over their reign.

"Then there's Philippe," Kate said with a sigh. "Jailed somewhere in the States, poor man. Addiction finally caught up with him. Attempted vehicular manslaughter while under the influence, or some such charge."

There but for the grace of God, he thought. "Attempted? So no one died?"

"Little consolation for the victims, I imagine. Philippe was to be out for Isa's next concert. Been cancelled, ya know."

"Yes, shame about her father. Good man."

"Ironic. He'd want to her to sing."

Luca didn't want to talk about Isa or dredge up his shameful past. Frankly, Kate's litany of tragedy began to depress him further. "Got any good news?"

She laughed, gulped down one whiskey, and motioned Sean for another. Her eyes looked as if they were trying to read Luca's face. She started and stopped before he finally spoke, "Well? Good news or bad?"

"That's just it. Depends on your perspective."

"Tell me. I'll judge for myself."

"Hear Telma Rossi's busted, flat broke. Walter cut her off completely. One too many escapades, I guess." A slight pink rose in her cheeks. "She's been taking on odd jobs here and there."

Luca understood why Kate, a friend of Isa, would look at Telma's bad fortune as good news—Isa's nemesis gets her comeuppance, divine retribution, karma. Luca didn't consider Telma a friend, but he sympathized with her plight. Her misfortunes had familiar echoes.

Kate cleared her throat. "Here's a piece of news that's not controversial. Danny, Tommy, and Miguel visited Dublin this past summer. All lookin' fit and best of buddies."

"Good to hear. And you? What goes well for Kate Maureen Mahoney?"

She blushed; a girlish grin lifted his spirits. "Gentleman's taken a fancy to me...and me to him. Owe it all to concert weekend."

Luca hoisted his glass. "Cheers. Happy for you."

She described how they met at Isa's last concert. He was an Englishman who'd migrated to Australia but found himself back in London as his company's local chief. "He's dreamy, rich...and available."

"Fantastic."

"Ripped Brigid and me apart, though. She can't stomach me fraternizing with the enemy. Hates the English, no matter that my man migrated to Australia. I get it. Owin' to the tragedy with her son, ya know."

Luca did not know. But, he didn't want to poke around in someone else's troubles when he had more than enough of his own. He remembered Brigid as a cheerful soul with a streak of playful mischief. Her secret tale of woe proved again to him that demons haunted everyone. "Sorry. A pity that sadness spoils her joy for you."

She inhaled and slapped her knee. "Enough of my chattin'. Tell me about Luca Caruso."

Luca described his business dilemma, omitting the illegal and unethical details. Kate and a couple of whiskeys coaxed his tale of relationship woe with Isa. "Tell you what," Kate said. "I'm here for a Lighthouse course. Meets in Russell Square. How 'bout you come along?"

Chapter 36

Wearing only briefs, Luca stood in his bedroom, staring into the wardrobe. What did one wear to a course intended to bare the soul and strip away layers of deceit?

"Save time if I turned up naked," he mumbled aloud, swigging the last of the vodka tonic. "Best just grab something that fits," he added, catching his plump profile in the dressing mirror.

Lighthouse? The promise of motivation, inspiration, and empowerment, among other things, sounded fanciful. Five decades of life taught him that anything that seemed too good to be true probably was. But Kate Mahoney, a certified Lighthouse Beacon, whatever the hell that was, wouldn't take no for an answer. "May just be the blasted banquet your starvin' spirit needs darlin'," she said when Luca begged off. "If it sours your stomach, spit it out." After he offered a tepid *yes*, Kate's strong arm didn't loosen. She called three times before the meeting.

Declining Kate's offer to pick him up in a cab, Luca boarded a Central Line train at the Holland Park Underground. Although logic told him that London's ten million souls had their own complicated lives to fret over, fear whispered to him that fellow passengers knew his desperate mission. Were those judgmental sneers, smirks of ridicule, or merely the reflection of his neuroses? Such angst was irrational, foolish, but he couldn't help himself. Perhaps paranoia and anxiety counted among the ailments that Lighthouse could fix.

As the train rocked and clattered under London, waves of regret crashed against Kate's promised rescue. What exactly was this miracle cure she endorsed with devotional rapture? Self-help, self-awareness, self-directed therapy, or merely self-delusion? He heard about cults and other pseudo-psycho programs imported from America with the same frequency as diet fads and rock stars. Kate spoke of Lighthouse's California pedigree with orgasmic delight. At best, he reasoned, Lighthouse was a social pyramid scheme that threw parties and gave away gold Range Rovers to zealous recruiters like Kate who snared fresh "Seekers." At worst, no party, no car—merely a dangerous bunch of charlatans who opened the Pandora's box of his mind and set him adrift with swirling demons.

Kate insisted the program was none of those things. Her continued addiction to self-help books, however, wasn't the best testimonial. Success rate for the Seekers he knew personally was fifty/fifty. The program didn't save Philippe from the rocks; the libidinous Frenchman sat in a cell someplace in the States, still victimized by addictions. Isa certainly fulfilled her dream and mounted the San Benedetto stage *twice*. But at what cost? *Self-actualization* was the ten-pound word she bandied about like common slang. It may have fortified her creative juices and empowered her to sing, but it didn't rid her of insecurities. What good was strength and independence if they turned vulnerability into a dreaded enemy and repelled love?

But what the hell; compared to Willy, his thug J, and Telma, Lighthouse was a sugar pill—might not help, but couldn't hurt. Philippe's plight was a wake-up call. Lucky for him his drunk driving didn't kill anyone. Luca drank too much, that he knew. However, drowning in alcohol was more pleasant than facing the tough decisions before him.

A drink lifted his spirits. After two or three, worries faded, pushed to the netherworld like black mattress monsters that vanished with the sun. The light-headed fogs brought bliss. Instead of the dread that stomped through his head in steel-toed boots, boundless possibilities floated with a swift tread. Oh, how he longed to speed toward that soothing refuge. His oft-repeated ritual—glass, bottle, cap, pour, sniff, swig—*ah*. Alcohol was the friend that never failed, delivering sweet escape…*every* time.

But how he loathed the mornings—headaches, numbness, lead feet clipped of Mercury's wings. Worst was the mind fuck, a tidal wave of regret that rushed into consciousness washing away seashells, and the sandcastles where he frolicked in his intoxication. The tide always returned, crashing over his head, erasing the footprints of escape. His only thought: how long must he tread water before the next low tide?

From Holborn station, Luca made his way up Kingsway, turning into Bloomsbury Place toward the British Museum and the spot where Kate planned to wait. When insisting upon a pre-Lighthouse rendezvous, she said, "We lose too many Seekers to last-minute jitters. Best I escort you the last few hundred yards." Isa, Kate added, had introduced her to the spiritual oasis of tea, coffee, and karma…as if that carried weight with him.

He spotted the shop directly ahead, a cup-shaped shingle protruded over the crowded pavement. Museum patrons with plastic gift bags and cardboard poster cylinders slowed his progress. The mass exodus suggested that the museum had only just closed for the evening.

As he stepped into the crosswalk, familiar cues alerted his senses. An amber glow from lead-paned windows warmed the graying twilight. Lively chatter teased his ears while robust earthy scents of ale and spirits stoked his nose. His tribe summoned him just as surely as if they fanned smoke signals and beat welcome drums.

With nary a hesitation, he turned into the Duke of Bedford pub, an oasis of tufted red velvet, dark oak, and busy wallpaper in shades of yellow and orange. "Whiskey and stout," he said after shouldering through to the busy bar. After the young barkeep, harried by the museum crush, handed over his drinks, Luca zigzagged to a stool at the far end of the room under a portrait of the pub's namesake.

He shared a table with an American family, fresh from the museum by the look of their packets. A teenaged son opened a cardboard tube and extracted his treasure, an art poster of the Elgin Marbles. As the father drank a lager and the mother sipped a shandy, they squabbled over the rightful owner of the Parthenon's antiquities. "Greece created them," said the woman. "But England preserved them for the ages," replied the man. "Wonder how much they're worth," added the boy.

The familial spat recalled an ongoing disagreement Luca had with Isa concerning the proper place of the past. Their debate, coincidentally, began at the British Museum, one of many London places they visited in the early days of their relationship. Luca felt England should return the friezes to Greece.

Isa argued to the contrary. "Surely," she said, "Elgin's Marbles arouse more visitors here than they ever could in Athens. Art's purpose is to inspire today, not mourn yesterday. Only the present matters, maybe the future, but never the past." This outlook explained why she didn't want to visit her childhood home in Buenos Aires and why she loved opera. "When I sing," she said, "the music comes alive. It's no longer lifeless notes on a dusty page."

Dodging the past, or in Luca's case, fearing it, was a common theme during their relationship. Just as Isa avoided her history, Luca struggled whether to tell her about the tragic accident that took the lives of his wife and daughter. If he loathed himself for what happened, what would Isa think of him? Her rejection of the past gave cover to his silence.

Over time, their relationship strengthened. His business was growing while Isa's singing improved and her consultancy thrived. They exchanged small gifts and love notes like giddy youths, smitten for the first time. The sex was amazing. Isa was happy, loving; she invited him deeper into her life, revealing the stories of Walter Benchley and other failed affairs. Not as dredging missions, but as examples of her break with the past. As his optimism surged for their future, he found himself opening up to her. His darkest secret bubbled to the surface. He had to confess.

Planning a quiet weekend, he intended to share the story. They drove to Clovelly, a quaint Dorset village with thatched roofs and a cobblestone main street that sloped down to the sea. His contacts gave him the name of a cozy restaurant with views of the water. But doubt and fear gripped him. Would he find the courage to tell her? He wasn't sure himself till the wine arrived at their table.

"You never ask about my prior life," he said to Isa as a way of priming the conversation. "Aren't you curious?"

She took his hand and kissed it. "Doesn't matter. Let's enjoy the moment. Everything's going so well. I love you—"

"And I love you," he said, interrupting her.

"Then why go poking around the past. Can't change anything."

"But our histories make us who we are."

"Precisely! That's what Lighthouse is helping me overcome."

"Overcome?"

"I've been trapped by my past—an overbearing mother, middle-child syndrome, Walter's betrayal, my ex-boss, an avalanche of insecurities…"

Her words trailed off; her joyful glow turned dour as she glanced at the moonlit sea. He often witnessed the pain in her face and the mood swing when she talked about those things. Her beacon was guiding her through rough waters, but it seemed clear to Luca that she still hadn't reached safe haven. So he never pried—he let her share on her terms.

As Luca topped off the wine, Isa turned to him. "Lighthouse helped me tap into my creativity. I can sing in front of an audience. But, there's still so much more to release. Luca please, for our sakes, let's not pry open the past—it's crippling. I'm finally becoming the person I believe fate always meant me to be. So, let's focus on the present and even the future. Don't dredge up history. I'm afraid of the consequences."

Luca suspected she didn't want to stir up trust issues with men. She admitted to walling herself away from any man who got serious. She told him in so many words that he was her grand experiment, her chance to come out of hiding. Fearing anything that pushed Isa into old patterns, Luca tiptoed around the past as if it were a landmine.

He didn't tell her about his wife and daughter. Perhaps he used Isa's plea as an excuse, a reprieve from exposing his demons. He convinced himself that he shunned the past for Isa, for love. That strategy deluded him…most of the time.

Perhaps fate brought Kate Maureen Mahoney and him together that prior afternoon in the Bloomsday Pub. Simmering guilt and alarm over his erratic behavior was guiding him to Lighthouse even more so than the pushy Irishwoman. He had to understand Isa, had to understand himself.

He jumped at the squeeze to his shoulder. "There ya are, darlin'. Ya misunderstood, didn't you? I said cuppa coffee, not pint of ale."

Luca cringed; his muscles tensed. He hadn't even noticed the departure of the American family. Turning, he lifted his head. Kate stared down at him. He detected neither judgment nor disappointment in her round, open face. He attempted to rise, but pressure from her hand kept him seated.

He sighed. "Oh, Kate. I'm sorry, so very, very sor—"

"No you're not."

"I am, truly I am."

She shrugged. "Sorry ya got caught, I'll grant you."

Only ducked in here for a quick one. Time got away from me, that's all. I apologize."

"No need. Ya are who you are."

He felt his forehead crease. Was this reverse psychology or velvet-gloved contempt?

"Wouldn't be judging me or trying to make me feel guilty, would you?" He infused his tone with jest to hide growing irritation.

Kate flinched, cocking her head as if she misheard. Then she let out a mighty roar of a laugh that brought smiles from others in the pub. "Heavens! That what ya think?" She plopped down beside him, moving her hand from his shoulder to his forearm, never losing physical contact. "Ya are who ya are. That's part of the Lighthouse creed. We don't judge others. Judge ourselves too much as 'tis. What others think of you, Luca, is irrelevant. Lighthouse helps you see that. But 'tain't easy. Each of us distorts our truths. Like lookin' at a reflection through a carnival mirror—psycho photo-shoppin'. We prop up false identities—cover tracks with toxic behaviors. Arrogance, bitterness, recklessness, and other nasties mask our truths, preventing us from being who we're intended to be."

She didn't have to say it, but he knew her litany of *toxic behaviors* included drink. "So how'd you find me?"

She squawked. "You're not the first Lighthouse recruit I've found carousin' with the Duke." Her eyes gazed up to the portrait of the pub's namesake. "Consider it an informed deduction."

He rolled his eyes. "Isa's concerts incubate gossip."

"Not gossip, *concern*. After yesterday's meetin'—in another *pub*, may I remind you, darlin'—I rang up some folks. Whether or not you want to believe, people do care about you."

"Who?"

"I for one. The American boys. Of course, Leech, Malcolm, et cetera. That's only the concert crowd. Surely there are others includin' Isa, even if she doesn't recognize it herself."

"What did the concert hotline say about me?"

"This calls for a drink." She stood up, looked toward the bar, and shouted, "Seamus, darlin', the usual please."

As they waited for her order, she shared news of family in Dublin and of her gentleman friend. Her stories, mostly tall tales, consisted of middles—few beginnings and rarely an end. She'd kissed the Blarney Stone for sure. But she was good company so he didn't care. Much better she talk about herself than shine the inquisitor's light on his dreary life.

"He'll have another round, handsome," she said to the publican, handing him Luca's empty glasses.

Luca looked at his watch. "What about the course? We'll be late."

Her hand batted the air. "There'll be another course tomorrow and another the day after that. You'll catch that life preserver when you're good and ready. Besides, I've been to so many Lighthouse courses, consider this private tutorin' for the wee price of a whiskey." She swigged her Jameson and spoke, "Now, where were we?"

"Sharing the word on the street about Luca Caruso."

She smiled and squeezed his arm again. "You're loved, darlin', you're loved. That's a fine place to start. Remember that. You've hit a rough patch. Business is down and you're hurtin'." Her fingertips tapped the whiskey glass.

"Certainly have done your homework."

"Aye, but there's one bit of missin' information." Her probing eyes fixed on him.

He thrust an open palm forward. "Ask away. Apparently, I'm an open book."

"Do you love yourself, Luca? Do you hang on to hope?"

Chapter 37

K ate spoke the truth. Lighthouse had another program the night following their rendezvous inside the Duke of Bedford pub, and the night after that. Luca didn't recall how many days and drunken nights passed before he made his way to the Hotel Russell to reach for the life preserver. But as he soon learned, grabbing the tossed rope was the easiest part of the rescue. More difficult was battling the surf, flailing toward the rescuers, and the actual climb into the boat. Hardest of all—a strong and resolute grasp to save from plunging back into the maelstrom.

As he began his paddle toward the rescue boat, Luca discovered that Lighthouse wasn't the answer, merely a means to an end. High Beacon Ardmore, the enlightened leader, provided the boat and threw the rope, but the rest of the journey was Luca's alone to captain. "Deliverance is within you—in your heart and mind," the ever-smiling Ardmore reassured his Seekers. "Make peace with yourself and listen to your spirit sing." Luca understood why Isa thought Lighthouse spoke to her.

The irony of rope—both lifeline and noose. Luca hoped he'd sense enough to grab ahold rather than hang himself.

The program's barrage of questions boomeranged back to the Seekers for answers. Wasn't that how most self-help programs worked? Guide, push, and prod but never direct. Lighthouse had a simple message. Inner conflict rippled throughout one's life with damaging and debilitating consequences. Life's battles ignited more often than not from internal sparks. Recovery, as with Dorothy's ruby slippers, was merely a heel-click away. But unlike fiction, the road from epiphany to rescue was neither immediate nor painless.

Several weeks after Luca's pub encounter with Kate, Jamie Stuart rang him up. He wanted to come by for dinner and a chat. Luca agreed to the meeting, but hung up the phone wondering what the Scotsman wanted. The last time he spoke with Jamie was in San Benedetto, at Isa's prior concert. Did the Scotsman's outreach have something to do with his evening at the Royal Opera House? Surely seeing him together with Telma explained Jamie's glare from across the auditorium. Or did Luca's wild imagination conjure up Jamie's judgmental sneer?

Among Isa's circle of close friends, Jamie was most likeable. His sense of humor and unpretentious manner, a rare mix in London, made him pleasant company. Jamie often made himself the butt of his jokes—an endearing quality in an alpha male. A ladies' and man's man, Jamie exuded testosterone. Luca placed him in the camp of Isa's staunchest allies. In the breakup, she claimed him. While Isa never confessed to such, Luca suspected she explored the secrets under the Scotsman's kilt.

Luca picked up the office phone, recognizing the line as the reception desk downstairs. Elizabeth's confident voice came through the receiver, "Mr. Stuart's here. Escorted him to the table. By the way, can I have him when you're done?" Her laugh rang in his ear as she disconnected but Luca was not amused by her pert remark.

He'd given prior instructions to sit Jamie at the back of the restaurant. The two men could chat in private yet Luca could still keep an eye on the operation that remained shaky due to a dearth of experienced staff.

As Luca approached the table, Jamie stood. *Here was a man who knew how to take care of himself.* He envied Jamie, a man his age. The Scotsman looked fit with a strong, taut face and clear, penetrating deep blue eyes. Doubts about intent vanished with a brilliant smile above a square jaw. He accompanied a firm yet friendly handshake with a collegial pat to Luca's shoulder.

"Great to see you, ole man," Jamie said, settling back down. "Join me in a whiskey?" he added, hoisting a glass.

"Thanks, only water," Luca replied, taking a seat and feeling his cheeks warm. "I'll have wine with dinner. Metering myself, that's all."

Jamie nodded. "Good man. Wish I had that kind of discipline. My wicked ways will catch up to me soon enough."

Is he serious? Jamie put paunchy middle-agers to shame. His six-foot frame and strong physique didn't look as if they were in any danger of sagging or shutting down. Female patrons, Luca noticed when monitoring the room, couldn't keep their eyes off him.

Even their menu selections were unfair. Jamie ordered fried calamari before moving to a hardy plate of veal and pasta. Luca, on the other hand, started with a hearts-of-palm salad followed by poached whitefish with a Mediterranean sauce of capers, olives, and artichoke hearts.

In the middle of their meal, the waiter left the table with Jamie's request for a second glass of wine. Elizabeth was the one to return. "Read your mind," she said to Luca with a wink. She placed Jamie's Sangiovese before him, and Italian sparkling water with lemon before her boss. The adept hostess was indeed clairvoyant. Luca nearly succumbed to an urge for a second glass of wine. "Allow me to choose your desserts," she added. A grin revealed to Luca her fiendish plot—panna cotta, tiramisu, zabaglione, or something equally as rich for Jamie, prunes and figs for him. Elizabeth winked, a flirtation most certainly meant for Jamie, Luca thought, before she sashayed away.

Luca watched Jamie's eyes follow Elizabeth gliding toward the kitchen. His annoyance rose as the Scotsman turned to him and said, "That flaxen-haired bird fancies ya."

Luca coughed up water. "You're joking. Look at me. I'm a mess."

"I must admit, did a double take when I spotted you at the opera. Didn't recognize you…'til I squinted. Ya were puffy, gray as a mackerel. But, you're lookin' better now, old man, much better."

Luca didn't take offense. Jamie spoke the truth. But it pleased him that Jamie had noticed a difference in his appearance in the nearly two months that had passed. Luca worked hard, changing his diet, cutting the drinking, and walking between his flat and the three restaurants.

Jamie studied Luca's face. "What's your secret?"

"Fear of death."

Jamie laughed, as did Luca. "Sounds silly, but I mean it. The benefits of diet and exercise will vanish in one bingeing weekend unless I find the will to hang onto life. But the journey's just begun."

"Much success," Jamie said toasting with his wineglass. After sipping, he spoke in a serious tone. "Bet you're wondering why I'm here."

Luca nodded. "Frankly, I didn't expect this to be a friendly dinner chat."

"Suppose not. Truth is, I avoided you. Avoided Telma too. I was angry with both of you. Isa was in a terrible state—she needed her allies, needed to trust their loyalty. You know how that goes."

"All too well. Thank you for being there for Isa. Had to be rough on her. I'm sorry, truly I am. Don't know what came over me."

"I do. Telma. Or rather the combination of Telma and alcohol—explosive."

"Guilty as charged, I'm afraid. As much as I'd like to blame that devilish Argentine, she didn't hold a gun to my head, make me drink, and certainly didn't make me lose my patience when Isa needed me most."

"Don't beat yourself up, old man. Happens to the best of us. Why d'ya suppose Jamie Stuart never got hitched?" His poise and confidence informed Luca that the Scotsman enjoyed the opposite sex on his terms.

"How is she? Isa, I mean."

"Good as can be expected. Tryin' to pull her life together. Threw herself into music. Doin' pretty good in that regard. This third San Benedetto concert was going to be a triumph—"

"But then her father got ill."

"Means the world to her. Credits him with inspiring her to sing."

"How is he, his health?"

"About the same, I'm afraid. No change."

"But you're not here to talk about Papa Fabrini or Isa?"

Jamie shook his head. "No, I want to discuss Telma."

Luca flinched. "Huh?"

"Rang her up after I saw you two at the opera. Blasted minx made me buy her tea at the Ritz, then off to a West End musical. Imagine me at the Ritz, nibbling finger sandwiches and teacakes. Left hungrier and thirstier than when I got there."

"Still the mistress of manipulation."

"Never judged her, really. She hurt Isa but I blamed Walter. I was at school with him. Behind his proud British veneer is an insecure little boy. He scooped Telma up. The Telma I met at graduation is nothing like the woman you met in San Benedetto. She has good in her. It's just hidden under scars. That Regent's Park mess is all ancient history now."

"Guess you're right. In our short weekend, Telma struck me as a wounded soul. Bits of compassion and vulnerability there…if you can survive the arsenic and quicksand."

Luca expected a laugh, but Jamie turned dour. "She's broke, Luca. Fallen hard."

"So I heard." He remembered Kate's fast-forward catch-up of the concert crowd. "Seems she's taken up with some real-estate syndicate. She's after some property I'm developing. Probably sniffs easy money."

Jamie shook his head. "She's not tryin' to force ya to sell your interest for a hefty commission."

"Then why's she hounding me?"

"For you, she's doin' it for you. Knows your hurtin'." Jamie scanned the room. "Ya need a way out. Empty tables don't lie."

"I'm working on a plan—"

"Bet ya are. Willy Epson's not a solution. He's a bigger problem than you'll know what to deal with. Stay away from him. He's the devil."

"How'd you—"

"Telma told me."

"How'd she—"

"Does it matter? You're playin' with fire." Piercing eyes and raised eyebrows told Luca that Jamie chose his words. His double meaning was clear.

"Why's Telma interested in saving *me*?"

"Feels terrible about what happened between you and Isa. Wee bit of a guilty conscience, I imagine."

Luca scoffed. "That woman has no soul, let alone a conscience."

Jamie shrugged. "Can see how ya think that. Each of us has our demons. You know better than most."

Luca recalled his talk with Kate, the Lighthouse meetings, and the hardest of all conversations—those he had with himself in the solitary confessional of his bedroom. *Yes, I have demons. Who am I to judge?*

Jamie poked the tablecloth. "Telma's foregoing her commission. Upped the ante, hasn't she?"

"She knows the value."

"Bull shit, man! She's doin' that fer you…to entice ya to sell. My guess is she'll get fired for offerin' well beyond market value—pretty much told me so."

"But why?"

"To save you from yourself…and Willy."

"Did she send you?"

"She'd kill me if she knew I was here. She and Isa are alike that way—proud, stubborn. But Isa's very social, loves family, friends. She harnesses the nasty impulses to her advantage—*most of the time*—while Telma's still quite the wild mare."

Luca nibbled on a fig while Jamie, between fork fulls of two desserts, spoke of Telma with fondness. "She saved me from a horrible embarrassment. Maybe she had selfish motives—poor lass, can't help herself there. But in the end, she saved my bloody arse…Isa's too for that matter."

Luca stiffened. "Isa too? Tell me the story."

He watched Jamie's mind churn as he sipped an espresso. "Sorry, ole chap, can't divulge the details. Sworn to secrecy. Let's just say that concert weekend…people, camaraderie…the whole experience softened the quills of our dear Telma."

Luca tried to remember that horrible weekend. He spent much of the time angry with Isa or inebriated. Perhaps Jamie was right. Maybe Luca had seen a subtle shift in Telma from one day to the next. She could have taken advantage of him that last night, finding him drunk at the Tazza d'Oro. Maybe that was even her plan. But Isa's discovery of Telma and him was as much her own fault—fingers caught in her own fiendish trap.

"Telma's paid a hefty sum for her devilry," Jamie added. "Lost her millionaire mama's boy. Walter cut off her gravy train. Old friends shunned her. I was one of them. Her father died in Argentina. She's pretty much alone in the world."

Luca was unmoved. "So she's trying to make amends, buy friends?"

"Luca, I know what it means to lose everything—to go from plenty to the poor house—the whirlpool of emotion—guilt, despair, anger. Gotta give Telma the benefit of the doubt. I lost everything to Willy's scheming. Struggled to get back on my feet. I'm surprised Willy's avoided prison. But mark my words, one of these days, someone's gonna kill that devil."

Chapter 38

Rome—One Year Later

Luca's journey back to Rome began shortly after his eye-opening dinner with Jamie in London. After considering his options, Luca accepted Telma's offer for the South Bank restaurant. That single act seemed to break the spell of bad luck. Things began to fall into place almost too perfectly. The Australian syndicate agreed to buy the Covent Garden location and assume the Bayswater lease. The Aussies even offered to keep most staff, freeing Luca to leave London with a clear conscience.

The transactions freed him of debt and saved him from dealing with the devil. Willy wasn't at all happy, visiting Luca one final time before he signed the contracts. Willy arrived just after closing time, accompanied by J whose sinister sneer was as intimidating as a handgun. According to Telma, Willy was desperate. Having racked up excessive gambling debts, he needed Luca's "commission" to shed himself of J, who kept tabs on Willy for the Russian mob.

A cornered rat was the most dangerous. Luca's planned return to Italy offered a chance to escape the vermin.

Luca never dreamed that starting over at fifty could bring such satisfaction. Hard work and frustration, yes, but fun...*Never*. However, that's exactly how he felt, working twelve, fourteen, sixteen hours a day and loving every minute of it. Perhaps the weather had something to do with his surging optimism and infinite energy. Rome had a more livable climate than London—warmer, brighter, dryer—the difference between porridge and frittata, Burberry tweed and Armani silk, Bentley and Vespa.

Maybe his spirits soared because the city was home. Many Romans never moved away from their birthplace, living in the same flat from baptism to last rites. Finding himself in familiar surroundings after his self-imposed exile abroad comforted him. With nearly twenty years in London and ten before that in Milan, he saw his birthplace with the wide eyes of a tourist.

Fortune blessed him with a great flat. His godson's firm had transferred the young man to the Middle East. With the company covering his rent in Dubai, the godson let the flat to Luca at half the market rate. It didn't hurt that the young man's mother, Luca's aunt, mentioned his financial difficulties and reminded her son of the money Luca sent from London to support his engineering studies.

"Look after it, Luca," Cousin Luciano said. "By the time I get back to Rome, you can afford your own place. Pay me back in pasta."

Luca loved the breathing room of his new home—high ceilings, tall windows, and verandas that refreshed with sunshine and green space. The formal dining room fit a large, round table while a spacious living room had a fireplace, well-stocked bookshelves, and a baby grand piano. Although the bedroom balcony had room only for a café table and two chairs, the main terrace was roomy enough for a large dining table, two lounge chairs, and a sitting area set among raised beds of flowers and trees. The garden was his Eden. Beyond the terrace, the dome of St. Peter's loomed like an ornate, upside-down sugar bowl.

A few months after settling in, Luca opened a restaurant that he named O Sole Mio. Nothing fancy—pasta, checkered tablecloths, Chianti-bottle candles, and an audio loop of Sinatra, Dean Martin, and Louis Prima. Tourists spoke effusively about finding an authentic Italian restaurant—the kind of place they thought existed only in movies. Luca couldn't complain—the restaurant paid the bills. But he yearned for more, professionally and personally—a challenge beyond dishing out spaghetti Bolognese for Japanese, and English tourists, and of course going home to an empty flat.

The idea came to Luca by way of a loud couple from Toledo, Ohio who asked to see the chef. "Best lasagna ever," the woman said, licking her fork.

"Beats the crap outta the shit we made in class. Shoulda told Guido to come here to learn how to cook," griped the man poking the checkered tablecloth.

"Honeybear, the man's name was Massimo."

"If you say so. Pasta pushers are all the same…Oh, sorry," he added without a blush.

Luca held out his hand. "Luca Caruso. But feel free to call me Luigi."

The burly man stammered as his wife batted his hand. "He's playin' with ya, Fred."

The man's shoulders relaxed. His crooked smile looked forced. "Show him the card, Georgina," he said, sliding an overstuffed purse across the table.

After rummaging through her bag, the wife handed Luca a card that read *Massimo's Magnificent Day of Cooking*. The address was a residential area in the Jewish quarter.

The woman spoke with enthusiasm. "We cooked right in his kitchen. That was the best part. A real Eye-talian kitchen. What fun!" she exclaimed, clapping her hands.

Her husband groaned. "Massimo made out like a bandit—over a hundred apiece. Eight of us packed into his kitchen like sardines. Eight hundred euros to make pasta you can get from a box." The man had an annoying habit of pronouncing *pasta* with a short *a* like that in the word *fast* or *mast*. "Bet he feeds leftovers to family."

The wife giggled. "Gotta excuse Fred. Ever since we got to Europe, he's moaned about sticker shock."

The husband grimaced, before turning to Luca. "You got a cooking school? If not, ya should. You're missin' out on easy dough, and I don't mean pasta," he added with a roaring laugh.

The wife groaned. "Anyway, Signor Luca, we just wanted to tell ya that your food's head and shoulders above Guido's…er, I mean, Massimo's. Such a darling place, too," she added, craning her neck around the room. "Just like Epcot."

Luca's mind raced to the idea of eight hundred euros a day, as well as the opportunity to channel new customers to his restaurant. His dream of a chic eatery could become a reality. He had his eyes on a quaint little square off the Campo de' Fiori—the kind of place that attracted customers with discerning palates and thick wallets. A cooking school might make his dream come true in two or three years even if it meant dealing with people who mispronounced *pasta*, cut spaghetti with a knife, or distinguished wine solely by color.

Luca thanked the couple for their kind words. "No cooking school yet, but soon. Next time you come to Rome." Excusing himself, he sent over desserts and coffee with his compliments as he charted the future in his head.

The kitchen of Luca's flat wasn't ideal for cooking courses, but could work with slight modifications. As his Ohio muses suggested, the mere notion of toiling in a working kitchen under the supervision of a local chef had marketable charm. While Luca wouldn't necessarily snare foodies from Milan or Venice, his cooking day would appeal to novices from New Jersey, Nova Scotia, and Newcastle. He'd show them that they didn't need a commercial kitchen with high-end appliances and fancy gadgets to prepare good, authentic Italian food.

Luca seasoned his personal charm as well—shedding both pounds and his adopted English accent. Luca Caruso would look, sound, and, with the help of onions, garlic, olive oil, and herbs, smell the part of a Roman chef. He was selling an experience—hearty food, robust wine, and yes...Italian sex appeal.

In record speed, he cut through Italian bureaucracy and opened his cooking school one month after the Ohioans planted the seed. As the first order of business, he sent for Elizabeth. She'd proven invaluable in shutting down his London operations. The wise Aussies kept the bright, attractive woman on to manage through the transition. In fact, they insisted upon it. But Elizabeth was only too eager to jump ship. "I'll be on the next plane. If I had wings, I'd fly myself," she said over the phone. Her voice practically sang with delight. Luca thought her exuberance merely a reaction to the thrilling prospect of living in Rome.

Once settled in Rome, Elizabeth managed O Sole Mio with British efficiency, freeing Luca to set up the cooking school. Their teamwork was even better than their previous work together in London. Elizabeth anticipated his every need. If he had doubts, she swept them away. When he wavered on important decisions, she gave him the verbal equivalent of a kick in the arse.

The English transplant sparkled in Italy...*literally*. Damp, dreary London had masked her beauty. In the Mediterranean sun, Elizabeth's light blonde hair shimmered, and her blue eyes twinkled above charming freckles. Italian fashion uncovered her shapely figure. The rosebud bloomed into a lovely, exhibition-quality flower.

With Elizabeth in place, Luca was off and running. He marketed the culinary experience as *Caruso's Rome: A Day of Italian Cooking*, targeting English-speaking countries. The speed at which the business grew surprised him although Elizabeth said she never had a single doubt.

A typical class started with a meeting point in the Campo de' Fiori, Rome's most famous market. Although the area had become a draw for tourists, stalls still provided fresh produce for the quarter's residents. After introducing himself to eager students, Luca polled them for their preferred menu—each day, something different. Then, dishing out historical facts about Rome and culinary anecdotes, he marched them through the market to gather vegetables, fruit, and fish. The butcher, baker, and cheese maker were the next stops. Students, Luca quickly learned, enjoyed meeting local vendors, learning about the different foods, and watching him haggle for the best product at the lowest prices. Much of the theatrics were staged with friendly vendors to enhance the circus spectacle.

Arms laden with treasures, Luca led the enthusiasts to his flat, a treat clients compared with a backstage pass. After a menu overview and instruction in basic preparation technique, he put them to work. Fresh pasta was always a hit. Students started with flour wells, dashes of salt, and egg. Balls of dough soon became ribbons that Luca stretched through the apartment to the delight of white-spackled clients. Thin sheets of rich, yellow transformed into ravioli, lasagna, or spaghetti to suit the menu.

Other offerings included gnocchi from riced potatoes, fresh sauces, braised meats, poached fish, and croquettes of eggplant or zucchini. Every session ended with a banquet served, depending upon the weather, in the dining room or on the terrace. After several glasses of wine, customers staggered away in a gastronomical stupor singing the praises of Caruso and his marvelous day of Italian cooking. Client referrals were strong. Rome found itself with yet another Caruso who gave encores to great fanfare.

"Good to hear your voice, Luca. Wasn't sure if you'd remember. It's been nearly three years."

"Of course, of course I remember," Luca replied into the phone. His mind conjured up an image of the caller, Tommy Evers—blond and tall, an American Midwesterner with a wholesome face and good manners. "A benefit of Isa's concert. Connects—"

"Good people from around the world."

"True. Velcro connections." Luca recalled Kate's story of the boys' visit to Dublin and other tales of friendships sprouting from Isa's concerts. "Still with the pilot?"

"Yeah, Miguel and I are still an item. Though he doesn't fly much anymore. Works in management these days."

Luca tapped his forehead. "Right, right, safety, security, something like that."

"Wow, great memory. Yep, my guy keeps the skies safe."

"So, you're coming to Rome. I'd love to see you two."

"We'll have Danny Chance with us."

Luca remembered the little fellow. Fast talker, preppie dresser, and a bit high strung, but a big heart under a New York veneer. "Fantastic! What brings you boys to the Eternal City—a Roman Holiday?"

"Full-blown Italian tour. Venice, Florence, Rome. Then the train to San Benedetto."

"San Benedetto? Not exactly on the grand tour."

Luca heard hesitation in Tommy's voice, as if he regretted mentioning the town. "The third concert. Rescheduled from last summer because of Isa's father."

"That's right," Luca said, although he was out of the loop. "You can't miss that."

"Been to every one—not skipping any if I can help it. So, you're not…"

Tommy's words trailed off. He probably thought better of marching down that brambled path. Luca changed subjects, chatting about the boys' plans in Rome including hotel and free time. He gave Tommy the option of meeting at his restaurant for dinner or taking the full-day cooking class.

"Let's do both," Tommy replied with excitement. "Not every day we can learn real Italian cooking from a real Roman chef. Afterward, we'll eat at your restaurant…see how things should really taste."

"*Bene, bene.* Till next month, then. *Ciao.*"

Luca hung up the phone, smiling at the imminent reunion. He looked across the bar and through the restaurant's front window. Sun-drenched Piazza Santa Maria in Trastevere, with its ancient fountain and basilica, drew hordes of tourists. His new life energized him. Everything in Rome was brighter, less stressful. Seeing Elizabeth enter the piazza, Luca sighed. He couldn't keep his eyes off of her. She looked beautiful in a simple lavender and cream dress, her long blonde hair swaying with each confident stride. *Yes,* Luca thought, *London seems a dozen years in the past instead of merely a dozen months.*

Excited for his rendezvous with the Americans, Luca hustled through Piazza Navona toward the Campo de' Fiori. His breathing was labored. He barely had time to recover from a long morning run, shower, dress, and dash out the door. Elizabeth offered to meet the boys for him, but with a squeeze to her bare ass, he told her to stay in bed. Not only did she deserve to rest after her inspired performance of the prior night, she agreed to get the flat and kitchen ready for cooking day.

With his tarnished reputation from San Benedetto, Luca didn't want to spring Elizabeth, a girl half his age, on Isa's friends just yet. He didn't even know what to call their relationship: a fling, an affair, just plain sex. Their dalliance began a month after she arrived in Rome. Champagne on the moonlit terrace to celebrate the first cooking class turned into a night of passionate lovemaking.

The following morning, Elizabeth's voice rose after he dismissed their behavior as a mix of alcohol and exhaustion. "What a relief to know that sobriety and a little rest will cure us of our passion." Although she didn't speak to him for the rest of that day, the attraction proved too strong, and the sex too addictive, for them both. Although they spoke of wanting a deeper relationship, the intimacy that grows from baring souls and sharing desires eluded them.

Luca had offered to collect the boys at their hotel near the Vatican, but they wouldn't hear of it.

"No way," Danny Chance said, when Luca phoned their room. "We want the full experience—soup to nuts."

Luca made his way through the area of the market that housed the flower stalls and cheap trinkets toward the bronze statue of Giordano Bruno. The Catholic Church burned the sixteenth-century philosopher for suggesting, among other things, that the earth wasn't at the center of God's universe. The statue provided an ideal meeting point and the basis for a wry joke about overcooking.

He recognized the three Americans at once—all wore shorts and sneakers. Three years hadn't changed them much. Tommy stood out with his height and thick blond hair. At his side was Miguel, who with his olive complexion and dark features blended with the Roman natives. A snug T-shirt accentuated the pilot's athletic build, broad shoulders and strong arms. Nearby stood Danny, colorful in a pink polo shirt and lime-green shorts. Sunglasses hung on a lanyard around his neck.

Danny was arguing with a plump, apple-faced fruit peddler. From what Luca gathered, Danny grabbed fruit from a bin at the front of her stall. Slapping his hand, the woman presented him different peaches from the back—a customary practice. Flawless, plump, succulent fruit on display merely baited customers. Vendor and customer were both upset.

"Solo a guardare, solo a guardare," the woman in the babushka repeated.

Danny lifted his hands as if in surrender and shrugged.

"Only for show," she bellowed. "Only for show."

Luca rescued the embattled New Yorker, paying for the peaches and explaining Danny's confusion to the woman in Italian. She made a sour face that curled her mustache, and offered anatomical instructions that he didn't translate into English.

"What'd she say? What'd she say?" Danny asked.

"Enjoy your stay in Rome." Luca's polite translation prompted Danny to smile at the woman, even muttering thanks in Italian before Luca added, "As for the peaches, well…she—"

"Said you can shove them up your tight little ass," Miguel interjected, clasping Danny on the shoulders and adding a raucous laugh. "Least that's what it sounded like to me."

"Grazie, grazie, pesca ladro," the woman said in a dismissive tone labeling Danny a *peach thief*. Her rough, red hands shooed the four men away.

Luca pulled the boys from the stall and toward the statue. A bronze heretic was safer company than an irate Roman fruit monger.

Tommy slapped Luca's back. "You look great."

Danny eyed him up and down as if seeing him for the first time. "Yes, Mister Caruso, very fit. Don't take offense, but you look years younger. The transformation is amazing."

Luca patted his stomach. "Still a few pounds to go, but I've lost most of my belly."

"Rome definitely agrees with you," Miguel said. "Guessing you got a girlfriend."

"Or boyfriend," Danny said with raised eyebrows and a tilt of his head.

Luca felt his cheeks warm. The three boys nodded in unison.

"Who is..."

"No one, no one," Luca answered, waving his hand in the air before changing the subject. "And you, Mr. Chance. How about your current love interest?"

Danny's back stiffened. A peach fell to the ground. "Let's not go there."

Tommy slapped the New Yorker on the back and laughed. "With all the places you never want to go, it's a wonder you have a passport."

Danny's nostrils flared and he shook his head from side to side.

"Let's go," Luca said, grabbing Tommy's and Danny's arms. "What do you feel like eating today? Fish, chicken, veal?" They didn't respond, merely exchanged looks like a secret code. "What's wrong? Are you vegetarians?"

Tommy spoke, "You did say this was a private party."

"Yes."

"And you usually teach up to eight people?"

"Yes."

"Then there's room," Danny said.

All three beamed. But their gaze wasn't on Luca. Instead, their eyes glanced over his shoulder. He turned to find Jamie Stuart. And beside him, Kate Maureen Mahoney who stood, hands interlocked, with a distinguished older man who he took to be her English beau.

What other surprises were in store as the calendar edged toward concert weekend?

Chapter 39

Luca hadn't laughed so hard in years. Spending a day with concert friends, the term by which he referred to the charming collection of personalities met through Isa, invigorated him. At the onset of her musical journey, Isa couldn't have foreseen the real value of the concert. That magical weekend spawned friendships and romances among people who'd otherwise never mix.

Luca stood in the sun-drenched kitchen, his back to the sink and herb-garden windowsill. He beamed from ear to ear. Around the chopping block stood two gay chaps from Chicago, another from New York, a Glaswegian buck, a Dublin firecracker, and the newest addition, a wayward Londoner who immigrated to Australia and returned home again. Did that mélange have anything in common beyond admiration—no, *love*—for Isa, and joyous anticipation of the main concert and all of its delicious side dishes?

Musings on the benefits of Isa's social experiment had to wait. Luca needed to guide the international delegation, tipsy by that point, through the art of Italian cooking. His flat looked as if it were flour-bombed. White powder freckles dotted walls, furniture, and appliances. Pasta ribbons stuck to the refrigerator, television, and telephone. The devastation was extraordinary, but he had made the mistake of uncorking the Montepulciano at the start of the cooking adventure. One bottle quickly advanced to a second and third. In his regular sessions, wine waited until clients moved to the dining room to enjoy the fruits of their cooking labors. But these were concert friends.

For days afterward, grated cheese, oregano, and eggshells tickled his bare feet. He never figured out exactly how a zucchini got from the kitchen to the stereo. The course turned to carnival when Kate found his CD collection and blasted the flat with a music shuffle. They rolled gnocchi to the rock of Nek, deboned chicken to Laura Pausini, shaved Parmesan to Eros Ramazzotti, sliced eggplant to Andrea Bocelli, and danced around the apartment with pasta ribbons to Pavarotti. If she'd been there, the devilish imp Brigid Clancy would have elevated the chaos to a category-five hurricane.

Luca turned to Kate as she hovered over the pesto. "Only missing your other half. Is Brigid catching up with you in San Benedetto?"

He noticed her back stiffen. She exchanged glances with her English beau, Richard, busy spooning ravioli onto plates. "She's not coming."

"Not coming?" Danny replied. "That little leprechaun's half the show."

"And one of the few dance partners sized right for you," Tommy said. His wisecrack and tousle of Danny's hair drew a volley of herb confetti from the compact New Yorker.

Miguel frowned. "Won't be the same without her."

"I won't be missin' the wee minx," said Jamie. "Been stalkin' me since concert one."

Tommy and Danny cleared their throats and looked to Kate who turned as red as the diced tomatoes that topped the bruschetta.

Jamie winked toward the woman. "Of course Katie here did too, but she's nabbed her Prince Charming," he said with a wink to Richard. "'Twas Brigid who filled me with fright, what with those tiny hands, and twitchin' fingers. Wiggled their way into all my naughty bits." The kitchen echoed with laughter.

Luca looked at Kate. "Thought you'd mended things by now. Can't imagine you two apart." He recalled their conversation at the Bloomsday Pub over a year in the past—the hint of Brigid's demon that he left undisturbed.

Kate moved from the stove to Richard's side. He set down the serving spoon to grab the hand she moved toward him. Her lips quivered; her expression careened between anger and sadness. She pressed a knuckle to her eye to hold back a tear. "Brigid doesn't approve."

"Approve?" Several in the group asked.

"Of me," Richard said, before lifting Kate's hand to his lips for a gentle kiss.

Eyes turned to the trim, white-haired Englishman. The Australian sun had weathered his face and crinkled his eyes. He had the appearance and swagger of a dapper yachtsman. In the short time Luca hosted the concert friends, he decided that Richard was a decent chap. Years among Sydney's laid-back residents had smoothed his stiff British edges to an affable luster. Quick-witted humor escaped him with the ease of a late-night television host. He and Kate made a cute couple—middle-aged lovebirds.

Kate stopped Richard's clarification with a shake of her head. Instead, she spoke. "Brigid says I'm sleepin' with the enemy. Despises Brits, she does. Unhealthy if you ask me. Been over twenty bloody years."

"I feel terrible. Being the one to come between you two." Richard's tone and expression tinged with sympathy.

"Nonsense!" Kate snapped. "It's her obsession, her problem, not yours." No longer able to dam her tears, Kate dashed off to the bathroom, shaking off offers of help.

Culinary tasks ceased; everyone headed for wine. Until that moment, Luca had abstained, reasoning that he needed sharp reflexes to supervise novices with sharp knives. With glasses filled, the men circled Richard, an unspoken invitation to share the story.

"I understand Brigid's anger," Richard began. "I'd feel the same way if I lost a son."

The others froze, eyeing each other under creased foreheads. Tommy broke the silence. "What happened?"

"Senseless violence. Shot by a British soldier in Northern Ireland," Richard replied.

"Was he IRA?" asked Danny.

Richard shook his head. "No. Least I don't think so. That's where the story gets murky. Her son wasn't an armed member anyway, but I assume his sympathies leaned that way. Brigid's certainly do, as do Kate's for that matter."

"Why was he shot?" Miguel asked.

"From what Kate's shared, Brigid's son, also called Danny, by the way," Richard said with a smile toward the New Yorker, "was in Belfast visiting relatives. By dumb luck, there happened to be a parade, one of those silly sectarian walkabouts intended to chest-beat and agitate the other side."

"Saw those skirmishes on the news as a kid," Tommy said. "Never made any sense. Both groups goin' outta their way to provoke the other side."

Richard explained that Brigid's son found himself in the middle of a melee. An angry mob swallowed Danny Clancy. What triggered the violence was never clear. But the crowd started pelting the riot police and British troops with rocks and bottles. "Rubber bullet struck Danny in the eye. Killed him instantly," Richard said, bowing his head.

"Wrong place, wrong time," Miguel said.

"Maybe…maybe not," replied Jamie. "'Twas a sordid mess, the Troubles— *both* sides."

"The poor woman's held onto anger for two decades," Luca added. *Another haunted soul nagged by demons.*

"Sadly, the story doesn't end there," Richard continued, telling them that Danny's death enraged his younger brother, Brigid's only other child. He joined a militant band of the IRA. Agents caught him on the Dun Laoghaire to Holyhead ferry with materials that prosecutors convinced a jury were bomb components. "Spent ten years in prison," Richard added. "Now you see why Brigid blames the British for destroying her family."

"Never saw that side of her," Tommy said. "You'd think she'd show—"

"That's the beauty of the concert," Kate said, interrupting him as she returned to the kitchen. Her round face and deep blue eyes looked refreshed; her red curls puffed. "The magic of Italy. We abandon our cares for Isa's weekend."

Kate's comments reminded Luca of Telma. The hard-nosed bitch with the soft center confessed as much to him about her experience. He too glimpsed that festive mood although love and alcohol blinded him to many concert benefits.

"We didn't see Brigid's dark side when we visited Dublin," Danny said.

Kate looked to the ceiling as if conjuring up memories; dimples lit up her face. "A lovely time we all had, indeed, darlin's. Brigid and I were thrilled to show you off to our friends." Her expression changed as she looked at her companions. "That was right before the bottom fell out of…"

Richard squeezed her arm. "When you started seeing more of me in London."

Kate nodded. "When you boys visited Dublin, was as if concert weekend went on tour. Hooted and hollered like schoolchildren, we did… like we were in San Benedetto."

"As we've done right here in Luca's kitchen," said Jamie, tapping the chopping block with his fist.

Danny swirled his goblet, and watched the red wine trail down the glass. "You might say Isa's concert has legs."

"Hear, hear!" echoed off the white and black porcelain tiles of the small kitchen.

Luca ushered the novice chefs toward the outdoor terrace. "*Mangiamo, mangiamo. Andiamo.* Come, let's eat."

The following night, the concert friends planned to reunite at Luca's restaurant. As O Sole Mio prepared to open for dinner, Elizabeth teased Luca that he hadn't stopped grinning since his cohorts staggered away from his flat after a cooking lesson, six-course meal, and seven-bottle afternoon.

"You love those people," she said. "It's all over your face and in your step."

"Bet you'd have stuck around if you knew Jamie Stuart was going to be here. Private lessons, I imagine. Maybe even something about cooking." She fixed her eyes on him, a look of bemusement on her face. "Don't deny it. I remember how you ogled him at the restaurant that night in London," he added in a lighthearted tone with a gentle swat to her behind.

"I did no such thing. Sure I'll be happy to see him again, but I can't wait to meet the others."

"Brace yourself," he replied with a laugh. "When they get together, anything can happen... and usually does."

"A smashing good time."

"Hope our other customers think so. Maybe I should have closed to the public."

"Nonsense! From what you've said, the good cheer will lure customers to our door."

Elizabeth saw the positive of any situation. She brought energy into every room and lifted the sourest of spirits. In London, she witnessed Luca at his lowest, yet maintained faith in him. Although his heart tried to convince him that their significant age gap didn't matter, his head spoke otherwise. A relationship beyond sex was unsustainable. That was his excuse for holding back, but what was hers? *Yes,* Luca thought, *despite her denials, my lark will fly away one day to a younger, sturdier limb.*

The evening passed as he expected. Good camaraderie and great stories. After the other restaurant patrons left, Luca, Elizabeth and their guests pushed the tables to the sides of the room and turned up the music. The friends, drinking wine, grappa, and Limoncello, danced to American and Italian pop standards.

The concert friends embraced Elizabeth and she enjoyed every one of them. Luca caught himself staring at her. She was a combination of grace, confidence, and good humor. What feelings stirred within him—pride, admiration, love? Although Luca didn't intentionally hide their relationship, the night galloped forward like a wild stallion.

The subject surfaced only once. Luca found himself alone at the edge of the makeshift dance floor with Jamie. The Scotsman motioned to Elizabeth who, along with the three American boys, group-danced and sang along with Dean Martin to *That's Amore*. "Didn't I tell you the fair lass was smitten with you? She's blossomed into a stunner. And the way she looks at you. That's not someone who's merely peeling the boss's tatties."

Kate's exchange of her winded beau, Richard, for a dance with the reluctant Jamie saved Luca from a response.

Jamie's observation pleased Luca. So much so that he didn't get jealous when later in the evening, Jamie and Elizabeth chatted away as they slow-danced through four consecutive ballads.

"Can't believe we leave tomorrow for San Benedetto," Danny said, sipping Limoncello at the end of the evening.

Tommy nodded. "Hate to see our Italian holiday come to a close."

"You saved the best for last," Luca said.

Kate patted his hand. "Come," she said. "Go mad, fly away with us." Richard and Jamie nodded in agreement.

The Americans sat up. "Yeah! Join us," one of them said.

Luca shook his head. "Couldn't." He and Isa were through as lovers and friends.

"But it's concert weekend, a carnival. Come," Kate said before turning to Elizabeth. "Do make him come, sweetheart. It'll do him a world of good."

A glimmer in Elizabeth's eyes registered Kate's prophecy. Even if Luca were unconvinced, he saw his nurturing lark make up her mind that he should accompany his friends to San Benedetto.

"You come too, love," Jamie said to Elizabeth, receiving agreement from the others. But Elizabeth merely smiled as she topped off everyone's glasses.

Elizabeth shot down every one of Luca's objections. "Go! Have fun. Your friends want you there. I want you there."

"Come with me. Let me show you off."

"No," she responded. "One of us has to watch the restaurant, feed all the starving artists you've attracted."

"That I've attracted? I don't know if I like the thought of you mothering those writers. You have a weak spot for tortured souls and scruffy-bearded men."

Moving her hands to her hips, her expression turned serious. "You trust me…to keep things running, don't you?"

"You manage things better than anyone…including me."

"Right, settled then."

In a flash, Elizabeth grabbed Luca's overnight case from a closet and opened it on the bed. Drawers and armoire doors flew open. Luca stood by and watched as Elizabeth whirled through the bedroom with the same efficiency she displayed at the restaurant.

She was beautiful. Not an exotic, classic beauty like Isa or Telma. No, Elizabeth was pretty, a natural, wholesome look. A kind heart made her even more attractive. Luca guessed that Elizabeth was a woman who, like a maturing rose, would grow more radiant with age.

He scratched his head. "You wouldn't be trying to get rid of me?"

Bent over the half-filled suitcase, she stopped to look up. She smiled, yet something in her face—a clouding of the clear blue eyes, a quiver in the lip—hinted of something. She shook her head as if erasing any hidden message. "No, my dearest Luca. I'll be here…as long as you need me."

Moving behind her, he reached around her body and embraced her. She was warm and smelled of lilac soap and strawberry shampoo. "I'll always need you," he whispered in her ear. "Let me prove it to you, *now*." He caressed her back. Brushing aside her soft, flaxen hair, he nibbled the nape of her neck.

She moaned, but held firm. "Plenty of time for that when you get back. What time's the train?"

"Two," he said, before glancing at the alarm clock. "Oh my God, that's less than an hour away."

Elizabeth raced into overdrive as Luca collected the last of his things from the bathroom. He was out the door and inside a taxi in under a quarter hour. Even in heavy Rome traffic, the ride to Stazione Termini was no more than twenty minutes.

He dashed to the ticket window. The large clock above the clacking departure board indicated six minutes before two. With ticket in hand, he bolted toward the platform. He spotted an open carriage door. He'd been so damn focused on catching the train that he hadn't reflected on his mission. His heart beat faster as the train doors began to close.

Why am I going to San Benedetto? His foot landed on the first metal step. *Am I fool to think Isa will welcome me?* His hand reached for the pole that would lift him into the train. *What in God's name was I thinking?*

Instead of grabbing the pole, he let go of his desire. He stepped down on *Terra Firma*. The doors closed; the train lurched forward without him. His hand brushed down his face as he watched the blue cars accelerate one by one, down the track. Taking a deep breath, he turned toward the station. Emotion flirted with regret as his mind flashed with images of concert friends and Isa. A part of him still loved that woman. As irascible as she was, they were soul mates. He cared what happened to her.

He froze. In front of him stood none other than Telma Rossi, bag in one hand and finger wagging at an impassive porter weighed down by two bulging suitcases.

"Christ!" she blurted. "If you weren't such a sloth, I'd have made my train."

Her head jerked; her posture straightened. She spotted him. "Luca, dear Luca," she shouted, her wave animated. "You missed the San Benedetto train, too. Fate nudges us together once again. How fabulous… for *both* of us."

Chapter 40

"Still say our chance encounter demanded a cocktail, not this watery, overpriced latte," Telma said with a roll of her eyes. She sat across the table in Rome's Stazione Termini, hiding her quills under beige linen, fangs behind a half smile, and talons beneath a fresh manicure colored the same red as her full lips.

Detouring her away from the station bar and into the restaurant required Luca's finest persuasion skills as well as a bit of gentlemanly arm-twisting. His survival instincts kicked in. Alcohol provided temptation enough, but Telma's role as whiskey chaser was as dangerous as juggling nitroglycerin.

Luca stared into Telma's large, dark eyes. "Can't believe you're crashing Isa's concert again."

She sat back, lifting her chin. A smirk inched up the corners of her mouth; eyes fired with satisfaction. "*Querido,* who said anything about crashing?" With a flourish of her hand, she reached into a weathered Fendi handbag and produced a large envelope. "Here," she announced, flinging it on the table. "My personal invitation to Renoir's boating party."

"Huh?"

"Concert weekend. Isabella Fabrini's mirth-filled gala."

Luca gasped before glancing down. A glossy card protruded from torn folds. He recognized the caricature of a red-gowned diva that Isa created to brand the concert—*Concerto per e di Amici*—a concert for and of friends.

Telma pushed the packet toward him and purred, "See for yourself. Addressed to Telma Rossi, London."

"I-I'm st-stunned. Why in heaven would Isa invite—"

"*Moi,*" she interrupted, patting her chest. "The bane of her sad, small existence."

Luca inhaled, trying to find the words. "Bit strange. Surely you must admit, it's—"

"Like asking Lucrezia Borgia to pass the wine."

He laughed. Telma roared with laughter too, instantly releasing the tension. Regardless of one's opinion of the woman, Telma had few delusions of the bitchy persona she unleashed upon the world. He often scratched his head, wondering whether anyone had ever seen the real Telma Rossi, including the woman then seated across the table.

"I know, I know," she said. "Found it a tad odd too. Had Isa flipped her big-headed lid or was she luring me to San Benedetto with wicked intentions?"

Luca nodded. "The thought of a trap did cross my mind. You weren't exactly a model concertgoer last time—"

Another hearty laugh interrupted him. "The party guest who pissed in the punch bowl. That whole spotlight-stealing prank? *Pleeeze*, the weekend needed a little goose."

"I was thinking more along the lines of the naked boyfriend in bed routine."

She scoffed. "Ridiculous! You and I both know nothing happened."

"We may be the only ones who believe that." She shrugged, prompting him to add, "Hey, I'm not blaming you. I'm the cad who self-imploded. But, I understand how Isa and others see it differently. A smoking gun, after all."

She sighed. "If I'm to be judged guilty of the crime, don't deny me the pleasure of committing it. Imagine my delight if only you had fired your large, lovely Italian pistol," she cooed, pawing his hand.

Luca pulled away. *Was she joking?* He decided to laugh, pretending she was. "Real or not," he said, "you mean to say that despite the scandal, you're willing to ride into San Benedetto and enjoy Isa's hospitality?"

"If it's a trap, what the hell? Concert weekend may be worth a little amusement even if the joke's on me. As you say, I probably have it coming. But I won't go down without a fight."

He was still confused. "What makes you think the invitation's not a mistake?"

"Fate's melded together Isabella Fabrini and Telma Rossi. Neither of us can fight it. Why try?" She exaggerated a blink of her eyes, as she added, "Not unlike you and me, dear Luca. Besides, I consulted with Walter and Jamie before accepting the invite."

"And?"

"Jamie must have blabbed," she started, piquing his interest. "No one else knew about it…besides Walter and me, that is." Luca leaned closer; his expression must have signaled puzzlement because Telma snickered. "I rescued the last concert, *Querido*. Surprised?" She watched his face for a reaction.

"What?" *So this was the act of generosity that Jamie referenced over dinner in London.*

"Everything would have shut down before Isa trilled her first high C if Telma, Walter, and the Bank of England hadn't sprung into action." She lifted her latte, frowning at the glass as if it contained river water. "My kingdom for a double vodka," she whined, before launching into her story.

She described Jamie's pledge to bankroll the second concert and the collapse of his finances at the soiled hands of Willy Epson. She confessed to struggling with the decision. Had she bailed out the concert to provide a self-serving platform while Isa embarrassed herself? Was the payout a collegial nod to the concertgoers and choristers who welcomed her with goodwill? Or perhaps, the bank transfer was merely the price of entertainment, a cheap ticket for the all-inclusive carnival weekend. Three years after her generous act, Telma didn't give Luca a sense that even she understood her reasoning. At that moment, sitting across the table, she projected the joy of someone thrilled with the prospect of reuniting with good chums, much the way he delighted in his afternoon of cooking and breaking bread with concert friends.

"Why the Cheshire Cat face?" she asked toward the end of her story.

"Telma Rossi, you're a fraud."

She sat up. His indictment knocked the grin from her face. "Idiot's more like it," she said. "What did charity get me? I lost my millionaire, alimony…and now live as a common drone."

The words may have reeked of regret, but her expression and confident posture told Luca that she'd do it all over again. She had the demeanor, if not the hive, of a queen bee. He considered her charitable act on his behalf. Her brokered sale of one restaurant triggered a chain reaction of good fortune that saved him from trading his soul to Willy Epson. He suspected that honest work and success in supporting herself had changed Telma. Confidence and purpose pushed aside her insecurities.

"You're an enigma," he said. "You have the capacity for kindness, but recoil from any acknowledgment of your good deeds. As a beneficiary of your charity, I'm wise to your deceit."

She winced as if he'd lanced her heart. "Stop! If you insist on beatifying me, I simply must drown myself in a vat of vodka. I won't travel all the way to San Benedetto with someone who dissects my soul."

After all the talk about Telma and her plans to attend the concert, Luca had forgotten his intention. "I'm not going to San Benedetto."

"But I saw you miss the train. I thought for sure…"

"I jumped off. Decided against going. Simple as that."

Her eyes grew wide and her head perked up. "Now it's getting interesting," she said with a smirk. "No one steps off a moving train unless they have a tortured conscience." She raised her glass. "Praise the lord and watery coffee. I need every one of my endangered brain cells to hear your confession. Do tell, Luca Caruso. What little angel told you to jump off that train…and why?"

"Angel? More devil, I'd say. I stepped off that train and into *your* clutches."

"Satan's merely an angel with attitude. Quit sidestepping the question. What torments you?" Her face lit up like a child with birthday cake.

"Nothing, nothing at all." Telma certainly wasn't a confidante with whom he wished to share his struggle. He'd sort out his confused feelings for Elizabeth and Isa by himself.

She wagged a finger in his face. "Something urged you to go to Isa's concert, then something or someone broke the oars of your little adventure. Might that someone be an adorable blonde who followed you all the way from London?"

Her words jolted like a taser. He shouldn't have been surprised. Telma poked her surgically enhanced nose into everyone's business. And despite a rocky start to their relationship, the two women had become lunch chums of sort back in London. He didn't see it coming. Ignoring his warning, Elizabeth extended an olive branch to the temptress as Telma's role in pulling him from the fiscal flames became clearer. The irony didn't escape him. Elizabeth became the one playing with fire.

The clinking of Telma's spoon against the latte glass brought him back into focus. "Talk," she said. "Remember, I've seen you naked. Gives me certain privileges."

For the first time since running into the woman, Luca regretted bypassing the cocktail lounge.

"It's quite simple. I wasn't invited," he said, dodging the truth.

"No surprise there. After the way you acted last time," she said with a chuckle. "Consider yourself my plus-one."

"That's what the others offered," he said, describing the time spent with the concert friends in Rome. "I got caught up in the camaraderie, wanted to keep the party going. But then reason took hold."

"Reason? I never mess with the stuff. As toxic as passion and half the fun. Take my ill-fated engagement to Graham. Logic told me to marry a millionaire. What a farce that would have been, practically bigamy. He was already married…to his mother."

Luca chuckled. "Whatever happened to your fiancé?"

"Mama died and Graham found his balls. Settled in with a nice Mayfair florist. He and Simon are serenely happy, tiptoeing through the tulips. Reason did neither one of us any good. Won't do you any favors either. Come!"

"It'd be cruel if I showed up."

"Cruel if you don't. You crushed Isa when you didn't come to her first concert."

"I don't know. My life's here now."

"Listen, Luca. If you mean Elizabeth, she's been good for you, very good. There's no denying that. As for sharing a bed, good for you."

Luca flinched. But lying about his relationship with Elizabeth was futile, especially with the tigress before him.

Telma smirked. "High time, if you ask me. Poor girl's been pining after you for years. Knew it that first time she kicked me out of your restaurant. She's a nurturer. Certainly found the right man there. But what happens when your wings mend and you can fly from the nest?"

"But I think I love her." *Where did those words come from?*

"Probably so. And she loves you."

"Why give that up?" *Am I asking Telma or myself?*

"Isa loves you, too. And you love her, if you were both honest."

Luca shook his head, trying to sort through her words and his feelings. Leech had said essentially the same thing. If everyone thought they were perfect for each other, why didn't he and Isa see it themselves?

"Love's not a commodity to casually toss around. It's absolute, finite."

"Nonsense! There's that reason crap again—toxic. And when mixed with passion, whoa…" She whistled, pulsing her hand above the table. "I believe it's possible to love and be loved by more than one person. Just ask those Mormons."

"B-but, Elizabeth," he stammered holding his head.

Reaching across the table, Telma squeezed his arm. "You might just show your love for that young woman by setting her free."

Her words were no strangers to his thoughts. Elizabeth was a beautiful girl with a kind spirit. Their twenty-year age difference would grow more pronounced. Elizabeth and he both knew that she was looking for a father figure when she fell in love with him. There was nothing wrong with that. But what would happen when time turned him into a grandfather figure? Elizabeth said it didn't matter—he'd always need her…and she'd always be there for him. Was that being fair to her?

"She'll never leave you as long as she thinks you need her," Telma added with a tap to the table. "Poor girl. It's her curse. Confessed as much over lunch and vino."

"Curse? What in heaven's name are you talking about?"

Clasping her hands, Telma looked away. She seemed flustered. "Silly chatter. I don't know why I said such a thing." Turning back to face him again, Telma added, "You need an answer to your dilemma. Must taste the wine to see if you like it. Don't pour it down the damn drain. Don't run away."

She could easily have said "*again*, don't run away *again.*" Fast getaways cluttered Luca's past. After his wife and daughter died in the car crash, he fled country and career. After his breakup with Isa, he sought refuge in drink. More recently, he almost abandoned his financial responsibilities by casting his lot with Willy Epson. In every case, new troubles attached themselves to his fleeing coattails. Escape was futile. Maybe Elizabeth understood that too when she urged him to go to the concert. But running to Isa meant running away from Elizabeth. Telma was right. Luca should face his dilemma, find resolution, and stop running. He looked across the table.

His expression must have betrayed his thoughts. Telma nodded. "It's settled then. You're coming."

He inhaled deeply through gritted teeth. "I don't know. Do I dare?"

"You're already packed. Besides, I need a travel companion."

"Someone to carry your luggage, you mean."

Her lips curled into the grin of an angel with attitude. How the tide had turned. Here was Telma, an invited guest to concert weekend, while Luca Caruso cast himself in the unsavory role of party crasher.

As they entered the train compartment, Telma elbowed him and nodded forward. Seated in the car was none other than the amorous Frenchman.

Luca extended his hand. "*Bonjour,* you're Philippe Blanchette, right?"

The man looked up from his mobile phone, a befuddled expression on his face, more pale and gaunt than Luca remembered. "Phil," he replied in a flat tone. Apparently, his French accent drowned somewhere in the mid-Atlantic. He shook Luca's hand. "Phil White now, if you please." His demeanor seemed more staid, tamer than before.

Telma shimmied past, leaving Luca to secure her suitcases. She dropped onto the seat beside the still handsome man as Luca lifted her makeup case to the shelf above their heads.

"Phil?" she said, rubbing the Frenchman's arm. "Now it's getting interesting. Talk! Remember, I've seen you naked. Gives me certain privileges…"

Chapter 41

After boarding the train in Rome, Telma pressed herself against Philippe... or rather, the rebranded Phil White. She hung onto his every word. Luca couldn't blame her. The Frenchman's tale riveted him as well, but for different reasons. He might have shared a similar fate if Kate, Elizabeth, and Lighthouse hadn't steered him from the rocks.

As the train sped through the Umbrian and Tuscan countryside, Phil transfixed Telma and Luca with his journey through the judicial system that played out like scenes from American TV. With a blood alcohol level twice the legal limit, he drove his Jaguar convertible into a Manhattan intersection, broadsiding another car.

He shrugged. "Red lights, red flags. Never paid attention to either."

Sincerity drained the comment of humor. Instead the words evoked somber irony. The court found him guilty of attempted vehicular manslaughter. *The evidence*, Luca thought, *must have been damn good for a jury to convict that handsome face.*

"I thank God I didn't kill anyone. The two in the other car were battered up though," he added in a penitent tone. His face looked ashen, the chestnut-colored eyes lifeless.

"Was it horrible?" Telma asked. "Prison, I mean." Her eager expression willed an affirmative response laced with detail.

Phil shrugged. "Depends. Sex I got...plenty of it. Most drugs too. But alcohol? Not so easy to slip that in your crotch."

Telma glanced at the Frenchman's lap but kept silent.

Prison offered Phil an appealing reason to address his addictive personality. He shaved time from his sentence by volunteering to participate in a program for drug and alcohol abusers. "Identify your monsters, recognize the patterns that trap you, and pretend you give a shit what the other poor SOBs say. Bit like Lighthouse…but without fancy retreats, bonding exercises, and recruiting pushes."

"Sounds abominable," replied Telma.

Phil laughed. "Weren't called Seekers either. You're looking at H2984008."

Luca cringed. "Makes me appreciate your new identity all the more."

"Wasn't all bad," Phil added. "Got me to face hard facts…about my past, the future…my present." He drifted away in reflection, before shaking his head and saying, "Anyway, swapped stories, made friends, got business leads."

"Sounds like a gentlemen's club."

"Wouldn't go that far, Telma dear. Staring at bars and shitting on stainless steel's not Phil White's idea of the good life. But I met a few good guys among the chaff. More decent than half the blowhards you find at a so-called *gentlemen's* club."

Luca's dealings with Willy confirmed Phil's comment. The City power broker had the money, influence, and legal team to stay out of jail. Laws bent for posh suits. Willy faced a greater threat from street justice than he ever would from a British court.

"So you fled America, now what?" Telma asked.

"*Mais non.* A little business in San Benedetto, *oui*—new client. Then right back after the concert. America loves me—not so fond of the French, but Phil White's another story. I'm what they call a budding entrepreneur."

"What!" Telma exclaimed, sharing a quizzical look with Luca.

"Entrepreneur. *Un bon mot français*, a good French word."

"I know what it means," Telma replied. "Just puzzled how you fit the definition."

"Americans see opportunity in anything and seize upon it. If they fail, *c'est la vie*, try something else. Look at Apple, a garage computer. And now, digital picture books, glorified bulletin boards to chronicle every one of life's mediocrities."

"Again, my sweet," Telma said, squeezing him tighter, "what does any of this have to do with you?"

He lifted her hand to his lips and flashed a proud smile. "You're looking at the founder and president of Bridges."

"Bridges?" Luca asked.

"*Oui!* Nautical theme, like Lighthouse." Still clueless, Telma and Luca offered tepid smiles. "Not to mention," Phil added with a shrug, "all the bridges I stared at from my East River cell."

Telma's smile faded. "How inspiring."

"What is it you do, exactly?" Luca asked.

Sitting up, Phil puffed his chest. "Minister to wayward souls."

Good Lord. Had he become one of those American TV preachers who spent more time fussing with hairspray, shiny suits, and makeup than on God's work? Their *Good Word* had five letters, M-O-N-E-Y. Wouldn't take much effort to turn Phil into a blazing light for swarms of desperate moths.

"Admirable," Luca said.

Telma rolled her eyes. "Still don't know what the hell it is you do. Merely how *selfless* you've become," she said, not bothering to disguise the sarcasm.

Phil nibbled her earlobe. "Nothing selfless about it, *chérie.* I've tapped into a gold mine. Only cuffs I now wear are platinum." His dangling wrist revealed a shiny watchband.

Telma's eyes lit up like a cat's; she practically purred. She not only adored fine jewelry, but her French soul mate hadn't abandoned her race of greedy materialists. Their eyes widened as Phil explained his job, preparing convicted criminals for prison.

"So, you're a counselor of sorts," Luca said, impressed with the initiative.

"*Mais non,*" Phil replied with a shudder. "I'm no social worker or nursemaid. I'm a *consultant.* I sell experience—command a small fortune. My clients are scared shitless. Bigger they are..." He rubbed fingers together to imply wealth. "...The more they cry—frightened little babies losing silver spoons. Not only survival skills, I'm a shoulder to cry on, proof one can survive the ordeal and exit the other side."

"Makes complete sense," said Telma, looking very pleased.

"*Oui.* A path into prison and a path home again—*voilà,* Bridges."

Besides transition coaching to and from prison, Bridges offered add-ons—a one-stop shop for all your incarceration planning. For a pricey fee, Bridges handled house rentals and property management, furniture and car dispositions. Phil hired a staff to advise clients on an array of issues including guardianship, elder care, and financial planning. He was building an empire. Luca imagined a Frommer's-like series of guides—San Quentin, Dartmoor, Sing Sing.

For all of his talk about money, however, Luca sensed that Phil's mission fulfilled him. Perhaps just as Luca had done with cooking school, Phil found a higher purpose to give his life meaning.

"And who says crime doesn't pay?" said Telma, looking pleased with her quip.

Phil nodded vigorously. "*Oui, oui, absolument.* American corporations and capitols are factories of future clients."

"Gertrude Stein's *grosses têtes*—greedy, ambitious, big heads," Telma said, responding to her traveling companions' gasps with a scoff. "Please, I have read a book or two."

As the three shared a laugh, Luca considered that Phil didn't have to limit his scope. Corruption was a global commodity.

"What matters is that I'm useful, happy. Money's nice too," Phil said with a smirk.

He'd tapped into the American dream, really anyone's dream. Luca saw himself and the Frenchman as kindred spirits. Both had hit bottoms of sorts, Phil in jail and Luca in financial ruin. But instead of giving up, both men leveraged their experiences into new careers. Darwinian theory applied to modern life: adapt or die destitute.

Luca thought of Isa. Hadn't she done the same thing? Despite initial failure and doubt, she climbed onto that stage and sang her heart out, working tirelessly to train her voice and hone her talent. That's why he admired her. Maybe that's why he still loved her.

Phil and Telma carried on while Luca lost himself in reflection, returning to the conversation only upon hearing Telma's fury. "Bull shit! You can't say you *shouldn't* tell us, then *refuse* to tell us. That's cruel…and not how one plays the game." Slapping his thigh, she turned to the aisle and pouted.

Phil frowned like a hurt little boy. "Okay, okay," he said through pursed lips, "but you must promise not to repeat. They'll be at the concert."

Uncrossing her arms, Telma turned toward Phil. "Yes, yes, all that crap. Swear to God, hope to die and blah, blah, blah. Now tell us who's off to the slammer."

Luca laughed at her gangster-era slang, but his interest surged.

"I'm serious," Phil said, still agitated. "It's my livelihood."

"He's right, Telma. We should honor his request—a reasonable *quid pro quo*."

Telma sighed. "Agreed, then. All settled. We won't breathe a word." Rubbing her hands together, she bristled with anticipation.

Phil lowered his voice. "It's someone you know. A person who's been to every concert. A big fish, as they say."

Luca leaned forward. *Perhaps Willy was about to get his comeuppance.*

Telma sat up, unable to contain her excitement. She rattled off names, tapping her chin in tempo. "Hmm…Danny, Tommy, Miguel…no, no, no." Her head perked up. "Got it! That bitch Alexandra Novak. Ha, love to see the photo spread of the happy housewife in prison stripes." She clapped her hands and looked at Phil.

He shook his head. "No, but you're very close."

"Oh my God, Cowboy. Governor Brad Novak," Telma blurted, bouncing in her seat.

Phil nodded. He clenched his jaw; his face went white. Luca guessed that he regretted sharing the information with Telma, the paragon of indiscretion.

Phil explained how Alexandra reached out to him after finding his name on a list of consultants provided by Brad's lawyers. "She called it premature, but I heard the stress in her voice," Phil said. "Called it contingency planning, a doomsday scenario. Needed advice for a prison choice."

"They get to choose a prison?" Telma asked. "Sure you're not a camp counselor."

"She phoned back a few weeks ago. Said the governor would likely cop a plea."

"Cop a plea?" Luca asked.

"American lingo. You agree to guilt in exchange for a lighter sentence and perks like prison location, report date, fine reduction. It's all the rage among politicians these days. Saves the embarrassment of a lengthy trial and sometimes protects a guilty loved one."

Telma sighed with delight. "Bet the bitch's roots are going gray and her perky tits are sagging with the pressure."

Phil nodded. "Sounded to me like she's the one pressing for the plea deal."

The interruption of the beverage cart pushed the conversation to less sensitive topics. But something nagged at Luca, a detail about Phil's ordeal. He didn't know why he couldn't shake it, or what compelled him to have the answer. "Phil," he asked. "Who were the people?"

The Frenchman cocked his head. "Huh?"

"In the other car. Who were the people in the car you hit?"

His expression veered among pain, annoyance, and confusion. "Does it matter?"

"Don't know, probably not, maybe…I just need the answer."

"A woman, pretty young mother and her little girl—six or seven."

Silent, Luca stared out the window for the remainder of the ride.

Chapter 42

San Benedetto

When the train stopped, Telma grabbed her makeup case, tucked her arm through the Frenchman's, and headed out the door. Luca studied the pair as they pushed toward the vestibule—two sides of the same shiny, rough-edged coin. They made good friends, probably even satisfactory lovers, but any deeper bond promised disaster.

Luca struggled down the aisle, toting Telma's two overstuffed bags and sliding his modest case forward with his foot. Stepping down onto the platform, he wondered how San Benedetto had changed since his prior visit. And what about the people? Who among the concert crowd had weathered time's passage and who buckled under the strains of a spinning world?

Although prison kept Phil locked up for over two years, the wily Frenchman leapfrogged ahead. Their chance encounter seemed to reawaken his spark, a *je ne sais quoi*, or, to use his adopted jargon, his *swagga*. His brown eyes warmed to their former luster; his strut regained its confidence.

As for others, Telma remained in place, shifting from side to side. The Novaks faced a backward push. Kate danced forward with her English beau while Brigid found herself mired in an unhappy past. From their time together in Rome, Luca understood where life had taken Jamie, Danny, Tommy, and Miguel. But concert weekend had others whose unread histories piqued his curiosity.

Their extended embrace allowed Luca to catch up to Telma and Phil. After dropping the bags at their feet, he stretched and heaved a sigh.

"Thank God you shed all that pudge," Telma said, with a nod of her head. "A year ago, I'd have insisted on carrying my own bags. You still wheezed like an old mare and sweated like a Malay coolie."

"Telma, my love," Luca said with a gentle tap to her nose, "don't change, don't *ever, ever* change."

After he stopped laughing, Luca turned. He found Phil staring at him, a perplexed look on his face. "*Incroyable*. Never would have guessed you went through a chubby patch," he said with a slap to Luca's shoulder. "As a matter of fact, you look fantastic—younger, tanner, trimmer than at the last concert."

"*Grazie,*" Luca said, pleased with Phil's praise. He started to describe his journey back to fitness when a high-pitched shriek interrupted him.

"*Signora, signora!*"

The three turned toward the station house. An attractive woman hurried toward them, arms flailing in the air.

"Good heavens," Telma said. "Is that screeching cat calling my name?"

"Wouldn't mind if she purred for me," Phil said. "She's a stunner."

As the woman approached, something about her was oddly familiar, but Luca couldn't place her. Not only had he encountered many new faces at the last concert, alcohol robbed him of many lucid memories.

"Good Lord," Telma said, clutching Luca's arm. "Our caterpillar has become a butterfly."

Once the woman was upon them, Luca recognized her as the hotel clerk. Her name escaped him until Telma shouted, "Svetlana! You look fabulous. Brava, my dear, brava!"

The two women embraced with the joy of long-separated sisters. Still holding the other's hand, Telma stepped back to study her specimen. Svetlana's hair, now soft blonde, was swept to one side like the modern cuts one saw in Rome. Her yellow and cream-colored dress was simple linen, a fashion found in the pages of French or American magazines. While the clothes and hair gave her a confident air, her beauty was unmistakable. Makeup defined high cheekbones and large dark penetrating eyes, features hidden on Luca's last visit.

"Always charming to see the excesses of easy credit," Telma said, finally signaling her approval with upturned lips and soft nods.

Svetlana smiled; a sparkling grin revealed a dentist's recent craftsmanship. Twinkling eyes conveyed satisfaction and pride. Reaching forward, she touched Telma's antique pendant. "Everyone should have the chance to exchange dowdy for chic, signora, no?" Her voice lilted with giddiness.

Laughing like schoolgirls, the two women locked arms.

Phil imposed himself between them, took Svetlana's hand, and pressed it to his lips. "*Enchanté, mademoiselle,*" he said. "*Très belle, très belle.*"

Luca and Telma exchanged smirks at the resurrection of Philippe Blanchette. After pleasantries, Svetlana tugged Telma's arm and tucked it under hers. "Come," the young woman said. "I drive you to hotel."

As Luca stooped to pick up the luggage, Svetlana turned to him and Phil with a scrunched face. "Sorry, but my car, she only two-seater."

"No worries," Telma interjected before Luca or the Frenchman could speak. "The boys can follow in a cab. Hope you drive a convertible," she added as Svetlana led her to the street. "We're too delicious to hide from this starving little hamlet."

As the BMW Z-4 sped away from the curb, Luca and Phil made their way to the taxi stand, sharing the burden of Telma's bags.

Phil nodded toward the disappearing red roadster. "You know those things—dogs, dolls, babies—so ugly, they're cute. She's like that." Luca was glad *she* was out of earshot. "Not ugly, no, no, no," Phil added. "Telma's beautiful. *Non*, she's so prickly, you just want to nuzzle and squeeze, *n'est-ce pas?*"

The taxi driver's energetic greeting saved Luca from answering. While he wouldn't call Telma huggable by any means, perhaps Phil sensed the same vulnerability he saw in her—the frightened girl who sometimes looked out from dark Latin eyes. Luca wondered if she could ever stop acting to let the real Telma Rossi take center stage.

In the taxi, Luca learned that Phil hadn't booked at the Villa Europa by choice.

"Alexandra wants me close by."

Was she merely consulting him about prisons or was she laying the foundation for a "partnership" to fill the long, dry months between conjugal visits with her corralled cowboy?

"Villa Europa's pretty expensive."

"A write-off," Phil said with a smirk. "Flew first class from New York, too. That's where they hide the pretty flight attendants. Decent champagne and big lavatories," he added with lifted eyebrows.

Wine, women, and washrooms. Good to see that prison hadn't completely changed the amorous Frenchman.

Perhaps he read Luca's thoughts about his lavish spending. He wasn't the self-conscious type. "With money, no discipline. In America, I'm not *nouveau riche.* I'm white trash. Funny, *oui*, with my new name, I mean," he said, lifting his shoulders and blowing air through his pursed lips. "But business is different, even in America. Lunched with Danny Chance in New York. Wants to broker my new office and I wanted to pick his brain about tax deductions. We arm-wrestled over the check," Phil added with a snicker.

Getting out of the taxi, Luca pulled his wallet but Phil batted it down. "I got the fare," he said. "You and I, we discussed business, *n'est-ce pas?*"

"No, not white trash," Luca said, before closing the taxi door, "a true capitalist."

Inside the hotel, Telma and Svetlana chatted away on an upholstered bench in a corner of the lobby. They laughed, gasped, flinched, teared, swore, and laughed again, as women do when they haven't seen each other in years. Topics careened from fashion to hairstyles to celebrities to romance. In one breath, men were swine, in the next, prized princes. One would have mistaken the pair for best friends rather than two people who shared a long weekend three years in the past. Luca's entrance didn't stop the chatty reunion. Telma remarked how she approved of the new décor—a positive step toward stirring the tired hotel from its mid-twentieth century coma.

Svetlana relayed how she bought and refurbished the hotel with the help of a relative. "Rich uncles are the best," she said with gusto.

"Dead rich uncles are even better," Telma replied.

Luca listened with head shaking until a young woman appeared from a backroom and motioned him to the front desk. With a drab gray smock, uncombed hair, and the barest hint of lipstick, she resembled the former incarnation of Svetlana. After her warmest sneer and grunt, she slid a registration form toward him.

As he pushed the completed form back, arms embraced him. "Signor Caruso," Svetlana said. "So glad we could fit you in." She snapped her fingers and pointed her protégée toward the room keys. "You in 14. Signora Rossi in 12 again. Adjoining rooms, suite if you like," she added in a suggestive tone.

Not sweet at all. "Oh n-no, no," he stammered, looking from Svetlana to her stone-faced young clone.

From behind him came Telma's deep-throated groan. "Good Lord, I had my chance to deflower you last time."

Svetlana shrugged. "Our very last room. Between concert and spa regulars, all hotels booked."

"It won't do, just won't—"

Writhing gyrations against his back and side startled him. Telma ground her body into his. Her fingers slid through his hair and her hand fondled his rear end. She growled into his ear like a tiger. "Don't spoil my fun, lover boy. I want to rip off your clothes, throw you on the bed, and lick every inch of your hot, new bod."

The best way to deal with a prankster was to play their game. Leaning over, he nibbled her ear. "Let's finish where we left off, you little minx." He grabbed the key with one hand and swatted her backside with the other. Telma gasped, then laughed boisterously.

The desk clerk stirred, drawing his attention. She stared over his shoulder. He felt the presence. Someone had entered the lobby and stood behind him. With a broad smile, Svetlana said, "Signor Benchley. Hope you had nice walk. Your room now ready."

Telma's eyes widened; she turned pale. She released Luca's rear end, stood erect, straightened her jacket, and turned. "Why Walter—"

"My God, woman," he seethed. "You are shameless. Not that I should be shocked by someone who measures class in carats."

Luca expected Telma to inhale and take aim, either unleashing invectives at her ex-husband or mocking his indictment by throwing herself at Luca. Instead, she broke into sobs, grabbed her key off the counter, and bolted up the stairs. Slack-jawed, Luca stared after her.

"Listen, Walter," Luca said, sipping sparkling water as the brooding banker threw back a second whiskey. "For the hundredth time, there's nothing between us. Never was or will be."

Luca sat at the Tazza d'Oro, staring across the table, wondering why he was defending his innocence to the guilty cad. Not only had Walter jilted Isa, he had no claim on, or, to use his vernacular, collateral interest in Telma. Luca found the situation very odd.

After snapping fingers for a third whiskey, Walter rested his elbows on the table and rubbed his temples. "What a fool I was to come." He spoke more to himself than to Luca. "Everyone said what a grand time I'd have—concert, parties, Italy. And the first thing I see? My wife making a spectacle. *Déjà vu*. Preferred last time, when I didn't have to witness it." Café patrons and passersby stared at the two as alcohol raised Walter's volume.

"First off, there was no last time. Second, she's not your wife anymore."

Taking a few sips from the refilled glass, Walter looked at Luca through glassy eyes. "Truth is, I love that woman. Infuriating and selfish, but I love her. Realized it right away. Not in the park where Isa found us. No, that was pure fucking passion. But there's no fire without a spark. No, later that night, after I slithered back to the reception for a last blowout with Isa. I recalled our stroll before the lovemaking. Telma was a caring girl…sweet, vulnerable. Not the too-perfect ice sculpture you see today, no, a simple, sincere beauty. Why must she push everyone away, hide behind smoke and mirrors? Told me she didn't want children. Never told her that I learned the truth. She couldn't have children. Guess we both kept secrets. I loved…love her."

And with that confession the spinning world leapt forward. Not only for Walter who bared his soul, but also for the object of his latent affection. As he sat, silent witness to Walter's outpouring, Luca's eyes wandered up to the hotel balcony. Telma leaned toward them, hands clutching the railing. Her frozen expression told him she'd heard. Tears streamed down her face.

Luca handed him a napkin to dab his eyes. "Listen, Walter, you must tell—"

A commotion interrupted him. Danny, Tommy, and Miguel rushed into the café and huddled around the table.

"Amazing news," Danny said, winded.

"Can't believe it," Tommy huffed.

Luca looked up at them with wide eyes. "What happened?"

Chairs scraped the stone floor as the three pulled them to the table and sat.

"Willy Epson. He's dead," Miguel said. "Found him in his bathtub, in London."

"Accident or suicide?" Luca asked.

"My bet's on murder," said Walter.

Danny spoke for everyone, "Amazing!"

Chapter 43

As Luca paid for lunch, a swat to his bum preceded the familiar voice. "Heard you came, *bello*. Searched every purveyor of salad and fruit juice in town." Even without the accent, a gentrified Scouse, the licorice-laced breath, and lavender-scented fog announced his old friend.

"Let me get a good look," Leech said after their embrace. He patted Luca's stomach and squeezed his cheek. "Gigolo material. Posh too. Break my piggy bank for a go at you."

Happy with the praise, Luca ruffled his friend's hair, wisps of spun lavender silk.

"Careful. Glue's not dry."

Luca looked at his palm, but an animated laugh told him Leech was joking. He loved the quirky man, a solid friend who grounded him, but whose eccentricities lifted his spirits. "You're a grand sight," Luca said. "Been feeling, I don't know…out of sorts."

"Hope it's not this Willy Epson business everyone's fussing about. Already robbed us of at least one chorus member." His tone suggested carelessness on the part of the deceased that threatened to sabotage the concert.

Luca shook his head. Other than Willy's wife, few would defect from the concert. Willy aggrieved more people alive than dead. "Nothing to do with Willy. I'm doubting whether I should have come."

Leech's hand fluttered the air. "Stage fright, *bello*. Butterflies in the stomach, racing heart, clammy forehead. Know the signs only too well."

"San Benedetto is Isa's world, not mine."

"Nonsense! This is precisely where you need to be. With whom you should be. Told you as much many times. But no one listens to Leech."

"I don't want to spoil her concert..." *I could have said "again."*

"Listen, *bello,* Isa wants you here whether or not she knows it." Luca's eyes dropped to his feet, but Leech lifted his chin. "You've beaten yourself up long enough for Milan—paid in full. Leave Isa to me. I'll tell her you're here." Luca simply stared at him, his lips pursed. "Come with me," Leech said with a pat to his shoulder. "To the chorus rehearsal. Even let you treat me along the way. Music may civilize the savage, but *gelato* soothes the soul."

Luca recognized Leech's ulterior motives. The colorful man must have known that Luca would continue to second-guess his decision to come. The chorus would keep him tethered to the concert and more. Leech, he guessed, was betting on the therapeutic benefits of confronting fears—opera houses, singing, and Isa.

Italy in June is hot. The nineteenth-century theater without air conditioning was unbearable. Leech's scalp beaded before the two men climbed to the first floor.

"Praise the gods for that second scoop of pistachio," Leech wheezed over his shoulder. "I'd completely overheat without it."

They reached the top floor of the opera house by a series of wooden staircases. In their ascent, stairs narrowed, opulence diminished, and the temperature rose. Leech asked to catch his breath before they entered the rehearsal studio. He used the break to tell Luca that Malcolm was coaching Isa, Ivy, and the other soloists in the main theater. "Quite a big production it's become. Full scenes," Leech said through huffs and puffs. "Town is talking about turning it into a summer festival. You'll be proud of *your* Isa." He stared. Luca knew the ploy, a stall to gauge his feelings. Perhaps Leech could favor him by disclosing what his eyes revealed—he didn't know himself. "Turned into quite the performer, she has," Leech added. "Despite her perverse obsession with that...that...*Jenkins* woman." Luca thought the other man's head would burst.

Dust motes, like tiny confetti, flitted in the natural light coming from the chorus room. Directives barked by Lady Blatherwicke gave cover to Leech's panting and the creaking floorboards under their feet. Leech held a finger to his lips and flashed a mischievous grin as they turned their ears to the open door.

"Alto or soprano?" Lady B scoffed, "If you don't know your voice by now, my dear woman, frankly it doesn't matter…As for Bizet, those who don't speak French, which, I fear from your blank expressions, is most of you, be mindful. It's a lyrical language, meant to trill from the tongue, not drone from the bowels like German, English, or that American dreck that's snuck into my chorus…And above all, *none* of that bathtub business. Makes for juicy gossip, but until someone sets La Tragédie de Willy Epson to music, that tabloid trash has no place in our opera house…Do I make myself clear?" She pounded the floor for emphasis. A smattering of yes, *oui, sí, ja,* and yeah responded.

"Now," Leech said, tugging Luca's shirtsleeve and pulling him off balance. They practically fell into the room as the badgered choristers nodded to their taskmistress's commands. Luca felt the collective exhale as the huddled masses responded to the colorful entrance with smiles and chatter. He wondered if Lady B and Leech planned this theatrical point-counterpoint to browbeat the chorus into submission, the choral masters' variant of good cop, bad cop.

"Look who I found," Leech said, holding up Luca's arm. "A treat for the tenors."

The room erupted in applause. Luca recognized Kate, her beau Richard, the American boys, Isa's cousins from America, Gina's two daughters, and several others. Affirmation surged through his body like electricity. Concerns about leftover ill will from his undignified exit from the prior concert weekend vanished. As one smiling man waved him to an empty seat, Luca felt welcomed, and in an odd way, loved.

Everything will be fine, Luca thought. The ensemble was a group of amateurs, not a professional company. The program was a concert for friends and family, not full opera. And, San Benedetto's dowager theater was not La Scala. *Everything will be fine.* The words repeated in his head. But despite his mantra, his heart pounded and his palms sweated. The real test was yet to come—the spotlighted stage.

They practiced in stifling heat. Lady Blatherwicke, past eighty but still a commanding presence with perfect posture and silky white hair, insisted on giving bits of historical context to each piece. Some choristers yawned or shuffled their feet while the most passionate absorbed the lecture with earnest looks and busy pencils.

Miguel nudged Luca in the side, motioning with his chin to the bobbing head of Danny Chance. "Brown-noser."

"Came to sing, not listen to a bloody lecture," Richard said loud enough to attract a glare and menacing pencil thrust from Kate.

Energy rebounded when the sheet music was passed around. First, they recited lines, many fanning themselves with the scores. Lady B and Leech enunciated the words for those unfamiliar with the French and Italian. Mercifully, Isa and Leech restricted the program to two languages.

"Repetez après moi," Lady Blatherwicke lilted, holding up the music of Bizet's *Carmen.* "Repeat after me!"

Les voici! Les voici! Oui les voici!
Voici la quadrille!
La quadrille des toréros,
Sur les lances le soleil brille,
En l'air toques et sombreros!
Les voici, voici la quadrille,
La quadrille des toréros,
Les voici! Les voici! Les voici!

As the two handlers circulated, the chorus repeated the lyrics with the rote discipline of schoolchildren. Dropped, added, and mis-accented syllables were called out. Flagrant violators were forced to stand, their cheeks pressed by the inquisitors until the word flowed to satisfaction. After a few such passes, most wised up letting the native Italian and French speakers carry the piece. And so it continued with Verdi's "Anvil Chorus," Donizetti's "Chorus of Wedding Guests," and the short finale from Puccini's *Turandot* in which the chorus would accompany Isa and her leading man.

After two hours, Lady B raised her hands. A chipper tone and broad smile got their attention quicker than a banging stick. "These wonderful people deserve a break."

Leech barked. "Wonderful people, *yes*—wonderful chorus...*not so much.* They'll get a break once they sail through the Verdi without jabbering like the Babel glee club."

Leech the Bad relented after Blatherwicke the Good whispered in his ear. "Fine, fine, fine," he said, throwing up his arms. "Need a bloody cig anyway. Make that a pack."

Luca shuffled through the rows of chairs to catch up with friends congregating in the back of the room. Tommy and Miguel fanned the group with air pulled in from an open window. When Kate began to rifle inside her oversized book bag, the small group let out a collective groan.

"Please," Danny said. "Not more books."

Kate smirked. "Here," she said, pulling out plastic bottles. "Been in this blazing hot room before. Water we need, not self-help."

Richard turned to Luca. "Boys said they spotted you at the Tazza d'Oro. We worried you got cold feet when you missed the train."

"Simple carelessness." Luca didn't want to get caught up in another conversation as to whether or not he should be in San Benedetto. He cast the die by joining the chorus.

Tommy slapped his back. "Well, we're all glad you're here."

"*Sí señor*, your *Italiano's muy bueno*," Danny said in an accent more Spanish than Italian. He held up hands inked with lyrics. "Almost as *bueno* as *mio*. Amazing."

"*Buono, buono, signor. Grazie mille*," Luca replied over the laughter.

Kate cast a furtive glance around the room before lowering her voice to a whisper. "What do ya know of this Willy Epson business, darlin'?"

They huddled closer, afraid Lady B might catch them gossiping about the taboo topic.

"No more than what the boys told me at the café," Luca said, glancing at the three Americans.

"Wouldn't surprise me a'tall if it's murder," Kate said, raising an eyebrow. "Lord knows the devil had it comin.' Heard he dabbled into all sorts of nastiness."

Luca felt his face grow warm. While he never consummated the arson plot, guilt riddled him for having considered it—his curse of Catholic indoctrination. Telma and Jamie knew or guessed about his plans but he doubted either of them had said anything. Should it indeed be murder, would Luca's name surface in an investigation? "What's the latest?" he asked, trying to hide his anxiety.

The others tied together a loose account based on conversations and hyperactive imaginations molded from watching too many television mysteries. Two days before, police found Willy's naked body in the tub of his London home. Tabloids, ever anxious to dress down the City's elite, fed the public information from *unnamed* sources. An anonymous caller, the papers said, alerted police, claiming that Willy missed several meetings and failed to return phone calls. Investigators found a note of undisclosed content and authorship at the scene. While the investigation was still young, empty bottles of sleeping pills and whiskey suggested an overdose.

Kate glowered. "Blended, they say," her tone disapproving. "Scotch at that."

"Amazing if someone forced him to swallow the pills at gunpoint," Danny said.

Miguel rolled his eyes. "Maybe he simply drowned."

Tommy's voice dropped to a whisper, his tone dramatic. "Or was drowned."

Kate pulled a London tabloid from her bag, smuggled into the opera house by an English alto who had only just arrived from London. The paper showed pictures of Vicki Epson entering the Knightsbridge home. Captions labeled her the estranged wife. Citing *reliable* sources, the account disclosed that seven-time wed Willy began seeing an American woman whom police had yet to question. The newspaper teased with innuendo of gambling debts, a crumbling financial empire, criminal indictments, and underworld associates. Even though the police were careful not to label the house a crime scene, the paper grabbed readers with the provocative headline: *What Killed Willy Epson...or Who?*

"Lucky we were together in Rome," Luca said. "A collective alibi."

Tommy shook his head. "We don't know when he died. Murderer may have filled the tub with ice. Willy could have been thawing for days. Plenty of time for a culprit to flee the crime scene." The wholesome American was surely an Agatha Christie fan.

"Don't look at me," Richard said, "I didn't kill the bastard."

Kate looked frightened as she stammered, "B-Brad and A-Alexandra. They flew in from London last night."

"Many of us in this room were in London earlier this week including Isa," Richard added. "By that logic, any one of us could have murdered the man."

"Or *all* of you," Tommy said, eyes widening. "*Murder on the Orient Express.*"

Danny gasped. "Amazing. He could be right."

Miguel squeezed both men's shoulders. "Quite the imaginations."

"We've nothing to worry about until the police show up in San Benedetto," Luca said, knowing only too well that anything could happen during concert weekend.

They jumped at the pounding noise, turning to the front of the room. Instead of the law's long arm, they found the formidable bicep of Lady Blatherwicke wielding her stick. She trilled, "To song, *al canto, à la chanson.*"

"No time to waste," Leech added. He kept the choristers on their feet, leading them through breathing exercises as a healthy looking Signor Bertini took a seat at the piano and organized his music.

"Bend over. Reach for your toes. Breathe, breathe," Leech bellowed. "Inhale like wheezing beasts," he added, demonstrating the desired technique. Luca chuckled. With humped back and swaying arms, Leech looked like a pastel baby elephant.

They hung their heads, grunting like pigs in heat. A knock at the door preceded the Irish-accented voice, "Must be in the wrong place. Was told this was a chorus, not the bleedin' circus."

Luca looked up. There stood the squinty-eyed leprechaun. Round, as white as the moon, and topped with red curls, the face belonged to Brigid Clancy. Laughter and applause greeted the beloved imp.

"Too late to enlist?" she asked, looking toward Leech and Lady B. They ushered her in with cheers and energetic waves. Brigid radiated joy as they welcomed her as a returning family member. She looked tired, but content to be among friends. She sidled up to Kate. The two bristled, posturing as old friends do when they're uncertain how to make the first move after a lengthy estrangement.

"Damn it, ladies," Leech bellowed. "You know you want to make up. We'll get nowhere till you do."

With a pound of her stick, Lady Blatherwicke commanded, "Hug!"

The Dubliners embraced and the room erupted in cheers. Teary-eyed Brigid turned to face Richard's extended hand. "What do ya think I am?" she blurted. Gasps were followed by an awkward silence until the wiry Dubliner added, "I'm no cold English fish. Come here, darlin'." With a cackle, she pulled Kate's wide-eyed beau into a hug.

As many dabbed tears, Luca's phone vibrated. He read the text a half-dozen times. *Glad U here. Come 2 dressing room 2night 7, Luv I.*

Euphoria batted down worry. Just as Kate and Brigid had done,

Luca anticipated reconciliation with Isa. Signor Bertini plunked the piano and Luca sang opera for the first time in years. Bizet's "Toreador Song" repeated in his head, *L'amour t'attend! L'amour! L'amour! L'amour! Toréador, Toréador, L'amour t'attend!* —Love awaits you! Love! Love! Love! Toreador, Toreador, love awaits you!

Chapter 44

The town's church bell tolled six times when Lady Blatherwicke moved to Signor Bertini's side, grabbing his hands as they descended to the keyboard. "Enough for today," she said, flashing a smile to the room of tired choristers. "Go prepare for this evening's lovely pre-concert party."

Leech shook his head from side to side, appearing to stifle a grin. "Still have doubts. But you're improving, yes you are, my pets. We may mold you into a chorus yet."

"Slip the lyrics under your pillows. Fill your dreams with song," Lady Blatherwicke sang the words. She glared at Leech as if daring him to usurp her right to the last word.

He picked up the velvet gauntlet with a toss of his head. "But no encores, pets—mustn't oversleep. Be here tomorrow morning by ten sharp—coffeed, juiced, and croissanted."

With a look of disgust, Lady B looked from Leech to the chorus. "For those who asked, you may book lunch and spa appointments tomorrow for half one or later."

"If those two prattle on, we'll miss the whole bloody weekend," Richard grumbled.

As Leech inhaled for another volley, Lady Blatherwicke whispered something to Bertini. The pianist launched into the *William Tell* overture with tremendous verve. Leech jumped, almost out of his satin slippers before doubling over in a jolly fit. With Rossini's notes racing from the piano, giddy choristers practically galloped from the sweltering room.

Without revealing his reason for lingering, Luca sent the others ahead. They were only too anxious to escape the cramped room for a cool shower, cocktails, and the promise of a charming Italian evening. Before separating, the friends made plans for a rendezvous at the Tazza d'Oro and from there, a communal stroll to the party.

Concert weekend produced a contagion of camaraderie. Participants represented six continents. Luca wondered whether Isa understood that her music opened a magical door for so many. As prickly as she could be, Isa was nothing short of bloody wonderful.

At the back of the rehearsal room, Luca stared out an open window to the square below. Long shadows replaced the bleached light of the afternoon sun. Aided by a breeze, the heat ratcheted down a few degrees. He was happy he came. During rehearsal, especially when the music featured the tenors, Luca caught Leech and Lady Blatherwicke staring at him. He'd seen that look before, as an aspiring opera singer.

During one chorus rehearsal in Milan, the director's gaze lingered on him. Did he hit the wrong note? Was his pitch off? Despite self-conscious worries, Luca kept flying through the score. That's what they taught him. His voice soared with unusual confidence. The director, a former opera singer with a kind face but the piercing eyes of a hawk, kept staring. She studied him as if hearing his voice for the first time. The call came a week or two later, the rehearsal that led to his first solo at La Scala…and his last.

Lady Blatherwicke's stares conveyed the same message, recognition of a professionally trained voice. Leech's grins signaled that and more. The experienced teacher, no doubt, recognized the joy of a voice reconnected to a long-denied passion—opera. But Leech didn't know that Luca's breakthrough had as much to do with the heart-lifting text, a sign at last of Isa's forgiveness.

Sensing someone coming up from behind, he turned.

"Leave it to your ole mate to find the cure for your ailment," Leech said, puffing out his chest. "You're solo material. But you're just the crutch this hobbling chorus needs."

"No solos for me. An amateur chorus is all I can handle. Thanks for prodding me."

"Glad to help, *bello*, glad to help. One down, one to go," he added with a wink.

Luca knew he hinted at a meeting with Isa but didn't acknowledge the bull's-eye. If all the meddling Good Samaritans hadn't been at rehearsal, Luca might have questioned the text's authenticity. Isa sent it. That's what he wanted to believe. He'd find out for certain soon enough.

Leech pressed his shoulder, pushing him onto a chair. "Sit, sit, my dear man. Relish your return. Tomorrow night you take to the stage as a seasoned performer. And from there—"

"It's back to Rome."

Leech shrugged. "Perhaps. Until the party then. *Ciao, bello*." After kissing Luca's cheeks, he practically skipped into the hall humming the Rossini overture.

The room remained in shadow, crystal chandeliers and fabric-covered wall sconces switched off to reduce unnecessary heat during rehearsal. Only Luca's pounding heart and breathing interrupted the stillness. He glanced at his watch. Anticipation willed the minutes forward, but fear wished them back. Despite the cheery text, he dreaded the possibility of rejection. The Isa he knew distanced herself from anything she didn't understand. He shared the blame.

The tragedy that dogged his past kept him from Isa's debut, from getting close. Sex wasn't intimacy, romance only the tip of a relationship. He was making the same mistake with Elizabeth. His dark secret affected him in ways he didn't even understand.

A fine mess I've made of things. Luca had feelings for Isa, but Elizabeth, with soft flaxen hair, kind blue eyes, and a sweet smile, also claimed a piece of his heart. She rescued him. Telma recognized that Elizabeth tended to him like a child nursing a sick bird. Perhaps he had been selfish, letting her pamper him. Theirs was an easy, comfortable relationship. But it couldn't last.

Maybe Elizabeth saw the inevitable. Maybe she even desired a breakup but didn't want to be the one to let go. Hadn't she urged him to come to San Benedetto? Luca saw the exuberance with which she mothered the struggling artists who clustered around his restaurant for free spaghetti and sympathy. Did his rescuer crave the chance to nurse another broken wing, to fulfill whatever curse Telma spoke of in Rome?

Pity and guilt were flawed underpinnings for a relationship. The difficult discussion was long overdue. Her mended bird could fly. Love or not, he owed his rescuer the chance to be free.

As he watched stragglers among his chorus mates mingle in the piazza below, the faint sound of music from inside the theater reached his ears. A piano plunked the opening bars of Mimi's first aria from *La Bohème*. In the scene, the audience meets the opera's tragic heroine when she knocks at Rodolfo's door. Mimi seeks help to relight her candle. She introduces herself, showing gentleness, and then falls faint. Rodolfo falls in love.

Luca closed his eyes and kept still, hoping to channel every bit of sensory energy to his ears. Not every note survived the ascent. Those that did were crisp and confident. Isa's interpretation was flawless. She evoked Mimi's sweet, romantic spirit. He marveled at the effort she poured into her artistry. The ripened voice stirred dormant emotions, stoking his feelings as she sang,

> *Mi piaccion quelle cose*
> *che han sì dolce malìa,*
> *che parlano d'amor, di primavere,*
> *di sogni e di chimere,*
> *quelle cose che han nome poesia...*

> (I love all things
> that have gentle sweet smells,
> that speak of love, of spring,
> of dreams and fanciful things,
> those things that have poetic names ...)

The room suddenly felt too small. Seeking escape, Luca hurried down the stairs. Opening a door to an upper box, he peered into the theater and the stage below. Isa was radiant, her full dark hair and olive skin a stunning contrast to the ivory-colored silk blouse and pearl necklace. A red linen skirt showed off a still trim waist and shapely hips.

Her appearance transported him back nearly eight years, the night Isabella Fabrini first appeared at his restaurant to launch her operatic journey. Though she acted tough, he suspected a hidden vulnerability. She asked him to relight her table's candle—not unlike Puccini's Mimi. When he did, magical speckles of gold flickered in her dark, brown eyes. Her face glowed like an angel's in the candlelight, illuminating a charming fragility. She scoffed when he suggested she might be superstitious. He suspected her denial masked a fear of showing weakness. Admiring the mysterious woman's beauty and spirit, Luca fell in love. She made him wait several months before agreeing to go out with him.

From his perch in the upper reaches of the theater, Luca resisted the urge to applaud and shout *Brava!* Instead, he backed into the corridor and descended through two levels of boxes before reaching the ground floor. The dark lobby with its black and white marble tiles offered an oasis from the heat. Except for the performers on stage, visible through an open door, the theater was empty. Lemon, balsam, and scents from a barrage of other cleaning solutions batted down the dust of the ancient opera house.

A poster propped onto an easel next to the high-polished mahogany bar caught Luca's attention. Leech's haste in rushing him to rehearsal kept Luca from inspecting identical prints posted on each side of the theater's columned portico. The poster carried a banner, *Concerto per e di Amici*—a concert for and of friends—along with a caricature of the red-gowned diva. He caught his reflection in the antique mirror behind the bar. What did he see on his face—admiration, respect, love?

His gaze returned to the poster. Although merely a child's rendering, the drawing captured Isa's blend of beauty, determination, intelligence, and passion. Black and white headshots of Isa and Ivy smiled at the top of the easel. Below, a copy of the program and a photo of a swarthy tenor named Paolo Salvaggi.

Luca disliked the man at once. According to the program, the leering tenor had a duet with Isa from *La Bohème*, a second comic scene with both ladies, and one solo, "Nessun Dorma." For the concert's finale, the final scene from Puccini's masterpiece, Salvaggi would reprise the role of Calaf to Isa's Turandot along with the chorus. Luca stared at the man's face—weak chin, big ears. Maybe he merely filtered the image through the lens of jealous eyes, envious of a stranger who had the career for which Luca had trained? And as a result, *he* got to share the stage with Isa while Luca stood in the shadows.

Luca glanced through the open door, a clear view of the stage. Isa and her leading man acted out a scene—voices rose, arms swung, and heads turned with exaggerated movements. Not recognizing the piece, Luca stepped closer. But the scene wasn't opera; the stage drama was real.

"If I knew you'd have such a hissy fit, I never would have brought it up," Salvaggi shouted.

Isa moved toward him. "The concert's tomorrow night. This isn't the time to raise *creative differences.*"

Salvaggi heaved a dramatic sigh. "I assumed you cared about our audience as much as I do. My apologies, Isabella," he said with a hand flourish and bow.

Isa threw her head back. "Don't apologize to *me*. Apologize to yourself…for being such an ass."

Malcolm rushed between them, pulling the scruffy-faced tenor to the piano. Leech and Ivy circled Isa and edged her toward the other side of the stage. The two singers glared at each other across the divide. Was that sexual tension Luca sensed? Despite his suspicions, Luca grinned. Isa was tough. In a man, such traits were admired. He knew that some people found her overbearing. But when she flared her nostrils, raised her chin, and stomped her foot, Luca found Isa irresistible.

To get backstage, Luca took the corridor that ran behind the lower boxes. Shouts gave way to a piano and the opening measures of "Nessun Dorma." Music quieted the commotion. Luca recalled his last visit, Isa's second concert. He stormed out of the dressing room, triggering a series of unfortunate incidents that led to banishment from Isa's life and the near loss of his soul to Willy Epson. He shook the painful memory from his mind. His return to San Benedetto gave him another chance.

Seeing the half-open door as an invitation, Luca pushed into the dressing room. The clock between Mesdames Callas and Scotto showed straight-up seven. He inhaled, nerves soothed by the scent of Isa's familiar perfume. Scanning the room, his eyes landed on the wardrobe rack. He pictured his diva dazzling the audience in gowns of glittery green, scarlet red, and midnight blue. On the dressing table were tributes: roses of pink and yellow, lupines of blue and purple.

He didn't see it at first, a simple bouquet in the center of the table. But there they stood, freesias the color of snow. *How sentimental of Isa.* Surely she sent them to herself. He had no other explanation. *Nobody else would dare send their flowers*—certainly not the pompous, self-centered tenor who peacocked on stage. Curiosity inched Luca forward. Was there a card? As he lifted the vase, voices at the door reached his ears.

"You can't be serious, Isa. Salvaggi's a pompous ass. Said so yourself."

"He may be an egotistical prick, but he's bloody gorgeous. What can I say? I'm a slave to sexy voices and tight little bums."

The giggles cut off. Luca turned to face the door. There stood Isa, arms stiff at her sides, shock on her face. Before she could speak, her younger sister brushed past her.

Ana rose on tiptoes and kissed his cheek. "What a surprise. You look fantastic. Doesn't he, Isa? Doesn't Luca look fantastic?"

Isa nodded. She didn't move from the doorway. "Yes, marvelous. Didn't expect—"

"Expect you to sneak into a lady's dressing room. You naughty man," Ana said, slapping Luca's shoulder. His face warmed as he looked to his hands. They still clutched the freesias.

With eyes fixed on the flowers, Isa cleared her throat. "Thank you for the lovely—"

"Lovely surprise. Coming all the way to San Benedetto," Leech said, bursting into the room in a splash of color and a lavender-scented fog.

Luca looked from Leech to Ana to the still rigid, Isa. "I-I was pleased to get—"

"The chance to sing in the chorus," Leech interrupted with a pat to his back. "And what a voice this boy has. We're lucky to have him, lucky indeed, my pet," he added with a wink.

Isa's shoulders relaxed. She stepped closer, head tilted with a look of interest and confusion on her face "You're singing in the chorus?"

Luca nodded. "Leave it to Leech. You've certainly created something special here. Your music ripples far beyond this opera house. It's gorgeous. You're gorgeous."

As he spoke, Isa moved to the sofa, sat down, and kicked off her shoes. Her beautiful brown eyes never left his face. Her tone softened. "Kind of you to say so. I sometimes wonder if it's all been worth it."

With her softer, vulnerable side surfacing, Isa tapped the sofa. Ana grabbed the vase from Luca's grip, and Leech pushed him backward onto the couch. A warm conversation followed, punctuated by laughter. Despite Luca's hints, Leech and Ana never left him alone with Isa. Instead, like jittery chaperones, the two bounced the conversation from topic to topic like a stone skipping across a pond. He never had a chance to mention Isa's text or confess to his haunted past that kept him away from the first concert. But, he couldn't complain. He and Isa broke the ice; they bantered like old friends. But was there more to the thaw? The answer had to wait.

Malcolm and Salvaggi walked into the dressing room together. Talk turned to the program. Leech and Malcolm must have sensed Luca's growing anger. They nudged him from the room before he could punch the swarthy prima donna. But was his reaction jealousy or merely a desire to protect Isa? Luca didn't know.

"Wait!" Isa shouted, running from the dressing room. "Sit with me tonight."

In an exit far superior to that of his last visit, Isa sent Luca away with hope and a kiss.

Chapter 45

"Nessun Dorma" crooned from Luca's lips as he pushed open the opera house door and bounded into the piazza. The late evening sun warmed his face as a light breeze refreshed him. His fellow choristers had showered him with camaraderie, but Isa's kiss sealed his welcome to San Benedetto. He forgave passersby for thinking him the village idiot—grinning from ear to ear, skipping over cobblestones while singing Puccini.

The phone vibrated in his pocket. A second text rewarded hopeful eyes. *Gr8 2 C U. Til 2night, Luv, I.* The message, though terse, emboldened him. His path forward cleared. He only needed private time with Isa to share the burden of his family's accident, and beg her forgiveness for not telling her sooner. With that weight lifted, might they not have a fresh chance at love?

Salvaggi, he told himself, was merely a distraction, not a legitimate rival…or was he? Luca could compete note for note with Salvaggi's *sexy voice.* And as for a tight bum, Luca happened to hide his under loose-fitting trousers. *But the freesias, what if Salvaggi had sent them?*

Luca glanced at his watch—nearly eight o'clock. The party started at nine. Italian math added up to at least two hours. Most of the shops were closed but on the advice of a local resident anxious to rid herself of a giddy lunatic, he trekked to the Villa Europa.

The hotel was indeed the jewel of San Benedetto. Awnings of broad yellow and black stripes shaded sparkling windows above a drive that cut through a pristine lawn of lush green grass. He understood why Isa chose the hotel's banquet room for the post-concert party and why the place attracted guests as wealthy as the Novaks. Serpentining through a line of Mercedes, Bentleys, and other luxury sedans parked under a lanterned portico, Luca leapt up the marble stairs and through the revolving door.

The lobby was posh and comfortable, decorated in rich velvets and satins of red and gold. Scanning the room, he didn't see a flower shop. He made his way to the concierge desk where a pretty young woman in a navy-blue uniform was occupied booking spa treatments for a handsome Australian couple in town for Isa's concert. Luca waited, his back against a half-wall topped with brass planters filled with greenery. Behind him in the walnut-paneled bar came the voice of Phil White, his accent teetering between both sides of the Atlantic.

"…*c'est* possible, yes. Given your resources and influence, *oui*," Phil said.

"I want him to be comfortable. Someplace among *our* type of people." The woman spoke with an American accent, but the tone bespoke the arrogance common among all entitled classes.

"Prison isn't a country club, Alexandra. Brad should skip the tea dance."

Alexandra groaned. "Earn your fee, damn it."

Phil would always enjoy a steady stream of clients. Death, taxes, and crooked politicians were sure bets.

"Yes ma'am," Phil replied. He surprised Luca for not offering in-kind services. Maybe such perks were part of his after-sale program.

"One more thing," the American said, her voice growing fainter, more sincere. "Draw up a shortlist of women's prisons."

So both Novaks were getting a new home. Luca was pleased. Based on Isa's past comments, Brad was only guilty of following orders—Alexandra's.

"Your finest white freesias," Luca sang to the shop clerk. "Delivered to Miss Isabella Fabrini."

"The singer?"

"The one and only. The diva of San Benedetto."

"Perhaps a summer bouquet?" the woman said, pulling stems of red, yellow, and orange blooms. "I can do up something very special."

Luca shook his head. "Freesias, freesias, freesias, dear lady."

"How about yellow? I've got beautiful yellow freesias."

"White, signora. Like those," he said, pointing to the window display.

"It's just…" she said with a shrug, "I delivered white freesias to the opera house this morning. Special order."

Luca frowned. "I know all about that."

Her forehead creased. "And you want to send the same?"

"You're absolutely correct," he blurted. "What was I thinking?"

The clerk nodded, showing pleasure at the affirmation of her professional opinion. Then, squeezing her shoulders, Luca kissed the top of her head. "Send twice what you sent this morning. Make that your whole stock."

"*Sì, sì.* I understand." She sighed, surrendering to the whims of this mad man. "I was told they were her special flower."

"*He* said that?" Luca had a vision of Salvaggi ordering the flowers. He inhaled, expecting to smell the man's cologne that he thought brash, effeminate.

"*He?* No, signor. Miss Fabrini, she sent them."

Luca's muscles relaxed. He was right. Isa ordered them for herself—a sentimental nod to their relationship. His blood pressure calmed. Isa would swim in white freesias if he had his way. He penned a note requiring both sides of two cards before popping into another of the hotel's specialty shops for something to neutralize Salvaggi's advantage.

With his purchase tucked discreetly into a shopping bag, shrieks of laughter guided Luca toward the Tazza d'Oro. The reunion of the merry Dubliners brought a sense of wholeness to concert weekend. Since their teary-eyed hug, Brigid and Kate carried on like scheming schoolgirls. Refreshed and looking lovely in cotton florals, Brigid and Kate were entertaining Jamie and the three American boys.

As Luca approached their tables, he heard Brigid say, "Leave him be." A pat of her hand informed him she meant Danny Chance. The high-strung New Yorker often found himself teased. "If he claims the entire San Benedetto fire brigade's ogling him, who are we to say it isn't so? Let the little fella have his fantasies."

"Fair enough," Kate said, turning to the squirming New Yorker. "Which is the fireman ya fancy, Danny?"

"And is he the same fireman who fancies you?" asked Miguel.

Danny crossed his arms as if the grasp would keep him from shaking. "Let's not go there. But let me just say, the firemen who want me are hot, amazingly hot."

"Send your rejects my way. Don't mind leftovers a'tall," said Brigid. She'd informed everyone at rehearsal that her husband passed away six months earlier. Loneliness may have driven her to San Benedetto but she didn't forget to pack her good humor.

Luca begged off their offer. With that bunch, a *quick drink* was an oxymoron. As he made his apologies, a hand pressed his shoulder. He turned to see Kate's beau, Richard. The jovial Englishman looked quite the yachtsman in a blue jacket accented with a white and red ascot. Beside him stood another man of similar age and build, with a shock of white hair. But as Richard was tan, the other man was fair. Luca recognized him from the chorus rehearsal.

"Cheers, mate," Richard said. "Don't tell me you're leaving already."

Luca pulled at his shirt, wrinkled and limp. "Coming and going. Haven't made it back to the hotel."

Jamie thumped the shopping bag. "Hope your dinner jacket's not in there."

Spotting the bag, Danny's eyes widened. "House of Sforza. Amazing products—*sexy*. Didn't know there was one in town." He nodded his approval of the men's luxury brand.

Brigid lifted her eyebrows. "Care to show off your purchase or is it truly a sexy secret?"

Luca's face warmed. His hands pressed the bag closed. Richard came to his rescue by presenting his companion, "This is Nick, Isa's newest recruit. She's done marketing consulting for him."

As Nick made his introductions, his story sounded similar to those of others who found their way to concert weekend. Isa's passion for music and the prospect of a one-of-a-kind adventure hooked him. Italy was Disneyland for grownups. With a growing following, Isa was the Pied Piper of San Benedetto.

Scooting away from Brigid, Kate slid in an empty chair. "Come sit here, Nick." Tapping the seat bottom, she exchanged a conspiratorial glance with Richard.

"Careful, Nicky," Danny said, affecting an Irish brogue reminiscent of a cereal leprechaun. "Been caught 'atween those two 'afore. Keep a hand on yer dignity."

Brigid didn't dawdle in putting Nick to the test. "Another Londoner?" Her tone made the city seem like a dirty word. The friends braced for the answer.

"Guilty," he replied as he made his way to the offered chair.

Brigid groaned. "Well, I've accepted that one," she said with a nod toward Richard. "What's one more?"

"But my mum's a Doherty from County Wicklow," Nick added.

Brigid flashed a Cheshire Cat grin. "In that case, darlin', squeeze right in." Her eyes flashed with mischief as she turned to the diminutive New Yorker. "Danny Boy, now ya can keep your lusty fire brigade all to yourself." Her boisterous laugh brought all the eyes of the café to their little group.

Danny looked as if he wanted to crawl under the table as Luca bade them good-bye.

Halfway between the café and the hotel, Jamie called after him, "Tell the lovely Svetlana that I'll be pickin' her up in twenty minutes. Wore my kilt 'specially for her."

Brigid sighed. "Aargh! Every lass 'cept me gets to juggle your sporran." Her comment sent the comrades into fits of laughter.

Before stepping into the hotel, Luca glanced up to the balcony. White curtains billowed through the open windows of Telma's room. A figure caught his attention. But it wasn't the fiery temptress. Walter, bare-chested, pulled the window shut. Luca was happy for Telma. She spent her life stirring up trouble for others as a way to tolerate her own miseries. Luca recognized her capacity for goodness. Maybe she finally did as well. The prior concert moved her. Perhaps the current weekend would heal her.

Inside the lobby, Svetlana looked stunning. She wore a strapless red chiffon dress with black stiletto heels. Her makeup and hairstyle were simple yet elegant. After sharing Jamie's message, Luca ascended the stairs. He heard Svetlana counsel her protégée. "At the last concert weekend, Signora Rossi she tell me, Svetlana, work hard, dress smart, show some skin, and one day you be invited to such a posh party."

Showered and shaved, Luca stood naked in front of the mirror. Isa could do far worse than Luca Caruso. His yearlong regimen of diet and exercise rewarded him with a strong body and bolstered confidence. "You could pass for forty," he said, addressing his image in the mirror with a hearty chuckle.

He glanced at his clothes laid out on the bed. They represented his journey from feast to famine, quite literally. Last summer he couldn't squeeze into his trousers, now he swam in them. But he had a secret weapon courtesy of the House of Sforza—the latest in men's cologne. The clerk said the scent drove women crazy, a secret combination of musk, hormones, and botanicals.

The restaurant's outdoor terrace bustled with concert friends. Luca wasn't surprised when he didn't see Isa. She liked grand entrances. "It's expected of me," she confided to him years before. She played the role up for her fans. "People come for an all-inclusive concert," she said by way of explanation. "Complete with drink, drama, and diva."

Seeing the jovial assembly, he imagined Isa's thrill. Upon arrival, she'd pause to admire the collection of people—friends, audience, congregation, and beloved menagerie. At one table sat her business school chums, among them Brad who sat on one side of Alexandra, with Phil on the other. Jamie was there too with Svetlana. Luca suspected that the two seats reserved for Walter and Telma would remain vacant. Sounds coming from their adjoining room back at the hotel suggested they were enjoying their own party.

Opera people occupied another table: Leech, Lady Blatherwicke, Malcolm, Ivy, Silverstein, and the patriarch and matriarch of the family Bertini. Salvaggi the tenor was nowhere in sight. Luca imagined him soaking in a honeysuckle bubble bath and filing his nails. That image was preferable to any scenario that involved Salvaggi and the missing Isa.

At least three tables contained family. Luca recognized Ana accompanied by a wild-haired musician type, Gina with husband and daughters, and many cousins from Italy and the States. Isa's stylist, Maria, sat next to Mama Fabrini.

Clients, colleagues, and friends filled other tables. The loudest laughs came from the corner with the Dubliners, their London beaus, and the boys from America. Brigid's playful pawing of Nick signaled a diplomatic thaw. Tommy and Miguel brought three friends from Chicago. Like many who didn't know Isa directly, they came for a magical time.

Most gatherings of this kind happened only at funerals—too damn late to enjoy the party. But Isa lured them in her lifetime with passion and music. Papa Fabrini would be proud.

Buttoning his gray cashmere blazer, Luca headed toward the waving Dubliners. Ana and Leech intercepted him.

Ana kissed his cheek. "So glad you came."

"You're sitting with us, my sweet-smelling man," Leech said, pointing to his table. "I've saved places for you and Isa."

"I'll join you too," Ana said. "The Bertinis agreed to swap."

"And Salvaggi?"

Leech swatted Luca's shoulder. "Never mind him. By the time he gets here, there won't be a seat. He's lurking around someplace. Pure diva. Probably won't make his entrance until *after* Isa."

The revving of a powerful engine drew all eyes to the street. A low-slung Ferrari raced to the curb, before slowing to funereal speed. The entire terrace erupted into applause. Danny let out a New York taxi whistle. Brad hooped and hollered, releasing his inner cowboy, and Jamie stomped his feet. Luca's heart raced. In the passenger seat sat Isa, radiant with perfect smile, large dark eyes and jet-black hair. A low-cut dress and an equally vibrant red shade of lipstick matched the car's high-gloss finish.

Luca couldn't stop laughing. "Brilliant. Bloody brilliant."

"Boobies and scarlet," Leech whispered. "Work every time."

"Fantastic," Ana cooed. "Urged her to parachute in, but Ferraris are sexier."

Several people pressed toward the convertible. As two men jostled for Isa's door, the car sped off. A collective gasp went up from the crowd. Isa's laugh and scarf floated on the wind. As red taillights disappeared into the night, a second round of applause erupted.

Ana grabbed Luca's shoulder. "Go," she said, pushing him toward the curb. "The car will turn and come back. It's part of the tease. Be the one to greet her."

Luca made his way slowly through the crowd, but kisses, hugs, and handshakes delayed him. The engine revs got louder. He pushed ahead, finally elbowing through a frontline of broad shoulders just as the car pulled to the curb. He exhaled. Extending his arm for the handle, someone brushed his side. Flowery cologne stung his nose. Salvaggi grabbed the door handle. Luca hated him and his pathetic ploy to share in Isa's glory. After lifting Isa to her feet, Salvaggi raised her arm in a victory salute. The terrace gave them *both* a standing ovation. Luca loathed him even more.

With the same tag-team maneuvering Luca witnessed in the dressing room, Ana and Leech tried to extricate Salvaggi, but to no avail. He held onto Isa to milk his own adulation, imposing himself at the table between Luca and Isa. After complimenting Luca's choice of cologne, the pompous prick kept his back to him to fawn over the evening's star.

Leech whispered in Luca's ear. "Fiasco. But don't tie those baggy trousers of yours into a knot. Ana will work her magic."

True to his word, during dessert Ana spilled a glass of Limoncello onto Salvaggi's lap. As he raced to the toilet, the tag-team squeezed Isa and Luca together.

Isa leaned toward him for a kiss. After sniffing the air, her face puckered. "Delighted you're here, Luca. But do change that aftershave. It's the same god-awful scent as my tenor's."

Luca laughed off the comment. "Anything you desire. I'm simply thrilled to be here." He motioned to the crowded terrace. "I'm so proud of you."

Isa squeezed his hand. "These concerts have exceeded my dreams. Gina's girls are even singing this year. Papa would be happy. And everyone's having a grand time…including me."

"Nice of you to invite Telma and Walter."

"They deserve each other."

Luca studied her face. Neither her tone nor her expression held a note of sarcasm or anger.

"I mean it, really, I do," she added, responding to his stare. "They're suited for each other. Probably knew it all along. Sure she behaved abysmally last time, but concert weekend brings people together. Why not them? Besides, keeps her out of the spotlight," she added with a chuckle. "As for Walter, he'll probably be exhausted. May not be able to walk for a week." Her smile vanished. She looked at Luca with concern, "Oh, I hope that doesn't disappoint you…him and Telma, I mean."

He wanted to believe that jealousy crept into her voice.

He whispered, changing the subject, "Romantic of you to order white freesias." Isa looked puzzled, prompting him to add, "Saw them on your dressing table. The florist confessed that Miss Fabrini…"

Her eyes remained glued to his face, her head tilted. "I didn't send those flowers. I thought…"

Over Isa's shoulder, Luca saw Leech turn the same purple as his hair.

Ana gasped. "L-let me explain."

The incidents of the past several hours clicked through Luca's head. He whipped the phone from his pocket. What a fool he'd been...a garden of freesias and...He reeked of desperation as well as lady's perfume. He pulled up the last text, shaking his head at the message. Then he hit the key that called the texting phone number. Ringtones came from the space between Isa and her sister.

"That's your bag, dear," Isa said.

Ana looked ill as she reached for her purse. When she pulled out the ringing mobile, Luca waved his phone in the air. Ana's eyes widened; her cheeks lost their color.

"So there's my mobile," Isa said, turning toward her sister. "Been looking for the damn thing for hours." Snatching the phone from Ana's hand, Isa glanced at the caller ID screen. With a puzzled expression, she looked to Luca. She began to speak but her question went unanswered.

Smelling of lemon liquor, Salvaggi returned. Inserting himself between them, he remained standing and directed his comments to Isa, "I must speak to you about the concert, *now*." His harsh tone made Luca want to punch him, but Isa's response surprised him. She merely smiled and obeyed before the pair glided away into the warm summer night, arm-in-arm.

Luca's phone chimed again. Another text. Elizabeth needed him to call her as soon as possible. The euphoria Luca felt at rehearsal drained away. He'd come to San Benedetto to solve his dilemma but he was merely more confused than ever.

Chapter 46

Luca threw on a comfortable pair of jeans and a gray pullover before trudging down to the Saturday morning breakfast buffet. Anxiety had robbed him of sleep. He tossed in bed, his mind unsettled by a litany of events: Ana and Leech's failed attempt to play Cupid, Isa's manner and abrupt exit with Salvaggi, and his own distressing conversation with Elizabeth. Every scenario led to the same place, anger and frustration with his past decisions and troubling questions about his future. He called upon every ounce of self-control not to muffle his agitated thoughts with whiskey or wine. How long could he hold off answering those familiar demons?

In the newly decorated dining room, painted a cheery yellow with light blue stencils, Luca's hope of privacy withered within minutes of setting his bowl of yogurt and granola onto a secluded table.

"Why the dreary frown?" the voice above him asked. "It's concert day. Birds are chirping, church bells are ringing, flowers perfume the air. I feel god-damn wonderful, and I haven't so much as sniffed caffeine."

Luca shielded his eyes. Before him stood Telma, her hair pulled back and tied with a red scarf. Bright sunshine streaming into the room through white sheers gave her a halo. Something about her appearance struck him. Her loveliness wasn't a processed glamor that came from mascara, lipstick, and skin-smoothing cream, but a glow radiating from within. He'd never seen her look so natural, or happy, a stark contrast to his heavy heart.

"I mean this in the kindest way," Luca grumbled, "but your bliss nauseates me."

Telma sat without invitation, motioning the attendant for a cappuccino for herself and an extra-large refill for him. Her words came in a merciful whisper. "Seen that look before…glaring back at me in the mirror."

Trying to focus on her face, Luca emitted only a groan.

She patted his hand. "Tell me what happened."

Dare he bare his soul to the mischievous scamp? Tell her that his bed sheets were soaked with the fever of a broken heart? The disastrous events with Isa rushed from his lips in high-speed replay. He spared no detail—big, small...or embarrassing.

Telma sneered as he described Leech and Ana's Cupid-like machinations. "Amateurs!"

Luca cringed at his foolishness. How silly of him to think that a brief appearance could erase years of a neglected relationship.

"Instead of resolution, Telma, I find myself in a swirling storm of shit."

She laughed, not a mocking cackle but that gentle half laugh, half giggle intended to comfort, to tell Luca that he overreacted. "It's not as bad as all that. And Elizabeth," she added. "Have you heard from her?"

Despite his grogginess, he read Telma's face. *Of course, Elizabeth's urgent text wasn't spontaneous.* He steadied his head on steepled hands before staring over the basket of croissants and yellow tea roses. "*You.* You pulled Elizabeth's strings. Think you have me all figured out, don't you?"

Her dark eyes darted from side to side. She lifted the cup to her mouth, an obvious stall technique. A glistening forehead was a rarity for the woman who never perspired.

"Don't deny it. The message, especially the timing, has Telma Rossi written all over it." In retrospect, he should have guessed that Elizabeth's words echoed the sentiments that Telma advanced as they waited together in Rome for the train.

Telma set the cup on the table, rattling the saucer. Squaring her shoulders, she inhaled and smiled. Luca braced. He recognized the return of Telma the Bold. "Why should I deny it? I just...helped matters along, that's all."

"So says the petrol-reeking firebug. Your benevolence overwhelms me."

She gestured with her hand as if batting away the sarcasm. "Be honest. That conversation was long overdue. I'm sure you'll find some way to thank me for all my help."

His conversation with Elizabeth replayed in his head as it had done throughout the night with the church's clock as backdrop, chiming every quarter hour. After his humiliating retreat from the party, he phoned Elizabeth. He reached her in the restaurant's kitchen. She was preparing food boxes for their adopted artists, collegial banter and rock music audible in the background.

"What's so urgent? You okay? Everything all right?"

"Rome's not burning, my sweet," Elizabeth said, her voice its usual mix of energy and kindness. "You've only been gone a few hours."

He heard her take a deep breath before telling him to hold. She wanted to take the call in the privacy of the office. Those few minutes seemed to Luca an eternity. When she returned to the line, she spoke slowly, her sentences fragmented but deliberate. He figured the climb upstairs winded her. "W-wanted to make sure you arrived safely, met up with your concert friends."

After exchanging pleasantries and local weather conditions, the real conversation began. Words blurred with emotion. Elizabeth wanted him to be happy, wanted him to have his freedom. His protests were futile. "All I ask is that you think about it. Make sure," she said, "there, among your friends, *every* one of them." She meant Isa of course. Sweet Elizabeth was giving her once-injured bird permission to take wing. The call was surreal. Now Luca understood why—Telma. But despite the strangeness of the dialogue, why didn't he want the conversation to end? What did he leave unsaid?

Staring across the breakfast table, Telma dipped a pastry horn into a pot of honey. "She wants you to be free."

"Wants *her* freedom, you mean." What made him snap, say something as ridiculous as that? Elizabeth was nothing but caring, unselfish. He was the bastard who didn't deserve her…or Isa. Now he had neither.

"Christ!" Telma said with a roll of her eyes. "You're both too goddamn nice to speak your minds. Better to discuss it now while you're both young—or relatively so—and beautiful. Time and fate chip away at all things. Pick your partner wisely. Never know when it's the last dance."

Had that been Telma's excuse for bedding her ex-husband? Luca knew she was right, but her meddling infuriated him. The type of conversation he had with Elizabeth, the kind that dabbled in dangerous scenarios, never ended well. Those pesky *what-ifs* torment like a mosquito buzzing about your slumbering head. Before long, *what if* turned into *why not*.

Luca held up his hands in surrender. "Fine. So Elizabeth's given me license to be happy. I don't have the foggiest notion what the hell happiness looks like. Lucky, lucky Isa. She seems to have figured it out." He repeated Isa's lusty comments about Salvaggi and the sexual tension he sensed between them. "Strolled arm-in-arm into the moonlight, laughing, pawing each other. Isa nestled on his shoulder for God's sake."

"You have no choice but to speak to her. Otherwise," Telma added with a caress of his hand, "you'll be haunted by questions of what might have been."

After offering empathy, Telma arranged a breakfast tray to take to a still drowsy Walter. She laughed away Luca's digs about her resurgent wifely duty with sarcasm. "First the ring—bigger, brighter, gaudier than before. Then it's Weetabix, canned fruit, and instant coffee for my Romeo."

Although flashes of the old Telma surfaced, her balcony tears, and joyous return to the arms of her ex-husband suggested an expanding mellow center, pushing against a thinning veneer. Indeed, time and fate chipped away at all things. "You're a fraud, Telma Rossi."

"So you've said. And you're a songbird. Now get to that opera house and sing. Things will work out," she replied, before turning and wiggling her satin-robed behind.

Luca sighed. Perhaps he should hop the next train back to Rome, put Isa and his dashed hopes for reconciliation behind him. Or was Telma wise to order him to the opera house, an advance rather than another retreat? He recalled the happy hours before the party. In rehearsal, his voice awakened with unbridled joy. His spirit soared at the sight of Isa on stage and the sound of her lovely voice. But had the rapture of that moment clouded his judgment, confused him about his feelings for Isa…and Elizabeth?

He could think of no better way to sort things out and break the failed patterns of the past than to return to the opera house. Rejoining his comrades in song gave him another chance with Isa.

The walk to the opera house reminded him of those American musicals from the thirties—roving bands of gleeful innocents joining in arms to stage a show. Choristers streamed from the doors of San Benedetto's hotels and marched through the streets and passageways. The Dubliners, parading with their London beaus, formed a human chain as they paraded through the pedestrian zone. Tommy and Miguel tagged behind. Luca recognized others too, chirping and flitting to the theater.

Every concert needed an audience. Passing an upmarket café, Luca saw the Novaks huddled with Phil White. The erstwhile Frenchman looked as tired as his Armani suit and lavender shirt, the same attire Luca spotted him wearing the prior night. Had Alexandra pulled him from someone's bed—maybe her own—for the early morning consultation? The poor chap was earning money the hard way.

At a café amongst other concert weekenders, Luca found Jamie sitting at an outdoor table. Between sips of coffee, the hunky Scotsman complained that lemon brioche was no substitute for fried eggs, bangers, and beans.

"Just the chap I wanted to see. Gotta second?" Jamie asked, kicking a spare chair out from the table.

Luca looked at his watch and shook his head. "Maybe later. I have to get to rehearsal. Don't want to face the wrath of Blatherwicke."

"Sit. Just a minute. Promise."

"Can't. Sorry. Later. I'll get a message to you."

At the theater, Luca guessed that many of his chorus mates nursed hangovers. Several rubbed heads and staggered up the stage stairs as if their legs were lead weights. Looking pasty and squeamish, Richard and Nick bragged about closing the Tazza with Kate and Brigid. But unlike their bedraggled mates, the rosy-cheeked Dubliners strutted about the stage like excited hens.

"Sorry, my handsome man," Leech said by way of apologizing for the botched reconciliation. "Even ole Leech causes a fiasco now and then. Is there no hope?"

Luca shook his head. Leech patted his friend's shoulder before Malcolm called him to the piano.

The sound of kicked thuds drew all eyes to the back of the auditorium. With a loud bang and a whoosh, the door gave way. In walked a rumpled Danny Chance. He swaggered down a side aisle in the same cherry-red trousers, lemon-yellow shirt, and lime-green jacket, an outfit branded in the mind of everyone who gazed upon the New Yorker at the prior night's gathering. Perhaps the flirtations of the fire brigade weren't fantasies.

Danny, face as red as his pants, huffed up the stairs with pursed lips. He held up his hands as if to ward off questions. A spontaneous chant to the tune of Westminster chimes arose from a few choristers. Others joined in and repeated the refrain. "Let's not go there, let's not go there, let's not go there, let's not go there." Back slaps, hair tousles, and *atta boys* refreshed the Don Juan.

Rehearsal went well. Whether an adrenaline rush or the threat of public embarrassment, voices rose in beautiful harmony. With Italian and French lyrics written on index cards or inked on palms and forearms, the chorus pushed through. Leech and Malcolm looked relaxed and Lady Blatherwicke was downright giddy. A few people voiced concern—things were going eerily too well, some catastrophe awaited the merry songsters.

Toward the end of rehearsal, Isa, Ivy, and Salvaggi walked into the theater. Isa, dressed in white slacks and a red sweater looked remarkably refreshed as she blew kisses from her fifth row seat. Did her glow spring from the same source as Telma's? Salvaggi, wearing dark jeans and a black silk shirt, looked too smug to have spent the night alone.

Isa and Salvaggi joined the chorus on stage to rehearse the finale, a number that included the entire company. In the last scene from *Turandot,* the princess professes her love for Calaf, her persistent suitor. Luca seethed. The leading man and woman embraced too seamlessly to be mere performers.

At the conclusion, Leech climbed onto Malcolm's piano bench. Looking like a circus ringmaster, he clapped his hands and called for order. A stern expression faded into a broad smile as he declared, "Ladies and gentlemen, *mesdames et messieurs, signore e signori, habemus chorum.* We have a chorus."

Isa addressed the grinning ensemble, first in Italian, and then in English. "Friends, family. To paraphrase my muse, Florence Foster Jenkins, 'people may say we can't sing, but no one can ever say we didn't sing'." The stage erupted in jovial laughter before Isa's raised hands signaled for quiet. "But, my dears, you *can* sing. My admiration for your voices is surpassed only by my gratitude and love. You join the long line of people whose support made this amazing journey possible. Only one thing could make me happier than I am at this moment. If dear Papa...and C... Christina..."

Isa started to tear up. Resisting an impulse to console Isa with a hug, Luca instead fished in his pocket for a handkerchief. But once again, he was too late. After accepting a silk handkerchief from the extended arm of Salvaggi, Isa clasped his hand in hers.

Lady Blatherwicke was also crying but mustered enough strength to pound her stick releasing the teary-eyed chorus into the sunny afternoon. Some friends lingered, but Luca didn't have the stomach to see Isa and Salvaggi sing passionate words of love to each other. As Luca made his way up the aisle, Ivy grabbed his hand and winked. "It's not over until *you* want it to be."

As he kissed Ivy's cheek, he glanced over her shoulder. Up on the stage, locked in embrace, were Isa and Salvaggi. *It was over.* He turned to the door and walked to the Terme. He hoped a mineral bath and massage could relax his muscles and extract the toxic thoughts that the stuffy theater hadn't sweated out of him.

Chapter 47

Backstage before the concert, Luca inhaled deeply to control his breathing. He clasped his hands to stop his fingers from twitching. The tension kneaded away by the Terme's Eastern European masseuse crept back into his neck and shoulders. While the earlier rehearsal dulled some of the edge, spotlights, costumes, and the sight, smell, and sound of a live audience rattled his nerves.

He sensed the heart-throbbing exhilaration of his fellow choristers, squeezed shoulder to shoulder in the curtain's red velvet folds. Ancient odors mixed with the perfume and perspiration of the latest band of performers to strut over the theater's warped planks. Faces teetered from fear to exhilaration with an array of expressions in between. Some bit lips, some stared quietly ahead while still others chatted out of fear, or in the Dubliners' case, mere habit.

An array of emotions gripped Luca—fear, joy, awe, dread, and more. They rose from his core, weaving over and under one another before gushing to the surface. He wanted to run yet there wasn't any place he longed to be more than right there in San Benedetto. Singing in the chorus readied him to battle his twin demons. For years, guilt and shame paralyzed him, kept him from the stage, from life, and even from love itself. The concert gave him an opportunity to vanquish those fiends. And released of that burden, maybe then his heart and head would allow him to love in peace.

He watched Leech, adorned in eighteenth-century period costume complete with lavender-powdered wig, usher Isa onto the still-curtained stage. The star looked gorgeous in a glittery gown of sea green, an emerald and diamond pendant glistening above her cleavage. Deep admiration for all Isa accomplished swelled within him.

Several people snickered as Wolfgang Amadeus Leech inched Isa into position with the care of a museum curator. Kneeling on the floor, he fussed over the angle of her feet and the folds of her gown. Isa looked down and smiled. Even from that distance, Luca saw that her expression showed deep fondness for the colorful little man. She credited him with transforming her from guttersnipe to opera singer. Extending her hand, she steadied him to his feet and kissed his forehead.

They held hands for a minute or two, staring into each other's eyes. Luca couldn't hear what Leech said, but Isa nodded, chuckling before leaning in to give him a final kiss on the cheek. After a hand flourish and deep bow, Leech backed off the stage and disappeared into the shadows of the opposite wing, a look of contentment on his face. Isa's concerts had given the dear man the opportunity to come out from the shadows of mere teacher to share the spotlight as music director. His true love, Edwin, would be proud.

A few moments later, the curtain parted to thunderous applause. Leech's bulb of a head beamed from the pit. Although the concert hadn't yet begun, he was already dabbing his beaded brow with a lace handkerchief pulled from a cuff of purple satin. Isa stood still, perfectly erect, arms at her sides. She gazed into the dark void as if willing the theater and audience into submission. Her expression shifted. Anxious determination gave way to self-assured majesty as if the magic scepter of her muse, Madam Jenkins, anointed her. The transformation awed Luca. From the hush that fell over the house, he assumed everyone succumbed to the enchantment of the reluctant diva.

With a look of anticipation and baton frozen in the air, Leech waited patiently for his cue. Luca looked to Isa. Two deep breaths, a glint in the eyes, and a barely noticeable upturn at the edges of her lips preceded a slight nod to the pit. Then with a tap of Leech's baton, they were off. The orchestra, under the dashing Malcolm's direction, played their first notes in perfect synchronization, drawing a smattering of applause from those familiar with Cherubino's beautiful aria from Mozart's *The Marriage of Figaro*:

Voi che sapete che cosa e amor,
Donne, vedete, s'io l'ho nel cor

(You who know what love is,
Women, see whether it's in my heart.)

Luca marveled at Isa. She sang with the confidence of a seasoned performer. Her voice revealed maturity, a mastery of the lyrical runs as well as strength with the high notes. He admired her dedication, the effort put into vocal exercises to hone her craft and artistry. He took great pleasure in witnessing her make laughingstocks out of the naysayers who called her foolish to turn to opera at the age of forty.

As he listened to Isa mesmerize the audience, Luca recalled those early years. After taking on Isa as a student, Leech asked for help. The new pupil was giving him difficulty. So as he did when faced with other problem students, the teacher summoned his friend to his Rupert Street studio. Luca's operatic training and experience at La Scala impressed him. The former singer was eager to help as long as his aid didn't require performing on stage. Besides, from the moment he glanced into Isa's eyes at his restaurant, Luca knew she was special.

Before Isa's lesson, Leech closed Luca inside a bedroom with air fresheners and window fans intended to keep cigarette odors from polluting his studio. He swore Luca to secrecy, fearing damage to his reputation. What would the Royal Opera do if they learned that one of their recommended voice teachers consulted a restaurateur for coaching advice? Luca kept his confidence since his old friend kept his. As far as he knew, Isa never found out about their arrangement.

From that lair of chintz and Pall Mall menthol, Luca diagnosed Isa's problem. The fledgling singer lacked confidence; her ego needed stroking. The mature student required affirmation more than the young darlings set out to conquer the opera world by the age of thirty.

Luca's growing fondness for Isa drove him to deception. He told Leech that Isa's voice suffered from a multitude of issues; he had to return. Luca did so, again and again. At his insistence, Leech directed Isa to Luca's restaurant for the *artist discount*. She accepted Luca's subtle coaching delivered over spaghetti and Sangiovese. Their relationship blossomed. He bolstered her confidence, emphasizing the strengths he heard for himself squirreled away in Leech's smoking lounge. Isa allowed him to rub shoulders with opera, his great but lost love, and offered respites from memories of the family tragedy that dogged his past.

In exchange for his undercover missions, Leech granted Luca a special privilege, sneaking him into the Royal Opera House where he eavesdropped on rehearsals. From his own experience with chorus masters, he knew Lady Blatherwicke rode Isa, not to be cruel, but to thicken her skin, to prepare her for the tough, unforgiving world of performance.

Leech echoed as much to him. "Lady Blatherwicke," he said after Luca threatened to throttle the tyrant, "knows the stigma of failure and pain of criticism. Clawed her way back into opera after suffering a nervous breakdown." Although the woman scared Leech, he credited her with keeping him involved with the Royal Opera. She stood up to conservative board members who wanted to distance the prestigious company from the *excessively flamboyant* and *most common* voice teacher.

To soothe Lady Blatherwicke's blistering criticism, Luca showered Isa with kindness though he needed no excuse to do so. Inside a cloakroom adjacent to the rehearsal studio, Luca fell in love with Isabella Fabrini each time she tried, failed, and tried again. Her tenacity, drive, and passion moved him. But what endeared her to him most of all was the vulnerability she struggled so fiercely to hide.

Deafening cheers brought Luca back to the concert. His hands grew numb from clapping. But his joy faded as Salvaggi strutted onto the stage during Isa's bows, stealing applause meant as reward for the star's stunning performance.

"Clear case of premature adulation," Kate whispered in Luca's ear with a chuckle.

Isa extended her hand. With a warm smile, she pulled the interloper, dressed in a trim Italian tuxedo with bow tie the same green as Isa's gown, to her side. Who did Isa think of when she became Mimi and sang that first duet with Rodolfo, a song about the discovery of new love?

That could be me standing beside her, Luca thought.

Luca willed Salvaggi to fail. He wanted the prima donna to open his mouth and chatter like a chipmunk or fall flat on his arse. As he stared at center stage, Luca's fingers shook with tremors. Isa and Salvaggi communicated with their eyes. At the sound of Luca's heaving sigh, Kate and Brigid each grabbed one of his hands and clasped it in theirs.

Luca waited for the collapse. But just as Isa soared in song, so did the pompous tenor—equals. They played off one another, reading each other's mind, anticipating the next note—experienced performers. Their interpretation of the tender scene was flawless. Whereas Isa avoided showing vulnerability in life, she tapped her hidden insecurities to season the role of Mimi with its required fragility. The music moved Luca; he couldn't deny the chemistry between the two singers. Unable to take his eyes off of them, Luca mumbled something. Was it a groan or a whimper?

"He's merely adequate," Kate said, squeezing Luca's hand to her bosom.

"A pompous prig, that's what he is," Brigid said into his ear. "Bet there's English blood in him."

Consolation from their kind lies was short-lived. From behind the trio came Danny's voice, louder than a whisper and tinged with anger. "Pompous? Adequate? He's no such thing. The man's nothing short of amazing."

Leech looked to the wing with distress in his eyes as yells of *hush* echoed backstage. Danny bristled and lifted his chin, whispering, "Amazingly brilliant."

After the magnificent duet, Isa left the stage in triumph, leaving Salvaggi in the spotlight for his solo, "Nessun Dorma" from *Turandot*. Pavarotti's aria, as it became known after the 1990 World Cup, was one of the world's most recognized songs. The audience responded to the orchestra's introduction with applause, silencing with the tenor's first words:

Nessun dorma! Nessun dorma!

(None shall sleep! None shall sleep!)

Salvaggi's strong voice took command of the theater. As it did with Isa, the audience fell under his spell. Each note ascended to the celestial blue ceiling as if to delight the cherubs playing among the marshmallow clouds. Luca surrendered. He couldn't compete with him. Maybe he never could.

Elbowing between Luca and Brigid for a better look, Danny Chance exposed a tear-stained cheek before closing his eyes and sighing. Luca braced for the aria's end.

All'alba vincerò!
vincerò, vincerò!

(At dawn, I will win!
I will win, I will win!)

The prophetic words stung. The rival tenor had indeed won, not only Turandot the opera's princess, but Luca's princess as well.

Luca didn't have time to pine. The closing notes were the chorus's cue for "The Anvil Chorus." Isa resurrected the piece from a prior concert citing its popularity while trusting the maxim *sex sells*. Luca stripped to the waist, as did Miguel, Tommy, and a few of the younger, beefier men. Leech had urged Luca to join the ranks of the bare-chested gypsy blacksmiths. English Nick was a reluctant recruit. "Wanna get a peek at the goods," Brigid declared, pushing up his arm to volunteer, "before I put ya in my basket."

Luca's adrenaline surged—the first time before an audience in two decades. The audience went wild when the curtain opened to the chorus. Many of his singing mates struggled to stay in character. Brigid and Kate curtsied at center stage, flashing mischievous grins as they whirled around in gypsy skirts. Wolf whistles produced blushes from the half-naked male ensemble. Luca's face warmed. Despite an uneven tempo, spotty diction, and head-on collisions between preening peasant girls, the piece was a success as measured by audience applause and sheer delight. Luca couldn't remember the last time he had so much fun. The stage manager had to push the chorus to the wings to keep the program moving.

At intermission, Luca and the rest of the chorus, fresh from a triumphant staging of the "March of the Toreadors," mingled with the audience in the lobby. On the bar, a placard recognized Walter Benchley for sponsoring the refreshments. Luca almost spewed his champagne. Above Walter's name, scrawled in bold letters with red lipstick, was added *Telma &*.

Luca waited for Jamie, sipping champagne and making small talk with those pressed against him in the shoulder-to-shoulder crowd. He struggled to understand the animated couple from Warsaw. The woman spoke no Italian and peppered her scant English with Polish words. As he leaned closer to better hear her, someone—he didn't know who—shoved a piece of paper into his hand.

Apologizing to the Polish couple, he studied the note. It looked suspicious, words scribbled on the white space at the bottom of a sheet of music. He glanced at the signature—*Isa*. The writing appeared to be hers, but her sisters had similar styles. Not having seen their handwriting in years, he was easily fooled. Ana knew he was wise to her text scam. The message was simple enough—*Luca, please come to my dressing room at intermission.*

His heart leapt at the chance to finally speak with her. Jamie would have to wait again. But just as he bade the Polish couple a farewell, a hand gripped his forearm. He turned to find Jamie. His expression made Luca uneasy.

"There you are. Come, let's go outside where we can talk."

Luca wanted to beg off to see Isa but something told him that he should listen to what Jamie had to say. The men walked outside into the piazza, finding an empty spot in front of one of the concert posters.

"Well?" Luca asked.

"I don't know what you plan to say to Isa. That's none of my business."

"Now that we have that settled," Luca said as he made an effort to leave.

Jamie put his hand on Luca's shoulder. "Please, hear me out."

"Make it quick." Luca made no effort to hide his irritation.

"You should know that Elizabeth loves you, very much."

Luca flinched; his voice rose. "What do you know about Elizabeth?"

"Only what she told me herself. In your restaurant when we danced."

Luca's mind flashed back to that scene. He asked Elizabeth what the two spoke about. "This and that," she had replied without offering specifics. Now standing outside the opera house, Jamie was offering to tell him. Against his better judgment, Luca asked for details.

"Elizabeth says you've got it backward. About her, that is. Says you think she's sticking around out of pity. Because *you* need *her*."

"That's true. I'd be lost without her."

"Maybe so. But the truth is, she needs you. More than you know."

"What?"

"Till she met you, Elizabeth was lost. Bounced from one hard-luck bloke to the next. Called it her curse. Penance for turning her back on her father."

"What does her father have to do with any of this?" For all the years Luca knew Elizabeth, she never mentioned her family. Because of his own secret, he never pried.

"She thought he abandoned them. Truth is, her mother drove him away. She was the abuser—verbal, physical. He was too ashamed to tell the truth. Assault on his manhood and all that. Story came out only after Elizabeth's mother died. Liver failure, alcohol. By then, the father had disappeared. She's never found him."

Luca felts pangs of sadness for his lover. "Why didn't she tell me?"

Jamie shook his head. "Embarrassed. Scared of what you'd think. Family secrets."

The words pierced Luca like a knife. If Elizabeth were guilty of concealment, so was he. Of all people, he had no right to judge. "What else did she say?"

"She thought she lost you when you moved to Rome. Then you sent for her. Don't you understand, old man, she needed you? Maybe even more than you needed her."

"I wish she would have said something."

"Guessing you should have told her a lot of things too. Fact of the matter is she doesn't want you to stay with her out of pity. She won't stand in your way if you'd rather be with..." Jamie's nod to the opera house made his meaning clear.

Recalling Isa, Luca remembered the note. He had to go to her. Just maybe, he was on the cusp of sorting things out once and for all.

Chapter 48

With his mind muddled and his stomach churning, Luca made his way backstage. The concert energized him. He wanted to go on singing forever. On one hand, seeing Isa on stage with Salvaggi triggered jealousy. On the other hand, his conversation with Jamie stirred other emotions for Elizabeth. He was conflicted in his desires.

Luca's knock pushed the door open. A sickening sweetness overwhelmed his nose, stopping him as if he'd hit a wall. The room looked like a spring flower show. White freesias filled the dressing table. The floor bloomed with a garden of brimming vases. He heard the sniffles. Maria the hairstylist was in tears. Mascara streaked down Ana's cheeks. Although her back was to the door, he could see Isa dabbing her eyes. Horror set in. Had some catastrophe befallen the Fabrini family? Isa's distress pained him.

"Here he is," Ana said, managing a brave smile.

Maria, her face gripped with pain, thrust a hair pick toward him.

Isa spun the dressing chair to face him, her eyes teary and red.

Luca rushed forward. "What is it? What's happened?"

Isa shrieked with laughter. "You should see yourself."

He glanced at his reflection in the dressing mirror—eyes cutting in every direction, a face devoid of color, an expression of sheer panic. Isa kept laughing.

Hysterics had obviously set in. Luca grabbed her hand. "What's wrong?"

"Allergies, dear Luca, allergies. I've never seen nor smelled so many freesias."

Maria slapped his shoulder. "Monster," she blurted before falling into a sneezing fit.

"She won't let us move a single one," Ana said, standing on her toes to kiss his cheek.

Isa scoffed. "Not true. Leech and Malcolm say they'll make splendid decorations for the finale. Now out!"

After a silent exchange, Ana and Maria made for the hall but not before the hairstylist grabbed a tissue box and directed a final sneer toward Luca. The door closed with a thud.

"You've something you want to say?" Isa asked.

"Sorry about the freesias. I didn't mean…I mean, I forgot I—"

"I'm not talking about the freesias."

"You're not?"

She stood up, took his hand and navigated him around the vases that littered the floor like landmines. Isa patted a cushion, an invitation to join her. "If this sofa could talk, the stories. Now, speak to me."

Luca assumed that Leech, in a last-ditch effort to push them together, told Isa about the accident that claimed the lives of his wife and daughter. He had planned to tell her himself, the prior night, but things got all jumbled.

Isa caressed his hand, her voice gentle. "Please tell me."

There was no point keeping anything hidden. Secrets had scarred his life. He told Isa everything—his aspirations to be an opera singer, the big break at La Scala and the stormy night of the accident when he put career before family. "My own damn arrogance. Still racked with guilt. Now maybe you can understand why I couldn't come to your first concert. Their deaths were too raw. Couldn't stop blaming myself…not sure I ever will." The admission felt liberating.

Inching closer, Isa nestled in his arm dabbing his cheek. "You'll never forget. Makes you human, makes you the dear man you are. So brave of you to tell me." After a moment of quiet caresses, her eyes stared into his. "That's not why I sent for you."

After kissing his cheek, Isa stood. From the dressing table, she picked up two small pieces of paper and her phone. She held them toward him. "You had a lot to say yesterday."

Of course, his texts and the notes from the florist. He forgot how passionately he professed his love for her. He felt heat rising to his face.

She returned to the sofa and took his hand. "I love you too, Luca Caruso, always have."

Her admission surprised him. Though the words should have sent his heart racing with joy. Instead they filled him with anxiety. He was speechless. Emotions collided in his mind like bumper cars. He didn't want to make another tragic mistake that crushed hearts—Isa's, Elizabeth's, or his own.

Isa continued, "I'm as much to blame for our rocky relationship. Foolish me. Kept you at a distance, afraid to fail again in love. Singing gave me confidence, convinced me that I'm worthy of love." Moved by her show of vulnerability, Luca kissed her hand. "And, so are you," she added, "worthy of love I mean. You're a dear, kind man, my dearest Luca. Isn't it about time you forgave yourself?"

Luca bowed his head. Yes, moving to Rome, starting over, and satisfying his passion with Elizabeth made him happy but inner peace had eluded him. Since returning to San Benedetto though, he felt such serenity possible. Witnessing Isa's triumph and facing his fear of public performance filled him with optimism. Elizabeth's admissions conveyed by Jamie, the prospect of love, filled him with hope. Perhaps he could begin to forgive himself.

Liberation had an unexpected consequence. He loved Isabella Fabrini; came to San Benedetto to profess as much. But the events of concert weekend led him to a different conclusion. The woman with whom he wanted to share his life wasn't Isa. If she would have him, he wanted Elizabeth.

However, after his outpouring of love in text and note that accompanied the blasted freesias, how could he let Isa down? He couldn't do that to her, not now...

"Dearest Luca," Isa said. "I love you, but as a dear friend. Leech told me about your part in launching my singing career. Wanted me to know that you were a far better muse than Madam Jenkins." They shared a quiet laugh before she added, "I'm forever in your debt. Singing, you see, has fulfilled me. Given my life purpose."

She explained how San Benedetto officials had phoned that afternoon. The town had approved plans to turn her concert into the focal point for an annual summer opera festival. In addition, she was considering a lucrative offer from the Royal Opera. Lady Blatherwicke had convinced them to hire Isa as a community liaison to spread the message of opera and performance around Britain.

After Luca offered his hearty congratulations with a kiss to her cheek, Isa took his hands in hers. "I want us to remain friends. Hope I haven't disappointed you too much?"

"No, no, no, dearest Isa. You've made me the happiest man in the world." Luca lifted her hands to his lips. But the tender reconciliation didn't last. The door pushed open. Leech rushed in.

"Sorry, my pets." Looking at the couple, embracing on the couch, his face went from pink to bright red. He put his back to them. "It's a—"

"*Fiasco*," Isa and Luca said in unison before laughing.

Leech flinched. "Right you are," he said, turning to Luca. "Isa needs you, my handsome man."

"We've just been discussing that very thing," Isa said.

Luca laughed. "You can stop scheming. You, Ana, and the universe have pushed us together at last. Only not in the way you think."

Leech's eyes ping-ponged between the two of them. He flashed a smile but immediately frowned, pacing up and down, wringing his hands. "Stupendous, marvelous, but not now, my pets. It's our tenor. Utter fiasco. Salvaggi has left the building."

Isa jumped to her feet. "You're joking." To Leech's head-shaking reply, she shouted, "That twit!"

"I've got choicer words for him, my dear," Lady Blatherwicke said, entering the room on Malcolm's arm, "and an urge to bloody his head." She brandished her stick in the air.

Isa's hands gestured wildly. "What did he say?"

"No one's seen him," Leech whimpered, pulling his wig into a fraying mess.

"Let's ask Danny," Kate said, pushing into the crowding room. "Saw him and Salvaggi gabbin' away like sweethearts."

They paced among the freesias until Malcolm pushed Danny into the center of the melee. The New Yorker looked as if he were about to launch his *Let's not go there* deflection when Brigid barged into the fray.

"Danny Chance, by the power of Saint Brigid, I command you to fess up."

Danny stomped his foot. "You're an atheist."

Brigid's expression went from bulldog to pixie. With head bobbing and eyes squinting, she backed away and mumbled, "Quite right, quite right."

Isa grabbed a silver candy dish, waving it above her head. "Danny Chance, if you want to set foot in San Benedetto again…"

Danny exhaled; his face frowning in defeat. "Paolo and I hooked up last night. Then he wouldn't speak to me. I had to see him. Found him flying about his dressing room. I asked if…if he'd see me again. Said he couldn't. Had to catch a flight to London."

"London?" Luca asked.

Danny shrugged. "Royal Opera wants him. Their tenor cancelled, he said. Insisted he fly out tonight or no deal. You ask me, he deserves the chance."

"Improbable!" Lady Blatherwicke exclaimed. "What else did he say?"

"Some bigwig donor demanded the Opera use him for the role. Even knew how to track him down in Italy."

Isa broke the silence. "That bitch!"

Surprised by her choice of words, Luca looked at Isa. Then it hit him. Walter Benchley was one of the Royal Opera's largest benefactors. Luca recalled seeing his name in the program in bold letters. Walter's resources combined with Telma's mischievous ways were a dangerous combination.

"That scheming witch," Isa ranted. "Out to destroy my concert again."

Leech grabbed her clawing hands. "Isa dear, neither bitch nor witch. No, my pet, Telma's pure genius." He lifted Luca's arm. "Your tenor's right here."

And thus the opera sped to a satisfying end. Luca took to the stage as lead tenor for the second half of the program. Isa, Ivy, and he had a splendid time performing their trio. He and Isa enjoyed the gentle irony when the chorus sang to them, Donizetti's "Chorus of Wedding Guests."

And the finale?

The last scene from *Turandot* was joyous and grand indeed. Luca stood on stage in a sea of white freesias. As he waited for the hearty applause that met the curtain's opening to subside, he scanned the audience. Jamie and Svetlana snuggled together. Phil White and Ana made an adorable couple, drawing daggers from Alexandra's eyes. On stage, Miguel and Tommy held hands, Kate paired with Richard, and Brigid with Nick. In the wings, a husky member of San Benedetto's fire brigade held a bouquet of roses. Danny, dressed as the Emperor, waved to him and to Luca's shock, the fireman waved back. When Luca glanced up to the center box,

Telma stopped nuzzling Walter long enough to offer Luca an exaggerated wink.

The music began. Adorned in colorful silk worthy of Princess Turandot, Isa entered from a wing. She made her way to Luca's side and whispered in his ear, "I couldn't be happier than to have you, my dearest friend, beside me. Papa was right, *opera is life*."

Holding Luca in her hands, Isa lifted her chin and declared in song to the full house, "...*Conosco il nome dello straniero! Il suo nome è...Amor!*"— I know the name of the stranger! His name is...Love! The audience went wild. For the reconciled friends, the words held special meaning. Their paths weren't smooth or straight. But both had found peace in their choices. Each saw a bright future.

The moment was powerful yet sweet. When Isa looked at Luca, her beautiful brown eyes told him she spoke the truth. They embraced as the chorus sang "O sole! Vita! Eternità!"

> *Love!*
> *O sun! Life! Eternity!*
> *Love is the light of the world!*
> *The sun laughs and sings*
> *to our infinite happiness!*
> *Glory to you!...Glory!*

Acknowledgments

Many helped me with this novel. Among these, I extend my deepest gratitude to:

My spouse. Jim read and reread drafts with fresh-eyed enthusiasm, offering valuable insight and critique.

Editors, Julie K. and Meera D. They combed the manuscript with great care, saving my readers from sloppy text and me from eternal embarrassment.

Loyal friends who read early drafts, giving me helpful feedback and encouragement. Barbara, Gia, Jerry, MaryEllen, Kathrin, Connie, Jane, Lorna, Charlie, and Janice.

Voice experts, Sara P. and Scott A. Their expertise in opera and voice instruction was invaluable.

Writers groups. In Chicago, the Barrington Writers Workshop and the Off Campus Writers Workshop; in Brussels, the Brussels Writers Circle for sharing knowledge, respectful critique, and most importantly, camaraderie in a lonely profession. My published colleagues inspire with their talent and motivate with their persistence and tenacity. I thank especially, Catherine Q., for her expert counsel on point-of-view and narrative voice.

The University of Iowa Summer Writing Festival. The course not only educated me on craft and technique, but also allowed me to meet a cluster of dedicated writers with whom I've remained friends.

The friendly staffs of my favorite cafés who kept me fueled on caffeine and encouraged with smiles and interest. These include Chris and her colleagues at Starbucks in Arlington Heights, Illinois, and Karina and her outstanding staff at Bocca Moka in Brussels.

Sadie, our golden retriever, and Puhi, our Belgian "guest cat." Their furry company and unconditional love soothed many an episode of writer's doubt.

CPSIA information can be obtained at www.ICGtesting.com
Printed in the USA
BVOW06*1414050216

435573BV00006B/15/P

9 781478 766889

THE BIBLICAL IMPORTANCE OF ISRAEL

AND EVERYTHING ELSE THAT GOES WITH IT

Written by
Reverend Chris Wickland
2017

4

DEDICATION

I dedicate this book to all who have a love for Israel and God's word.

I want to thank…

Jesus

My Wife for her tireless patience with me

and all who have helped me on the journey.

Also a very special thank you to the ladies who worked hard on editing and proof reading this manuscript. I am in your debt.

CONTENTS

Introduction   Page 8

Chapter One   Bridging the gap   Page 11

Chapter Two   The Abrahamic Covenant   Page 16

Chapter Three   The Davidic Covenant   Page 25

Chapter Four   Bridging the Testaments   Page 29

Chapter Five   Israel after the Gospels   Page 39

Chapter Six   Acts to Romans   Page 43

Chapter Seven   Romans Part One   Page 46

Chapter Eight   Romans Part Two   Page 55

Chapter Nine   Romans Part Three   Page 62

Chapter Ten   Knock! Knock!   Page 68

Chapter Eleven   The Acts Council   Page 77

Chapter Twelve   You Foolish Galatians!   Page 81

Chapter Thirteen   So What about the Sabbath?   Page 96

INTRODUCTION

At the time of writing this book, I have been a believer in Jesus Christ for over 28 years. On my journey, I have flowed through the various streams of Christendom i.e. Anglican, Charismatic, and Pentecostal, encountering the unique points of emphasis within each stream. In my opinion, Anglicans are great on the social gospel, helping the needy and providing great services to the community. The Charismatic churches tend to be good at training and equipping believers for service, and have great imagination and creativity, to bring a timeless gospel message in a relevant way. The Pentecostals, on the other hand, love that 'old time' religion with an emphasis on the gifts of the Spirit, and have a desire to see signs and wonders through God's power and faith.

Within each of these streams or flavours of Christendom, I soon came to realise that in each one, the issue of Israel was looked upon with very different eyes. Some saw Israel as a perplexing oddity, others dismissed it out of hand, as being of no relevance at all; whilst others believed that Israel was the centre of all biblical prophecy. Then, of course, we have the extremes; from groups who are anti-Israel and racist towards the Jews, to the pro-Israel groups racist towards the Arab nations. More so, the extreme pro-Zionists, who, in their desire to become Jewish themselves, alienate the Gentile Christians and perplex the Jewish communities. Yet there are other groups of Christians who have no problem with the Jewish people, but do have a problem with the physical existence of the land of Israel, which they would prefer to be called, the more politically correct, 'Palestine.'

Meanwhile, caught in the middle of all this Gentile diversity, are the Jewish Messianic Congregations who are trying to retain their Jewish identity, whilst discovering their new identity found in Jesus the Messiah. As you can see, the issue of Israel is a big one, a 'hot potato' to some, and a heresy to others, and a real 'sticky toffee pudding' to many Christians!

Having had the privilege of rubbing shoulders with many believers from various streams within Christendom, I have gained an interesting perspective regarding Israel. Attending bible colleges that teach replacement theology, and through my own personal study of Charismatic, Pentecostal, and Jewish-Roots theologies, has brought me to the conclusion that many of the schools of thought hold great truth and revelation for the Body of Christ. Equally, though, all of them have extremes and errors. At the end of the day, all doctrines need to be balanced and held in tension. The problem with the Greek mindset of the western world, is that we love to compartmentalise, but with scripture this view doesn't always work. It is this western mindset which, probably, has led to much doctrinal schism in the Body of Christ throughout history. Please do not misunderstand me, I am not in any way endorsing the fudging of doctrine, so that we can all get along, I am simply encouraging us all to start to truly believe what we read in the Bible, instead of reading through the lens of culture or tradition.

Here is a question for you: Why do we have Calvinism, Arminianism, anti-law (Torah), pro-law (Torah), pre-millennial, post-millennial and amillennial Christians? Simply put, each camp has a theological mindset that reflects some truth of scripture. So, the answer is not, which camp is right or wrong, it is about skilfully pulling together the elements involved, to establish a robust working understanding of scripture as a whole. No one camp has the full picture, because the Body of Christ is so multifaceted, that no one movement can fully show forth the fulness of God on the earth.

So back to the primary question. What is the biblical importance of the land of Israel in our day? Well, to look at this, let us to go back to the Old Testament and take time to track through some of the covenants and discover what was promised within them. Then, we will move on into the New Testament to see what it says regarding those covenants and their fulfilment. In other words, we will let scripture speak for itself. We will look at the nature of the Old Covenant and the New and, hopefully, this will help many readers grasp a more informed understanding of law and grace. We will also look at some of the errors in replacement and 'Hebraic theologies', as well as slaying a few 'sacred cows'. This could get messy!

My aim is to present a biblical, not a 'doctrinally biased', case for the importance of Israel. I would encourage you to read with an open mind, putting aside prejudice or bias, whilst taking a fresh look at this subject through the lens of scripture. So, whether you are 'pro-Zionist' or not, let's wipe the slate clean and rebuild our theology and understanding from scripture alone. I am sure we will discover something fresh and new along the way.

Finally, I am a Gentile Christian and happy to be so. I have no interest in becoming a Jewish believer, any more than I would want to influence Messianic believers to move away from their Jewish roots. The Apostle Paul makes it very clear, if you are Jewish stay Jewish, if you are Gentile stay Gentile. (1 Corinthians 7:18). This book is a simple call for us to come back to scripture and take a fresh look at the *Biblical Importance of Israel*, step by step.

CHAPTER ONE

BRIDGING THE GAP

To understand the Bible fully, we need to look at it as one whole unit; and not as an 'Old' and 'New' Testament. The problem we have with the Bible being so compartmentalised, is that it can stop the flow of scripture, as can the chapter breaks. For example, we assume that because the chapter has finished, so has the flow of the narrative, causing us to miss out on some fundamental teachings that flow from one verse to the other. I have enjoyed reading bibles that have no chapters or verses, just the written text. One of the notable joys being the logical flow of the text, in many cases making better sense when not broken down and compartmentalised.

The one page in the whole Bible which I feel ruins the flow and consistency of scripture is the page which says, *'The New Testament.'* Please don't misunderstand me, I am fully aware that we are in a new covenant based on better promises, with a better mediator, but that one page gives people a mental license to think the old is irrelevant. It's amazing how one page stops the flow of the narrative.

Let me give you an example of flow and context between the Old and New Testaments. Let's take the book of Revelation as an example. Now this book, taken by its own authority, without consulting the Old Testament, is probably the most bizarre and frightening book in the whole Bible. It will make no sense to a Christian who only reads the New Testament. However, when one realises the book has over 400 Old Testament references, perplexing ideas start to become clearer.

Let's look at an example:

Revelation 12:1-2 *'And a great sign appeared in heaven: a woman clothed with the sun, with the moon under her feet, and on her head a crown of twelve stars. She was pregnant and was crying out in birth pains and the agony of giving birth.'* ESV

The question which needs to be asked about this passage, is who or what is the woman? What do the sun, moon and stars have to do with her? To answer this question, we need to use the principle of *'First Mention'*. In other words, the Bible will mention something and then keep building upon that original theme, so that when it reappears there is no need to keep asking what it means. So, we see who the woman in Revelation is by going right back into the beginning of our Old Testament.

Genesis 37:9-10 *'Then he (Joseph) dreamed another dream and told it to his brothers and said, "Behold, I have dreamed another dream. Behold, the sun, the moon, and eleven stars were bowing down to me." But when he told it to his father and to his brothers, his father rebuked him and said to him, "What is this dream that you have dreamed? Shall I and your mother and your brothers indeed come to bow ourselves to the ground before you?"'* ESV

This passage gives us the interpretation of Revelation chapter 12. The sun is Jacob, the Moon is the mother of Joseph, and the eleven stars are Josephs eleven brothers who later become tribes. Thus, the woman in Revelation represents the Jewish Nation as a whole, made up of the twelve tribes of Israel.

Now, some of you may have spotted a discrepancy in the text. In Revelation Chapter 12 there are twelve stars, however, in Joseph's dream there are only eleven. Why? Well, Joseph is one of the twelve tribes of Israel, and in the dream eleven of the twelve are bowing down before him, so eleven brothers plus Joseph equals twelve.

From this simple piece of detective work, and by looking at the Bible as a complete book, we are enabled to decode parts of scripture which would otherwise seem random and out of place. Sadly, an idea prevalent in today's church, is that the Old Testament has been done away with, thus leading to the conclusion: don't bother reading it!

By treating the Bible as one whole book we can unlock some wonderful revelations. Let's look at another example from the book

12

of Revelation. This time we are going to find the New Testament in the Old Testament.

Revelation 4:5   *'Out from the throne come flashes of lightning and sounds and peals of thunder. And there were **seven lamps of fire** burning before the throne, **which are the seven Spirits of God;'*** NASB

In this text, we have the seven lamps which are (or represent) the seven Spirits of God. This all seems to be a bit 'far out' for our minds to cope with, but it will get easier when we anchor it into things we can understand.   However, before we do, we need to look at a few more verses from Revelation.

Revelation 1:4 *'John to the seven churches that are in Asia: Grace to you and peace, from Him who is and who was and who is to come, and from the **seven Spirits** who are before His throne,'* NASB

Revelation 1:12   *'Then I turned to see the voice that was speaking with me. And having turned I saw **seven golden lampstands;'*** NASB

Revelation 1:20   *'"As for the mystery of the **seven stars** which you saw in My right hand, and the **seven golden lampstands: the seven stars** are the angels of the **seven churches,** and the **seven lampstands** are the **seven churches.'*** NASB

So, let's take all these unusual texts and bed them into a context from the Old Testament.   Firstly, what is the seven or sevenfold Spirit of God? To answer this question, we need to turn to Isaiah 11:2

'And the spirit of the LORD shall rest upon him, the spirit of wisdom and understanding, the spirit of counsel and might, the spirit of knowledge and of the fear of the LORD;' KJV

This passage reveals to us the sevenfold or seven Spirits of God. It is actually the Holy Spirit with seven attributes. He is the Spirit of the Lord. (He proceeds from the Father and the Son. (See Romans 8:9)

13

He is the Spirit of wisdom.

He is the Spirit of understanding.

He is the Spirit of counsel.

He is the Spirit of strength.

He is the Spirit of knowledge

He is the Spirit of the fear of the Lord.

From the text in Revelation we understand that the seven lampstands represent the seven churches. Now, prepare your minds for a paradigm shift! We see the New Testament hidden in plain sight, within the Old Testament.

Number 8:1-3 *'Now the LORD spoke to Moses, saying, "Speak to Aaron and say to him, When you set up the lamps, the **seven lamps** shall give light in front of the lampstand." And Aaron did so: he set up its lamps in front of the lampstand, as the LORD commanded Moses.'* ESV

This lampstand which was built for the Tabernacle of Moses, was a replica of the one in heaven, which we have just read about in the book of Revelation. The Mosaic Tabernacle was built to the heavenly pattern.

Hebrews 8:5 *'They (The Priesthood) serve a copy and shadow of the heavenly things. For when Moses was about to erect the tent, he was instructed by God, saying, "See that you make everything according to the pattern that was shown you on the mountain."'* ESV

The huge Menorah in the Tabernacle of Moses was built to reflect the heavenly Menorah which represents the seven churches. So, in the Old Covenant of Moses, the New Covenant and the seven churches, the seven angels and the seven-fold Spirit of God were being revealed in plain sight for all to see. However, because the Jewish priesthood had no New Testament reference, they could not see the revelation right before their very eyes.

I hope now, you can see why I have laboured the point. The Bible needs to be understood in its entirety, not by covenant or dispensation alone. Let scripture interpret scripture. Sometimes, you need the Old Testament to understand the New, and other times you need the New to shed understanding upon the Old.

CHAPTER TWO

LAYING THE FOUNDATION

THE ABRAHAMIC COVENANT

One of the most important themes linking the Old and New Testaments together is that of 'covenant'. It runs like a weave in a tapestry, holding the whole picture together. Without covenant, we do not have a New or an Old testament. Without an understanding of covenant and the covenant nature of God, we cannot fully grasp the nature of scripture, and more importantly, the nature of God Himself. To understand the biblical importance of Israel, we have to understand covenant and the God who introduced it.

There are three key Hebrew words we need to be familiar with, when looking at the nature of covenant. Firstly, the Hebrew word *'Berit'* is often translated as 'covenant'. This word is strongly linked to key words such as 'promise,' and 'pledge.' The other Hebrew word is *'Chesed'* which is God's covenantal favour toward His people. This word is often translated as grace, loving kindness, and favour. Alongside *'Chesed'* we also have the word *'Shalom,'* which denotes fullness of life, peace, joy, health, vitality and prosperity. To have access to God's *'Chesed'* and *'Shalom,'* we have to be in *'Berit,'* covenant with Him first. In fact, all the main blessings of God can only come through being in covenant with Him. The New Testament equivalent to these words are *'Diatheke,'* (Covenant) *'Charis,'* (Grace) and *'Eirene'* (Peace).

There are six primary covenants God has made with man. They are known as the Adamic, the Noahic, the Abrahamic, the Mosaic, the Davidic and the Messianic covenant. These covenants span all of the Bible, they are very important and we do need to grasp and understand them, but the two key covenants which we need to focus on for the moment are the Abrahamic and the Mosaic.

16

The Abrahamic covenant is probably the most important one to look at, as it is the main covenant that, as Gentiles, we are grafted into.

The first thing we should note, is that Abraham was both Gentile, and later, Jewish. Let's look at what Joshua 24:2 says about Abraham in his early days before meeting the One True God.

'And Joshua said unto all the people, Thus saith the LORD God of Israel, Your fathers dwelt on the other side of the flood (river) in old time, even Terah, the father of Abraham, and the father of Nachor; and they served other gods.' KJV

So, firstly, before Abraham was called by God, he and his family worshiped other gods. In other words, he was a pagan and a Gentile. Now, this is actually quite important to understand, because the Abrahamic Covenant is as much for the Gentile man and woman as it is for the Jewish man and woman. I will expand upon this more later.

Abraham's call to the One True God begins in Genesis Chapter 12. Within this call of God are some key themes we need to spot and latch onto. Remember, the New Testament will confirm what is being shown here in Genesis, so we need to pay close attention to what is being revealed.

Genesis 12:1-3 *'Now the LORD said to Abram, "Go forth from your country, And from your relatives And from your father's house, **To the land** which I will show you; And I will make you **a great nation**, And I will bless you, And make your name great; And so you shall be a blessing; And I will bless those who bless you, And the one who curses you I will curse. And in you all the families of the earth will be blessed."'* NASB

These three verses contain so many wonderful gems, it would take several books to cover them all, but for the sake of this book, I want to focus on the areas I have highlighted. Pay careful attention to the language. Remember, this is God speaking to Abraham. He is told to go to a LAND and it is 'there' that he, Abraham, will be made into a NATION.

Here we encounter our principle of *First Mention.* The Abrahamic covenant, which is ratified and re-ratified throughout the book of Genesis, includes within it, a people group and a physical land area for that people group to live in!

Genesis 12:7   *'The LORD appeared to Abram and said, "**<u>To your descendants I will give this land</u>**." So he built an altar there to the LORD who had appeared to him.'* NASB

Here again we have God stating very clearly to Abraham that his descendants will be given the land by God Himself. It is, in part, a legal stipulation on God's behalf of the covenant, and its fulfillment. Remember we are letting scripture speak for itself.
Let's take a look at Genesis 13:14-15.

*'The LORD said to Abram, after Lot had separated from him, "Now lift up your eyes and look from the place where you are, northward and southward and eastward and westward; **<u>for all the land which you see, I will give it to you and to your descendants forever.</u>**'* NASB

We are now getting into some interesting language here. Again, God is confirming the covenant, and again re-stipulating that Abraham's descendants will be given a piece of land which will belong to them forever. Now, when terms like 'forever' are used we have to address exactly what 'forever' means.

Many from a replacement theological background would state that Israel broke the covenant with God and so God moved away from Israel to the Gentiles. There is a slight problem with this view. The replacement camp look only at the legal terms of the Mosaic Covenant with all its strict guidelines of blessings and curses. If Israel broke covenant with God under the Mosaic administration, then all manner of terrible things would befall them, even expulsion from the land of Israel itself. (See Deuteronomy 28:15-66)

The New Testament scriptures show us that the Abrahamic Covenant is still very much 'up and running'. (Galatians 3:13-14 & 29) The book of Hebrews is very clear that the Mosaic administration has closed and a better covenant is now operating. (Hebrews 8:13)

The apostle Paul makes this very clear in Galatians 3:17 *'What I am saying is this: the Law, which came four hundred and thirty years later, does not invalidate a covenant previously ratified by God, so as to nullify the promise.'* NASB

This scripture makes it very clear that the Mosaic Covenant in no way invalidates the Abrahamic Covenant. This is a very key scripture that we cannot overlook.

Another erroneous assumption about the New Covenant, is that it replaces Israel with the Church. There is a problem with this view, so let's take a look at where the New Covenant is first mentioned.

Jeremiah 31:31-33 *'"Behold, days are coming," declares the LORD, "when I will make a **new covenant** with **the house of Israel** and with **the house of Judah**, **not like the covenant** which I made with their fathers in the day I took them by the hand to bring them out of the land of Egypt, **My covenant which they broke**, although I was a husband to them," declares the LORD. "But this is the covenant which I will make with **the house of Israel** after those days," declares the LORD, "I will put My law within them and on their heart I will write it; and I will be their God, and they shall be My people.*

This is such a powerful piece of scripture which, if simply believed, would answer many of our questions. So now it's time to slay a 'sacred cow' or two!

Firstly, God is speaking this prophecy to Israel not the Gentiles. Remember, the New Covenant is first and foremost for the Jewish people. (see Romans 1:16) Secondly, this prophecy is addressed to *the house of Israel* and *the house of Judah.* This is very important as Israel was a divided nation at the time of Jeremiah. Judah and Benjamin were known as the Southern Kingdom located around Jerusalem, the other ten tribes who broke away after Solomon died, moved into the northern territories and became known as Israel. Therefore, this prophecy can only be referring to the whole nation of Israel. God does not need to make a New Covenant with the Gentiles because we never had an old one to start with. THIS IS A JEWISH ONLY PROPHECY.

The next point to note, is that this is not a *renewed covenant,* it is a NEW covenant. There are some in the Hebrew Roots camp that try to stress the covenant of Moses continues today in a renewed fashion, but there is a problem with this interpretation. Let's look at the passage again.

*""Behold, days are coming," declares the LORD, "when I will make a **new covenant** with the house of Israel and with the house of Judah, **not like the covenant** which I made with their fathers in the day I took them by the hand to bring them out of the land of Egypt,*

The text is very clear. It cannot be a renewed covenant, simply because God states that the new covenant will *not be like the covenant* which He made with their fathers in the wilderness. This is not renewed, it is a brand new covenant, based on the promises to Abraham not the covenant of Moses.

[[There will be some who would argue the Mosaic Covenant has not been annulled because of what Jesus said, "Do not think I came not to abolish the law and prophets." (Matthew 5:17) This question will be answered in detail in a later chapter.]]

The next question which needs to be asked is "When did the New Covenant come to the Jewish people?" To find the answer to this we need to go to the gospels.

Luke 22:20   *'After supper he (Jesus) took another cup of wine and said,* **"This cup is the new covenant between God and his people**--*an agreement confirmed with my blood, which is poured out as a sacrifice for you.'* NLT

It is at this Jewish Passover that Jesus reveals the New Covenant as prophesied by Jeremiah. Jesus the Passover Lamb, who was about to be slain for the sins of the world, made a New Covenant with the people of Israel. Remember all of Jesus' disciples were Jewish, the whole Bible was written by Jews. Salvation really did come to and from the Jewish people. It was to the Jewish people that Jesus established the New Covenant! Remember, Gentiles do not have an Old Covenant, so they don't get a New Covenant! We Gentiles just get grafted into what is known as the Messianic Covenant. Although we call it the New Covenant, it is only truly New for the Jewish people!

Now back to our text in Genesis.

Genesis 13:14-15 *'The LORD said to Abram, after Lot had separated from him, "Now lift up your eyes and look from the place where you are, northward and southward and eastward and westward;* **for all the land which you see, I will give it to you and to your descendants forever.'**   NASB

Taking into consideration all that we have just looked at, and knowing that the Abrahamic Covenant is still running; this promise in Genesis **'for all the land which you see, I will give it to you and to your descendants forever.'** must simply mean what it says: Forever means forever. But this is still a very simplistic argument. So, we are going to look at more passages of scripture and then link them to the New Testament so that the reader will see for themselves that the promises to Israel are still in effect.

Although these scriptures are really showing us the Jewish element there are also others which reveal God's plan for the Gentiles as well.

21

Genesis 17:16 *'I will bless her, (Sarah) and moreover, I will give you a son by her. I will bless her, and she shall become nations; kings of peoples shall come from her."*

The Hebrew word for *'nations,'* is *'goyim.'* This is where we get the word Gentile from. The Abrahamic covenant is so encompassing it deals with the Jewish people, gives them a country to populate; but it also stipulates that Gentiles will be included. This is completely in sync with New Testament teaching, which will also be covered in a later chapter.

As time moves on, the blessings of the Abrahamic Covenant pass onto Isaac the son of Abraham. We see this in Genesis 26:3-4

*'"Sojourn in this land and I will be with you and bless you, for **to you** and to **your descendants** I will give all these lands, and I will establish the oath which I swore to your father Abraham.'* NASB

Again, here we have God confirming the covenant and passing it onto the next line in the family tree. The promises are consistent; the land where Isaac was living was for him and his descendants, and it would be God who would give it to them.

Later this same blessing is passed onto Jacob:

Genesis 28:3-4 *'"May God Almighty bless you and make you fruitful and multiply you, that you may become a company of peoples. "May He also give you **the blessing of Abraham**, to you and to your descendants with you, **that you may possess the land** of your sojournings, **which God gave to Abraham."***

Some key points to look at here; the blessing of Abraham has been given to Jacob, he and his descendants will possess the land, a land which God gave to Abraham.

In Genesis 35:9-12 We have the same covenant language from God being spoken over Jacob who is now called Israel.

'Then God appeared to Jacob again when he came from Paddan-aram, and He blessed him. God said to him, "Your name is Jacob; You shall no longer be called Jacob, But Israel shall be your name." Thus He called him Israel. God also said to him, "I am God Almighty; Be fruitful and multiply; **A nation and a company of nations** *shall come from you, And* **kings shall come forth from you.** **"The land which I gave to Abraham** *and Isaac,* **I will give it to you, And I will give the land to your descendants after you.***"* NASB

From Israel will come *'a nation and a company of nations.'* What does this mean? From Jacob/Israel will come a nation, the Jewish nation, and also from the Seed of Jacob will eventually come The King who is called the Messiah. Through Him the Gentiles will also be grafted into the commonwealth of Israel.

Galatians 3:16 *'Now the promises were spoken to Abraham and to his seed. He does not say, "And to seeds," as referring to many, but rather to one, "And to your seed," that is, Christ.'* NASB

Ephesians 2:12- *'In those days you were living apart from Christ. You were excluded from citizenship among the people of Israel, and you did not know the covenant promises God had made to them. You lived in this world without God and without hope. But now you have been united with Christ Jesus. Once you were far away from God, but now you have been brought near to him through the blood of Christ. For Christ himself has brought peace to us. He united Jews and Gentiles into one people when, in his own body on the cross, he broke down the wall of hostility that separated us.'* NLT

In the Genesis 35 passage we again have the ratification of the covenant which stipulates a physical land for a physical people group: **"The land which I gave to Abraham** *and Isaac,* **I will give it to you, And I will give the land to your descendants after you.***"*

So, in conclusion to this chapter, we see clearly that the Abrahamic covenant deals with the Nation of Israel, the Land of Israel and also contains a policy to allow the Gentiles to enjoy the covenant.

Remember a key scripture which underpins the validity of the Abrahamic Covenant in the New Testament is Galatians 3:17:

'What I am saying is this: the Law, which came four hundred and thirty years later, does not invalidate a covenant previously ratified by God, so as to nullify the promise.' NASB

The Abrahamic covenant still stands today, and has not been replaced or invalidated. We will look further at this in a later chapter, but for now a good basic foundation has been laid for the biblical importance of Israel.

CHAPTER THREE

THE DAVIDIC COVENANT

The next theme we need to look at is the Davidic Covenant. The reason behind focusing on the Abrahamic and the Davidic Covenants will become apparent when we start to study the gospels.

In the Abrahamic covenant, we had several promises that kings would arise from within Israel as a people group. The Davidic covenant is the fulfillment of that promise with additional promises, which ultimately points towards The King of Kings, the Messiah, and His second coming as Eternal Ruler and King over all the earth.

The Davidic covenant is again one which contains so many additional subjects, we could easily get side-tracked with all the other wonderful aspects, such as the Tabernacle of David etc. For this chapter, we will be looking at the context of Israel, the people, the land and the ultimate Jewish King, Jesus.

The promise of this covenant is mentioned in 2 Samuel 7:11b-13

'...and I will give you rest from all your enemies. The LORD also declares to you that the LORD will make a house for you. "When your days are complete and you lie down with your fathers, I will raise up your descendant after you, who will come forth from you, and I will establish his kingdom."He shall build a house for My name, and I will establish the throne of his kingdom forever.' NASB

In this passage God promises to raise a dynasty, a house of kings, to David. The line of kings that will come throughout the ages will be descendants of David and thus, Jewish. It is also apparent that this passage contains strong Messianic overtones. The text keeps referring to an individual who will ultimately establish an eternal kingdom, something a mere mortal could not do. Whoever this King would be, (which we know to be Jesus), would have to be Jewish and born of the family line of the original King David, the line of Judah.

The next text to look at is found in Jeremiah 23:5-6

*"'Behold, the days are coming," declares the LORD, "When I will raise up for David a righteous Branch; And He will reign as king and act wisely And do justice and righteousness **in the land**. "In His days Judah will be saved, And Israel will dwell securely; And this is His name by which He will be called, 'The LORD our righteousness."*
NASB

This is a very interesting prophecy because it states very clearly that the Righteous Branch of David will reign as King and work righteousness in the Land. Which land? The land of Israel.

"'In His days Judah will be saved, And Israel will dwell securely; And this is His name by which He will be called, 'The LORD our righteousness."'

Jesus is the means by which Israel will be saved, but now it starts to get a little 'sticky'. Obviously, only a small portion of Israel received Jesus as Messiah when He walked the earth. Jesus did not come to earth as a ruling King, but as the Suffering Servant. This is where the early Jews made an error in looking for the ruling powerful King as prophesied in the Davidic Covenant. They did not realise that before they could receive this great King, they would first have to receive the Suffering Servant. The Jewish people basically got their prophecies mixed up. They were expecting the prophecies pertaining to the second coming of the Messiah, but failed to see His first coming as the humble Suffering Servant, the Lamb who would take away the sins of the world.

The prophecy in Jeremiah 23:5-6 states very clearly that Judah will be saved and Israel will dwell securely. If this is the case, then it has to be an end time scripture. Firstly, for the reasons already given about Jesus returning as King. Secondly, the New Testament bears witness to this prophecy as still yet to be fulfilled, and one which has not been fulfilled in any way historically. So, no preterist (historically fulfilled) argument will stand here.

Romans 11:26 *'and so all Israel will be saved; just as it is written,* *"THE DELIVERER WILL COME FROM ZION, HE WILL REMOVE UNGODLINESS FROM JACOB."* NASB

This single text is a real conundrum for those in the replacement camp, because two key elements are mentioned. Firstly, Israel as a people group, and secondly, Zion is mentioned, which refers to Mount Zion in Jerusalem. According to the Psalms and many other Old Testament texts, Mount Zion is where the Messiah will reign when He returns.

Also, another key aspect to Jeremiah's prophecy is the mention of the two kingdoms. Israel being the Northern Kingdom and Judah being the Southern Kingdom. In other words, this prophecy is rooted in history and cannot be 'super-spiritualised' to mean something else. This prophecy is absolutely for Israel as a nation and the New Testament passage in Romans bears witness to this.

The King of Israel must be Jewish by birth and so must be born in Israel.

Deuteronomy 17:15 *'you shall surely set a king over you whom the* *LORD your God chooses, one from among your* **countrymen** *you* *shall set as king over yourselves; you may not put a foreigner over* *yourselves who is not your countryman.'* NASB

It needs to be noted here that Jesus' Jewish identity does not vanish because He is back in heaven. God is the One who raised up the Jewish people and set their culture through the Law of Moses. Jesus, who is God, was born into the Jewish culture, so after He ascended into heaven He still retains His Jewishness. In fact, everyone retains their ethnicity when they go to heaven. Let's see what scripture has to say on this.

Revelation 21:25-26 *'Its gates will never be shut at the end of the day, because there will be no night there. And into the city will be brought the glory and honour of the **nations**.'* Berean Study Bible

This passage from revelation is talking about the New Jerusalem and the New Heaven and the New Earth. You will note that the *'glory of the nations'* is brought into this city. The Greek word for nations is *'Ethnos.'* This word is also rendered ethnicity. When we enter the New Jerusalem even though we are one new man in Christ, we still retain our ethnicity which we were born with from the earth.

By the very doctrine of the incarnation, (Jesus becoming clothed in human flesh) Jesus is now fully God and fully man. His resurrection body, although no longer mortal, still retains the scars from the crucifixion (John 20:27) and He still retains His ethnicity, which is Jewish. This concept is a real stumbling block for some Christians, they just cannot cope with the idea of their Saviour being eternally Jewish. Remember God designed the Jewish nation. He gave them their laws and cultures and way of life. So, which came first the chicken or the egg? The chicken of course.

Remember Jesus didn't go through a Jewish phase of life, He is the eternal King of the line of David.

2 Samuel 7:11b-13
'...and I will give you rest from all your enemies. The LORD also declares to you that the LORD will make a house for you. "When your days are complete and you lie down with your fathers, I will raise up your descendant after you, who will come forth from you, and I will establish his kingdom."He shall build a house for My name, and I will establish the throne of his kingdom forever.' NASB

CHAPTER FOUR

BRIDGING THE TESTAMENTS

We have so far, laid some key foundations from the Abrahamic and Davidic covenants, which will help us to see clearly what transpires as we look at the Gospels.

We know from the Abrahamic covenant, that God promised to make Israel a nation and give them a land to live in. This would be an eternal promise.

Genesis 13:14-15
*'The LORD said to Abram, after Lot had separated from him, "Now lift up your eyes and look from the place where you are, northward and southward and eastward and westward; **for all the land which you see, I will give it to you and to your descendants forever.**'*
NASB

Subsequently, God swore to David that He would raise up a King from the house of David. This king would come from Israel, and would be essentially Jewish.

2 Samuel 7:11b-13
'...and I will give you rest from all your enemies. The LORD also declares to you that the LORD will make a house for you. "When your days are complete and you lie down with your fathers, I will raise up your descendant after you, who will come forth from you, and I will establish his kingdom."He shall build a house for My name, and I will establish the throne of his kingdom forever.' NASB

So, now, it is time to look at the Gospels to see the relevance and importance of the Abrahamic and Davidic covenants, which were partially fulfilled with the birth of Jesus, the Jewish Messiah and Saviour of the Gentiles.

MATTHEW'S GOSPEL

The first book in the New Testament is the Gospel according to Matthew. Interestingly, of the four Gospel accounts, Matthew's is the most Jewish in flavour. It is a great way to start the New Testament! It is very easy to forget that the whole Bible was written by Jewish believers, especially as our westernised translations often fail to highlight the Jewishness of the text. So, for example, the book of James in the New Testament, is actually called the book of Jacob in the Greek manuscript. Really? Yes really! These issues, sadly down play the Jewishness of the text, even from the Greek manuscripts.

The book of Matthew starts off in a very Jewish style, with something that is very important within Jewish culture: a genealogy. For Jewish people, it is important to know their family tree and where they come from. Jewish identity was found in the context of family, not in personal status or fame.

In Chapter 1 verses 20 to 23, Joseph, Mary's husband to be, has a dream:

*'"She will bear a Son; and you shall call His name Jesus, for He will save **His people** from their sins." Now all this took place to fulfil what was spoken by the Lord through the prophet: "BEHOLD, THE VIRGIN SHALL BE WITH CHILD AND SHALL BEAR A SON, AND THEY SHALL CALL HIS NAME IMMANUEL," which translated means, "GOD WITH US."* NASB

In these verses we see some interesting language: The birth of the child will save *'His people'* from their sins. Who are *'His People?'* Some may argue that we are all God's people, thus claiming that this passage is not specific to Israel. However, that is not what Jesus says, in Matthew 15:24: *'Then Jesus said to the woman, "I was sent **only** to help **God's lost sheep--the people of Israel**.'* NLT

Jesus' primary mission was to the Jewish people, therefore we recognise from this passage, that God is talking about His People, the nation of Israel. This is also borne out in other texts from the New Testament:

Romans 1:16 *'For I am not ashamed of the gospel, for it is the power of God for salvation to everyone who believes, **to the Jew first** and also to the Greek.'* NASB

The Gospel was always, first and foremost, to the Jew and then to the Gentile. This is only right as God was in covenant with the Jewish nation and not the Gentiles. Paul again, makes this clear in Ephesians.

Ephesians 2:12-14 *'In those days you (Gentiles) were living apart from Christ. You were excluded from citizenship among the people of Israel, and you did not know the covenant promises God had made to them. You lived in this world without God and without hope. But now you have been united with Christ Jesus. Once you were far away from God, but now you have been brought near to him through the blood of Christ. For Christ himself has brought peace to us. He united Jews and Gentiles into one people when, in his own body on the cross, he broke down the wall of hostility that separated us.'* NLT

Looking back to our text in Matthew, you may notice that the angel of God concludes Joseph's dream with a quote from Isaiah 7:14. This is a specific Messianic prophecy given <u>to</u> Israel <u>for</u> Israel.

"BEHOLD, THE VIRGIN SHALL BE WITH CHILD AND SHALL BEAR A SON, AND THEY SHALL CALL HIS NAME IMMANUEL," which translated means, "GOD WITH US." NASB

One thing is very clear. God has not rejected His people, He is fulfilling prophecy and being faithful to His prophetic promises. Now, let's move onto Matthew 2:6. Here, we have a prophecy from Micah 5:2.

'And you, Bethlehem, land of Judah, are by no means least among the rulers of Judah, for out of you will come forth One leading, **who will shepherd My people Israel.** *"'* ESV

This is a wonderful prophecy about a leader who will be a true shepherd to the people of Israel. This is a comforting affirmation of Psalm 23:1 *'The LORD is my shepherd, I shall not want.'* NASB.

Jesus confirms the Micah prophecy and hints at His divinity in John 10:11. *'I am the good shepherd. The good shepherd lays down his life for the sheep.'*

The Micah Prophecy also has eschatological (end times) overtones referring to Jesus' second coming. This is not unusual where a single prophecy can have a dual fulfillment.

For example in Daniel 9:27 we have a prophecy about the Abomination of Desolation:

Daniel 9:27 *'The ruler will make a treaty with the people for a period of one set of seven, but after half this time, he will put an end to the sacrifices and offerings. And as a climax to all his terrible deeds, he will set up a* **sacrilegious object that causes desecration**, *(Abomination of desolation) until the fate decreed for this defiler is finally poured out on him."* NLT

This prophecy was fulfilled in the Maccabean revolt in 167 to 160 BC. A wicked king named Antiochus Epiphanes issued decrees to end Jewish religious practice. He then went into the Holy of Holies in the temple and erected his own statue. To all intents and purposes, this prophecy from Daniel was well and truly fulfilled.

However, in the Gospels, this prophecy is re-quoted by Jesus, implying that it still had not been fulfilled in all it's fullness.

Matthew 24:15-16 *'"The day is coming when* **you will see what Daniel the prophet spoke about**--*the sacrilegious object that causes* desecration *(Abomination of desolation) standing in the Holy Place." (Reader, pay attention!) "Then those in Judea must flee to the hills.'* NLT

This scripture is then taken further by the Apostle Paul, who alludes to it being fulfilled by the anti-christ:
2 Thessalonians 2:4 *'He will exalt himself and defy everything that people call god and every object of worship. **He will even sit in the temple of God**, claiming that he himself is God.'* NLT

Let's come back to our prophecy (Micah 5:2) quoted in Matthew 2:6:

*'And you, Bethlehem, land of Judah, are by no means least among the rulers of Judah, for out of you will come forth One leading, **who will shepherd My people Israel.**'* ESV

Those in the replacement camp, often use the Micah prophecy, to justify that trying to connect the gospels to the Old Testament is irrelevant. Even though the scripture clearly speaks of Israel, they still hold this view, because they believe, God has divorced Israel and replaced them with the Church. They would base their argument on Jeremiah 3:8 :

Jeremiah 3:8 *'She saw that I divorced faithless **Israel** because of her adultery. But that treacherous sister **Judah** had no fear, and now she, too, has left me and given herself to prostitution.'*

We need to remember two things. Firstly, when Jeremiah speaks of Israel, he means just the Northern 10 tribes, who were eventually taken off the map and forcibly relocated by the Assyrians and become known as The Ten Lost Tribes.

Secondly, God made a promise to both Israel and Judah that He would make a new covenant with them, Jeremiah 31:31:

*'"Behold, days are coming," declares the LORD, "when I will make a new covenant with the **house of Israel** and with the **house of Judah**,'*
NASB

Scripture cannot be broken, there is no 'wiggle room' here. God has an intentional plan for both Israel (The Northern Tribes) and Judah. (The Southern Tribes) as one nation.

LUKE'S GOSPEL

Our next section of scriptures to look at will come from the Gospel of Luke. The first main passage is in Chapter 1, when Gabriel appears to Mary to tell her that she has been chosen by God to bear the Messiah.

Luke 1:30-33   *'And the angel said to her, "Do not be afraid, Mary, for you have found favour with God. And behold, you will conceive in your womb and bear a son, and you shall call his name Jesus. He will be great and will be called the Son of the Most High. And **the Lord God will give to him the throne of his father David**, and **he will reign over the house of Jacob forever**, and of his kingdom there will be no end."* ESV

This is a wonderful passage of scripture, which strongly ratifies the covenantal language of the Davidic Covenant as seen in 2 Samuel 7:11b-13

*'...and I will give you rest from all your enemies. The LORD also declares to you that the LORD will make a house for you. "When your days are complete and you lie down with your fathers, **I will raise up your descendant after you, who will come forth from you, and I will establish his kingdom." "He shall build a house for My name, and I will establish the throne of his kingdom forever.**'*
NASB

The language in Luke 1:30-33 is very specific to the people of Israel. Jesus will be given the throne of His father David and He will rule forever. This is a fulfilment of many prophecies in the Old Testament.

Gabriel also states that Jesus will reign over the house of Jacob **forever.**

Here is an interesting thought, why do you think Gabriel mentioned the house of Jacob instead of the house of Israel? I, personally, think it is because he wanted to make his message clear. Remember, Israel was known as the Northern kingdom, and so Gabriel's use of the term 'House of Jacob' can only mean all the physical descendants of Jacob, thus including, all the twelve tribes. There could be now no misinterpretation or super-spiritualising of the text, such as 'spiritual Israel'.

The next scripture in Luke's Gospel is taken from what some denominations call the 'Magnificat.' This is Mary's, psalm-like proclamation, telling of the goodness of God towards His people. Again, we see strong national language in verses 54 and 55.

Luke 1:54-55 *'**He has helped his servant Israel**, in remembrance of his mercy, as he spoke to our fathers, **to Abraham and to his offspring forever.**"* ESV

Through the coming birth of Messiah, God has helped His servant Israel in fulfilling the eternal Covenant to Abraham and his descendants.

It is fair to say, that the bridge between the two testaments is still strongly Jewish in flavour. The covenants of old are being re-ratified and confirmed by angels and prophecy. God seems to be extremely interested in the affairs of Israel and is still confirming the promises He made to the forefathers of long ago. There are most certainly, no hints that God has divorced Himself from His people. Also, we still need to bear in the mind the principle of 'first mention'. All the scriptures we are looking at find their roots in the Old Testament, thus for the most part, the original meaning still stands true.

For some, from a replacement background, there may be a case for God rejecting Israel, not so much when Jesus was born, but later when Israel rejected Him as their Messiah. This is a fair point, which will be addressed in a later chapter. At the end of the day, we must trust the integrity of scripture, and not try to make it fit our personal beliefs. This means we may all have some repositioning to do theologically.

The next passage in Luke is a fulfillment of prophecy and a proclamation of God's faithfulness and covenantal loving kindness. This psalm of praise comes from the lips of Zachariah, the father of John the Baptist.

Luke 1:68-75 *'"Praise the Lord, **the God of Israel**, because **he has visited and redeemed his people**. He has sent us a mighty Saviour from the royal line of his servant David, just as he **promised** through his holy prophets long ago. Now we will be saved from our enemies and from all who hate us. **He has been merciful to our ancestors by remembering his sacred covenant--the covenant he swore with an oath to our ancestor Abraham.** We have been rescued from our enemies so we can serve God without fear, in holiness and righteousness for as long as we live."'* NLT

The areas in bold, highlight the obvious references to the Davidic and Abrahamic covenants. There is absolutely nothing here to imply that God is displeased, angry, divorced from, or not interested in Israel. This is tender, covenantal language of love and hope to Israel in a time of difficulty, when they were under the occupation of Rome.

The problem with these particular scriptures is that, they are cloaked in the veil of '*The Christmas Story.*' We have all sung these scriptures as children, and we have all seen Christmas cards with the three wise men and baby Jesus in a manger! As nice and quaint as that is, the familiarity to the Christmas story can blind us from the glaringly obvious. We can be so overly familiar with the story, that we just don't see the obvious truth, that God is fulfilling Jewish prophecy.

Let's look at another famous passage in the Christmas story, where the angels appear to the shepherds who were watching their flocks by night.

Luke 2:10-11   *'But the angel said to them, "Do not be afraid; for behold, I bring you good news of great joy which will be for all the people; for today in the city of David **there has been born for you** a Saviour, who is **Christ the Lord' NASB***

So, an angel appears to a few shepherds (not on a bleak midwinters night!) and gives them this amazing proclamation.   *'...**there has been born for you** a Saviour, who is **Christ the Lord..'***   Notice the statement 'Born for you.'   To a Jewish person, they would have known that this was a fulfillment of a famous passage in Isaiah.

Isaiah 9:6-7   *'**For to us a child is born, to us a son is given**; and the government shall be upon his shoulder, and his name shall be called Wonderful Counsellor, Mighty God, Everlasting Father, Prince of Peace. Of the increase of his government and of peace there will be no end, on the throne of David and over his kingdom, to establish it and to uphold it with justice and with righteousness from this time forth and forevermore. The zeal of the LORD of hosts will do this.'*   ESV

*'**For to us a child is born, to us a son is given...'***   The text is very clear. The child born was both a national and prophetic fulfillment for the people of Israel.

Some may start to question where the Gentiles fit into all of this! Remember, salvation comes from, (and to) the Jew first, then to the Gentiles.

John 4:22   *'You worship what you do not know; we worship what we know, **for salvation is from the Jews**.'*   ESV

Isaiah 49:6 *'He says, "You will do more than restore the people of Israel to me. **I will make you a light to the Gentiles, and you will bring my salvation to the ends of the earth.**"'* NLT

Romans 1:16 *'For I am not ashamed of this Good News about Christ. It is the power of God at work, saving everyone who believes--**the Jew first and also the Gentile.**'* NLT

These scriptures are all confirmed at Jesus' circumcision, when an old devout man called Simeon gives a prophecy to Mary and Joseph:

Luke 2:28-   *'Simeon was there. He took the child in his arms and praised God, saying, "Sovereign Lord, now let your servant die in peace, as you have promised. I have seen your salvation, (I have seen your Yeshua) which you have prepared for all people. **He is a light to reveal God to the nations,(Gentiles) and he is the glory of your people Israel!**"* NLT My parenthesis added.

This text, again spells out that Messiah was born to be the Glory of the people of Israel and to reveal God to the Gentiles. This text cannot be super-spiritualised to mean 'spiritual Israel'. There is a clear distinction in the language. Gentiles and Israel. To place these two people groups side by side is very important to note. In fact, up until this time, in the Bible, there were only two people groups: Jews and Gentiles. However, after the crucifixion there are now three people groups on the earth: Jews, Gentiles and the New Creation which is the Church, the One New Man in Christ.

In summary, the scriptures speak very clearly regarding God's heart for Israel and His promises to them. It is very apparent that God had not divorced Israel at the time of the birth of Jesus, as some have implied. In fact, the language is so Old Covenant and so based on ancient biblical prophecies, that it is a wonder why we have often failed to see it!

In the next chapter, we will start looking at Israel in light of the book of Acts and the letters of Paul, through to the book of Revelation.

CHAPTER FIVE

ISRAEL AFTER THE GOSPELS

So far, from the Gospels, we have established the validity of Israel. However, there are several key texts, which some from a replacement background, would cite as an argument to invalidate Israel. These will be fairly and logically considered in a later chapter. However, for now, let us look and see what is said about Israel, in the New Testament.

Remember, the principle of 'first mention'. The term 'Israel', is nearly always used, in both the Old and New Testaments, to refer to an original people group, who were the descendants of Abraham, Isaac and Jacob. As the Bible was written by Jewish authors certain key words and phrases will remain synonymous throughout the whole text. They would not randomly change meaning over night with no prior 'first mention' principle being applied. The Bible is the Word of God. It is amazingly designed and does not negate or contradict itself.

Nowhere in the Gospels, did Jesus, or anyone else, actually make the statement, that the Church is the new Israel. Yet, some may still argue, that Jesus alluded to it in Matthew chapter 21:33-46
'"Hear another parable. There was a master of a house who planted a vineyard and put a fence around it and dug a winepress in it and built a tower and leased it to tenants, and went into another country. When the season for fruit drew near, he sent his servants to the tenants to get his fruit. And the tenants took his servants and beat one, killed another, and stoned another. Again, he sent other servants, more than the first. And they did the same to them. Finally, he sent his son to them, saying, 'They will respect my son.' But when the tenants saw the son, they said to themselves, 'This is the heir. Come, let us kill him and have his inheritance.' And they took him and threw him out of the vineyard and killed him. When therefore the owner of the vineyard comes, what will he do to those tenants?" They said to him, "He will

*put those wretches to a miserable death and **let out the vineyard to other tenants** who will give him the fruits in their seasons."*

Jesus said to them, "Have you never read in the Scriptures:

"'The stone that the builders rejected has become the cornerstone; this was the Lord's doing, and it is marvellous in our eyes'?

*Therefore, I tell you, **the kingdom of God will be taken away from you** and given to a people producing its fruits. And the one who falls on this stone will be broken to pieces; and when it falls on anyone, it will crush him."*

***When the chief priests and the Pharisees heard his parables, they perceived that he was speaking about them.** And although they were seeking to arrest him, they feared the crowds, because they held him to be a prophet.'* ESV

So, in looking at this parable, it is clear, firstly, that Jesus is speaking to the Jewish people and the religious leaders of the day, and secondly, the people of Israel are 'The Vineyard'. So, this parable is essentially about, who is going to be entrusted to look after them. In verse 43, Jesus makes it very clear that the 'vineyard' would be handed over to new tenants. The only people who seem to be bothered by this, are the religious leaders, because it is about them, not the people of Israel. The next question that needs to be addressed, is who did Jesus give the keys of the Kingdom to?

Matthew 16:2 *'I will give you the keys of the kingdom of heaven, and whatever you bind on earth shall be bound in heaven, and whatever you loose on earth shall be loosed in heaven."'* ESV

The keys were given to the twelve disciples who became the twelve apostles. Now, this power to bind and loose is not, necessarily, talking about binding demons, in this instance. It is referring to the rabbinical authority which the rabbis had in interpreting scripture and

40

overseeing and shepherding the people of Israel. So, Jesus is stating here, that He is now taking the keys away from the rabbinical authorities and giving them to His twelve apostles. This should become very apparent in the book of Acts. All the original apostles were Jewish and all apart from Paul, were sent out to the Jewish people. The "Church" was pioneered by the Jewish Apostles. Just because history shows that the Gentiles outgrew the Hebrew believing congregations, does not in any way invalidate the Jewish foundation stones of our faith. Neither does it justify writing off Israel as a people group. Still not convinced? Let's take a look at the New Jerusalem in heaven and see who's names are on the gates and foundation of that city.

Revelation 21:12-14 *'It had a great and high wall, with twelve gates, and at the gates twelve angels; and names were written on them, which are the names of **the twelve tribes of the sons of Israel**. There were three gates on the east and three gates on the north and three gates on the south and three gates on the west. **And the wall of the city had twelve foundation stones, and on them were the twelve names of the twelve apostles of the Lamb.**'*

There is no way around this whether you believe the New Jerusalem to be the new 'spiritual Israel', or a literal city in heaven, either way, it's foundations and gates are based on Jewish patriarchs and apostles. The foundation of the city in heaven and the Church on the earth are Jewish. So, with this information, we can now look at a verse in the book of Acts. that is a classic for those seeking to prove that God has replaced Israel with the Church.

Acts 1:6-8 *'So when they had come together, they asked him, "Lord, will you at this **restore the kingdom to Israel?**" He said to them, "It is not for you to know times or seasons that the Father has fixed by his own authority. But you will receive power when the Holy Spirit has come upon you, and you will be my witnesses in Jerusalem and in all Judea and Samaria, and to the end of the earth."'* ESV

Here, the disciples are speaking to Jesus, in His resurrected form, and they think possibly, now is the time, (or at least soon) that He will defeat the Romans and restore the Kingdom of Israel to its rightful place. In answering the question, Jesus did not, in any way imply that Israel would cease to be a nation. He simply answered their question, by stating, that it wasn't for them to know the times or seasons which the Father has fixed.

The apostles knew that Israel needed to be restored as a Kingdom with her own sovereignty again. They knew from biblical prophecy that this was going to happen and they wanted to know if 'now' was the time. Jesus answers the question by not answering it! *"It is not for you to know times or seasons that the Father **has fixed**...'* Israel has a fixed time of restoration. In other words, God has a date locked in future history when Israel will be finally restored.

CHAPTER SIX

MARCHING ONWARD - ACTS TO ROMANS

The next passage of scripture to look at comes from Acts chapter 3. The context is that a lame beggar has just been healed and can now walk. This, naturally, caused a stir amongst all the people at the Holy Temple. So, Peter being a great evangelist and preacher takes the opportunity to deliver a great sermon to the interested crowd.

Acts 3:19-26 *'Now repent of your sins and turn to God, so that your sins may be wiped away. Then times of refreshment will come from the presence of the Lord, and* **he will again send you Jesus, your appointed Messiah***. For he must remain in heaven until the time* **for the final restoration of all things, as God promised long ago through his holy prophets.** *Moses said, 'The LORD your God will raise up for you a Prophet like me from among your own people. Listen carefully to everything he tells you.' Then Moses said, 'Anyone who will not listen to that Prophet will be completely cut off from God's people.' "Starting with Samuel, every prophet spoke about what is happening today. You are the children of those prophets, and* **you are included in the covenant God promised to your ancestors***. For God said to Abraham, 'Through your descendants all the families on earth will be blessed.' When God raised up his servant, Jesus,* **he sent him first to you people of Israel,** *to bless you by turning each of you back from your sinful ways.'"* NLT

This is a powerful passage of scripture and a great sermon from Peter. It's bold, it's strong, full of conviction and passion. Like all the other passages we have looked at, it is filled with strong covenantal language. There is nothing in this text which implies God has now moved on from Israel. In fact, just the opposite! *'he will again send you Jesus, your appointed Messiah.' (V:19).* In clear language, Peter is addressing the fact that Jesus is the appointed Messiah, whom the Jewish people have been waiting for. He also answers the question, as to when the kingdom would be restored to Israel (Acts 1:6), in verse 21: *'For he (Jesus) must remain in heaven* **until the time for the final** *restoration of all things, as God promised long ago through his holy prophets.'* Where the text states the *'restoration of all things,'* it is referring to, the restoration of Israel and the kingdom of God being established upon the earth, as the Messiah reigns from Mount Zion in Jerusalem. There may be a few from the replacement persuasion, who would argue that, God has now rejected the people of Israel, because they crucified their Messiah. Yet, Peter's sermon gives no hint of this.

Another part of Peter's sermon here in Acts we see very strong covenantal language being used again. *'You are the children of those prophets, and* ***you are included in the covenant God promised to your ancestors.' (V:25).*** The text is very clear, Peter, as the Apostle to the Jews, is imploring his Jewish brothers to accept, that Jesus the Messiah is the fulfillment of the Law and the Prophets, of which they are included, not rejected.

The Apostles Peter and John, went to the temple daily, teaching the doctrine of the resurrection from the dead through Jesus, and so, were arrested by the temple guard. In Acts chapter 4, they are brought before the religious leaders to give an account of their behaviour.

Acts 4:11 *'This Jesus is the stone* ***that was rejected by you, the builders,*** *which has become the cornerstone.'* ESV

This is an interesting verse. Note; it is the religious leaders 'the builders' who rejected the Messiah, not the Jewish people. Having said that, historically, we know that many of them, later, did reject Jesus. That still does not mean that God has rejected the Jewish people any more than He has the Gentiles. I know many Gentiles who have rejected Jesus, but I also know that God has not given up on them. The logic has to swing both ways. You cannot point the finger at the Jewish nation any more, or less than you point it at yourself. Remember it was both Gentiles and Jews that killed Jesus the Messiah, as this was all part of God's ordained, redemptive plan.

Acts 4:27-28 *'"In fact, this has happened here in this very city! For Herod Antipas, Pontius Pilate the governor, the Gentiles, and the people of Israel were all united against Jesus, your holy servant, whom you anointed.   But everything they did was determined beforehand according to your will.'* NLT

Throughout Church history, the Christians have been guilty of a terrible persecution of the Jewish people, including accusing them of 'Deicide' (Murder of God). Yet, the text in Acts is very clear, we are all guilty of putting Jesus to death. If it wasn't for sin, He would not have needed die.   Also, we need to remember, Jesus was not murdered, He went to The Cross as a willing sacrifice, to pay the penalty for our sin. Jesus saved us <u>from</u> God's wrath and saved us <u>to</u> Himself as beloved children.

CHAPTER SEVEN

ROMANS PART ONE

It is now time to start looking at the Letters of Paul in the New Testament. His teaching reveals a great deal of theology regarding Israel, which we need to pay careful attention to and handle with great care.

We now cast our gaze over the incredible book of Romans, focusing upon chapters nine through to eleven. From here on, this book will look more like a commentary, as we take the time to go through important verses line by line.

Romans 9:1-5 *'I am speaking the truth in Christ—I am not lying; my conscience bears me witness in the Holy Spirit—that I have great sorrow and unceasing anguish in my heart. For I could wish that I myself were accursed and cut off from Christ for the sake of my brothers, my kinsmen according to the flesh. They are Israelites, and to them belong the adoption, the glory, the covenants, the giving of the law, the worship, and the promises. To them belong the patriarchs, and from their race, according to the flesh, is the Christ, who is God over all, blessed forever. Amen.'* ESV

Here, we see the heart-felt anguish of the apostle Paul for his own people, Israel. Paul was a Jew from the tribe of Benjamin, a Pharisee and studied under Rabbi Gamaliel. He was an incredible intellect, skilled in both Greek and Hebrew. Yet, Paul readily laid aside his knowledge and culture, as they would not benefit him, in his calling as the apostle to the Gentiles. However, we continue to see, throughout his letters, that Paul never gave up his Jewishness. To have been sent to the Gentiles and still have a heart for his own people must have been hard for him. He was very often misunderstood by his own kind and at the same time, perplexing to the Gentiles. Paul truly had, a difficult calling, that few today could ever really understand. He loved the Gentiles, yet loved Israel.

In the opening verses of Romans 9, Paul tells us that he would willingly go as far as giving up his salvation for the sake of his own kinsmen, according to the flesh. Now, we need to pay attention to Paul's language; when he says, *'according to the flesh,'* he is referring to the natural race of the Jewish people, not those who are now born again believers in Jesus. He has a passion, zeal and love for his own kinfolk and so desires them to know their Messiah.

Paul then lists the credentials of the Jewish people. Bearing in mind he knows that his audience is going to be mostly Gentile.

Romans 9:4-5: '*They are Israelites, and to them belong the adoption, the glory, the covenants, the giving of the law, the worship, and the promises. To them belong the patriarchs, and from their race, according to the flesh, is the Christ, who is God over all, blessed forever. Amen.'* ESV

The Jewish people have a wonderful culture and a timeless legacy. They are the people with whom God chose to make covenant. He gave them the Torah, (Law) the prophets, and the 'Writings'. Even the Messiah, Jesus, came from the Jews as a people group. Paul could see their wonderful heritage, but he also saw many of them rejecting Jesus, which troubled him a great deal. To come so close to redemption, with all the covenants and the Law, yet to miss it in respect of the Messiah, must have broken Paul's heart.

We are now starting to move into the wonderfully deep waters of Pauline theology. If you find them hard to understand, then rest assured, even the apostle Peter makes a comment about Paul's teachings:

2 Peter 3:16 *'speaking of these things in all of his letters. Some of his comments are hard to understand, and those who are ignorant and unstable have twisted his letters to mean something quite different, just as they do with other parts of Scripture. And this will result in their destruction.'* NLT

So, as we continue in Romans 9, we come to verse 6, a very telling statement:

'But it is not as though the word of God has failed. ***For they are not all Israel who are descended from Israel;'*** ESV

This verse is a tricky one and can be interpreted in several ways. The text leads into a discussion about true Israel and natural Israel. True Israel being those who are of the faith of Abraham, i.e. those who have a living faith in Jesus, and natural Israel are those who are just born Jewish.

It is this verse that may lead the replacement camp to speculate that the Church is now the new 'Spiritual Israel', thus the true Israel of God. Now here, I have to be honest and admit that there is some truth to this statement. Paul validates this in other scriptures.

Ephesians 2:12- *'In those days you (Gentiles) were living apart from Christ. You were excluded from citizenship among the people of Israel, and you did not know the covenant promises God had made to them. You lived in this world without God and without hope. But now you have been united with Christ Jesus. Once you were far away from God, but now you have been brought near to him through the blood of Christ. For Christ himself has brought peace to us. He united Jews and Gentiles into one people when, in his own body on the cross, he broke down the wall of hostility that separated us.'* NLT

Although this text can be interpreted to mean, that all who believe in Jesus, through faith, are the true Israel, I think contextually, Paul is still talking about Israel the people group, not the Church. The reason I say this, is because the verses continue with Jewish ideas and Paul gives a clear differentiation between Jew and Gentile throughout this chapter. So, in short, Paul is stating, that not everyone who goes to church is saved; not everyone born a Jew, is a true Jew of the Faith.

The next statement Paul makes is even more difficult to fathom, as we get into theological terms such as election, covenant and

48

predestination. Many have pondered over these verses and have come to various conclusions. Personally, I think the following verses do lead to a more predestined will and choice of God, than not.

Romans 9:10-14 *'And not only this, but there was Rebekah also, when she had conceived twins by one man, our father Isaac; for though the twins were **not yet born and had not done anything good or bad, so that God's purpose according to His choice would stand, not because of works but because of Him who calls,** it was said to her, "THE OLDER WILL SERVE THE YOUNGER." Just as it is written, "JACOB I LOVED, BUT ESAU I HATED." What shall we say then? There is no injustice with God, is there? May it never be!'* NASB

Paul is clearly talking about the Jewish people and is now bringing up the concept of God's choice and election. God chose Jacob even before he had done anything good or bad, so that God's purpose according to His choice, would stand. In other words, God gets to choose those upon whom He wants to show mercy. This is borne out as consistent with other passages. Our salvation is based on God's choice and His work, not our works of the flesh. The only choice we get, is to say 'yes' or 'no.'

John 6:44 *'**For no one** can come to me unless the Father who sent me **draws them to me**, and at the last day I will raise them up.'* ESV

Romans 9:14-16 *'Are we saying, then, that God was unfair? Of course not! For God said to Moses, "I will show mercy to anyone I choose, and I will show compassion to anyone I choose." **So it is God who decides to show mercy. We can neither choose it nor work for it.'*** NLT

Ephesians 2:8 *'For by grace you have been saved through faith. And this is not your own doing; **it is the gift of God,**'* ESV

Romans 9:18 *'So you see, **God chooses** to show mercy to some, and he chooses to harden the hearts of others so they refuse to listen.'* NLT

Acts 13:48 *'When the Gentiles heard this, they were very glad and thanked the Lord for his message; and all who **were chosen** for eternal life became believers.'* NLT

I will be honest with you, these scriptures make for tough reading and raise some very deep questions. Suffice to say, Paul is laying a theological frame work. The Just lived by faith in the Old Covenant just as much as we now live by faith in the New Covenant. We are never saved by following rules. We are justified by faith alone, and even that faith is a gift from God. Paul brings this out in more detail in the following verses.

Romans 9:23-24 *'He does this to make the riches of his glory shine even brighter on those to whom he shows mercy, **who were prepared in advance for glory. And we are among those whom he selected, both from the Jews and from the Gentiles**.'* NLT

Now, whether, you like predestination or not, one thing is apparent in these verses, God is electing and predestining both Jew and Gentile to salvation. So again, God has not forsaken His covenant people.

In the subsequent verses in Romans, Paul starts to compare the Gentiles with the remnant of Israel, being saved, in a comparative side by side approach.

Romans 9:25-26 *'Concerning the Gentiles, God says in the prophecy of Hosea, "Those **who were not my people**, I will now call **my people**. And I will love those whom I did not love before." And, "Then, at the place where they were told, 'You are not my people,' there they will be called '**children of the living God.**'"* NLT

This is a wonderful scripture in Romans, which is a re-quote from the Old Testament book of Hosea. Paul is stating that God would call a people, who are not His people, and make them His own children. This is God's work of redemption to the Gentiles. Now, Paul in the next few verses wants to focus back to the Jewish people.

Romans 9:27-29 *'And concerning Israel, Isaiah the prophet cried out, "Though the people of Israel are as numerous as the sand of the seashore, **only a remnant will be saved**. For the LORD will carry out his sentence upon the earth quickly and with finality." And Isaiah said the same thing in another place: "**If the LORD of Heaven's Armies had not spared a few of our children**, we would have been wiped out like Sodom, destroyed like Gomorrah."'* NLT

These verses, like most re-quotes, can have dual meanings. Paul is using an Old Testament prophecy to state that a small number of natural Israel have been predestined to salvation. This small predestined number of Jews is known as the Remnant. These verses, also, have an eschatological meaning.

From many of the prophetic writings a picture emerges, that prior to the Day of the Lord, there will be a huge war against Israel in the Middle East. Israel will be scattered to the surrounding nations of Jordan, Syria, Babylon etc. At some stage during this war the Messiah will return and the physical remnant of Israel that remain alive, will recognise the Messiah as their saviour. So, we can see these verses have dual prophetic aspects to them. Also, prior to the Day of the Lord, possibly during the great invasion against Israel, there will be a spiritual revival in Israel:

Joel 2:28-32 *'"It will come about after this That I will pour out My Spirit on all mankind; And your sons and daughters will prophesy, Your old men will dream dreams, Your young men will see visions. "Even on the male and female servants I will pour out My Spirit in those days. "I will display wonders in the sky and on the earth, Blood, fire and columns of smoke. "The sun will be turned into darkness And the moon into blood **Before the great and awesome day of the LORD** comes. "**And it will come about that whoever calls on the name of the LORD Will be delivered; For on Mount Zion and in Jerusalem***

There will be those who escape, *As the LORD has said,* ***Even among the survivors (The Remnant KJV) whom the LORD calls.***

The prophet Joel's famous prophecy was only partially fulfilled in the book of Acts. The full context of this passage will be fulfilled, just prior to the Day of the Lord, when Jesus returns. This prophecy, although generic to Gentiles is also specific to Israel. This again, shows God's plan for His people Israel. God has not done away with Israel. God is faithful to the promises he made to Abraham and David.

It is interesting as we conclude Romans Chapter 9, that Paul states how Israel 'missed it' with God. It was not because of rebellion or disobedience. Rather, they were no longer being justified by faith, like Abraham. They had become locked into a wrong way of thinking. They thought they could justify themselves through legalistic observance to the Torah (Law of Moses). The truth is that only God can justify and make us righteous, not ourselves. The only way to obtain justification and God given/imputed righteousness is, simply, by faith alone.

Romans 9:30-33 *'What does all this mean? Even though the Gentiles were not trying to follow God's standards, they were made right (righteous) with God. And it was **by faith** that this took place. But the people of Israel, who tried so hard to get right (righteous) with God by keeping the law, never succeeded. Why not? Because they were trying to get right (righteous and justified) with God **by keeping the law instead of by trusting in him (by faith)**. They stumbled over the great rock (Jesus) in their path. God warned them of this in the Scriptures when he said, "I am placing a stone in Jerusalem that makes people stumble, a rock that makes them fall. But anyone who trusts in him (believes in Him by faith) will never be disgraced."*
NLT (My parenthesis added to make the text even clearer).

For those not sure what 'being justified' means, it is a legal term. To be 'made just' or 'justified' means, that the judge declares you to be innocent of all charges against you. Only God, through the

52

substitutionary sacrifice of His Son Jesus, can cleanse us of all sin allowing us to be declared justified, innocent and free from the death penalty. Thus, there is no condemnation for those in Christ Jesus.

2 Corinthians 5:21 *'He made Him who knew no sin to be sin on our behalf, so that we might become the righteousness of God in Him.'* NASB

Romans 8:1 *'Therefore there is now no condemnation for those who are in Christ Jesus.'* NASB

When we understand that we are justified by faith in Christ alone, we understand Paul's issues with the Jewish people. They were trying to justify themselves and be made righteous by observing a set of laws, and not by their faith in Him.

This leads to an obvious question. "If you cannot be justified by observing the Law, but only by faith, why even obey the Law?" Simple. Jesus sums it up in John 14:15 *"'If you love me, obey my commandments.'* NLT

Obedience to God and His Word must always come first from a place of love and faith. You cannot put the cart before the horse on this issue. It is God who justifies us, not our good deeds. We do good deeds in response to the fact that He first loved us and so now, we in return, love Him.

We see this beautifully illustrated in the story of the woman caught in the very act of adultery. She was brought before Jesus to see what He would do; because according to the Law, both she and the man involved would have to be stoned to death. Jesus then responded by stating, "he who has never sinned can throw the first stone." In other words, only Jesus was the One worthy to throw the stone, but look what He says to the woman…

John 8:10-11 *'Then Jesus stood up again and said to the woman, "Where are your accusers? Didn't even one of them condemn you?"*

"No, Lord," she said. And Jesus said, **"Neither do I. Go and sin no more."** NLT

Jesus shows compassion to the woman by saving her from certain death. He shows her mercy, love and forgiveness; but then comes the key. *"Go and sin no more."* It's the love of God that leads us to the Law of God. It's the grace of God that empowers us to live the righteous life. We receive the righteousness Jesus clothed us in, by faith. The faith that gives us the robes of righteousness is a gift from God.

Ephesians 2:8 *'For by grace you have been saved through faith; and that not of yourselves, it is the gift of God;'* NASB

So, no man can boast in his works to get saved. We are saved by grace through faith. We are justified by faith, not obedience. We are sanctified by His Spirit and the fruit of our sanctification is obedience. Don't ever confuse sanctification with justification. This is where the Jews and many Christians have made a serious error. Justification is always by faith. We are obedient from the place of being justified by His love and then we choose to live the sanctified life (being set apart for God) by co-operating with God's Spirit to live a life yielded to His word.

Paul confirms this thinking in Romans 3:31.

'Well then, if we emphasise faith, does this mean that we can forget about the law? Of course not! In fact, only when we have faith do we truly fulfil the law.' NLT

CHAPTER EIGHT

ROMANS PART TWO

I live and minister on the south coast of England, which happens to be a hotbed of replacement theology. Having been a pastor for a while, I get to hear some outlandish things that go on in God's house (the Church). I have probably been guilty of committing a few outlandish and unpopular things myself! However, when I hear accounts of Christians asking their church leaders if they can pray for Israel and be told 'NO!' I find this, frankly, bizarre and a little disturbing. If it was voiced that Christians wanted to form a group to pray for the Palestinians, I can rest assured that the answer would be a 'yes' and rightly so. If it had been raised that a group of Welsh Christians wanted to pray for Wales, yet again there likely would have been no problem, if not a few chuckles behind closed doors, but why no to Israel?

The issue of Israel really does cause a 'niggle' to the flesh with many and there are several reasons why the reaction is so acute. As a pastor, I often have to ask myself, why I react emotionally to certain situations and why I suddenly feel threatened and insecure in particular conversations. Very often I find that my reactions are down to incorrect assumptions, lack of knowledge or just good old-fashioned insecurity.

So, we can see why church leaders sometimes embargo prayer meetings for the Nation of Israel. Let's see what the Apostle Paul has to say on this subject.

Romans 10:1 *'Dear brothers and sisters, the longing of my heart and my prayer to God is for the people of Israel to be saved.'* NLT

There's an old saying, "If it's good enough for Paul then it's good enough for me." There are a good handful of passages that encourage us to pray for Israel, but the majority come from the Old

Testament. So, if we are dealing with people who are 'New Testament only' Christians, we should only quote New Testament verses in fairness to them. The verse from Romans 10:1 is a pretty good one to quote, because it clearly shows the apostle Paul's heart for his own people. He is, clearly, not praying for a "Spiritual Israel," he is earnestly desiring the salvation of his own kinsmen the Jewish Nation of Israel.

Romans Chapter ten now takes us into the wonderful theology of 'salvation by faith' alone, verses 'works' based self- salvation of which Israel was guilty. I would just like to make it very clear here, that you can be just as much a legalist in the New Testament as you could in the Old. In the Law of Moses there are 613 commandments but did you know that in the Messianic Covenant (New Covenant) there are 1,050 commandments. So, the number is not the issue. The real issue is a motivation by faith, in the 'heart' of the believer, and not legalistic observance. We need to be very careful, that we do not look down on the Jewish nation of the past. Christians struggle as much today with legalism as do the Jews.

Habakkuk 2:4 *'Look, his ego is inflated; he is without integrity. **But the righteous one will live by his faith**.'* HCSB

Romans 10:2-4 *'I can testify about them that they have zeal for God, but not according to knowledge. Because they disregarded the righteousness from God and **attempted to establish their own righteousness**, they have not submitted themselves to God's righteousness. For Christ is **the end of the law** for righteousness to everyone who believes.'* HCSB

Now, if you are sharp enough, you may have spotted a problem with the Romans 10 text. There is nothing wrong with the text from a translation point of view, but there is a seeming contradiction here. *'**For Christ is the end of the law** for righteousness to everyone who believes.'* Jesus stated in Matthew 5:17 that He did not come to abolish or do away with the Law. So, how can the same Jesus who spoke those words now claim to be the end of the Law? This isn't

56

really a problem or a contradiction if we take some time in examining the Matthew and Romans passages closely. Remember, Jesus said that scripture cannot be broken (John 10:35).

Matthew 5:17 *'"Do not think that I have come to abolish the Law or the Prophets;* **I have not come to abolish them but to fulfil them***.'* ESV

In Matthew 5:17 Jesus says He came to fulfil the Law (the Torah) and the prophets, and not do away with them. Let's take a look at the Greek word 'fulfill' to get a better picture of what Jesus was saying. The word is *'Playro-o.'* It means to satisfy, finish the task, accomplish, to make complete, render to perfection, to fulfil and be obeyed as it should be. So let's put this together and amplify the Matthew 5:17 text.

'Do not think that I have come to abolish the Law or the Prophets; I have not come to abolish them, but to satisfy, to fulfil and obey it as it should be and thus fulfil the righteous requirements of the law.

Now, let's take a closer look at Romans 10:4.

'For Christ is the **end** *of the law for righteousness to everyone who believes.'*

The Greek word for *'end'* is *'Telos,'* this is from the word *'Tello,'* The word, basically, means the goal or target. This puts a different meaning on the term '**end** of the law.' A better rendering of this passage would be *'Jesus the Messiah is the* **goal and target** *of the law for righteousness to everyone who believes via faith.'*

I like the way the CJB puts it. *'For* **the goal** *at which the Torah aims is the Messiah, who offers righteousness to everyone who trusts.'*

I want to make it very clear here, I have no agenda to bend the text to make it say something I want it to say. We know that scripture cannot be broken and cannot contradict itself, so although the verses we looked at do seem to contradict one another, a simple look at the Greek will iron out the seeming contradiction. We now end up with a slightly different view point, to the one that we, perhaps, started with.

In Romans 10:5-6 we see two kinds of righteousness being paralleled. The righteousness through observance of the Torah (Law), or the righteousness obtained via faith.

*'For Moses writes that **the law's way** of making a person right with God requires obedience to all of its commands. But **faith's way** of getting right with God says, "Don't say in your heart, 'Who will go up to heaven?' (to bring Christ down to earth).'*

Verse 10 *'If you confess with your mouth that Jesus is Lord and believe in your heart that God raised him from the dead, you will be saved.'* NLT

The New Living Translation renders this very clearly: The Law's way of making a person righteous is by complete observance of it. However, faith's way is about simply believing. The principle applies to both Jew and Gentile. We are only ever justified by faith, one is never justified by Torah observance; indeed, it is impossible to do so. Only one Man, who was God incarnate, managed to fulfil the Torah and obtain it's righteousness for us.

2 Corinthians 5:21 *'For our sake he (God) made him (Jesus) to be sin who knew no sin, so that in him **we might become the righteousness of God.'*** ESV My Parenthesis added to help with the context of the text.

Because of the death and resurrection of Jesus Christ, we are now clothed in His garments of righteousness. When God looks upon us He no longer sees us as 'old sinners'. He now sees His son and His righteousness in, and upon us. This is how we can come boldly to the throne of grace. We need to be as righteous as God, to come into His Holy presence; this is a part of the wonderful work He did for us on the cross.

Hebrews 4:16 *'Let us then with confidence draw near to the throne of grace, that we may receive mercy and find grace to help in time of need.'* ESV

One may well be asking what all this has to do with the biblical importance of Israel. This book's title is *'The biblical importance of Israel **and everything else that goes with it**.'!* This book has already established the fact that Israel is still significant to the plans and purposes of God. However, if we consider Israel and her people, we then have to address all the issues and baggage that goes along with them. When I say baggage, I am referring to all the odd and crazy extremes that Christians can end up entangled in!

The next interesting verse we will look at is Romans 10:12-13

'For there is no distinction between Jew and Greek; for the same Lord is Lord of all, bestowing his riches on all who call on him. For "everyone who calls on the name of the Lord will be saved."' ESV

Now, someone from a replacement background may state that there is no distinction between Jew and Gentile, thus, God is no more interested in the Jew than the Gentiles.

What this verse actually shows, is that there is no favouritism. The Jews, even with their birth-right and legacy of history, still have to believe in Jesus by faith, the same as the Gentiles. In other words, there is no backdoor or special dispensation to salvation if you are Jewish. God treats all alike in this matter. To be justified before God has to be by faith in Jesus. Israel has not been replaced or done away with, but, in respect to faith, she is now on a level playing field with the Gentiles. Let's not forget, however, that Paul makes a very clear distinction between Jew and Gentile.

Romans 1:16 *'For I am not ashamed of this Good News about Christ. It is the power of God at work, saving everyone who believes--**the Jew first** and also the Gentile.'* NLT

God offers His rewards of salvation to the Jew first and then to the Gentile. That statement may offend some, but it's only fair. The Jewish people have been in covenant with God for a long, long time, and most Gentiles have never had any covenant with God. It stands to reason that He will offer His rewards, first, to those whose forefathers were the prophets and patriarchs. However, this also works in reverse:

Romans 2:9 *'There will be trouble and calamity for everyone who keeps on doing what is evil--for the Jew first and also for the Gentile.'* NLT

One thing I have found to be true is that, whatever argument we try to apply to the Jew, we will also have to apply to the Gentile. This works both positively and negatively. So, when we state that God abandoned the Jewish nation because she rejected God, we then have to apply that statement to ourselves as Gentiles. It cannot work just one way. If God abandoned the Jewish nation as replacement theologians state, then God will also abandon a faithless Church, who no longer follows in the teachings prescribed in scripture. If God is a covenant breaker to Israel, then you can bet your last dollar that God will break His covenant with the Gentile Church! The good news is that God is in no way a covenant breaker! When we are faithless, He is faithful. God will never abandon His church and He will never abandon Israel.

Romans 10:18-21 *'But I ask, have the people of Israel actually heard the message? Yes, they have: "The message has gone throughout the earth, and the words to all the world." But I ask, did the people of Israel really understand? Yes, they did, for even in the time of Moses, God said, "I will rouse your jealousy through people who are not even a nation. I will provoke your anger through the foolish Gentiles." And later Isaiah spoke boldly for God, saying, "I was found by people who were not looking for me. I showed myself to those who were not asking for me." But regarding Israel, God said, "All day long I*

60

opened my arms to them, but they were disobedient and rebellious."'
NLT

This is a really exciting passage of scripture. Again, the replacement camp may use this scripture to justify the notion that Israel was given a chance and they blew it; so now God chooses the Gentiles instead. However, there are some things to consider here before we jump to any conclusions. God is now using the Gentiles to provoke Israel to jealousy. Why? because He wants them to see what they are missing. Why? So, they will accept Jesus as their Messiah. Why? So that all the Law and the Prophets can be fulfilled in their lives. Let's be honest here, Israel were disobedient and rebellious and yes, they rejected the Gospel of salvation through Yeshua (Jesus). So, is it game over for Israel? Has Paul stated that Israel have gone their own way and its over for them? No! Look at the very next verse in Romans 11:1.

'I ask, then, **has God rejected his own people, the nation of Israel? Of course not!** *I myself am an Israelite, a descendant of Abraham and a member of the tribe of Benjamin.'*

I could end this book right here on this verse alone. God has not rejected His own people, the nation of Israel. It's right there in black and white. This verse alone ends the argument positively, about the biblical importance of Israel, and as well, raises more questions to answer! Such as: What is God's plan for Israel, how does the New Covenant fit into this, what are the issues of Law and Grace? Why does the apostle Paul affirm the Law then seemingly speak of it in a negative light, why is the letter to Galatians so seemingly anti-Jewish? These are all good questions, and will be looked at in the next few chapters.

It's now time to look at one of the most fascinating chapters of the New Testament, Romans chapter eleven.

CHAPTER NINE

ROMANS PART THREE

We established at the end of the previous chapter that God has not finished with His people Israel. Equally in Romans 11, the Apostle Paul gives another teaching that is both challenging and difficult to understand. Our best response, is to just accept that Paul really did know what he was talking about! He was moving then, in a realm of revelation from the Holy Spirit, that few people will ever have the privilege or burden to carry.

Paul gives us his view, in no uncertain terms, regarding the whole rejection issue, in Romans 11 verse 1, and sets the tone for the whole chapter:

'I ask, then, **has God rejected his own people, the nation of Israel?** *Of course not! I myself am an Israelite, a descendant of Abraham and a member of the tribe of Benjamin.' NLT*

Paul now continues his discourse, regarding the people of Israel and how a remnant has been chosen by God's grace. In verse two he re-clarifies that God has not done away with Israel:

Romans 11:2: *'God has not rejected his people whom he foreknew. Do you not know what the Scripture says of Elijah, how he appeals to God against Israel?'* ESV

If any Christian is still persuaded by the replacement position, then they are going to have to do some pretty clever exegesis to get around these two verses in Romans 11! The golden rule is that scripture cannot be broken.

In the next few verses Paul addresses some challenging concepts. God has chosen to save a remnant of Israel *by* His grace whilst hardening the hearts of others *to* His grace.

Romans 11:2-8 *'**God has not rejected his people** whom he foreknew. Do you not know what the Scripture says of Elijah, how he appeals to God against Israel? "Lord, they have killed your prophets, they have demolished your altars, and I alone am left, and they seek my life." But what is God's reply to him? "I have kept for myself seven thousand men who have not bowed the knee to Baal."* **So too at the present time there is a remnant, chosen by grace**. *But if it is by grace,* **it is no longer on the basis of works;** *otherwise grace would no longer be grace. What then?* **Israel failed to obtain what it was seeking. The elect obtained it, but the rest were hardened,** *as it is written, "***God gave them** *a spirit of stupor, eyes that would not see and ears that would not hear, down to this very day."* ESV

As we read through these verses, we realise that God has chosen and elected some, within Israel, to salvation and others He has hardened. The obvious question is, why? We will look at Paul's answer later, but for now let's look at the key elements. Firstly, God has not rejected His people Israel. Secondly, God has chosen a remnant at this present time by His grace to receive salvation. Thirdly, God has hardened the hearts of many Jewish people to not receive the Gospel.

Romans 11:11 *'**I ask then, why did they stumble so as to lose their share? Absolutely not!** However, because of their trespass, salvation has come to the Gentiles to make Israel jealous.'* Berean Study Bible

Here in verse 11, Paul states again for the third time, in this chapter, that Israel have not been cast off and rejected. They have been hardened as a consequence of trying to justify themselves, through legalistic observance of the Law and in rejecting their Messiah. So, like it or not, Israel's hardening has been a blessing and a benefit to the Gentiles, but remember, just because they are hardened for a season of time, does not mean they have been replaced. Infact, Paul goes on to say in verses 12 and 13, that, if the hardening of Israel benefits and enriches the Gentiles, how much more blessed will the Gentiles be when they, Israel, are fully included again.

Romans 11:12,13   *'Now if their trespass means riches for the world, and if their failure means riches for the Gentiles,* **how much more will their full inclusion mean!'**
'For if their rejection means the reconciliation of the world, **what will their acceptance mean but life from the dead?'** ESV

Now we turn to the following verses in Romans 11, which speak of the gentiles, being grafted into the Olive Tree.

Romans 11:16-18   *'And since Abraham and the other patriarchs were holy, their descendants will also be holy--just as the entire batch of dough is holy because the portion given as an offering is holy.* **For if the roots of the tree are holy, the branches will be,** *too. But some of these branches from Abraham's tree--***some of the people of Israel--have been broken off. And you Gentiles**, *who were branches from a wild olive tree,* **have been grafted in**. *So now you also receive the blessing God has promised Abraham and his children, sharing in the rich nourishment from the root of God's special olive tree.* **But you must not brag about being grafted in to replace the branches that were broken off. You are just a branch, not the root.'** NLT

I chose to use the New Living Translation here, as it expounds clearly the underlying theology of being "grafted in." As said before, it is extremely important to understand which covenant we have been grafted into, that being, the Abrahamic covenant. There is no mention anywhere in the New Testament, that we have been grafted into the Mosaic covenant. This is a very important distinction, emphasised by Paul in his letters to the Romans and Galatians, and will help us understand some of the questions pertaining to Law and Grace, that will be answered in a later chapter.

The Olive Tree mentioned here, is both Israel as a people, and the covenants which underpin them. The root of the tree is specifically the Abrahamic covenant. The branches are the people.

Now, because of the severity and goodness of God (Romans 11:22), some of the natural branches have been cut off, to make room, for the

64

grafting in of branches from the wild olive tree. We (Gentiles) by nature, are not supposed to be grafted into the natural tree, but because of God's goodness, He has permitted us to be included into the covenants of Israel. Now, as mentioned in previous chapters, God always intended to bring the nations, the Gentiles, to salvation, through the Jewish people. Salvation comes from the Jewish nation, as Jesus said to the woman of Samaria.

John 4:22 *'You [Samaritans] do not know what you worship; we [Jews] do know what we worship, for salvation is from the Jews.'* AMP

Back to Romans 11, I see a passage of scripture, often overlooked, which is incredible in all that it offers to the Gentiles.

Romans 11:17: *But some of these branches from Abraham's tree-- some of the people of Israel--have been broken off. And you Gentiles, who were branches from a wild olive tree, have been grafted in.* ***So now you also receive the blessing God has promised Abraham and his children***, *sharing in the rich nourishment from the root of God's special olive tree.* NLT

So, because we are grafted into the root of the tree, we now have access to the wonderful Abrahamic covenant and all its incredible blessings. If more Christians paid attention to all that is contained in the Abrahamic blessing, I am sure there would be a greater degree of appreciation and thankfulness to God for His Jewish people and the covenants. To be ignorant, or disconnected from the understanding of the Abrahamic covenant, is like chopping off your leg and trying to run. It breaks my heart that I myself and much of Christendom, have been robbed of the full understanding of this blessing. Sadly, this is the fruit of replacement theology, evident in much of the Church today.

Paul continues by encouraging the Gentiles, that, in Christ, they have equal rights to the covenant, then warns them against becoming arrogant and proud against the Jew.

Romans 11:18   *'**But you must not brag about being grafted in to replace the branches that were broken off. You are just a branch, not the root.**'* NLT

Romans 11:18   *'Do not boast over the branches and pride yourself at their expense. If you do boast and feel superior, remember it is not you that supports the root, but the root [that supports] you.'*   AMP

Romans 11:20-21   *'They were broken (pruned) off because of their unbelief (their lack of real faith), and you are established through faith [because you do believe].   So do not become proud and conceited, but rather **stand in awe and be reverently afraid**. For if God did not spare the natural branches [because of unbelief], **neither will He spare you** [if you are guilty of the same offence].* AMP

Paul then, gives a warning that is simply not taken seriously enough in today's Christian church:

Romans 11:22 *'Consider therefore the **kindness   sternness** of God: sternness to those who fell, but kindness to you, provided that you continue in his kindness. **Otherwise, you also will be cut off.**'* NIV

I would not even dare to surmise what "the Gentiles being cut off" would look like, but I know enough that I shudder at the thought! We may like to use all manner of theology to soften the blow of this passage, but what if it actually means what it says! After all, God did cut off some of the Jewish people before, so why not the Gentiles? This passage shows us the kindness of God toward the Gentiles, as a result of His sternness to the Jewish people, but this will not be forever, they will be grafted in again.

Romans 11:24 *'You, by nature, were a branch cut from a wild olive tree. So, if God was willing to do something contrary to nature by grafting you into his cultivated tree, **he will be far more eager to graft the original branches back into the tree where they belong.**'* NLT

66

God is eager and wanting for His chosen people Israel to come back into covenant with Him. God has deliberately hardened them, so that the Gentiles can be grafted in. Herein lies a mystery: when the fulness of the Gentiles has come in, then all Israel shall be saved.

Romans 11:25-26 *'I do not want you to be ignorant of this **mystery**, brothers and sisters, so that you may not be conceited: Israel has experienced a hardening in part until the full number of the Gentiles has come in, and **in this way all Israel will be saved**. As it is written: "The deliverer will come from Zion; he will turn godlessness away from Jacob.'* NIV

Romans 11:29 is a well- known verse often quoted for various reasons.

'For the gifts and the calling of God are irrevocable.' ESV

However, the primary context of the verse is regarding Israel. When God calls and elects, His calling becomes irrevocable. His promises to the patriarchs are everlasting and will not be revoked.

Romans 11:28 *'Many of the people of Israel are now enemies of the Good News, and this benefits you Gentiles. Yet they are still the people he loves because he chose their ancestors Abraham, Isaac, and Jacob.'* NLT

Paul wonderfully concludes his argument with this parallel: Israel's disobedience resulted in the Gentiles being shown mercy through the Jewish Messiah, Jesus Christ. Now, in turn, Gentile believers in Christ, are able to show the same mercy back to Israel, so that together we may all receive God's mercy.

Romans 11:30-31 *'Once, you Gentiles were rebels against God, but when the people of Israel rebelled against him, God was merciful to you instead. Now they are the rebels, and God's mercy has come to you so that they, too, will share in God's mercy.'* NLT

CHAPTER TEN

Knock! Knock!

With a twist of historical irony, the issues that the first century church had to face, were actually to do with the biblical relevance of the Gentiles. The initial first century church was Jewish. As we have seen, all the believers were Jewish, the apostles were Jewish, everyone was Jewish! All was kosher, until the day the apostle Peter had a vision described in Acts Chapter 10, when a group of Gentiles knocked at his door! A whole new chapter for the early church subsequently ensued, causing all manner of problems that needed to be addressed. Letters were written to various congregations, giving instructions and teachings for all believers on how they were to behave, as well as warnings about heresy and incorrect teaching.

To understand the epistle to the Galatians, which we will look at in Chapter 12, we will find that initially it seems quite anti-Jewish; we need to grasp the historical backdrop as to why the epistle was written and what it was warning against. Without this knowledge, we can easily slip into error.

Often, as I have had discussions within Jewish communities, I have noted that many were not so offended by Jesus as I would have thought. Some even acknowledged Him to be a good Torah observant Jew. The problem they had, was with the apostle Paul, who, from a Jewish perspective, seemed to be offensively anti-Jewish and even the one responsible for starting a new religion. This, we know, is not the case.

In this chapter I will address some of the questions often asked about Paul; and will set in place the historical backdrop, so we can understand the issues and problems, which the early church encountered and had to deal with. Hopefully, this will also dispel the romantic myth that somehow the early church got it right all of the time. Sadly, like us today, they also made many mistakes! They had problems, just as we do, with our schisms, divisions and doctrines.

KNOCK KNOCK!

The church in Jerusalem was flourishing, and although persecution was growing, many Jewish people were coming to recognise Jesus as their Messiah. Miracles, signs and wonders were aplenty, and all was going well until the apostle Peter's vision and the subsequent knock at the door. Little did anyone realise what this would lead to! That simple vision and knock at the door would lead to the birth of the Gentile church, which now spans the globe and has influenced much of history in the last 2000 years. What a difference a day makes!

The account is recorded In Acts chapter 10. Cornelius, a Roman army officer, living in Caesarea, had an alarming vision of an angel. The angel gave him the name and address of Simon Peter and told Cornelius to summon him. So, he sent a household slave and a military aid, to go find Peter's abode and ask him over for a polite chat, cup of tea and a fig roll!

Meanwhile, the apostle Peter is taking it easy and praying on the roof of the house, when suddenly he goes into a trance.

Acts 10:10-16 *'And he became hungry and wanted something to eat, but while they were preparing it, he fell into a trance and saw the heavens opened and something like a great sheet descending, being let down by its four corners upon the earth. In it were all kinds of animals and reptiles and birds of the air. And there came a voice to him: "Rise, Peter; kill and eat." But Peter said, "By no means, Lord; for I have never eaten anything that is* **common** *or* **unclean**.*" And the voice came to him again a second time,* **"What God has made clean, do not call common."** *This happened three times, and the thing was taken up at once to heaven.'* ESV

This is an interesting verse to look at, because there is far more going on here than meets the eye. Most commentators state, that God was speaking to Peter only in respect of Gentiles and food. This is not exactly true. The Greek text is quite clear on this and even the English translation alludes to it. The issue is not about what is 'unclean', but what is 'common'. The voice says to Peter very clearly to not call 'common' that which has been made 'clean'. So what does all this mean?

The animals shown in the vision were all unclean and forbidden according to the Torah. The word for 'unclean' in the Greek is *'akathartos.'* It directly correlates to the Greek Old Testament rendering, when referring to unclean foods as prescribed in Leviticus chapter 11.

The other word of interest is the word 'common.' In the Greek text 'common,' is rendered 'koinos', which simply means 'that which is common.' It was never used biblically in the context of something being unclean. However, there is historical evidence that shows the pharisaical traditions stated that something clean can be rendered 'common' if touched by something unclean. The thinking in the days of Jesus was that the Gentiles were 'common' and even 'unclean' because they ate and touched things which were forbidden by the Torah. Thus, the Pharisees taught that to stay ritually pure, a Jew had to not only stay away from that which was 'unclean', but also from that which was 'common'. This is why Peter states in the vision, that he had never eaten anything 'common' or 'unclean.' What is interesting is the answer Peter receives from the voice.

Acts 10:15 *'And the voice came to him again a second time, "**What God has made clean, do not call <u>common</u>.**"'*

The Voice has nothing to say about that which is forbidden, only that which is 'common'. Thus, God is nullifying the teaching of the pharisees, not the Torah. The full implications of this are then revealed when two Gentiles knock at the door. That being, Gentiles are not to be called 'common' when they have been made 'clean'.

So, what about dietary laws? For the Jew, God ONLY expects them to not eat that which is forbidden by Torah. Anything else added to Torah, by additional food laws, is actually going beyond Torah and into the traditions of men. So, the vision is stating, that Jews can eat all kinds of common food, however, they are still not allowed to eat forbidden food as prescribed by Torah. So, there is some truth to the idea of dietary laws changing, but it had more to do with the tradition of the elders, than the Torah.

Another misunderstanding is in Mark's gospel, where Jesus declares all foods 'clean' (see Mark 7:2 & 18). Please note, He is not referring to the dietary laws as prescribed by the Torah. The context of the passage is regarding the washing of hands in a way prescribed by the Pharisees. The tradition is, that if Jews did not wash their hands in a certain way, then the food would become either 'common' or 'unclean'. Jesus was stating that neither was true; and thus, declared all food allowed in the Torah, would remain 'clean' irrespective of whether they washed their hands or not.

Now, some people may find all this a little disturbing. If Jesus had declared all food 'clean', in the way we would understand, then Jesus would have been stoned by the Jews for being an apostate! We know Jesus did not break the Law, He fulfilled it. The only laws He did break, were the pharisaical traditions of men, which made the word of God of no effect.

It is at this point that we now need to reflect upon all that has been said and consider a few questions for Gentile believers. The apostle Paul makes a very clear distinction between Jew and Gentile.

1 Corinthians 7:17-18   *'Each of you should continue to live in whatever situation the Lord has placed you, and **remain as you were when God first called you. This is my rule for all the churches.*** (NLT)
*Was anyone **at the time of his call** already circumcised? Let him not seek to remove the marks of circumcision. Was anyone at the time of his call uncircumcised? **Let him not seek circumcision.**'* ESV

Paul is very clear that this should be a RULE IN ALL THE CHURCHES. If you are circumcised, at the time of your calling, then stay circumcised. If uncircumcised, then do not become circumcised.

In other words, if you were Jewish at the time of your calling to salvation then remain Jewish and if you were a Gentile stay Gentile and seek not to be Jewish. This was a golden rule, a rule which was set in all the churches in the first century. I cannot stress enough, the importance of that rule for today's church. What makes the church beautiful is her multifaceted glory. She is made up of Jew, Gentile and all manner of different cultures and nationalities. The apostle Paul goes to great lengths in some of his epistles to tell Gentiles to remain Gentile. Jews should remain Jews and not seek to be like a Gentile. We will cover more on this subject in a later chapter. But for now, I want to come back to the issue of 'clean' and 'unclean' food.

So, does what we eat in any way effect our walk with God, our salvation, or even His holiness? No. Let's look at the words of Jesus on this matter.

Mark 7:19 *'Food doesn't go into your heart, but only passes through the stomach and then goes into the sewer." (By saying this, he declared that every kind of food is acceptable in God's eyes.)'* NLT

Now remember the context: this passage is not about declaring all food 'clean' from a Torah point of view, Jesus was criticising the traditions of the Pharisees. However, the spiritual truth of the text is actually true for all believers. What we eat merely goes into the stomach and passes out again. It is not food that defiles our soul (heart) or spirit, it's what comes out of our heart that contaminates our soul and spirit. If food, in any way, could effect the state of our soul or spirit, then there would be no need for the work of the Holy Spirit, we could simply be holy by what we eat. Eating food in the Old Covenant made Israel ceremonially 'clean' to enter the presence of the Lord in the Tabernacle. In the New covenant, we are way beyond being merely ceremonially clean. We have not only been made clean, but made into a new creation in the likeness and image of the second Adam. The fact that we can even enter boldly into the throne room of grace, means we are made as Holy as God. (See 2 Corinthians 5:21)

Does eating a pork sausage in any way diminish God's holiness or presence within us? Can what we eat effect our salvation, the finished work of the cross? Absolutely not! However, I personally believe that a Jewish believer should be FREE to enjoy Kosher and to uphold and honour the Mosaic administration and customs if they so desire.

Remember, the apostle Paul never states that Gentile believers are grafted into the Mosaic covenant, rather we are grafted into the Abrahamic Covenant. According to the book of Hebrews, the Mosaic system has come to a close and is fading away.

Hebrews 8:7 *'For if that first covenant had been faultless, there would have been no occasion to look for a second.'* ESV

Hebrews 8:13 *'When He said, "A new covenant,"* **He has made the first obsolete.** *But whatever is becoming obsolete and growing old is ready to disappear.'* NASB

We are now under a New Covenant based on better promises.

Hebrews 8:6 *'But now Jesus, our High Priest, has been given a ministry that is far superior to the old priesthood,* **for he is the one who mediates for us a far better covenant with God, based on better promises.'** NLT

Also, the writer of Hebrews, re-quotes the Jeremiah 31 prophecy stating very clearly that there is now a New Covenant, which is NOT LIKE the covenant made with the forefathers. In other words, it is not a renewed covenant as some try to say. It simply cannot be because Jeremiah states that the New Covenant will NOT BE LIKE the original covenant.

Hebrews 8:9 *'This covenant* **will not be like the one I made with their ancestors** *when I took them by the hand and led them out of the land of Egypt...'* NLT

It has been argued, that Jesus has not come to do away with the law, thus the texts in the book of Hebrews Chapter 8 are being misunderstood. The error of thought comes into play when we state that the whole of the Mosaic Torah is THE ROYAL TORAH OF GOD.

James 2:8   *'If you really fulfil **the royal law** according to the Scripture, "You shall love your neighbour as yourself," you are doing well.'* ESV

The mosaic Torah enshrined the Law of God (ROYAL TORAH OF GOD). Built around that Law was the mediatorial system which contained various laws, customs and ceremonial cleansing laws, which have now been replaced by a better mediatorial system. Thus, the Law is eternal (not invalidated) and is now written on our hearts and minds, and the systems of the mediator are now based on better promises.

So, for example:
We no longer require the Aaronic priesthood:

Hebrews 8:6   *'But now Jesus, our High Priest, has been given a ministry that is far superior to the old priesthood, for he is the one who mediates for us a far better covenant with God, based on better promises.'* NLT

We no longer require the sprinkling of animal's blood or water:

Hebrews 10:22   *'let us go right into the presence of God with sincere hearts fully trusting him. For our guilty consciences have been sprinkled with Christ's blood to make us clean, and our bodies have been washed with pure water.'* NLT

We are not required to be ceremonially pure, through ritual cleansing, in order to enter the tabernacle:

Hebrews 9:13   *'Under the old system, the blood of goats a and the ashes of a young cow could cleanse people's boaₙₑ.. ceremonial impurity. Just think how much more the blood of Christ will purify our consciences from sinful deeds so that we can worship the living God. For by the power of the eternal Spirit, Christ offered himself to God as a perfect sacrifice for our sins.'* NLT

We no longer require a Mosaic- based temple system as we ARE the temple. All this has been replaced with a new priesthood and a new order which is the order of Melchizedek.

1 Peter 2:5   *'And you are **living stones that God is building into his spiritual temple**. What's more, **you are his holy priests**. Through the mediation of Jesus Christ, you offer spiritual sacrifices that please God.'* NLT

Hebrews 7:14-22   *'(for the law made nothing perfect); but on the other hand, a better hope is introduced, through which we draw near to God. And it was not without an oath. For those who formerly became priests were made such without an oath, but this one was made a priest with an oath by the one who said to him: "The Lord has sworn and will not change his mind, 'You are a priest forever.'" This makes Jesus the guarantor of a better covenant.'* ESV

Hebrews 5:9-10   *'In this way, God qualified him (Jesus) as a perfect High Priest, and he became the source of eternal salvation for all those who obey him. And **God designated him to be a High Priest in the order of Melchizedek.**'* NLT

Remember, the Law is eternal, but it is the mediatorial systems which have been replaced.   Also, many of the laws within the Mosaic system revolved around the tabernacle or temple. The One New Man, Jew and Gentile in Christ, is now the temple of God and so the Mosaic system has been superseded with a better mediatorial system, a better priesthood and a better temple. However, remember the heart of the Mosaic system is the Law and the Law is eternal.

One of the misunderstandings I see in some congregations of the Jewish roots movement, is that Torah is placed seemingly higher than Jesus, and the New Testament Scriptures. It is important that we divide the word of God correctly and see ALL scripture as Torah and the Prophets, not just merely the Law of Moses and the Old Testament. It is also important to understand the nature of the New Administration in The Messiah. We are no longer under Moses, but under the new mediatorial system of Jesus the Great High Priest in the order of Melchizedek.

From a New Testament perspective, the first five books, which are the four gospels and the book of Acts, reflect the first five books in the Old Testament. The gospels reveal to us the fresh interpretation and application of The Law in a new and wondrous way. The book of Acts is similar to the book of Numbers, in that it records the journey of the people of God; and all the wonderful and fearful things that happened with God in the midst of His people. Additionally, the Epistles are letters (equivalent of O.T 'Writings') written to the early church to help them understand the nature of the New Covenant, the New Creation, in Christ Jesus, and how to live out our most holy faith. The book of Revelation is the last book in the New Testament and concludes the cannon of the Prophets. The Old Testament has the Law, the writings and the Prophets. The New Testament also has The Law, the writings and the Prophets.

CHAPTER ELEVEN

THE ACTS COUNCIL

It would be prudent for us to now look at the book of Acts Chapter 15. For the Gentile believing community this is a very important part of scripture to study.

It is true to say, that Gentiles, when they come to faith, have a slightly different path to walk than our Messianic Jewish brothers. Many Gentile Christians today, simply assume they are free to do what they like, but are unable to justify their position with any real authority, other than a glib statement about their position in the New Covenant. In reality, we have a lot of freedom in Christ, but there are still prohibitions in effect that some ignore or are ignorant of.

There must be a tension in the believer, of being justified by faith alone, whilst walking in obedience to the scriptures from a place of love and intimacy with God. This tension, or tightrope, must be walked carefully. Personal preferences and leanings will inevitably determine how we walk this out. Some people prefer Laws and principles and so may gravitate more towards legalism (self-justification), and others may tend toward antinomianism where they do not like any kind of law.

To put this chapter into context, we need to be aware that Gentile believers were the problem in the early, predominantly Jewish congregations.! They were somewhat of an enigma, no one really knew what to do with them! However, there was a faction of believing Jews called the 'Circumcision Party' who to be honest, didn't party very much, they were exceptionally serious and quite militant in their approach to both Jewish believers, and the new Gentile converts. They believed, that Gentiles were not truly saved or covenant members of Israel unless they received the sign of circumcision and obeyed the Law of Moses. In other words, they were trying to convert Gentile believers to Judaism. We have to be mindful today that we do not do the same thing to Jews who come to know Jesus/Yeshua as their Lord and Saviour, by trying to enforce Christian traditions on them. Remember the advice the Apostle Paul gives us in 1 Corinthians 7:17-18

*'Each of you should continue to live in whatever situation the Lord has placed you, and **remain as you were when God first called you. This is my rule for all the churches.** (NLT)*
*Was anyone **at the time of his call** already circumcised? Let him not seek to remove the marks of circumcision. Was anyone at the time of his call uncircumcised? **Let him not seek circumcision.**'* ESV

This scripture is clear, that even as One New Man in Christ, the church is still made up of various cultures. We convert to Jesus, not to another culture.

Now, Let's take a look at Acts 15 in detail and deal with this whole Jew and Gentile problem.

Acts 15:1 *'But some men came down from Judea and were teaching the brothers, "**Unless you are circumcised** according to the custom of Moses, **you cannot be saved.**"* ESV

This is an interesting scripture, in that, it highlights religious assumptions regarding some of the Jewish believers. Circumcision was indeed a requirement of the Abrahamic Covenant and confirmed in the Mosaic Covenant. However, these Jewish believers, showed a lack of understanding of 'justification by faith alone', which is the very heart of the Abrahamic and Messianic Covenants. I also find it both interesting and sad, when I see extremes of this today in certain factions of the Jewish/Hebrew roots movement. Many of them are Gentiles who have converted to Judaism. Also, some of the believers in this movement are often militant towards Gentile Christians, stating that they have to observe circumcision and all the law of Moses.

Acts 15:2 *'Paul and Barnabas disagreed with them, arguing vehemently. Finally, the church decided to send Paul and Barnabas to*

Jerusalem, accompanied by some local believers, to talk to the apostles and elders about this question.' NLT

This hard-line view from the 'Circumcision Party,' was causing a lot of division within the church amongst both the Jewish and Gentile believers. Naturally, Paul and Barnabas were dragged into this debate as they were the most prominent Jewish preachers at that time. Not only were they the apostles sent out to the Gentiles, but they were also accused of preaching a different doctrine.

Acts 21:21 *'But the Jewish believers here in Jerusalem have been told that you are teaching all the Jews who live among the Gentiles to turn their backs on the laws of Moses. They've heard that you teach them not to circumcise their children or follow other Jewish customs.'* NLT

No one had a problem with whatever Paul was teaching the Gentiles. The controversy centered around what they ***thought*** he was teaching the Jews!

Acts 15:4-5 *'When they arrived in Jerusalem, Barnabas and Paul were welcomed by the whole church, including the apostles and elders. They reported everything God had done through them. But then some of the believers who belonged to the sect of the Pharisees stood up and insisted, **"The Gentile converts must be circumcised and required to follow the law of Moses.**"* NLT

We see here in verse 5 the premise for the Acts 15 church council meeting, regarding whether or not Gentile converts should be circumcised and follow the law of Moses?' The rest of Acts 15 is a fascinating discussion regarding this topic. The conclusion to this council appears from verse 19 onward:

Acts 15:19 *'"And so my judgment is that we should not make it difficult for the Gentiles who are turning to God. Instead, we should write and tell them to abstain from eating food offered to idols, from sexual immorality, from eating the meat of strangled animals, and from consuming blood.* ***For these laws of Moses have been preached in Jewish synagogues in every city on every Sabbath for many generations."*** NLT

This was then summarised in a letter and sent out to all the congregations throughout the land.

Acts 15:28-29   *'"For it seemed good to the Holy Spirit and to us to lay no greater burden on you than these few requirements: You must abstain from eating food offered to idols, from consuming blood or the meat of strangled animals, and from sexual immorality. If you do this, you will do well. Farewell."'* NLT

A big sigh of relief for all the Gentile men, no circumcision! So, did the Jerusalem council answer the two questions?   The first answer is very clear, Gentiles do not need to be circumcised.   The second answer is a little clearer. The Gentiles were required to observe some basic dietary and moral requirements as a starting place, as it was important for both Jew and Gentile to live in harmony.   So, Paul's admonition to both Gentile and Jewish believers in the same congregation was to be kind, loving and respectful to one another, in all matters of conduct i.e., what they did and ate in front of one another.

Now it's time to take a look at the letter of Paul to the Galatians.

CHAPTER TWELVE

YOU FOOLISH GALATIANS!

We now come to the most seemingly anti-Jewish, anti-Torah book in the whole bible! It is also probably the only letter where Paul's frustration against the 'Circumcision Party,' (The group of believing Pharisees), comes to the fore. He tells them to go all the way and emasculate themselves (Galatians 5:12), while having a rant at the Gentile believers for trying to justify themselves with Torah observance!

From a Jewish perspective, the apostle Paul seems to be so anti-Jewish that he is an offence to his own people. In today's world, Paul is still very much misunderstood. He is called bigoted, sexist, anti-Jewish and commonly thought of as the one who started a new religion called Christianity. However, a little bit of digging in the scriptures will reveal how much he truly loved the Jewish people, loved the church (Messianic Congregations) and that he never stopped being Jewish.

So, the Circumcision Party had been to Galatia and caused quite a stir! They went into the churches, trying to get the Gentile believers to become, Torah observant and agree to being circumcised. In other words, they were trying to convert Gentile believers to Judaism. This was something which was strictly warned against by Paul:

1 Corinthians 7:17-18 *'Each of you should continue to live in whatever situation the Lord has placed you, and **remain as you were when God first called you. This is my rule for all the churches.*** (NLT)
*Was anyone **at the time of his call** already circumcised? Let him not seek to remove the marks of circumcision. Was anyone at the time of his call uncircumcised? **Let him not seek circumcision**.'* ESV

The letter of Galatians opens with the usual greetings from the apostle Paul and a brief doxology of praise to God. However, by the time we get to verse 6 Paul is going straight for the jugular!

Galatians 1:6 *'I am astonished that you are so quickly deserting him who called you in the grace of Christ and are turning to a different gospel,'* ESV

Wow! That is a really stinging and strong line from Paul! He is not happy at all with what had been going on in the Galatian church. From their perspective, they probably thought they were doing the right thing. They wanted to be good obedient Gentile believers and wanted to please God; and so started implementing Jewish traditions and Torah observance into their lifestyle. They probably thought that God would be pleased with them for observing the Torah.

Now, it needs to be said here that there is nothing wrong for Jew or Gentile to want to live according to parts of the Torah. The problem is when people are told that faith in Jesus is simply insufficient and requires further obedience to make one justified in God's eyes.

I know that this will raise some interesting questions, but let's keep it simple. If you are truly following Jesus you will want to live a righteous life. We cannot in any way add to the finished work of the cross or make ourselves more special and loved in God's eyes, by strict obedience to a code of law. Remember, it was whilst we were still sinners that God loved us and died for us (Romans 5:8), not when we became Torah observant.

Faith in Christ is first and foremost about relationship and love; from there comes obedience. Jesus said, "If you love Me you will obey my commandments' (John 14:15). It is also the love of God that leads us to the Law of God. This is made wonderfully clear in the story of the woman caught in the act of adultery. (John 8: 1-11) According to the law of Moses, those who commit adultery had to be put to death. So, all the Pharisees and Sadducees stood around the woman waiting to stone her. Jesus then said these incredible words, "He who is without

82

sin, throw the first stone." (v:7) It quickly became apparent that everyone had sinned in thought, word and deed. Jesus was the only one left. Interestingly He was the ONLY one worthy to throw the stone. Indeed, He is the One who gave the Law, He is the Word made flesh, but He chose mercy and love over legalistic cold obedience.

John 8:10-11 *Then Jesus stood up again and said to the woman, "Where are your accusers? Didn't even one of them condemn you?"* "No, Lord," she said. And Jesus said, "Neither do I. **Go and sin no more**." NLT

Jesus did not condemn the woman, He loved her with the love and compassion of the Father, then from the place of love, He led her to the law of God. When I say the law of God, I am referring to the basics of morality and right living according to all scripture, not simply the law of Moses.

James 2:8 *'If you really fulfil **the royal law** according to the Scripture, "You shall love your neighbour as yourself," you are doing well.'* ESV

It needs to be noted, that the Law of Moses was given after Israel's redemption, not before. I often see misguided believers battering unbelievers with the law of God, thinking that it will get them to repent. Redemption only comes through the power of the Gospel, the kindness and mercy of God. (Romans 2:4)

From the place of redemption, we then lead people into discipleship. Thus, in simple theological language, justification leads to sanctification. Or in layman terms; once we get saved (that's justification), we become disciples and work out our salvation through the indwelling power of the Holy Spirit (that's sanctification). Simple! So, let's get back to Galatians.

Galatians 1:6 *'I am astonished that you are so quickly deserting him who called you in the grace of Christ **and are turning to a different gospel,**'* ESV

What I find shocking in this verse, is what Paul states about a 'salvation based on works' gospel. He calls it a different and false gospel. This is very strong language, and it needs to be strong. Paul then goes a step further by pronouncing the curse of God upon those who preach a different or false gospel.

Galatians 1:8 *'**Let God's curse fall on anyone**, including us or even an angel from heaven, who preaches a different kind of Good News than the one we preached to you.'* NLT

From verses 13 onward, Paul starts listing his credentials as a Pharisee and about his former life in traditional, rabbinical Judaism. Thus, implying if anyone knew about life as a Pharisee under the Law, he was the one.

Galatians 1:13 *'You know what I was like when I followed the Jewish religion--how I violently persecuted God's church. I did my best to destroy it. I was far ahead of my fellow Jews in my zeal for the traditions of my ancestors.'*

I am going to quote from Philippians here, to emphasise the truth Paul is trying to get across to his readers and us today, about how the gospel of grace far exceeds attempted salvation by works of the law.

Philippians 3:1-9 *'Whatever happens, my dear brothers and sisters, rejoice in the Lord. I never get tired of telling you these things, and I do it to safeguard your faith. Watch out for those dogs, those people who do evil, those mutilators **who say you must be circumcised to be saved.** For we who worship by the Spirit of God are the ones who are truly circumcised. **We rely on what Christ Jesus has done for us**. We put no confidence in human effort, though I could have confidence in my own effort if anyone could. Indeed, if others have reason for confidence in their own efforts, I have even more! I was circumcised when I was eight days old. I am a pure-blooded citizen of Israel and a member of the tribe of Benjamin--a real Hebrew if there ever was one! I was a member of the Pharisees, who demand the strictest* *obedience to the Jewish law. I was so zealous that I harshly persecuted the church. **And as for righteousness, I obeyed the law without fault. I once thought these things were valuable, but now I consider them worthless because of what Christ has done.** Yes, everything else is worthless when compared with the infinite value of knowing Christ Jesus my Lord. For his sake I have discarded everything else, counting it all as garbage, so that I could gain Christ and become one with him. **I no longer count on my own righteousness through obeying the law; rather, I become righteous through faith in Christ. For God's way of making us right with himself depends on faith.** I want to know Christ and experience the mighty power that raised him from the dead. I want to suffer with him, sharing in His death,'* NLT

At first glance, this looks like Paul is anti-Torah, but actually, we know, he loves the Law of God. What he hates is the erroneous doctrine that 'works' based righteousness is how to be saved/Justified. Paul had somehow, managed to obey the Law completely, so much so, that he was blameless (verse 6). Yet, it did him no good from a salvation/justification point of view. THE LAW DOES NOT SAVE/ JUSTIFY, ONLY JESUS SAVES AND JUSTIFIES. The Law was not given to offer salvation. It was offered to those who were already in covenant with God. The law is about sanctification, not justification. Sadly, at some point in Jewish history, the Torah became perverted by the religious leaders into a means of works-based salvation. The Law was given to show the sinfulness of man and the holiness and goodness of God, it was never a means of salvation or justification.

Romans 7:7 *'What shall we say then? Is the Law sin? May it never be! On the contrary, I would not have come to know sin except through the Law; for I would not have known about coveting if the Law had not said, "YOU SHALL NOT COVET."'* NASB

Romans 7:12 *'So the law is holy, and the commandment is holy and righteous and good.'* NASB

Jesus fulfilled the law in its entirety, so that those who believe in Him are seen as totally righteous in God's eyes (2 Corinthians 5:21). It is a righteousness obtained by faith in Jesus, not a system of rituals or rules. In other words, you cannot bribe God with good behaviour. You cannot get into heaven with good deeds. You get right with God only through faith in the atoning work of Jesus the Messiah.

Also, from a point of salvation, we now look to Jesus, the Person who lived the Law in love, grace and truth. He is our example of right living; a man in relationship with God, through the Holy Spirit, who loves mankind and loves the Word of God. This is the example we follow.

It needs to be understood, that the Torah was weak in certain areas. It was weak in that it could not save, and of itself it could not change us from within. Indeed, our old sin nature took the commandment of God, which was meant to bless us and perverted it, so that it brought about death instead. So, the Torah is good and holy, but our sin nature perverted it, so that the Torah brought death instead of life.

Romans 7:8-13 *'**But sin**, seizing an opportunity through the commandment, produced in me all kinds of covetousness. For apart from the law, sin lies dead. I was once alive apart from the law, but when the commandment came, sin came alive and I died. **The very commandment that promised life proved to be death to me.** For sin, seizing an opportunity through the commandment, deceived me and through it killed me. **So the law is holy, and the commandment is holy and righteous and good.** Did that which is good, then, bring death to me? By no means! **It was sin, producing death in me** through what is good, in order that sin might be shown to be sin, and through the commandment might become sinful beyond measure.'*
ESV

I find it very interesting, how Paul continues to state that the Torah is good, holy and righteous. In some parts of Christendom today it appears that the Law of God is considered as a perverse set of scriptures, which God was glad to have finally done away with!

Nothing could be further from the truth! The Law is good, holy, righteous, spiritual and eternal.

Romans 7:14 *'So the trouble is not with the law, **for it is spiritual and good.** The trouble is with me, for I am all too human, a slave to sin.'* NLT

Paul makes it very clear, that the only way we can be spared from the curse of the Law and destruction, is to accept the righteousness Jesus gives us when we receive by faith, His free gift of eternal life.

Galatians 3:13-14 ***'Christ redeemed us from the curse of the law*** *by becoming a curse for us—for it is written, "Cursed is everyone who is hanged on a tree"—so that in Christ Jesus the blessing of Abraham might come to the Gentiles, **so that we might receive the promised Spirit through faith**.'* ESV

It seems very clear in Galatians Chapter 2 that the 'Circumcision Party,' were quite an intimidating group. Many Jews, including Peter, were happy to eat with Gentile believers until the Circumcision Party arrived, then they would separate themselves from the Gentiles and eat only with Jews. This shows how strong minded the Circumcision Party were, bearing in mind Peter was the very one who had the vision about not calling 'Common,' that which was made 'Clean,' (See Chapter 10). It was this kind of hypocrisy the apostle Paul had to strongly condemn.

Galatians 2:11-14 *'But when Cephas (Peter) came to Antioch, I opposed him to his face, because he stood condemned. For before certain men came from James, he was eating with the Gentiles; **but when they came he drew back and separated himself, <u>fearing the circumcision party</u>.** And the rest of the Jews acted hypocritically along with him, so that even Barnabas was led astray by their hypocrisy. But when I saw that their conduct was not in step with the truth of the gospel, I said to Cephas before them all, "If you, though a Jew, live like a Gentile and not like a Jew, how can you force the Gentiles to live like Jews?"* ESV

Paul is not criticising Jewish believers for being Jewish, he is pointing out that they should be biblical, and not continue to walk in the traditions of the Pharisees. Following the rabbinical/pharisaical traditions of the day meant they had to separate themselves from the common and the unclean. Paul was adamant that Gentile believers are not common and they are not unclean. They are justified by faith, grafted into the covenant of Abraham, with Israel and are circumcised in heart. It seems some of the Jewish believers were reverting back to old Jewish traditions which were in opposition to the Gospel. It was for THIS they were chastised by Paul.

Galatians 3:13 *'So that in Christ Jesus the blessing of Abraham might come to the Gentiles,* **so that we might receive the promised Spirit through faith.'** ESV

Ephesians 2:11-13 *'Don't forget that you Gentiles used to be outsiders. You were called "uncircumcised heathens" by the Jews, who were proud of their circumcision, even though it affected only their bodies and not their hearts. In those days you were living apart from Christ. You were excluded from citizenship among the people of Israel, and you did not know the covenant promises God had made to them. You lived in this world without God and without hope.* **But now you have been united with Christ Jesus. Once you were far away from God, but now you have been brought near to him through the blood of Christ. For Christ himself has brought peace to us. He united Jews and Gentiles into one people when, in his own body on the cross, he broke down the wall of hostility that separated us.'** NLT

As we move into Chapter 3 of Galatians, Paul reiterates again that salvation is a work of the Spirit of God by faith, not the flesh.

Galatians 3:1-3 *'O foolish Galatians! Who has bewitched you? It was before your eyes that Jesus Christ was publicly portrayed as crucified. Let me ask you only this:* **Did you receive the Spirit by** **works of the law** **or by hearing with faith?** *Are you so foolish?*

Having begun by the Spirit, **are you now being perfected by the flesh?'**

The term 'works of the law,' is a specific phrase Paul uses to denote legalism, i.e, where people follow a code of conduct to justify themselves unto righteousness.   However, the standard of righteousness we are required to attain, is none other than God's own righteousness, far beyond our comprehension, and is <u>completely impossible</u> to even come close to by works of the law.

To become as righteous as God, one simply needs to believe by faith in Jesus and that is it!   Done! Complete! Over! Finished forever! Those who walk by faith are the true sons of Abraham.   Because Gentile believers are children of Abraham by faith, there is absolutely no reason why the Jewish believers should treat them as anything less.

Galatians 3:7 *'The real children of Abraham, then, are those who put their faith in God.'* NLT

Again, Paul is stating the same facts about self-justification and faith.

Galatians 3:11 *'So it is clear that* **no one** *can be made right with God by trying to keep the law. For the Scriptures say, "It is* **through faith** *that a righteous person has life."* NLT

Paul is again making it very clear that the Torah is good, but it cannot impart salvation to us.

Galatians 3:21 *'Is the Law then contrary to the promises of God? May it never be! For if a law had been given which was able to* **impart life***, then righteousness would indeed have been based on law.'* NASB

Now, we get to some tricky verses!

Galatians 3:23-25 *'Before the way of faith in Christ was available to us, we were placed under guard by the law. We were kept in protective custody, so to speak, until the way of faith was revealed. Let me put it another way. The law was our guardian until Christ came; it protected us until we could be made right with God through faith. And now that the way of faith has come, we no longer need the law as our guardian.'* NLT

I chose to use the New Living Translation here, as it clearly reveals the meaning of the text. These verses speak of a custodian. An example of what Paul is writing about here is found in many royal families. A boy, for example, who will one day become king, is put under a guardian, or custodian. This guardian will teach the boy how to be a king, how to govern, how to act and respond. He will teach him all the basics of life as a royal. However, the boy cannot give orders to the guardian until he reaches a certain age or his father dies; thus, he is under the law of the guardian. This is what happened for the people of Israel. The guardian, the Torah, was preparing them for the coming Messiah, who would be the ultimate sacrifice and pay in full, the price for sin and cleanse them from all defilement. The Torah, through the offerings, the tabernacle, and the ritual cleansing, was always pointing to the future work of Jesus, who would one day completely fulfill and satisfy them. Paul explains this clearly in Galatians 4:1-7.

Now we get down to some 'nitty gritty' in Galatians chapter 4, regarding days and feasts. There are some who would argue that these verses are talking about pagan days and months. However, I would disagree from a context point of view. The main thrust of the letter to the Galatians, was regarding the erroneous doctrine of justification through Torah observance. So, the verses referring to feast days would, more likely, be to do with Torah feasts than not.

Galatians 4:8-11 *'Formerly, when you did not know God, you were enslaved to those that by nature are not gods. But now that you have come to know God, or rather to be known by God, how can you turn back again to the weak and worthless elementary principles of the world, whose slaves you want to be once more?* **You observe days and** *months and seasons and years!* *I am afraid I may have laboured over you in vain.'* ESV

Here, Paul is trying to show the Galatian congregation that their old, worldly pagan ways are similar to what they are doing now (i.e. observing feast days). Religion, for the most part, is a manufactured and man-made process of rules and regulations to observe, appease and please God. The Galatians were becoming slaves to a religious system, that would never make them right in God's eyes. Only the blood of Jesus can do this.

I am now going to link Galatians 4:8-11 with two other scriptures in respect of observing days and seasons:

Colossians 2:16-17 *'Therefore let no one pass judgment on you in questions of food and drink, or with regard to a festival or a new moon or a Sabbath.* **These are a shadow of the things to come, but the substance belongs to Christ.'** ESV

Romans 14:5 *'In the same way, some think one day is more holy than another day, while others think every day is alike.* **You should each be fully convinced that whichever day you choose is acceptable.'** NLT

These verses are similar, but have different contexts. Yet, there is a question here, which needs to addressed! "What is the conscience or motivation for a Gentile to observe feast days, seasons, new moons and sabbaths?" Paul is clearly talking about Jewish feasts here, but he is questioning the heart reasonings for observing or not observing them. Were they trying to justify themselves to God, to complete their salvation? Paul is adamant on this issue: salvation is a one hundred percent finished work. Observing feasts will in no way embellish that already-finished and complete work. We cannot add or take away anything from the work of the cross. It is finished!

However, Paul is clear that if you want to observe a feast day, you can, but if you don't want to then don't. The feasts themselves add nothing to our salvation, they are shadows of the age to come and impart deeper revelations regarding their fulfillment in Yeshua (Jesus). The Galatians were most likely observing feast days and sabbaths for all the wrong reasons.

I have heard it said on several occasions, that unless the church gets back to her Jewish roots, she will never see revival or the power of God. I would like to challenge those who hold this view.

Firstly, church history simply does not agree with this. Some of the greatest awakenings and revivals this world has ever seen had nothing to do with getting back to their Jewish roots.

Secondly, I don't believe Messianic or Jewish roots congregations have seen any more of the miraculous, revival or huge growth, than any other God fearing church.

Thirdly, the apostle Paul says it wonderfully in Galatians 3:5

*'I ask you again, does God give you the **Holy Spirit and work miracles among you because you obey the law?** Of course not! It is because you believe the message you heard about Christ.'* NLT

The miraculous power of God is not released through observing Torah, Sabbaths or feasts. The church does not need to get back to a Torah formula to see the power of God flow in our congregations. Today, the reason why the church in the west has lost her power, is simply because she no longer prays! When I say pray, I mean real passionate, faith-filled prayer, in line with the Word of God. If you want revival then pray! Every revival and awakening in church history happened when people prayed in desperation for God to move in power.

When we start to read these letters of Paul in context, we begin to understand that Paul is not anti-law, he is just anti-foolish Galatians! The Torah is good, holy and spiritual and teaches us many things about the nature of God, but it is not able to save us, nor is it a magic

92

formula for revival. Only Jesus and His Holy Spirit can do all of that. The early Jews had elevated the Torah to an almost God-like place and believed that external observances were the way to holiness, even salvation in God. Sadly, I see the same philosophy today. I have met some in the Hebrew roots movement who are overly obsessed with Torah. Personally, I think they have moved into an unhealthy place. Jesus and His gospel are above all! Everything else is positioned below Him. We don't ignore the Law or the Old Testament, but it's all about balance and tension in the outworking of our faith. One of the greatest revelations in the New Testament, is that we are a **New Creation**, a new species (2 Corinthians 5:17). Yet, sadly, many believers would rather focus on the flesh and not upon the inner realities of the Spirit, and so, veer far away from the whole of God's Word. There are many churches so disconnected from the Old Testament scriptures that they are not even read or preached on. This is such a travesty. Extremes at both ends of the spectrum must break God's heart.

2 Timothy 3:16 *'**All Scripture** is breathed out by God and profitable for teaching, for reproof, for correction, and for training in righteousness,'* ESV

So, I appeal to all my brothers and sisters throughout all of Christendom: ALL SCRIPTURE IS GOD BREATHED. In other words, ALL SCRIPTURE IN THE BIBLE IS THE WORD OF GOD. Not just the bits you like, it is all God breathed. So, it all needs to be read, digested, meditated upon and preached upon. So, for all the Old Testament fans, you need to read your New Testament. For all the New Testament fans, you need to read your Old Testament. We need to teach the whole counsel of God in our congregations. Not just Torah, not just all the end time prophetic teaching and certainly not just grace. It needs to be balanced, incorporating all scripture. This is what makes for a healthy congregation.

In the world of modern media, we can find anything we are looking for. We have such a wonderful plethora of great bible teachers to access online, we are truly blessed. However, in my opinion, those media platforms also give some people a voice that should otherwise stay quiet!

I have seen some very interesting and very clever teaching from the extremes of the Hebrew roots movement, stating that Gentiles should get circumcised! In my opinion, they use all manner of clever devices to bend and twist scripture, with lots of assumptions and a plate full of zeal to finish it all off!

I have a golden rule, keep it simple! So, should Gentiles ever get circumcised in respect to faith in Jesus/Yeshua? Simply put, No! As Paul says in the following verses:

Galatians 5:2-12 *'Take note! I, Paul, tell you that **if you get yourselves circumcised, Christ will not benefit you at all**. Again I testify to every man who gets himself circumcised that he is obligated to keep the entire law. **You who are trying to be justified by the law are alienated from Christ; you have fallen from grace**. For through the Spirit, by faith, we eagerly wait for the hope of righteousness. **For in Christ Jesus neither circumcision nor uncircumcision accomplishes anything; what matters is faith working through love.** You were running well. Who prevented you from obeying the truth? **This persuasion did not come from the One who called you**. A little yeast leavens the whole lump of dough. I have confidence in the Lord you will not accept any other view. But whoever it is that is confusing you will pay the penalty. Now brothers, if I still preach circumcision, why am I still persecuted? In that case the offence of the cross has been abolished. **I wish those who are disturbing you might also get themselves castrated!'** HCSB*

Paul then shows the Galatians, a more excellent way to fulfil the Torah/Law of God: by loving God and loving one another.

Galatians 5:13-15 *'**For you have been called to live in freedom**, my brothers and sisters. **But don't use your freedom to satisfy your sinful nature**. Instead, use your freedom to serve one another in love.*

94

For the whole law can be summed up in this one command: "Love your neighbour as yourself." But if you are always biting and devouring one another, watch out! Beware of destroying one another.' NLT

We have complete freedom as believers in Jesus, but that freedom is never a license to sin. Rather, our freedom is to live lives that truly glorify God, and glorify His Holy Word; by lifestyle, conduct and the love we have for people. After all, it is the love we have for one another which will reveal to the world that we are Jesus' disciples.

John 13:34-35 *'A new commandment I give to you, that you love one another: just as I have loved you, you also are to love one another. By this all people will know that you are my disciples, if you have love for one another."* ESV

I want to finish this chapter with Paul's final thoughts on this issue in Galatians.

Galatians 6:15-16 *'It doesn't matter whether we have been circumcised or not. What counts is whether we have been transformed into a new creation. May God's peace and mercy be upon all who live by this principle; they are the new people of God.'* NLT

CHAPTER THIRTEEN

SO WHAT ABOUT THE SABBATH?

Every now and then, I meet with people who are passionate for God's word, His Grace and His Law. This is a good thing and I always enjoy meeting and chatting with such people. However, there is sometimes a sticking point with some of these good folk: the issue of the Sabbath and the Jewish feasts.

I remember chatting with a brother, who was talking about how the church should not be celebrating pagan festivals, such as, Christmas. Half way through his discourse, I stopped him and said, "This is not about Christmas, this is about one thing: the Sabbath." The brother looked at me with surprise and then agreed. He then went on to state, that, in his opinion, the church should be worshiping on a Saturday, not on a Sunday, and needed to get back to her Jewish roots.

I have stated in the previous chapter, that there is no issue for believers to celebrate, or not celebrate Jewish feasts, as they are types and shadows of the age to come.

Colossians 2:16-17 *'Therefore let no one pass judgment on you in questions of food and drink, or with regard to a festival or a new moon or a Sabbath.* **These are a shadow of the things to come, but the substance belongs to Christ.**' ESV

Romans 14:5 *'In the same way, some think one day is more holy than another day, while others think every day is alike.* **You should each be fully convinced that whichever day you choose is acceptable.**' NLT

Personally, I think it is good to celebrate some of the feasts as they richly connect us to the roots of our faith, and also reveal a great deal of symbology about Jesus and His atoning work on the cross. I feel that much of the church would do well to celebrate the feasts of The

Lord, as they are prophetic in nature and some are yet to be fulfilled. So, if you were thinking of the feasts as some old antiquated, irrelevant celebration, you would be greatly mistaken.

There are many Gentile Christians who are now connecting to their Jewish roots and this is beneficial and deeply valuable. Invariably though, when we go down the path of rediscovery we can end up hitting some bumps in the road! For example, in the pursuit to live a holy life, we could well end up judging those who don't quite live as we do. Jesus was very hot on this issue!

Matthew 7:1 *"**Judge not, that you be not judged.**" For with the judgment you pronounce you will be judged, and with the measure you use it will be measured to you. Why do you see the speck that is in your brother's eye, but do not notice the log that is in your own eye?'* ESV

Feeling righteous because we are observing feasts, is another trap to be avoided, but the truth is, feelings should be completely irrelevant to the believer, as we walk by faith not by sight. Also, we know, that our righteousness was obtained two thousand years ago at the cross. What is done is done; we cannot add or take away from Jesus' work of salvation. It is a finished work! Jesus has given us His (one hundred percent Torah observant) righteousness, and because of this we are, in Him, the very righteousness of God.

2 Corinthians 5:21 *'For our sake he made him to be sin who knew no sin, so that in him **we might become the righteousness of God.**'* ESV

Another common example is the issue of the Sabbath and the church worshiping on a Sunday. At this point, we need to pause and take a serious look at what the bible says about this.

Firstly, I want to correct a common mistake that Gentile Christians can make regarding Sunday and the Sabbath. Sunday is not The Sabbath, it has never been, and never will be! The Sabbath is locked into the order of God's word and creation. It was always a Friday evening to Saturday evening and nothing will ever change that! So, I need to make it clear to my Messianic Jewish brothers and sisters, why the church celebrates on a Sunday.

Sunday, traditionally, became known as 'The Lord's Day.' It was mentioned by the apostle John, in the book of Revelation; and alluded to in the book of Acts:

Revelation 1:10 *'I was in the Spirit **on the Lord's day**, and I heard behind me a loud voice like a trumpet.'* ESV

Acts 20:7 ***'On the first day of the week**, when we were gathered together to break bread, Paul talked with them, intending to depart on the next day, and he prolonged his speech until midnight.'* ESV

Now, it needs to be made very clear here, that just because the 'The Lord's Day,' was considered potentially important, it in no way negates the importance of the Sabbath.

The fact that the Gentile Church preferred to celebrate their faith on the Lord's Day is evident throughout Church history, whilst the Jewish believers continued with their Sabbath celebrations. In 110AD, an early church father, Ignatius of Antioch, is recorded to have said, of the Lord's Day:

"If, then, those who had walked in ancient practices attained unto newness of hope, no longer observing Sabbath, but living according to the Lord's life ...no longer observing the Sabbath, but living in the observance of the Lord's [Day]"

There are various other sources which also confirm this, but suffice to say, the Lord's Day is not the Sabbath and neither does it replace it. It was during the middle ages and the great Reformation, that Sunday became known as the Sabbath of the Gentiles. Sadly, this is simply not the case, and Gentile believers need to understand, that this issue is a real hot potato for our Messianic Jewish brothers and sisters. Sunday is not the Sabbath. It never has been and it never will be!

98

I remember a few years ago, while meditating on the passages of Genesis chapter one, I received a wonderful revelation which helped me to understand the deep significance and importance of the two sacred days: the Sabbath representing salvation and rest and the Lord's Day, creation and New Life.

Day one, is a Sunday, this was the day creation began, a day of divine revelation and new creation. It was the day when Jesus as the Creator, was revealed to this natural realm.

Genesis 1:1 *'In the beginning, God created the heavens and the earth.'* ESV

John 1:1 *'In the beginning was the Word, and the Word was with God, and the Word was God.* ESV

Genesis 1:3 *'And God said, "Let there be light," and there was light.'* ESV

John 1:4 *'In him was life, and the life was the light of men.'* ESV

John 8:12 *'Again Jesus spoke to them, saying, "I am the light of the world. Whoever follows me will not walk in darkness, but will have the light of life."'* ESV

Day one, is also the day on which Jesus rose from the dead. So, Sunday represents new life and new creation. As this universe began on a Sunday, I believe so too will the next heaven and earth. Many believe the earth is around 6000 years old (or at least man has been around that long), and when Jesus returns, He will rule and reign for a thousand years giving the earth a thousand year sabbath rest. At the end of the seventh thousandth year of sabbath rest the clock resets back to the beginning of the week when a New Heaven and earth will be created.

2 Peter 3:8 *'But do not overlook this one fact, beloved, that with the Lord one day is as a thousand years, and a thousand years as one day.'* ESV

Revelation 20:6 *'Blessed and holy is the one who shares in the first resurrection! Over such the second death has no power, but they will be priests of God and of Christ, and they will reign with him for a thousand years.'* ESV

Isaiah 65:17 *'"For behold, I create new heavens and a new earth, and the former things shall not be remembered or come into mind.'* ESV

The Sabbath day represents the Sabbath rest and finished work of salvation, which was completed fully at the foundation of the world.

Hebrews 4:3-4 *'For we who have believed enter that rest, as he has said, "As I swore in my wrath, 'They shall not enter my rest,'"* although **_his works were finished from the foundation of the world_**. *For he has somewhere spoken of the seventh day in this way: "And God rested on the seventh day from all his works."'* ESV

The Lord's day represents the new birth and the new creation. We need both days, not just one or the other, they are as important and as significant as each other. They also represent Jew and Gentile side by side. So, for those who judge other believers for celebrating the Sabbath or the Lord's day, be careful, as both days hold great significance. Without Sunday, (the Lord's day) you can not have the Sabbath. Think about it for a minute. We only have a Sabbath at the end of the creation period (at the end of the week). The beginning (Sunday) is as important as the end (sabbath), and Jesus is the beginning and the end.
Thus, the first and last day of the week are equally valid and important.

Revelation 22:13 *'I am the Alpha and the Omega, the first and the last, the beginning and the end."'* ESV

Hebrews 12:2 *'Looking unto Jesus **the author and finisher of our faith**; who for the joy that was set before him endured the cross, despising the shame, and is set down at the right hand of the throne of God.'* KJV

The next question we need to tackle is whether or not the Sabbath is mandatory. Some would simplistically argue that it was a part of the ten commandments, so it is a given, that we have to observe it. However, there is a sticking point with this view, in that, although it was a specific law of the Mosaic covenant it was not previously mandated in biblical history.

In the Abrahamic covenant, there was no stipulation regarding the Sabbath, however, it was made a mandatory covenantal sign of the Mosaic covenant, and if broken it would be considered as apostasy and the guilty one would have to be cut off from the people and even put to death.

Exodus 31:13- *'"Tell the people of Israel: 'Be careful to keep my Sabbath day, **for the Sabbath is a sign of the covenant** between me and you from generation to generation. It is given so you may know that I am the LORD, who makes you holy. You must keep the Sabbath day, for it is a holy day for you. Anyone who desecrates it must be put to death; anyone who works on that day will be cut off from the community. You have six days each week for your ordinary work, but the seventh day must be a Sabbath day of complete rest, a holy day dedicated to the LORD. Anyone who works on the Sabbath must be put to death. **The people of Israel must keep the Sabbath** day by observing it from generation to generation. **This is a covenant obligation for all time.**'* NLT

So, we can clearly see from the text, that under the Mosaic administration the covenant seal was the mandatory observance of the Sabbath, but up until that time, it had just been a day of memorial.

Remember, in the New Testament there is absolutely no mention of being grafted into the Mosaic covenant, only the Abrahamic, and also, the Mosaic administration has come to an end.

Hebrews 8:13 *'In speaking of a new covenant, **he makes the first one obsolete**. And what is becoming obsolete and growing old is ready to vanish away.'* ESV

The Law has not been done away with, but the Mosaic mediatorial system has. The mediatorial systems had to do with priesthood, cleansing, animal sacrifice and certain ceremonial and covenantal stipulations. Those systems have been replaced with a new and better mediatorial system. We now have a Great High Priest, a better sacrifice and better covenantal benefits. The mandatory observance of sabbath was a specific covenantal stipulation of the Mosaic administration.

So, should the Christian observe the Sabbath? The answer is yes and no. The Christian does not have to mandatorily observe it, as it is not a covenantal stipulation of the new covenant. Remember what scripture teaches on this:

Colossians 2:16-17 *'Therefore let no one pass judgment on you in questions of food and drink, or with regard to a festival or a new moon or a Sabbath. **These are a shadow of the things to come, but the substance belongs to Christ**.'* ESV

The feasts are shadows of the age to come, not mandatory stipulated covenantal observances. Because the Sabbath is a feast of the Lord and was a part of the order of creation before the law, I thus have to conclude, that observing Sabbath is actually a good thing to do, **if** you wish to. Some may argue with this view, but we have to keep looking to scripture for the answer.

Romans 14:5 *'In the same way, some think one day is more holy than another day, while others think every day is alike. **You should each be fully convinced that whichever day you choose is acceptable**.'* NLT

102

Now that we have looked at the Sabbath, which is one of the feasts of the Lord; what should we do in respect of all the other feast days? Again, the reality is, that we may well be celebrating them in the age to come. So, it makes sense to learn about them now and enjoy them for what they are and all they symbolise. Staying connected to our Jewish roots is a real blessing for Gentile believers.

It is my opinion, the Gentile church has lost much revelation of her Jewish roots, and is now sadly, far removed from the covenant to which she is grafted into. I liken some of today's church to the supermarket society. We buy our groceries with very little thought as to how they were grown and processed. Sometimes, I enjoy cooking food using farm shop vegetables just to remind me, that food does not come out of a tin, but out of the ground! I think the Gentile church could also do the same with her Jewish roots!

It is time for all believers, Messianic and Gentile, to bridge the disconnection and push down the barrier, which Jesus so painfully removed by His blood two thousand years ago. Remember, it is by the love we have for one another that the world will know we are Jesus' disciples.

So finally, what is the purpose of the Law? Paul answers this question in the opening passage of 1 Timothy chapter one.

'Now we know that the law is good, if one uses it lawfully, understanding this, that the law is not laid down for the just but for the lawless and disobedient, for the ungodly and sinners, for the unholy and profane, for those who strike their fathers and mothers, for murderers, the sexually immoral, men who practice homosexuality, enslavers, liars, perjurers, and whatever else is contrary to sound doctrine, in accordance with the gospel of the glory of the blessed God with which I have been entrusted.' ESV

My final thoughts to the reader of this book come from the Words of Jesus.

John 14:15 *"'If you love me, you will keep my commandments.'* ESV

May God bless and richly prosper you all.

Pastor Chris Wickland

BOOKS FOR FUTHER STUDY

The Complete Jewish Study Bible by Hendrickson Bibles
The Orthodox Jewish Bible by Dr Phillip E. Goble
Israel in the New Testament by David Pawson
Torah and The New Covenant by Daniel Gruber
Jewish Roots (Understanding Your Jewish Faith) by Daniel Juster
The Jewish Jesus by David Hoffbrand
The Jewish New Testament Commentary by David H. Stern

BOOKS BY CHRISTOPHER WICKLAND

Faith School (Learning to walk by faith the easy way)
The Biblical Importance of Israel and everything else that goes with it
The Blessing of Abraham (soon to be published)

CONTACT THE AUTHOR

If you wish to contact the author of this work please feel free to email this address.

livingwordchurches@yahoo.co.uk

www.livingwordchurchnetwork.uk
www.chriswickland.com

A PRAYER FOR SALVATION

If you feel after reading this book, that you would like to know Jesus as your Lord and Saviour, please simply pray this prayer of salvation.

Dear Lord Jesus. Come into my life and be my Lord, my God and my friend.
Forgive me for all my sins, wash me clean, change me and set me free.
Let me never be the same again.
Jesus I believe You died for me. Thank you that you rose from the dead, and now pray for me from heaven.
Help me to live for you, to become a disciple and fulfil everything You have called me to do.
I thank you that I am now forgiven and a child of God.
In Jesus Name. Amen

To grow in your new life as a Christian you need to follow a simple plan…

Get yourself into a good local church. Make new friends and grow in your faith with others.

Read your bible daily. This will be a form of spiritual food to help you grow in your new faith. It's recommend that you start with the gospel of Mark.

You are now in a relationship with The Living God. Like any relationship you need to talk. Start talking (praying) to God today.

Printed in Great Britain
by Amazon

81041938R00068